PRAISE FOR
MONICA BURNS
AND HER NOVELS OF "CUTTING-EDGE ROMANCE"

"This sizzling hot historical and its compelling characters will leave you panting for more! Monica Burns writes with sensitivity and panache. Don't miss this one!"
—Sabrina Jeffries, *New York Times* bestselling author

"[Monica Burns's] excellent love scenes and bold romance will have readers clamoring for more." —*Romantic Times*

"A cinematic, compelling, and highly recommended treat!"
—Sylvia Day, national bestselling author

"The love scenes are emotion-filled and wonderfully erotic . . . Enough to make your toes curl." —*TwoLips Reviews*

"Elegant prose, believable dialogue, and a suspenseful plot that will hold you spellbound." —Emma Wildes

"Historical romance with unending passion." —*The Romance Studio*

"Wow. Just wow." —*Fallen Angel Reviews*

"A satisfying read, complete with intrigue, mystery, and the kind of potent sensuality that fogs up the mirrors." —*A Romance Review*

"Monica Burns is a new author I must add to my 'required reading' category . . . Everything I look for in a top-notch romance novel."
—*Romance Reader at Heart*

"Blazing passion." —*Romance Junkies*

Assassin's
HEART

MONICA BURNS

BERKLEY SENSATION, NEW YORK

THE BERKLEY PUBLISHING GROUP
Published by the Penguin Group
Penguin Group (USA) Inc.
375 Hudson Street, New York, New York 10014, USA
Penguin Group (Canada), 90 Eglinton Avenue East, Suite 700, Toronto, Ontario M4P 2Y3, Canada
(a division of Pearson Penguin Canada Inc.)
Penguin Books Ltd., 80 Strand, London WC2R 0RL, England
Penguin Group Ireland, 25 St. Stephen's Green, Dublin 2, Ireland (a division of Penguin Books Ltd.)
Penguin Group (Australia), 250 Camberwell Road, Camberwell, Victoria 3124, Australia
(a division of Pearson Australia Group Pty. Ltd.)
Penguin Books India Pvt. Ltd., 11 Community Centre, Panchsheel Park, New Delhi—110 017, India
Penguin Group (NZ), 67 Apollo Drive, Rosedale, North Shore 0632, New Zealand
(a division of Pearson New Zealand Ltd.)
Penguin Books (South Africa) (Pty.) Ltd., 24 Sturdee Avenue, Rosebank, Johannesburg 2196,
South Africa

Penguin Books Ltd., Registered Offices: 80 Strand, London WC2R 0RL, England

This book is an original publication of The Berkley Publishing Group.

This is a work of fiction. Names, characters, places, and incidents either are the product of the author's imagination or are used fictitiously, and any resemblance to actual persons, living or dead, business establishments, events, or locales is entirely coincidental. The publisher does not have any control over and does not assume any responsibility for author or third-party websites or their content.

PRINTING HISTORY
Berkley Sensation trade paperback edition / September 2010

Library of Congress Cataloging-in-Publication Data

Burns, Monica.
    Assassin's heart / Monica Burns.—Berkley Sensation trade paperback ed.
        p.   cm.—(The Order of the Sicari series ; 2)
    ISBN 978-0-425-23652-9
    1. Psychokinesis—Fiction.   2. Rome (Italy)—Fiction.   I. Title.
    PS3602.U76645A86 2010
    813'.6—dc22
                                                                    2010020084

PRINTED IN THE UNITED STATES OF AMERICA

10 9 8 7 6 5 4 3 2 1

For Beverly Castellano
You loved the concept of my Sicari heroes.
I only wish you could have seen them come to life on the page.
You are greatly missed.

Acknowledgments

With gratitude to Kati Dancy for her meticulous attention to detail and her demand for excellence. A special thanks to Ida Plassay for continuing to tutor me in Italian, and Maria Rosa Contardi for answering questions about Rome's current landscape, as well as her expertise in Italian and Latin. And a nod of gratitude to Billi J. Jones-DiMatteo, Nicole Burnham, Joyce Tenney, Lynne Connolly, and Binnie Syril (a network connection goddess). I couldn't have made the climax scene in the Pantheon realistic without each of your observations about this incredible monument.

Chapter 1

LYSANDER woke to screams. Pain was the next signal he was still alive. The cut on his thigh ached with the force of a charging bull ramming a horn into him. The screams intensified. They sounded like an animal's high-pitched squeals of terror and pain. His gut twisted. Dominic? Or Peter? He instantly reached out with his mind, and tried to figure out how many Praetorians were in the other room. Not a single emotion or thought.

Christus, how long had he been out? His telepathic ability had never been that strong, but at least he should have been able to know how many of the *bastardi* were out there. A salty taste on his tongue said his mouth was full of blood. He spit it out onto the floor and opened his eyes. The darkened room was not much bigger than a storage room. Nylon rope bound his wrists, pulling his arms up over his head in a painful stretch. He tugged on his restraints gently.

Merda, he hurt. How long had he been hanging here? The screams on the other side of his prison's door rose on a wild crescendo until they died down to low piteous cries. Praetorians had refined their torture skills during the Inquisition. Technology had just updated those skills. A cold, vicious bite of unfamiliar emotion tried to surge through him. He suppressed it.

No one survived Praetorian torture sessions, and the remains of the Sicari he'd seen said they'd died agonizing deaths. He closed his eyes in a desperate attempt to shut out those gruesome images. Think about something else. Phaedra. The ugly emotion building inside him eased slightly. *Deus*, she had a gorgeous mouth. And her hair. Soft as silk. Threading his fingers through that dark silk last night . . . last night. He winced as grief lashed at him. Maybe the Elysium Fields would let him re-create those incredible moments with her as often as he wanted.

Beside him, a soft whimper of fear forced him to turn his head. *Marta*. A few feet away, he saw his healer tied to the wall. Praise Jupiter, at least *she* was still alive. In the next breath, he remembered what happened to healers. Guilt gnawed at him with savage glee.

"Marta?"

"I'm scared, Lysander." The terror in her voice almost made him give in to his own fear.

"I know, *cara*."

"They took Peter first."

It was a simple statement, meant only to inform, but it sent more guilt slicing through him. This was his fault. He should have known something was wrong the minute they entered the warehouse.

"Marta—"

"Let it go, Lysander. You're not to blame." Her forgiveness ate away at him, but he ignored it.

"We're getting out of here." His fingers explored the knot of nylon holding his wrists together in a painful grip. Sailor's knot. Immediately, he visualized the rope slipping apart in opposite directions until it released him. Nothing happened. In the near darkness, he saw Marta turn her head toward him.

"It won't work." The words were a quiet sigh of defeat. "They gave the three of you some type of drug to suppress your telekinetics. Dominic tried to free himself all the way up to the last minute, but he couldn't. We're going to die here."

No. The Praetorians wouldn't let her die. She was breeding stock.

He buried the thought and returned his attention to the rope holding him hostage. Closing his eyes, his fingers helped him memorize the way the rope was tied. The screams in the other room gained momentum again, and almost as if they came from a distance, he heard Dominic's thoughts. A whisper more than anything else. Nothing clear. The drug had to be wearing off. But would it wear off in time to get him and Marta out of here?

The thought heightened his desperation to free himself. There wasn't anything he could do for his friend, but maybe he could get Marta out of here. Save her from a fate worse than what he would end up enduring. Even knowing that didn't make it easy to shut out the screams.

Almost as if she could read his thoughts, her fear vibrated through the room like an instrument being played with a wild fury. It reinforced his belief that his abilities were returning. He focused his attention on the knot, concentrating hard on mentally undoing the twisted fibers.

Dominic's screams grew louder—bouncing off the walls of the room at a frightening level. A sickening dread clawed at him. Concentrate. His friend was as good as dead. He had to focus on getting Marta out of this torture chamber. Overhead, he felt a slight movement in the rope.

Triumph rolled through him. He wanted to tell Marta, but he didn't. It would be cruel to raise her hopes only to see them crushed if he didn't succeed in time. The thought made him work harder. The rope nudged its way free a tiny bit more. In the back of his mind, he heard Phaedra's voice whispering encouragement.

He was certain it was a figment of his imagination, but it bolstered his courage in a way nothing else could. He'd be damned if he was going to lose her, just when he'd found her. He turned his attention back to the rope, only to sense what seemed to be Phaedra's fears for him. Impossible. He knew full well it was simply his mind compensating for the pressure he was under right now. The mind did strange things when it was under stress.

Once more, he focused on the rope, blocking out everything but the nylon knot. After several minutes, the mental drain made him ease up on his concentration. *Christus*, this was almost as hard as when he'd taken Cleo's dare as a kid to unlock the cabinet holding the Order's sacred Assent of Office parchments. This time his failure wouldn't be the *Indictio*. And right now, he'd willingly take on that hard labor. He visualized the rope's knot unraveling when a sudden shift in emotions echoed in the back of his head. Dominic's shrill screams swelled even louder in the small prison then abruptly went silent. A dark emotion slithered through his veins.

"Lysander."

The minute Marta said his name, he turned his head toward her. The resignation on her face filled him with rage, guilt, and fear. He'd failed. He was going to die, and Marta—he shut down the images of what she was going to endure.

"I'm still here, *cara*."

"They're coming."

"I know," he said hoarsely.

He frantically pictured the knot above his head falling open, releasing him from its hold. When that didn't work, base animal instinct took over, and he sawed at the nylon with his wrists in a hopeless effort to free himself.

"Lysander? I won't let them breed me," she whispered, almost as if consoling herself. "I'll find a way to keep that from happening."

"*Fotte*," he roared as the door to their prison flew open.

Blinded by the sudden light streaming into the room, he stretched out with his thoughts to determine how many Praetorians there were. Two. Fear and rage swelled inside him as he continued to saw at the rope with his wrists. Someone rushed at him, and his last thought was of Phaedra before the light in the room blinked out.

He awoke to find himself in restraints on a hard surface, his head locked into place by a leather strap. The rafters directly above him said he was still in the warehouse. The soft clink of metal tools hitting against each other made him want to turn toward the sound, but he couldn't. A quiet chuckle echoed in his mind, and he instinctively threw up a shield against the mental probe.

"Do you have a name, Unmentionable?"

The pleasant tone of the man's voice didn't ease the sudden fear crawling across his skin. It increased it. He closed his eyes and tried to stem the emotion that threatened to drown him. No. He couldn't give in to the terror. It would drain his ability to keep this *bastardo* out of his head. He swallowed hard and tried to focus on something pleasant. Something the Praetorian couldn't use against him.

Flowers. When was the last time he'd bought flowers for someone? The thought was idiotic, but he could sense the Praetorian's irritation as his mental barrier kept the man from probing deeper.

"Come now, Unmentionable. Tell me your name."

"Why? It doesn't really matter, does it?" An image of Phaedra slipped past the shield.

"Not really, but it does personalize the experience." There was a note of amusement in the man's voice that said he'd seen Phaedra. It sent a bolt of rage through him.

"I'm sure it does," he snarled as he opened his eyes to meet the flat gaze of the Praetorian. He rolled saliva and blood around in his mouth and spat it at the man. "Lysander Condellaire, *Primus Pilus* of the Order of the Sicari, son of Aurelia and Massimo Condellaire."

"A *Primus Pilus*. I'm honored." The man pretended to brush off a fleck of the spit that had not even come close to him. "It's not often I have a First Spear to administer redemption to. I am Nicostratus. Your judge *and* jury. As a heretic, you may repent at any time."

He didn't answer. Something said this *bastardo* liked to talk to his victims, and he wasn't going to give the son of a bitch that satisfaction. In fact, he was going to fight hard not to give the man *any* kind of response, no matter how bad—a red-hot needle of pain scraped its way across his skin. He nearly bit his tongue off to keep from screaming out loud.

Instead, he dug his fingers into his palms, and his body jerked violently against his restraints. It was impossible to escape the needle's persistent fire or the excruciating pain. When it stopped, he found himself breathing raggedly with relief—ready to sob. A moment later, his body bucked hard against the straps holding him down.

Ever so slowly, the skin on his face gave way to the man's cruel touch. Nerve endings sent horrifying signals to his brain at their sudden exposure to the air. He almost wept from the pain, but swallowed the cries he wanted to let loose.

"You're a brave man, Condellaire. It's not often I encounter an Unmentionable capable of holding back his cries when I strip his skin."

Lysander opened his eyes and he choked on a rush of bile as

Nicostratus showed him a strip of flesh dangling from a pair of small forceps. He swallowed the bitter fluid in his throat, but not before a wave of helplessness crashed over him. The emotion sent him spiraling down into a dark place where he wanted to hide from what was happening to him. No sooner did he hit the bottom of that hellish pit than he fought back. He bucked his body against his restraints.

"*Fotte* you, you Praetorian *bastardo*," he mumbled, each word more agonizing than the last as the movement of his lips tugged at the exposed muscles on his cheek. In his mind, he visualized his fist driving itself into the man's face.

His effort was rewarded by Nicostratus's head flying backward from the invisible punch. In less than two seconds, the man recovered and quickly reached for something on the tray next to the table. Needle in hand, the Praetorian pushed up Lysander's sleeve and proceeded to inject him with something.

"You're stronger than I thought. But this should keep you in check," Nicostratus said with just a hint of anger. The man started to push Lysander's sleeve down but stopped. "Well now, what have we here? A birthmark?"

The man's voice was coaxing in a way that sent an icy sensation creeping over Lysander's skin. An instant later, the exposed nerve endings on his cheek lit up in a bitter blast of fiery pain. *Christus*, the Praetorian was patting him on his exposed muscle. He fiercely bit down on the groan rising in his chest. When he didn't answer, the man made a small noise that indicated curiosity.

"Tell me, Condellaire, did your mother ever explain where this mark comes from?"

"My father, you *bastardo*."

"Your father. I see."

A whisper of sound drifted through his head. The son of a bitch was trying to read his mind again. Desperately, he fought to fortify the shield around his thoughts and filled his head with nonsensical images. Anything to block the man's probe. He would *not* let his mind betray the guild or the Order. The Praetorian's thoughts strengthened in an effort to dig deeper.

Lysander shored up the fragile wall he'd built inside his head with images of his mother. Determination and willpower helped him to pull every memory of his mother he could find inside him. The Praetorian chuckled. It wasn't a pleasant sound. Rather it encouraged the helplessness that had taken root in his stomach and spread through every muscle in his body.

The man's mental probe withdrew and Lysander's muscles shuddered into a limp state, his ability almost on the edge of failure. *Christus*, he couldn't fail. He wouldn't give this *bastardo* that satisfaction. The sound of metal against metal told him the carving was going to begin anew. Eyes closed and fists clenched tightly, he locked his jaw in preparation for the fiery needle to carve its way into his skin again.

"This is for not knowing me, boy."

Puzzled by the statement, the tension in his body eased just before the laser hit his skin. One thin stream of fire after another flew across his eye in an X pattern. Deep in the back of his mind, he started to sob from his inability to save his friends or himself from this hell. He was powerless, and the knowledge crushed him. Somewhere he heard the sound of screaming, and he realized it was him as the laser continued its terrible path across his cheek. He sank into the pit.

When he came to, he immediately wished he could crawl back into oblivion. He automatically opened his eyes, and the action shot a bolt of lightning deep into the back of his head as his eyelid pried itself off his seared eyeball. It pulled another roar of pain from him. Nicostratus laughed.

"Now then, my son. We need to talk, as we don't have much time."

"Just end it, you sorry *fotte*." The pain it cost him to speak made him slide toward the dark edge of the abyss, and he closed his eyes again.

"I'm not going to end it, Lysander. I couldn't kill my own son." The words ripped through him with the same painful force of the laser the man had used on him. This son of a bitch wasn't just insane, he was sadistic.

"*Merda di toro.*"

"No, it's true. I'm as surprised as you are. And I find it interesting that no one told you about your mother and me. We had a . . . well, let's say she resisted my charms."

Pain made his thoughts sluggish. Resisted. Was the *bastardo* saying he'd raped his mother? Not possible. The man was taunting him in an effort to break him down. The Praetorian made one more attempt to break the last defensive wall he'd built around the Order's strategic information. Unable to think straight, an image of Phaedra filled his head, and he clung to the memory of the night before. Nicostratus made an insulting noise.

"Ah, yes, that reminds me of how I fucked your mother. If I'd known she was ready to breed, I would have taken her with me."

"You're a liar." Each word sent fire shooting up into his brain, and it took him a moment to realize he was sobbing the words.

"No, my boy. Take a look."

Lysander tried to keep his eyes closed, but fingers pinched his eyelid, forcing open the only eye he had left. He stared at the mark on Nicostratus's arm. Immersed in agony, he couldn't focus. Despite his uncertainty as to what he was really looking at, he wanted to throw up. Deep inside him, a vague thought registered the image, but he refused to believe it. He tried to shake his head.

"What?" he whispered, barely able to speak.

"Look closer, Lysander. It's proof I'm your father."

"A mark?" He closed his eye, praying for oblivion. Fingers pinched his eyelid again.

"The eagle. Do you see it?"

He groaned as he blinked and focused on the mark the man had on his arm. The *bastardo* had lost it. That mark wasn't an eagle—it was a bird. *His* mark was an eagle. His mother had said it belonged to his father.

"Your's . . . bird. Not . . . eagle." He barely got the words out as he hovered on the brink of consciousness.

"Look again, boy."

Suddenly, there were two arms with matching eagles in almost identical spots thrust in front of him. They blurred. He was seeing double, that's all. The helplessness reached his heart, tearing it apart like a rabid animal. He stared, his mind trying to comprehend what he was seeing.

"No." He didn't have the strength to shout, and the Praetorian laughed.

"But of course it's true. I knew the minute I probed your mind. How else do you explain your extraordinary ability to resist my repeated probes for information? A true Sicari might show some resistance to me, but they would not be as strong as you." Nicostratus made a soft sound of amused disapproval.

"Not true," he rasped then roared with pain as the Praetorian bastard lightly tapped his skinned cheek again.

"You would have made a fine Praetorian, my boy. Your ability to defy the pain you're in is exceptional."

The laser hit his skin again from his ear down to his jaw. The pain pulled a pitched scream of agonized terror from him, and he fell backward into a black pool of nothingness—his last thought was of ancient Rome and Phaedra running to meet him. He was home again.

He had no idea how long he'd been out, but when he awoke, everything was silent and dark. Was it nighttime in the Elysium Fields? He tried to sit up. The slight movement sent fire streaking through every cell in his body. He started to cry. The Praetorian had left him here to die. Alone. His own son.

He grew still with horror. He wasn't Sicari. He was Praetorian. The obscene thought pulled a cry of denial from him. His mind hovered on the brink of despair. Impossible. It couldn't be true. But they shared the same birthmark. The whisper of truth curled through his head. He wouldn't believe it. The *bastardo* was lying. A teardrop rolled over his skinned cheek, and it pulled a sob of anguish from him.

"*Fotte. Fotte. Fotte.*"

It was a roar of fear and helplessness, as well as a cry of agony. More tears flowed over his bared muscles, until the pain sent him back to that dark place again.

Voices filtered their way down into the pit, and he shuddered with terror. They'd come back for him. Like a wild animal anticipating more torture, he tugged at his restraints, ignoring the fire that consumed his body. He wouldn't be able to keep the son of a bitch out of his head this time. He heard running feet, and then he smelled the soft scent of a woman. Marta?

"*Dulcis matris Deus*." Cleo leaned over him, her cool hand brushing across his forehead. Horror widened her eyes as she stared down at him. In the next instant, she spoke into her mike. "Lysander's alive, but I don't know for how much longer. He needs the *Curavi*. *Now*."

He couldn't hear the response she got, but a sudden image of Phaedra filled his head. She was here. A subtle warmth filled him as her fear and worry for him whispered sweetly across his mind. *Deus*, he needed her right now. Needed to feel her touch. Her hand in his, her healing—*no*.

The sound of feet pounded on the warehouse floor once more, and first Ares then Phaedra came into view. He'd never seen a more beautiful, yet terrifying, sight in his entire life. He couldn't take part in seeing her lovely face marred by his injuries. Couldn't let her see the monster inside him. Terror lanced through him as she reached for his hand. Tormented, he tugged at the restraints. If she touched him—tried to heal him, she'd see him for what he was. He couldn't let that happen. Couldn't let her perform the *Curavi*.

"No. No *Curavi*."

Cleo clamped down on his arm. "*Christus*, he's out of his mind with pain."

"For the love of God, Cleo. Tighten those restraints." Panic laced through Phaedra's voice. "I can't heal him if he's fighting me. I'll heal the lesser injuries first. Then we can transport him. When we're home, I'll . . . I'll do what I can for his other wounds."

He saw her swallow hard and recognized her fear. The idea of her taking on his injuries was a nightmare, but he knew without a doubt that when she touched him she'd be able to see all the darkness inside him. He was too weak to keep her locked out of his thoughts if she touched him. She'd see. She'd see everything because the pain was too horrible to prevent her from learning the truth.

"*No*," he roared. "*No Curavi*."

The strength of his voice echoed loudly in the room, and he heard Ares utter a vicious curse while Cleo grasped his hand in a death grip. Fear and horror darkened Phaedra's eyes as she bent over him. Her mouth brushed across the ear on his unmarked cheek.

"Let me do this for you, *carino*," she whispered in a sweet, gentle voice. "I'm not afraid."

"*No*. Refuse the *Curavi*."

He tried to shake his head as he forged through the pain and ground out the words forcefully. Couldn't let her see. Her parents' murder . . . hated Praetorians . . . couldn't bear her hatred. He felt himself slipping off into oblivion and climbed up the cliff back into the pain. She'd heal him without his permission if he didn't protest.

"Listen, you dumb son of a bitch." Cleo's voice was harsh. "You let Phaedra heal you or I'm going to rip you a new one. You hear me?"

"No . . . dead already." And he was. He was Praetorian, and if anyone found out . . . he'd rather die.

"Give me your hands, Lysander. With your permission, I must touch you to heal your injuries." There was a frantic desperation in Phaedra's voice, but it only made him clench his hands into tight fists.

"I. Refuse. *Curavi*."

His voice wasn't loud, but it was strong and determined. He heard someone nearby release a vicious sound. Ares. His *Legatus* forcefully pushed Cleo aside to grip his arm.

"Take the goddamn *Curavi*, you sorry *bastardo*," his guild leader ordered in a fierce voice.

Something wet hit his unscarred cheek, and his gaze shifted from Ares to Phaedra. In the dim light, he could see tears clinging to her lashes. He wouldn't hurt her. Wouldn't let her see he was everything she hated. He loved her too much. He couldn't let her see that *or* his shame. He released a sob of pain.

"Is. My. Right. *Refuse*. *Curavi*." Each word was a labor of effort to say.

"*No*," Phaedra exclaimed violently. "I'm not about to let you die, you dumb *bacciagalupe*. Ares, make him take the *Curavi*."

"No. My. Right." He hovered on the edge of light and dark.

"I can't, Phaedra. If he'd been unconscious, it wouldn't be a problem, but he's refused. There's nothing I can do." Ares's voice was fierce with disgusted anger.

"Please, Lysander. Don't refuse me." His cheek grew wet as Phaedra bent over him, her mouth against his ear. Her hand bit into his arm, and he felt a pulse of energy as she pleaded with him. "Don't try to save me from the pain. Let me save you. I want to do this for you. I don't want you to die."

The heat in her hand grew stronger, and a roar built in his chest. With a wild cry, he bucked against the restraints holding him in place. Restraints that proved he'd been powerless against the Praetorian, but he wasn't helpless anymore. He had the right to refuse the *Curavi*. And for her sake, he wasn't about to let her heal him.

"Get the fuck away from me. I don't want your goddamn healer's touch. I refuse *Curavi*." The blast of words made him pay a dear price as a cloak of needles wrapped itself around him, digging into every part of his body. He saw the agony flare in her beautiful brown eyes, and deep inside a voice cried out for her. The only thing that kept him from taking his words back was the darkness welling up inside him. He was Praetorian. There was nothing that could change that. But it was his secret. A truth he couldn't share with anyone, not even the woman he loved.

Chapter 2

DEMETRI. Phaedra awoke with a start. She'd been dreaming again. No, more of a nightmare, because she'd been scared. The fragments of the dream were like dark tendrils she recognized but couldn't really see. The only thing she remembered clearly was that she'd been in ancient Rome. Lysander had been there as well, but how or why, she couldn't remember. It wasn't the first time she'd had this type of dream. But it had never made her feel this disoriented and scared before.

Even her bed felt wrong. She shot upright. It wasn't her bed. It was a sleeper chair in Lysander's hospital room. A quick glance at her watch said she'd been asleep about two hours. That made for a total of about four hours in the last thirty-six. Her ability was always weaker when she didn't get enough sleep or if she drank too much. And she wasn't sure her touch would be strong enough to help Lysander if he woke up, let alone if he actually agreed to her performing the *Curavi* this time.

Her gaze focused on the still figure in the hospital bed, and the soft sound of the heart monitor filled her ears as if it were a booming church bell. Between his internal injuries, sword wounds, and the side of his face stripped of skin, he was lucky to be alive. Bandages covered most of his face, while she could see the black sutures on his lower lip. A white sheet and blanket covered the rest of his visible injuries.

An overwhelming need to touch him swept through her, and she left her chair to move toward the bed. She brushed her fingers through his short blond hair. He looked so helpless, something she instinctively knew he'd hate. He shouldn't be here. He should be completely healed.

She closed her eyes for a brief moment. Why had he refused the *Curavi*? What had possessed him to reject her healer's touch? The only answer she could think of was that he didn't want her to suffer what he had. He'd been afraid for her. A tear slid down her cheek. Didn't the man understand she was willing to go to the depths of Tartarus for him?

The delicate creak of the room's heavy oak door drew her attention away from Lysander as she saw Ares enter the room. She immediately averted her head, and with a furtive swipe of her hand, she dried her damp cheek. A strong hand clasped her shoulder, forcing her to turn around.

"I just talked to the doctor. He's going to be okay," Ares said. "He can have plastic surgery to eliminate most of the damage."

The words eased some of her fear, but not all of it. He'd been through a Praetorian torture session. Something few Sicari had ever survived. The physical trauma was repairable, but the emotional toll it extracted was high. A large number of survivors had deliberately thrown themselves into combat situations where there was no hope of survival. The thought of that happening to Lysander terrified her.

"Hey, you don't have to stay here," Ares said gently.

"No," she whispered and looked at the wall clock. "There may still be time. It's not been quite twenty hours since we found him. There's still a four-hour window. It might be enough."

She'd not explained her reasons for coming with Lysander to the Order's central headquarters in Genova, Italy, but Ares had agreed to her demand without any objection. Her brother probably thought she was hoping to convince Lysander to accept the *Curavi* once he woke. Doctors could repair his face, but she was the only one who might be able to give him back his sight, and there wasn't any guarantee she could do that for him. But there was a window of time for healing wounds, and it hardly ever extended past twenty-four hours. The longer the time frame, the less likely the *Curavi* would work. Ares frowned at her.

"Phae, you're the best healer the Order has, but the odds are he's already past the turning point, and not even you can heal him then."

"Maybe, but I need to at least try." She shook her head at her brother's exasperated expression.

"If Lysander rejected the *Curavi* when he was close to dying, what makes you think he'd accept it now?"

"I don't, but if he wakes up in time, I have to try." She didn't look at Ares. Instead, she turned away from the bed and went to stand at the sliding glass door.

Designed with an eye toward a patient's physical and spiritual needs, the secluded and fortified hospital gave the Order's patients access to sunshine and fresh air as part of their recovery process. A large garden stretched its way outward from the small patio adjoining Lysander's room. In the early-morning light, the beauty outside was a stark contrast to the pain and darkness she knew Lysander was experiencing.

Deus, she hated the *bastardi* who'd done this to him. For almost two thousand years, the Praetorians had hunted the Sicari. At one time, the Sicari had been a part of the Praetorian Guard. Like their enemy, they'd served as bodyguards to the Caesars of ancient Rome, they'd had wealth, position, and power. But the Guard had split at the time of Constantine I, and those in power had cast out a select group of brothers. They labeled the outcast Sicari. Assassins.

They called the Sicari heretics, and yet like the vermin they were, the Praetorians hid from the world behind the robes of the Carpenter's church. Using the banner of righteousness, they'd sought to exterminate the Sicari, inflicting terrible atrocities on her people as well as the innocent. A soft groan drifted through the air to pierce her thoughts. She whirled around to see Ares move quickly to the bed, his hands on the bed rail, bending over his friend.

"Hey, how you feeling, *amici*?"

"Like *stronzo*." Lysander's voice was so soft she had to strain to hear him.

"Yeah, well you could be feeling a lot worse," Ares joked. From where she was standing at the door, she saw Lysander suddenly grab her brother's hand.

"Marta?"

The one word question was little more than a hiss of air, and she saw Ares struggle to come up with an answer. They'd found Dominic and Peter, but the Sicari woman was gone. Marta would live, but in a living hell. The Praetorian *bastardi* would rape her constantly both for physical pleasure and in an effort to impregnate her. Any children Marta bore would be taken from her. The males raised in the Praetorian Collegium and the females murdered. The woman would have been better off dying in that warehouse. Without hesitating, she went to the opposite side of the bed.

"They took her," she said, hating herself for it. She should have lied to him, but he would eventually learn the truth. Stretching out her hand, she lightly touched him on the shoulder. With a violent jerk, he retreated from her hand.

"*No.*" His dark growl was fierce and intense.

"Take it easy, pal." Ares gently grasped the warrior's arm. "It's just Phae. You're safe here."

"Leave, *now.*"

He didn't say her name, but she knew he meant her, and the demand sent pain slicing through her until she swayed on her feet. Fingers wrapped tightly around the cold metal of the bedside rail, she met his gaze with her heart pounding like mad in her chest. Something wasn't right. She could almost feel the erratic swell of his emotions crawling across her skin. It was unlike anything she'd ever experienced before. Nothing was truly discernible except the bleak darkness that consumed him. Wild and thrashing, it was frightening in its intensity.

Deus, it would eat him alive if he didn't release it. It wasn't unusual for her to feel or see emotions or images when she healed someone. If she healed him, he might be able to release some of the dark emotion inside him through her. The thought of taking on that horrifying darkness sent a streak of terror slithering down her spine like a serpent poised to strike. She shuddered. It didn't matter. She could do this. She could do it for him.

"Ares, leave us." Her soft command whispered across the bed, and Lysander almost managed to jerk upright.

"*No.*" This time his objection was stronger, more forceful. Determined to get him to agree to the *Curavi*, she glared down at him.

"Lie back down, you dumb *bacciagalupe.* You're going to rip out some stitches or worse, your IV," she snapped fiercely. "Ares, get the hell out of here, *now*."

The furious response silenced both men, and without another word, Ares left the room. Alone with Lysander, she held on to the metal bar of the bed guard for dear life and stared down at the stranger in the hospital bed. Her voice died in her throat at his granite expression. *Dulcis matris Deus*, what had they done to him, and would she survive the knowledge?

"Leave, Phaedra." Cold and detached, the command made her flinch.

"Not until you let me try to heal you." She fought to keep her voice steady, yet resolute. "There might still be a chance I can—"

"You don't know when to give up, do you?" His voice was husky with pain, but there was an odd note in his voice that had her nerve endings standing on end.

"No. Not if I believe I can help you."

"I don't want your help." He shifted in the bed slightly, a grunt breaking past his lips. She had to stiffen her body to keep from reaching out to touch him.

"I know you're worried about my pain, but it comes with the territory. I promise you, I won't melt." Her words tugged a soft laugh from him. It was a cruel sound, and it made her flinch.

"Stop trying so hard, Phaedra. There's no need to get sentimental on me." The chiseled expression on his face didn't reveal anything. "We both know you can't give me back my eye."

"You don't know that, and we won't find out if you don't at least let me try."

"Why?"

"Why?" she gasped. "Because I want you whole again."

"You want me whole again." He repeated her words with a sarcasm that cut deep.

"That's not what I meant, and you know it."

She grabbed his forearm in anger. He knew damn well what she was trying to say. She wanted to erase the horror he'd endured. She wanted to try and ease the darkness she sensed in him. Free him from the inner pain that was gnawing at him like a mad dog. An invisible pressure pried her fingers off his arm.

"Look, all I want is *you* out of this room and away from me," he said in a disgusted voice.

She shivered. He was hurt. That was all. He'd seen the horror on her face last night. He knew what a healer went through during the *Curavi*. He had to have known that first sight of him had triggered fear. It was why he'd refused her touch. It's why he was rejecting her now. He was looking for a reason to get rid of her. But she wasn't going to let him get away with it.

"*Christus*, do you really think it matters to me what you look like?" She smacked the cold stainless steel barrier between them with desperate fury. "I don't give a damn what you look like as long as I'm with you."

Her words hung in the air for a long minute as he just stared at her, his expression slowly easing into one of amusement. It sent a wild streak of fear winding through her.

"With me?" His snort of laughter held a note of cold cruelty that made her clutch at the bed rail in a frantic effort to stop her trembling.

"Yes, the other night . . ." Her voice trailed off for a second as a sneer tugged at his mouth and his eyebrow went skyward. When he didn't speak, she stumbled forward. "I thought that . . . you and I—"

"Come on, *bambina*." His green eye held an insolent gleam as he raked his gaze from her face to her breasts then back up again. "The sex wasn't bad, but did you *really* see it going beyond a one-nighter?"

The words hit her with the force of a hard slam to the training mat. She couldn't move. All she could do was struggle to find a way to absorb the blow. Her grip on the steel rail tightened to the point she was certain she would bend the metal. He was lying. He had to be. Didn't he? She stared at the amused condescension on his face, her stomach lurching with a nausea that made her want to throw up.

"If you're doing this because you think last night changed things between us—"

"Look, *dolcezza*, it was just one fuck. Let's not make it into something bigger than that."

If his words weren't crippling enough, the boredom in his voice was the same as if she'd taken a Praetorian blade in her back. The pain of it made her legs buckle beneath her until the only thing holding her up was her deadlock on the metal rail of the bed guard. Desperation snarled its way through her as she stared down at him.

"You bastard," she breathed as humiliation churned her stomach so hard she thought she'd throw up what little food she had in her stomach.

She turned away from him slowly, her legs feeling rubbery. His face was almost out of her vision when she thought she saw a flash of agony cross his face. She paused to look back, but she realized she was wrong. He still wore the same contemptible smirk. Unable to bear looking at him, she stumbled out into the hospital corridor. Ares was walking toward her and tried to stop her. She brushed him off and headed for the main entrance. The sooner she was back in Chicago the better. There were Praetorians to kill, and maybe, just maybe, she'd get lucky enough to find a way to end her misery. The glass doors of the hospital entrance opened with a quiet swish, and she walked out into the sunshine knowing the life she'd thought she had was over before it had even begun.

Chapter 3

"*I intend to marry him.*" *Cassiopeia stared across the atrium at the tall Roman general conversing with her father. Beside her, Octavian Julius Valeria frowned darkly.*

"*It's a ridiculous notion, my pet. Maximus has nothing to offer in the way of family or fortune. You should marry me.*"

"*I don't love you, Octavian. But I do love Maximus.*"

Her gaze never left Maximus. She was grateful for the cool night air that streamed in through the opening in the atrium's roof and the cross currents that pulled a soft breeze into the peristylium. Watching Maximus made it much warmer in the house than it was. The sight of him filled her with an ache that heated her blood with Apollo's fire until it settled between her legs in a rush of liquid warmth.

"*Romans don't marry for love. We marry to keep the patrician houses strong.*" *Octavian's tone was sharp, telling her he wasn't happy at all.*

"*And Maximus will make the Atellus name stronger when father adopts him. Maximus Caecilius Atellus. Just the sound of it rings with great strength. Our sons will ensure my father's name continues, and I shall have Maximus. It's an excellent arrangement.*"

"*I've known Maximus for a long time. The man has an aversion to marriage.*" *Octavian snorted with amusement.* "*What makes you think you can change his mind.*"

"Because I intend to make him fall in love with me."

Across the room, Maximus laughed at something her father said, and that familiar tug on her senses increased. His plebeian family hailed from the northern part of the Empire, and the Gaul influence showed in the dark blond hair he wore short. Although she couldn't see his green eyes from here, she knew how striking and unusual they were. He might not have patrician blood, but he had the air of one. His strong nose and sensual mouth lent itself to the impression that he was a noble. Venus could not have designed a man more delicious if she'd tried. Normally, he wore his military uniform when he visited her father, but tonight he was dressed in the fine robes indicative of the position Emperor Maxentius had given him in the Senate. She preferred his uniform. It showed off his strong, sinewy legs and the strength of his arms. Arms that held the promise of all measure of delights. She wanted to see all of him bared before her.

"If this is an attempt to have me express my feelings in poetry reminiscent of Ovid, I will do that if necessary," Octavian said quietly. When she didn't answer, his voice sharpened. "Don't be a fool. He's not good enough for you, Cassiopeia."

Slowly turning her head, she studied the anger on Octavian's face. It was unlike him to be so quarrelsome with her. Octavian had been the one to introduce Maximus to her father. Eager to appease her friend, she touched his arm lightly.

"Octavian, how can you say such a thing? Maximus is your friend."

"Friendship is one thing. Marrying into a patrician household is something completely different."

She frowned. Was her childhood friend right? As one of the senior statesmen in the Senate, the name of Gaius Quinctilia Atellus was associated with fairness and levelheaded thinking. But would he object to Maximus as a son-in-law? No. He liked her handsome Roman general very much. If anything, her father would welcome Maximus into the family with open arms. The only thing needed of her was to convince Maximus to fall in love with her. She shook her head.

"You disappoint me, Octavian. I never thought you would be in

the camp of those who prefer the patrician class to remain pure. The fact that Maximus is your friend only makes it worse."

Without allowing the man to utter a response, she moved away from him. As hostess, she found it necessary to stop and greet several prominent guests she'd invited at her father's request. It seemed to take an interminable amount of time to make her way around the shallow, water-filled impluvium with its resplendent mosaic to where her general and her father stood. When she finally reached the two men, she saw Maximus grow rigid with tension. His physical reaction made her bite back a smile. He was aware of her more than he cared to admit. "Father," she murmured a greeting as she kissed his cheek before she turned to the man she intended to conquer. "General, I'm delighted you could join us."

Her hands outstretched, she forced him to take her hands in his. They were large hands, rough and strong. The hands of a soldier. She wanted to feel their roughness against her skin. As she stood on tiptoe to kiss his cheek and then the other, he had no choice but to lower his head toward her. Her cheek brushing against his, she pressed her mouth against his ear.

"There isn't a woman in this room who can take their eyes off you. Including me."

At her whisper, he pulled back abruptly, his eyes narrowing as he stared down at her. The vivid green of his gaze studied her for a long moment before he looked at her father. She glanced over her shoulder to see her father barely restraining his amusement.

"Forgive my daughter, Maximus. I've given her free rein for so long, it's impossible to control her."

"Perhaps it's simply a matter of finding the right hand to gentle her."

The amused note in Maximus's voice sent irritation spiraling through her. This wasn't the way he was supposed to respond to her. She suppressed her annoyance and forced a smile to her lips as she summoned Adela to her side with a wave of her hand.

With only a small command, the freedwoman hurried away to find the dancers hired as the evening's entertainment. As music filled the room, she looked up at Maximus and offered him her most *beguiling smile. His green eyes darkened, and she quickly turned her gaze to the erotic dance being performed in front of them. Suddenly, she realized it might be difficult to make him dance to her tune.*

Another senator hailed her father from across the room, and he excused himself, leaving her alone with Maximus. Tension as finely taut as a spider's web wove through her as she watched the dancers. After a long moment, she braved a quick glance up at him. To her surprise, he was openly studying her, and she could feel the heat of a blush cresting over her cheeks.

"You blush like a vestal virgin, my lady." The whisper was almost a caress against her skin, and the sound of his voice sent the blood pounding through her veins.

"Do I?" she choked out.

"Most certainly," he said with a soft laugh that made her legs go weak. "It enhances your beauty."

"You think I'm beautiful?" Startled, she looked up at him in surprise.

No one, not even her father had ever said she was beautiful. A look of hunger swept across his face and it sent a thrill whirling through her. Strong fingers bit into her upper arm as he quietly pulled her away from the festivities, through the peristylium, and into one of the empty rooms reserved for the family's use. The scent of the flowers in the large garden that was the peristylium drifted into the small room as he pulled the privacy curtain closed behind them. Her heart skipped a beat, and she breathed in Maximus's raw male scent as he advanced on her until her back came up against a cool marble column. She was certain it was her imagination, but she could almost feel his fingers caressing her throat before they trailed their way down to the valley between her breasts. The fanciful sensation made her nipples grow hard as unripe cherries.

"You've been playing with fire for several weeks now, mea mellis," he growled. "Exactly what is your game?"

She'd seriously misjudged her attraction for him. He was far more devastating alone. She swallowed hard and shook her head. "I don't play games."

"Then what is it you want from me, Cassiopeia?" The flicker of emotion in his piercing gaze sent her pulse racing.

"You. I want you for my lover." Unspoken emotion charged the air, and she knew better than to elaborate any further.

He jerked upright with a shake of his head. *"You're a senator's daughter."*

"And this figures into the equation how?" she said in an annoyed tone. She'd expected him to scoff at a relationship, not to point out their different social stations.

"I'm a simple soldier."

"Are you saying that in service to the Empire you've been injured in some way that prevents you—"

In a split second, arms solid as oak pulled her into the heat of his body. He felt as good as she had imagined he would. Hard, sinewy, and all male. Her body ached with need as his erection beneath his robe pressed into the apex of her thighs. Desire spiraled through her and she shifted her hips forward, wishing there was nothing between them to prevent him from sliding into her. His mouth plundered hers, and she sighed as his tongue forced its way past her lips in a kiss filled with passion. He was hers. She knew that with even more certainty now. Almost as if he could read her mind, he released her and put several feet between them. His breathing was ragged as he studied her in the low light.

"You're playing with fire, mea dulce.*"*

"No." She shook her head and closed the distance between them. She curled her hand around his neck then pulled his head down and brushed her lips against his. *"I know what I want. And I want you."*

He kissed her hard before his mouth trailed a hot path over her jaw and down the side of her neck. *Deus,* the man's touch was all she'd imagined. She trembled in his arms in anticipation. The desire building inside her forced her hips forward to brush against his hard length beneath his tunic. Heat pooled between her legs. She drank in the rough, male smell of him. If this was what love felt like, what heights would her desire for him take her to?

The thought sent a shudder through her. It was still possible to lose him. He desired her, but could she make him love her? What if she failed? She refused to consider the possibility. She would win. She would have this man's heart. There was no other option for her.

His hands skimmed up her arms to tug at the fragile material that was her gown. It gave way beneath his rough fingers until the bodice fell to reveal a breast. Ever so slowly, his mouth caressed its way from her shoulder to the taut nipple. He suckled her for a delicious moment then eased his lips back up to her throat.

"Please, Maximus."

"There will be no going back, mea dulce."

"I have decided. You have no choice," she whispered.

She was floating and she realized he was carrying her to one of the couches. By the gods, he was going to make her his right now. Her heart tightened with love and joy. Now he might feel only desire, but love could not be far behind. The soft pillows of the couch pressed against her back. With a gentleness that was at odds with his soldier's hands, he pulled her gown up to her hips.

Heat spread its way across her thigh as his fingers undid the cloth concealing her core. A guttural noise rolled out of him as he exposed her to his eyes. His throat bobbed violently as he swallowed. Against her skin, she felt his fingers tremble. Amazement swept through her as her gaze met his. There was something else besides passion glowing there. It reassured her that she'd made the right decision to force his hand. His touch parted her, and she arched up against his fingers . . .

ROME, ITALY
PRESENT DAY

The buzzer on the alarm clock shattered the dream, and Phaedra groaned with disappointment as she slapped the snooze button to eliminate the annoying sound. She desperately wanted to go back to sleep. It had been such a deliciously wicked dream. The only problem was her body ached for the man in her dreams. Lysander.

Damn, it had been more than a year since he'd brutally rejected her that night in the Order's Genova medical center. Why was the man still haunting her dreams? She winced. She knew why. Just because he'd crushed her heart, it hadn't stopped her from loving him. She was as big a fool as they came. Why couldn't she get the man out of her heart *and* her head? The thought tugged a groan out of her. And these dreams. They made no sense at all. Why would she be dreaming about the first Sicari Lord and his wife, Cassiopeia?

For that matter, why did Maximus look like Lysander *before* the Praetorians tortured him? She rubbed sleep out of one eye with the heel of her palm. Whatever the dream was trying to tell her—and dreams always meant something—all she wanted was the man she'd fallen in love with more than a year ago. A sigh of resignation whispered out of her. Whatever those Praetorian *bastardi* had done to him, they'd destroyed that man. The man in that hospital bed hadn't been the same man who'd made love to her.

Her thoughts drifted back to that horrible morning. Pain forced her eyes closed. Hearing those cruel words from him had been the most humiliating moment of her life. But worse was the pain that had come with it. She'd left the hospital numbed to anything but her desire to strike back. To make him hurt as bad as he'd hurt her.

And she'd worked hard to do that from the moment he came back to Chicago. Every chance she had, she flung her barbs at him as if they were darts. But he never acted as if any of her sharp jabs had hit their mark. That is until the night of Julian's *Rogalis*, his memorial service. The moment she'd blamed Lysander for her friend's death she'd wanted to take the words back. Her words had finally found their mark, and the anguish on Lysander's face had twisted her insides in a way that said she had gone too far. Out in the small sitting room, the sound of the apartment door opening and closing with a loud bang echoed into the bedroom.

"Phae, you awake?"

She groaned. Cleo. Didn't the woman ever sleep? Her friend had picked her up at the Order's private hangar at Rome's International Airport when she'd arrived late last night, and now she was up before her. She adjusted the spaghetti strap of her camisole nightshirt and slid out of bed. Her friend wasn't about to let her sleep any longer. Not that she'd be able to. She was going to be on tenterhooks until she talked to Lysander and asked him why he'd summoned her to Rome. Even more importantly, she was going to do something she *never* did. Apologize.

She grimaced at the thought. Apologies meant she'd screwed up. And even if the words had been said in the height of her own grief and remorse, he'd not deserved the blame she'd laid at his feet. Clearing the air between them would make the difference between this assignment being tolerable or unbearable. The room's cool air made her shiver, and she reached for her robe as she headed toward the sitting room. The sight of Cleo seated on the couch, chewing on a bagel, tugged a smile to her lips.

"Did you bring anything for *me* to eat?" Her question made the Sicari fighter turn her head to look at her, a grin on her lovely features.

"Absolutely." Cleo pointed to a small plate of fruit and cheese. "All I could find in the fridge was some Romano. It's a tad salty, but the fruit should take the bite out of it."

Beautiful enough to be a cover model, her friend was tangible proof of their Roman heritage. Mysterious dark eyes, midnight black hair, and a smile that could charm even a Praetorian. But then Cleo was more interested in killing the Sicari's sworn enemy than charming them. An opinion Phaedra held with even more vehemence than her friend did. The *bastardi* had stolen her childhood and hurt the man she loved. As far as she was concerned, the only good Praetorian was a dead one.

Phaedra curled up at the opposite end of the couch and reached for an apple. After a couple of bites, she leaned forward to take some Romano off the plate. The hard cheese had a kick to it and was a little salty like Cleo had said. Still, the Italian cheese was one of her favorites, specifically for its sharp bite.

"So, what do you think this is all about?" Cleo sent her an arched look.

"What kind of question is that? We're in Rome because Atia thinks the *Tyet of Isis* is here."

"Mother has always thought the *Tyet of Isis* was here in Rome, and you know *damn well* that's not what I'm talking about." Her friend snorted. "For the past year Lysander's been emphatic about not having you on any of his teams then suddenly, whoosh, you're on his team here in Rome."

"You'll have to ask him that question." She shrugged and took another bite of her apple.

The last thing she intended to do was let Cleo know how confused she was by this change in him. But had he really changed? When she looked back over the past year without anger fueling her perceptions, she was coming to realize he'd always had her back.

On the three occasions they'd actually served on the same reconnaissance team, his sword, not her partner's, had always been the one to save her at the last second. Then there was the night Ares had run the gauntlet. Running through a corridor of armed Sicari warriors wasn't supposed to be painless. The brutal punishment for breaking one of the major laws of the Order had almost killed her brother. For a healer to touch a survivor during the first twenty-four hours was a punishable offense as well. But breaking the rules ran in the family. After healing Ares's internal injuries, she'd been weak as a kitten.

Lysander had been the one to see she got back to her room. The man had actually carried her there. A moment that had delivered her into the Elysium Fields only to be pulled back into Tartarus far too quickly when he'd left her alone. And he'd not betrayed her to Atia, the *Prima Consul*. He'd kept her secret when the Order's leader questioned them about the whole incident.

If he didn't care about her, why would he do all that? Was it because he was Ares's friend, or was there something more to his behavior than she realized. *Deus*, she really was a fool to think that. She suddenly realized Cleo had asked a question and was watching her like a hawk. She frowned as she met her friend's intense gaze.

"What?"

"I asked if you were okay with all of this?"

Without even trying, she could easily read Cleo's concern. While her healing ability was the strongest of her Sicari skills, Phaedra also had the ability to sense emotions in others. It was like emotional radar. Sometimes it gave her only a sense of someone's intentions, while at other times she could read emotions buried deep beneath the surface.

Cleo wasn't probing, she was just worrying about her as any friend would, and they'd been friends a long time. It had been Cleo's mother, Atia, who had taken her and Ares in after the Praetorians had massacred their parents. The memory of those terrifying moments flashed in front of her eyes.

The priest's closet her mother had pushed Ares and her into as she kissed them good-bye. The sound of her mother's screams as she was being butchered. The peephole she'd peered through to see her mother's murderer. The face of the Praetorian that had haunted her all these years. His cruel laughter as he'd reached out with his mind, trying to read their thoughts and discover their hiding place.

From the age of six, she'd learned how to shield her thoughts from Praetorians, but her skills and Ares's hadn't been fully developed then. The man had known it. He'd known it was simply a matter of time before he found them. The only thing that had saved them was another Praetorian ordering the murderer to leave.

"This whole thing really does have you shaken up, doesn't it?" Her friend frowned with concern.

"It's a job, Cleo. Nothing more."

"If that's true, then why do you keep zoning out on me?" Cleo said with a snort of disbelief.

"I've just got a lot on my mind."

"Right. So what are you going to do about it?"

"Do about it?" She knew exactly what Cleo was referring to but refused to go there.

"You need to talk to him about it."

"About Julian's *Rogalis*?" She grimaced and dodged the true intent of Cleo's remark.

"I'm not talking about that, and you know it." Her friend glared at her. "I'm talking about that night in the warehouse."

The statement immediately threw Phaedra back into the past, the pain of it sweeping through her like a wildfire. The sight of Lysander lying on that metal slab, his entire body reflecting a man on the edge of death. When she'd reached him, she'd expected him to be unconscious, but to see him alert and in agony had been devastating. Then when he'd refused the *Curavi*—she swept the memories aside.

"There's nothing left to say."

She recognized the hollow note in her voice. It represented that piece of her that was missing. Cleo was right. There was a lot more she wanted to say. But Lysander didn't want to hear it, because he just didn't care. Her heart contracted as she remembered his cruelty that night in the hospital.

"Oh, puhleeze." Cleo released a soft snort of disgust. "I know you better than that. Both of you. That man didn't refuse the *Curavi* for the hell of it. He was protecting you that night."

The apple crunched as Phaedra bit into it. The sound reminded her how bruised and battered she'd felt the morning she'd left Lysander's hospital room. The pain had eased, but the numbness was still there after all these months. A painful sign that she was still in love with him.

"Even if what you're saying is true, he's not willing to discuss what happened, and neither am I," she said with a glare at her friend.

"Oh, really?" Cleo snapped.

"Yes, *really*. I don't know what makes you think there's more to this than what I'm telling you."

"Well, let me think . . . oh, right, the two of you have been at each other's throats since . . . since that night in Englewood. No wait—*you've* constantly eviscerated the man, while the dumb son of a bitch has just taken it without blinking."

"We've always argued. You know that."

"But it's different now."

"Different how?" She tried to sound nonchalant, but her friend narrowed her beautiful eyes at her.

"There's something under the surface of it all. It's not something I can put into words." Cleo's perceptive observation made her cold with panic.

"The reason you can't put it into words is that there is *nothing* different."

"That's bullshit," Cleo snapped as she sent her a dark glare. "Ever since that night at Julian's *Rogalis*, it's been like watching two wildcats snarling their way through some sort of mating ritual."

"You've got one hell of an imagination," she bit out through clenched teeth. The analogy had only served to increase her anxiety level. If Cleo saw it, did Lysander? "Now if you don't mind, I need to shower then check in with the *Primus Pilus*."

"*Va bene*," Cleo said with a stubborn grimace as she stood up. "But I'm right about all of this, and you know it."

"I'll just leave you to your delusions," she lied as she glared upward at her friend.

"*Christus*, you're as stubborn as Lysander. I'm betting the minute the two of you have it out with each other you're going to be in bed together faster than someone can say *fotte*." Speechless, Phaedra watched Cleo smile with satisfaction. "Interesting. Phaedra DeLuca doesn't have a comeback for a change.

"I don't have a comeback because you sound like a lunatic."

"Not really. In case you haven't noticed, whenever the man thinks no one's watching him, he can't take his eyes off of you." Cleo arched her eyebrows and popped another grape into her mouth.

Phaedra froze at the other woman's statement, her heart skipping a beat. Was it possible Cleo was right? But if he cared, why didn't he do something about it? Why would he have shut her out the way he had? It didn't make sense.

"Have you thought about seducing the man?" Cleo's voice filtered through her thoughts.

"*What?*" She gaped at her friend's mischievous expression. Appalled at the direction of the conversation, she shook her head vehemently. "*No.* Absolutely not."

"Not willing to risk failure, eh?"

Riled by the comment, she clamped her jaw shut before she said something else she'd regret. The notion of seducing Lysander was far too tempting a thought—not to mention a hopeless one. The fact was she *wasn't* willing to risk failure. Failure would mean an even greater heartache than she was experiencing now. She shook her head.

"I'm not going to let you provoke me into doing something stupid. So drop the subject."

Clearly disappointed, Cleo grimaced as the small desk clock chimed the hour, and she immediately sprang to her feet. "*Crap*, I've got to run. *Ciao, bambola.*"

With that final parting shot, her friend was gone, leaving her in a state of confusion. Left alone, Phaedra stared at her surroundings with a sense of fear. Could she do what Cassiopeia had done in her dreams? What would happen if she tried to seduce Lysander as Cleo had suggested. Did she have the courage to even try? She blew out an angry sigh of disgust.

She was crazy. *No*, Cleo was crazy. Falling into bed with Lysander was something she did only in her dreams now. Dreams where he was Maximus and he loved her. But that's all they were, just dreams.

Chapter 4

ROME, SEAT OF THE ROMAN EMPIRE
310 A.D.

HE *watched her. From the open doorway of the small spa, he stud-*
ied the voluptuous curves of her body as she stepped out of the
marble bath. A slave tried to cloak her in a pristine white cloth, but
with an elegant wave of her hand, she took the towel and sent the
servant away. Tendrils of hair the color of a midnight sky escaped
the makeshift knot on the top of her head to caress the nape of her
neck.

Outside, the final heat of the day had eased, leaving Rome cool.
But in here, his body burned hotter than Apollo's chariot blazing its
way into the west. Marble cooled his shoulder as he leaned against
the hard column of the bath's entrance. The stone's chilly smooth-
ness did nothing to quench the fire in his blood or stop his cock
from growing hard at the sight of her.

Arms folded across his chest, he drank in the beauty of her full
curves. The olive bronze of her skin shimmered beneath the layer
of water skimming down her back before it danced off her softly
rounded buttocks. The lushness of her body shot a familiar ache
through him. Cassiopeia, daughter of Gaius Quinctilia Atellus,
Roman senator, was his.

There had always been women in his life, but the idea of leaving
a wife behind if he died in battle wasn't a worry he'd been willing to
accept. Of course, that was before she chose him. What had made

*her choose him over all others? He was a soldier. A plebeian by birth.
Far removed from the patrician clan she belonged to. It was doubtful he would ever know the reason why. He could only thank the
gods that she had chosen him.*

*His gaze greedily swept over her, his body reacting as it always
did whenever he was near her. He suppressed a sudden growl of
desire as she bent over to pat her legs dry with the linen towel. The
view from this angle was more than enticing—it was erotic. He
remained where he was. He had no desire to rush tonight. If he did
do so, she'd know he would be gone at dawn.*

"Really, husband. Must I beg you to lie with me?"

*Cassiopeia turned to face him, her sultry expression of amuse-
ment making his erection even harder. He folded his arms across
the breastplate of his military uniform and shook his head as he
smiled at her teasing.*

*"Never, mea amor. I simply wanted to watch you and take plea-
sure in the knowledge that you're mine and no other man's."*

*The linen cloth she held slipped out of her hand and pooled at her
feet. With the grace of one of the gazelle's he'd seen in Africa, she walked
toward him. The moment she reached him, she pressed her hand into
his forearm. The touch sent a pulse of gut-wrenching emotion racing through him straight to his heart. How he loved this woman. A
somber look flitted across her features. He tried not to listen, but her
thoughts rushed at him with the speed of a charging lion. The first
of her thoughts reached him. She knew he was leaving. Her mind
screamed a protest, but she remained calm and composed on the outside. The hardest thing for him was the images he saw in her head.
Her imagining him being injured or killed on the battlefield.*

"When?"

*Her voice was tranquil almost, but he heard the note of fear in
the single-word question. He sighed. Even if she had never learned
about his special skills, she would have been able to read him almost
as well as he could read the minds of others.*

*"Tomorrow," he murmured as he touched her cheek. The
moment she blanched, he shook his head. "It's only for a few weeks.
Maxentius wants me to visit one of the provinces to ensure the gov-
ernor is doing his job."*

"The emperor relies on you too heavily. He forgets that you and I have been married less than a year."

"Most soldiers are ready to leave their brides much sooner than I have been willing to part with you." He chuckled as he gave her a quick kiss. "Besides, we both know that my return will be even more pleasurable than tonight will be."

He envisioned his hands grasping her waist then sliding upward so his thumbs brushed over the tips of her breast. The soft purr rolling out of her throat made him smile as her gaze met his. Pleasure made her lovely lips part in sensual invitation as his mental touch slid down to her cunny, and his invisible caress stroked through the velvety-soft folds between her legs.

As her eyes fluttered closed, she whimpered from his invisible caress. Eager to love her, he quickly removed his uniform. The red cloak attached to his breastplate fell to the floor where it deadened the sound of the chest armor. His fingers quickly undid the leather laces of the brass-studded leather skirt he wore, and it followed the breastplate to the floor. The leather was a stark contrast to the brightly colored cloak. Her eyes flew open as his concentration slipped. In silence, she knelt to help him finish undressing. Warm hands caressed the back of his calves as she removed the sandal boots that covered his feet and calves. The last of his uniform, a red tunic, flew off his head, leaving him bare to her.

With a gentle touch, she caressed him with a reverence one might expect from a priestess of Vesta. She looked up at him, and the depth of love in her expression sucked the wind from him. A second later, she had him in her mouth. Pleasure and need melded into one stark emotion that engulfed him like fire. With exquisite skill, her tongue and mouth loved him until each caress pulled him closer to an edge only she could take him to. His sac drew up tight underneath him and he uttered a sharp cry . . .

LYSANDER Condellaire shot upright in bed. The vivid reality of the dream still haunting his senses, he jerked his head first in one direction and then another, searching for any sign that he might not be where he expected to be. The morning sun and the sound of traffic outside his window reassured him he was still in the Sicari installation in Rome. He glanced downward and grimaced at the pool of white fluid on his stomach.

"*Fotte.*"

He climbed out of bed and moved into the bathroom to clean himself up. When he'd finished, he gripped the sides of the free-standing basin and stared at the grotesque reflection in the mirror. He hadn't had a dream that intense since the last time he'd visited Rome, the week before . . . he threw up a wall to fight off the memories threatening to take over. With a skill he'd become adept at, he shoved his thoughts back into the dark hole where he'd buried them. The single green eye of the half man, half monster in the mirror glared back at him. With a low hiss of anger, he shoved one hand through his dark blond hair as he wheeled away from the sink and turned on the shower.

For as long as he could remember he'd had dreams of ancient Rome and the Roman plebe who'd worked his way up the ranks to the rank of *Legatus*. He'd even had glimpses of the woman before, but never like this. Never this vivid. This arousing. And not until now had the woman been a dead ringer for Phaedra DeLuca. His mind embraced the image of the Roman woman again, and he shuddered.

He stepped into the shower's spray of hot water. Eye closed, he let the water sting his face. It was just a dream. It was his mind's way of compensating for his wish to have Phaedra back in his bed. That one night of incredible sex between the two of them was going to have to be enough to last him a lifetime. With a deep growl, he grabbed the bar of soap and scrubbed at his body. Anything to take his mind off the erotic dream and Phaedra's role in it.

When he emerged from the bathroom a little later, he pulled on the standard black leather pants and dark shirt he always wore on duty. During the summer months, it would have been necessary to rethink his clothing, given the heat factor. But the air still had a bite to it in late February—even in Rome. He stepped out of the small bedroom into the sitting room. Designed as a temporary residence, the apartment offered up just the right amount of amenities for rest, work, and relaxation.

"Come in," he commanded sharply at the sound of a knock on his door.

A young woman entered the room with a tray of food. Although he hadn't called for breakfast, the *Vigilavi* were excellent at anticipating the needs of their employers. Most of the *Vigilavi* had served the Sicari for generations. Their forebears were people the Sicari had saved from different life-or-death situations. They were an integral part of the Order's structure, and their contributions in law enforcement, academics, medicine, and other areas were invaluable.

With an abrupt gesture, he silently ordered her to set the tray on the table out on the balcony. The sunshine made it warm enough for him to enjoy eating outside. The woman moved quickly to do as he instructed. The speed with which his thoughts reached out to search hers didn't surprise him. It was a natural ability. An ability his mother had warned him never to reveal to anyone. She'd died on his sixth birthday, the day after giving him her warning, and it had reinforced her advice.

What irritated him was that his unintentional probing showed he wasn't in control, and it emphasized the intrusive nature of his action. A wave of disgust sailed through him as he quickly broke the link. The connection hadn't been strong, but it had been enough for him to see the stark image of the girl with her lover.

He used to find it easy to prevent his telepathic ability from sifting through the thoughts of others. But ever since that night more than a year ago—*merda*, that was the last thing he wanted to think about at the moment. Infuriated by his lack of control, he flicked his hand and watched as several files flew off the nearby desk and into his hands. Still irritated by his thoughts, he followed the girl out to the balcony. As she gestured at the tray, Lysander nodded his thanks.

"May I bring you anything else, *il mio signore?*" Her formal deference made him grimace.

The title of *Legatus* wasn't something he'd asked for. Atia had made him *Legatus* strictly to lead a hand-picked team of Sicari in search of the *Tyet of Isis*. He'd tried to convince the woman that Ares was better suited for the task, but she'd emphatically dismissed the idea. Lysander knew the *Prima Consul* would eventually put

Ares back in charge of the Chicago guild. He'd merely been keeping his friend's spot warm for him until the Order's leader reinstated Ares as *Legatus*. In truth, he preferred being Ares's *Primus Pilus*. Life was a lot easier as his friend's second-in-command.

"*No, grazie.*"

"*Molto bene.* My name is Irini. If you change your mind, please just ring." With that cheerful reply, the girl left the room. Stomach rumbling, he pulled out a chair and sat down. The Colosseum was visible from where he sat, and there was a familiarity about the monument that called to him with a strength that seemed more than simple recognition. *Merda.* He was imagining things. He had a fondness for ancient Rome's history, and his mind was manipulating that fact. Just like in his dream.

The image of Phaedra, naked at his feet, had barely formed before he slammed the door on the vivid mental picture. He reached for a *panino* and slathered jelly on it. Focus. He needed to keep the mission front and center in his thoughts.

The remainder of his team had arrived last night after he went to bed, and by tomorrow, he'd have everyone working to isolate the possible hiding place of the *Tyet of Isis*. The *Prima Consul* always played her cards close to her chest, but Atia was convinced the artifact was here. She'd even told Lysander that she was reasonably certain the artifact was a small box decorated with carvings or paintings of an Egyptian knot called the *Tyet of Isis*, hence the artifact's name. Other than that, there wasn't much to go on, but when he'd called to ask Emma some questions about the search two nights ago, even she'd been pretty convinced the artifact was here in Rome.

He glanced at the file on top of the stack he'd set on the table. He didn't even need to open it. The *Prima Consul*'s personal bodyguard, Ignacio Firmani, had trained Cleo Vorenus. It was one of the reasons why he'd asked for her specifically. Atia hadn't been pleased that he'd selected her daughter for the mission, but she'd not overruled him. When it came to combat, they'd worked together so long they knew exactly when and where the other needed help in a tight spot. She wasn't just like a sister to him. She was the kind of partner who always had his back. He took another bite of his roll, followed by a drink of the quickly cooling cocoa.

Cleo had been the first one to find him that night in the warehouse, and weeks later, she'd been the one ordering him to either live or just die so everyone else could get on with their lives. He'd chosen to live, despite losing Phaedra. The image of her beautiful face pushed its way into his thoughts. It was gone in an instant as a loud knock announced Marco Campanella's arrival. The man quickly crossed the small living room to join him on the balcony.

"*Scusi, il mio signore,* but you wanted to see the files of the last team members when they arrived."

Lysander nodded at the man he'd chosen for his *Primus Pilus.* It hadn't escaped his notice that the younger man had Julian's temperament without the rash nature. Had that been why he'd given him the role of *Primus Pilus?* His First Spear? Was it his way of trying to atone for Julian's death? He clenched his teeth at the thought. No. Choosing Marco to act as his second-in-command hadn't been done out of guilt. The man had earned the right to be *Primus Pilus* on this mission.

His expression solemn, Marco handed off the files he carried before stepping back to wait quietly as Lysander reviewed them. Lysander had consulted with the *Prima Consul* on potential members for his team, and everyone he'd requested had arrived two nights ago. The newest arrivals had been handpicked by Atia herself without his consultation.

He didn't like it, but as *Prima Consul* she was well within her right to do so. He was fortunate her earlier career had been as a fighter. It gave her greater insight on how to build a balanced team, unlike a fat politician such as Cato. The worm. He opened the first file.

"Have you reviewed these yet?" He already knew the answer.

"Yes, *il mio signore.* Violetta Molinaro is a skilled fighter with strong intuitive skills. She has limited healing abilities, but she has a talent for closing her thoughts off to Praetorians."

Lysander nodded at the man's assessment of the Sicari woman's skills. Even his friend, Ares, couldn't match the woman's talent to avoid Praetorian detection. What bothered him was that her healing abilities were so limited. Atia knew they were in the heart of Praetorian country. He needed a healer on his team. A good one.

He flipped open the next chart. Luciano Pasquale. He released a noise of satisfaction. The man's reputation was excellent. He had a way of getting a job done. Quietly. Lysander flipped opened the last chart and his heart slammed in his chest.

"*Il Christi omnipotentia*. The woman's gone mad," he exclaimed as he stared at Phaedra's file.

"*Il mio signore?*" Curiosity filled Marco's voice, and Lysander shot the other man a quick glance.

"It's nothing." He shook his head. "Team assignments. Angelo and Maria Atellus stay together, but they're not to do any nighttime reconnaissance without backup. Partner Pasquale with Cleo. You'll work with Molinaro. DeLuca will work with me. I want everyone assembled in the conference room at two o'clock. That should be enough time for the late arrivals to overcome their jet lag."

Out of the corner of his only eye, Lysander saw his *Primus Pilus* hesitate. He turned his head and sent the younger man a hard look. One mistake in his career didn't mean he'd allow his *Primus Pilus* to question even the smallest decision he made. With a sharp bob of his head, Marco left him alone on the balcony.

Lysander turned back to the file in his hand. What in Jupiter's name was Atia thinking by sending the Order's most valuable healer into the heart of Praetorian territory? Of course, he should have asked what she was thinking the minute she put *him* in charge of this mission.

The last assignment he'd led had ended in two fighters tortured to death and a Sicari woman taken for breeding purposes, leaving him the sole survivor. In the far recesses of his mind, he heard the shrieks of his friend Dominic or were they the sound of his own cries? He grimly silenced the screams. The memory of that failed assignment made him inhale a deep gulp of air before he released it in a loud whoosh.

Based on that information alone, he was beginning to question Atia's sanity. Something that could jeopardize the woman's role as *Prima Consul*. The job was for life unless the leader of the Sicari

Council retired or someone proved them unfit for duty. Right now, he was thinking maybe someone needed to at least question Atia's judgment if not her sanity.

The papers in front of him detailed Phaedra's experience, her capabilities, and her weaknesses. He bit down on the inside of his cheek as he stared down at the information. He didn't have to read Phaedra's qualifications. He knew them well. With a vicious swipe of his hand, he slapped the file closed against the wrought iron table.

"Goddamn it, I don't need her here."

That wasn't true and he knew it. Of all the healers in the Order, Phaedra was the best, and someone with her abilities would be a valuable asset to the team. His fingertips brushed across the ravaged tissue that barely covered the muscles of his face. She'd actually been willing to heal him that night in that hellhole a year ago, but he'd rejected her attempt.

Phaedra had believed he'd been afraid to watch her suffer his injuries during the healing process. That was partly true, but even if he'd given in to her pleas that night, not even *her* abilities could have destroyed the monster hiding beneath the surface.

Worse, she would have seen him for what he was during the healing process. Many healers experienced not only the injured's physical pain, but the emotional trauma of the event as well. He hadn't been willing to risk that with her. He closed his eye, all too aware of the empty, misshaped socket on the other side of his nose.

The Order had offered him plastic surgery, but he knew it wouldn't have changed anything. He knew what he was. What he saw in the mirror every day served as a constant reminder of the ugliness in him. A monster he'd never known until it had revealed itself that night. It made him vigilant against letting that darkness hurt his friends or the Order itself.

He shoved his way out of his chair, and it toppled over backward as he stepped out of the sunlight and into the small living room. Enough. He wasn't going to let the past, or Phaedra DeLuca, get in the way of him accomplishing his task. A taunting laugh surfaced in the back of his mind.

With a grunt of anger, he returned to the bedroom to snatch his eye patch off the nightstand. It wasn't a necessity, but he'd found the patch helped minimize the initial impact his scarred face had on most people. Then there were the occasions when it served to make unsavory characters uncomfortable. The circular leather piece settled into place over his sunken eye socket, and he walked back into the sitting room as a sharp rap hit the small apartment's door.

"Enter," he ordered, expecting Irini had returned to pick up his breakfast tray.

In the next instance, his entire body went rigid with surprise as Phaedra entered the suite. Desperately, he tried to ignore the fact that every nerve ending in his body was on fire with tension.

She'd woven her ebony hair into a braid that ran down the middle of her back to a spot an inch or so past her shoulders. The memory of that dark hair spilled out around her on a pillow made the knot growing in his throat expand and tighten. Her complexion was flawless, and her skin was the golden brown typical of southern Italy natives. Like him, she wore the standard work uniform of the Sicari Order, only on her, it clung to curves that stirred up sensual images he knew best to leave buried.

But it was her eyes that always managed to draw him in and hold him paralyzed. They were a warm brown with gold flecks that flashed whenever she was angry or excited. Slanted just enough to give her an exotic look, they were narrowed at him right now. A sign she was assessing the situation. He immediately acknowledged the fact that at any minute he'd be drowning in deep waters.

Chapter 5

PHAEDRA was still mulling over Cleo's words as she headed toward Lysander's apartment in the Rome safe house. In some respects, Cleo had been right about the underlying tension between her and Lysander. That tension had intensified the moment she'd condemned him at Julian's *Rogalis*.

She'd stood there in front of that funeral pyre furious that Julian had allowed his pain to overrule his judgment. Her friend had gone looking for trouble all because of her. Watching the flames of Julian's cremation, her guilt and anger had destroyed her ability to think straight. Everything had slammed into her like a freight train. Her guilt over Julian's death, the pain of Lysander's rejection, and her own inability to get on with her life.·

It had made her want to strike out at whatever entered her line of sight. And the minute Lysander stepped toward her at that funeral pyre she'd exploded with rage. His pity was the last thing she wanted, and it had made her lash out as savagely as possible. The instant she blamed him for Julian's death, she'd regretted her bitter words.

The anguish on his face had said he was blaming himself not just for Julian's death, but for the two warriors who died in that Englewood warehouse in Chicago. But Julian's death hadn't been his responsibility. It had been hers. That moment had changed her. For the first time, she had an insight into what Lysander had to be living with every day.

The anger bottled up inside her had been washed away until the only thing left was the ache that came with loving him. From that point forward, she'd stopped looking for ways to taunt him. If he'd been puzzled by her new restraint, he'd never allowed it to show. And now he'd asked for her. Hope wasn't something she could afford with Lysander, but that didn't stop it from growing in her heart.

The fact that he wanted her on his team for the Rome assignment was enough to make that emotion bloom like a fragile flower. She didn't understand why, but he'd suddenly changed his mind about having her on the same team with him. It was a complete about-face from the past year when he'd gone out of his way to *avoid* having her assigned to any of his missions.

Her knuckles rapped on the door of Lysander's apartment. If the man had meant to throw her off stride by bringing her to Rome, he'd succeeded. She couldn't remember the last time she'd been so frigging nervous. His deep voice ordered her to enter. Swallowing her fear, she moved through the door.

The sight of him standing in the middle of the room sent her heartbeat skidding out of control. If she'd been a racecar suddenly shifted into high gear, her heart couldn't have gone any faster. There was an odd look on his face that she could have sworn was fear before his expression froze into granite. What could the man possibly be afraid of where she was concerned? Every nerve ending in her body tugged on her to get as close to him as she could. She resisted the pull as he folded his arms across his chest.

The movement emphasized sinewy shoulder muscles rippling beneath the black T-shirt he wore. A rush of fire sped up her spine until her neck was hot beneath her braided hair. Unable to help herself, her gaze slid downward to the solid line of his powerful legs encased in snug black leather. The memory of those strong legs sliding against hers made her jerk her gaze back to his face. That didn't make her feel any better because that beautiful green eye of his was watching her like a hawk.

He faced her head on, his features polar opposites of each other. One profile a horrible mass of scarred tissue and muscle, the other side was that of a beautiful angel capable of seducing a woman with just one glance of that piercing green gaze of his. Something he'd managed to do quite easily a year ago. The black patch over his scarred eye added to the hard, dark edge of emotion he exuded as he stared at her in silence, waiting for her to speak. *Deus*, the man made her nervous as hell. She fought to get her pulse rate under control.

"We need to talk," she snapped. *Christus*, that wasn't a good start.

"About?" His uncooperative tone made her tighten her lips.

"Damn it, why do you always have to be so cryptic?" The man was more than that. He was exasperating. "You're worse than Ares."

"I'm flattered."

"It *wasn't* a compliment."

He arched his eyebrow in an arrogant fashion at her frustrated remark but remained silent. She drew in a deep breath then exhaled. This was *not* going well at all. She was supposed to be apologizing to him, not antagonizing him. She centered herself in an attempt to create some calm inside her.

"Okay, let me start over. We have . . . a history, you and I. This isn't Chicago, and since you asked for me on this assignment, I thought it best we clear the air between us."

"I didn't ask for you," he said harshly.

If he'd struck her, she couldn't have been more stunned. How could he say he hadn't asked for her? She was here. She'd received the e-mail, and her name had been on the passenger list for the Order's Learjet that had flown her here.

"I don't understand . . . as *Legatus*, you picked your own team. I was told to report here."

"The *Prima Consul* added fighters to the list I submitted. I didn't put your name on my list."

The skin on her face grew cold as the blood drained away. He'd not asked for her. *Deus*, could she have ever been a bigger fool? Her head was spinning, and she didn't know which way to turn. Rejection was becoming a habit she could do without. Had he let her come all this way just to tell her she wasn't wanted? She went rigid at the thought.

"So why didn't you tell Atia to take me off the roster?" she bit out.

"I didn't know she'd assigned you to my team until my *Primus Pilus* gave me your file a little while ago," he said quietly.

For a moment, she could have sworn there was a gentle note of apology in his voice. She immediately discarded the notion. It was just wishful thinking on her part. The man was being polite, nothing more. But she didn't want him to be polite. She wanted him to say the past year had been nothing more than a big mistake. She wanted to hear him say he cared about her and had pushed her away because he'd not wanted to see her hurt. That's what she wanted him to do.

He didn't do any of that.

Instead, he rubbed the back of his neck and stared down at the floor in a contemplative fashion. Her imagination had the audacity to suggest that her presence had thrown him off balance. She tried to dismiss the idea but couldn't. The man was almost stone hard with tension, and it had to be because she was here. If they were going to be walking around on eggshells with one another, then she needed to go home. But the truth was she didn't want to go home.

"Send me back to Chicago then." She heard the break in her voice, but he didn't seem to notice.

"Atia had her reasons for sending you here. She's not likely to send you home," he said smoothly, but she could see he was uneasy about her being here. "As for the past. It's just that, the past."

She flinched at his words. It wasn't *just* the past. It was as real and vivid to her as if it had happened yesterday. Only a man who didn't care about her could use those words. She drew in a sharp breath as she bent her head to avoid looking at him. The last thing she needed was for him to see how vulnerable she was where he was concerned.

"Then I guess I'm staying."

"If you're worried I'll treat you differently than the others— *don't.*"

His words had a sharp edge to them that said he'd somehow been offended by her comment. She jerked her head up to see his green eye studying her with an emotion that made her heart skip a beat. He blinked and it wasn't there anymore. Had that been a flash of desire in his gaze or was she imagining things?

The knot in her throat swelled. She was an idiot. When was she going to learn that things weren't going to change? She kept looking for anything that might give her hope, but she kept coming up empty-handed. It was time to move on, but she wasn't sure how. Maybe the best way to do that was to do what she'd come here for. Apologize.

"I didn't just come here to clear the air between us." She hesitated, uncertain how to proceed.

"It's not like you to hold back, Phaedra," he said with a trace of cynical amusement. "Just say what you have to say."

Christus, the man wasn't making this easy. She didn't blame him for being wary of her. The verbal lashings she'd given him over the past year weren't something she was proud of, but she couldn't take them back. At the same time, she knew he wasn't completely blameless. He'd been a *bastardo* to let her go that morning thinking they'd shared something special. And she was the idiot who kept praying he'd lied.

"I wanted to say thank you for . . . you were good to me when Julian died." She saw him stiffen with surprise. Clearly, her words weren't what he'd been expecting.

"I know how much he meant to you."

There it was again, that stiff note in his voice. Almost as if it pained him to talk about Julian. Maybe it did. It definitely wasn't an easy topic for her.

"Julian was my friend. You did what you could to make things easier for me, and I'm grateful." Her gaze met his, and she bit her bottom lip at the impassive expression on his face. "And I'm especially grateful for you not telling Atia that I healed Ares after he ran the gauntlet."

"It was easy to do. I didn't see you heal him," he growled.

The dark expression on his face made her mouth go dry. Tension vibrated between them in a way that was tangible. She could feel it sliding over her skin until she wanted to run from the room. But she charged ahead.

"But you knew. You saw me after the fact. You even carried me back to my room—"

"Where's all this leading, Phaedra? I've work to do."

"I wanted to talk to you about the night of Julian's *Rogalis*."

"There's nothing to say," he bit out between clenched teeth as his body grew even more rigid with tension. "You spoke the truth."

"*No.*" The vehemence in her voice was startling as she turned and walked past him to stand at the door leading out onto the balcony. "I'm to blame for what happened to him, not you. He wouldn't have disobeyed your orders if I hadn't rejected his offer of the blood bond the night before."

Her words were a hard blow to his midsection. Julian had asked her to be his wife. Is that what they'd been arguing about when he'd encountered them in the gym the night before Julian died? Why had she rejected the Sicari fighter? *Il Christi omnipotentia*, was it possible she still cared for him despite the vicious way he'd rejected her at the hospital?

His heart stopped at the thought before it resumed. The muscles in his face grew taut, which made his demonic side protest with a sharp sting. He didn't have the right to ask that question. Besides, her acidic barbs over the last year had illustrated how much she despised him.

"That night wasn't the first time Julian disobeyed orders. He was impulsive." He ground out the words.

"But I accused you . . . blamed you, and I . . ." She swiped at her cheek.

Dulcis Jesu, she was crying. Phaedra never cried. She hadn't even cried at Julian's *Rogalis*. He was certain his arms were going to show bruises from the way his fingers were digging deep into his skin as he fought back the urge to go to her. A second later, she inhaled a deep breath. "I was wrong to blame you that night, and I'm sorry."

In the next instant, she was racing toward the door. Stunned by her apology, he stood there frozen. Phaedra hated being wrong, and she hated apologizing even more. Saying she was sorry to him had to have cost her dearly. The fact that she was leaving suddenly pierced his consciousness. He sprang forward and intercepted her just as she reached the door.

The minute his hand grasped her arm, she whipped around in a defensive posture, her palm slamming into his chest. Her unexpected reaction caught him off guard, but he quickly blocked her next blow. In an experienced move, his foot kicked forward to hook around the back of her legs and knocked her off her feet. The moment she started to fall backward, he followed her and tugged her into his chest. Holding her close, he twisted his body and envisioned hitting a soft mattress. When they hit the floor beneath the invisible padding, she was on top of him.

His first thought was the memory of the last time she'd been this close to him. Then there had been nothing between them, just hot skin. Fire streaked through his blood until he could feel the beginnings of an erection. *Merda*, he should have let her fall. She was skilled in hand-to-hand fighting and she would have easily recovered. The soft sound of her ragged breathing grazed his senses until his heartbeat matched the pace of her frantic breaths.

It surprised him she didn't scramble away from him. Instead, she stayed exactly where she was. A pleasurable weight on his body. The scent of her was an aphrodisiac to his senses. She smelled like a warm summer breeze with just a hint of apple, tart and fresh. His gaze met hers, and there was a flash of awareness in the liquid warmth of her eyes that created a primal response throughout his entire body.

The soft pink of her lush mouth tugged at him, and without meaning to, he envisioned kissing her. A sigh of need whispered out of her, and he stiffened as she lowered her head to tentatively brush her mouth over his. The caress breached a wall inside him, and his hand cupped the back of her neck to pull her closer.

She came willingly, and in the next instant desire engulfed him in a blaze of heat that only she could quench. Her lips parted against his, giving him free rein to explore the inner sweetness of her mouth. He couldn't remember the last time he'd tasted anything this wonderful. Sweet and hot, her tongue swirled around his in a silent demand for more.

Seconds later, her lips were setting his body on fire as she trailed her mouth down his throat. Her teeth nipped lightly at his skin, pulling a growl of pleasure from him. *Deus*, he wanted her worse than the last time he'd made love to her. Everything came rushing back at him as his hand caressed every inch of her he could reach.

He'd not forgotten how good it was between them, but he didn't remember it being this intense. There wasn't a thing about her that didn't make him crave more. The scent of her filled his nostrils as he remembered how good she'd felt when he'd slid into her velvet heat.

She gasped, and he realized she'd felt him stroking her inner core with his thoughts.

She immediately lifted her head to stare down at him. Passion lit those gorgeous brown eyes of hers as she rubbed her hips across his stone-hard erection in an erotically suggestive move. It dragged a tortured groan from him, and she rubbed against him again, making his cock ache for her. He drew in a sharp hiss of air and rolled her over onto her back.

With desire raging in his blood, he lowered his head to kiss her hard. His blood thickened and roared in his veins as she met his demanding caress with equal fervor. *Christus*, he needed to find a way to regain control of the situation. His senses immediately shut down the thought as the scent, taste, and feel of her pulled him back into a place he didn't want to leave. Her mouth left his and lightly trailed across his marred flesh. He stiffened at the touch. There was a tenderness in the caress that tightened a vise around his heart.

"Lysander, please." Her whisper was almost like a prayer and it slammed into him with a force that sucked the air out of his lungs.

Fuck. He was out of his mind. He'd been right on the edge of making her his again. With a growl of fierce anger, he quickly rolled away from her. In a single fluid move, he was on his feet. Surprise widened her eyes before a haunted look swept across her face. It was the same expression she'd worn when he'd sent her away at the hospital.

Unable to bear looking at the pain in her face, he whirled away from her. One hand running through his short hair, his brain churned frantically to come up with some logical explanation for kissing her. He'd been trying for the past year to make her believe he didn't care about her, and now he'd come close to making love to her.

How in Jupiter's name was he going to make her believe things hadn't changed without her hating him? That was the point, wasn't it? No, he didn't want to hurt her again. And he was certain he was about to do just that when he turned around to face her. *Damn*.

An impassive expression on her face, she had risen to her feet and stood ramrod straight, staring at a point over his shoulder. Except for the wild pulse fluttering in her neck, anyone else would have thought her well composed. He knew better. But her response to him seconds ago still surprised him. Over the past year, he'd worked hard to make her despise him. He'd thought he'd succeeded, but now he wasn't sure, and the knowledge scared the hell out of him.

"I ask *Indulgentia, il mio signore*. I have no excuse for hitting you."

"*Christus,*" he muttered. She sounded like she expected him to sentence her to the *Castigatio* for striking a *Legatus*. With a sharp gesture, he dismissed her statement. "Forget it. I have."

She flinched, and he immediately regretted his sharp tone. He'd made it sound like he'd already forgotten what it had been like touching her again. Nothing coherent formed in his mind to say, and he just stared at her in silence. The tension between them was an invisible thread stretched taut, and the minute it snapped, it was going to hit him like a baseball bat.

"About just now—"

"Forget it. I have." She coldly threw his words back at him.

Her bitterness was a sharp-edged blade gutting him with delicate precision. It went right to his middle then slid upward to his heart and cut it out of him. *Merda*, he deserved her wrath. He'd managed to hurt her again. If this was what it was going to be like working with her every day, he was in trouble.

Maybe he needed to pair her off with Pasquale. No. The only person he trusted to keep her safe was himself. The question to answer was whether to tell her now or later that they were going to be partners for the duration of the mission. He glanced at her impassive features. Somehow, he didn't think she was going to react well to the news. Later. He'd tell her later.

"May I go?"

The sudden husky note in her voice wound his muscles up tight. *Christus*, was she on the verge of tears again? He couldn't let her go like this. There had to be some type of explanation he could give for his behavior. The only thing he could think of was the one thing he wasn't about to say. He ignored the temptation to deny her request. Instead, he gave her a sharp nod of permission and watched in silence as she darted out the door. He was going to have Atia's head for this. The *Prima Consul* was playing games with not only his life, but Phaedra's as well.

Chapter 6

ATIA Vorenus entered the main door of the Santa Maria sopra Minerva and paused just inside the doorway. The church rested on the site of one of the ancients' temples—Minerva, goddess of wisdom. The irony of her presence here was not lost on her. She'd given her bodyguard the slip some time ago, and if Ignacio knew where she was, the man would have a heart attack. Even as recent as twenty years ago, her presence in this church would have placed her life in jeopardy. She was still at risk if she really thought about it. The capture of the Order's *Prima Consul* would mean a promotion for any Praetorian. Something Ignacio was going to drone on about when he finally caught up with her.

The Santa Maria sopra Minerva was all the more alarming simply because of what it had been so long ago. Masquerading as holy men, the Praetorians had used this particular place as a breeding ground for their ethnic cleansing of the Sicari. The *bastardi* had abused the Carpenter's teachings for centuries, convincing others that it was a divine task to root out evil. An evil they'd labeled Sicari. This very church had produced some of the more zealous of inquisitors during the Middle Ages, all of them Praetorian. Even the great Galileo had not escaped their wrath, as his trial had taken place here.

She tensed as she saw a clergyman enter the nave and move to the front of the altar. Immediately, she closed her thoughts off, but not before the man turned to study the place of worship. She inhaled a sharp breath of trepidation. Capture meant her death. She was too old to be used as breeding stock, but the Praetorians would try to cull every piece of knowledge they could from her before they killed her.

Despite her aversion to showing the Carpenter disrespect with the pretense of penitent worship, she stopped at the ornate fount a short distance into the nave to avoid drawing any attention to herself. Better to pretend than be found out and possibly lose her life. Dipping her fingers into the water, she genuflected in the direction of the altar with an unspoken apology. Somehow, she didn't think the Carpenter would mind.

The pretense done, she quickly skirted the back row of pews to follow the aisle along the north wall. She moved with the speed and silence she'd learned in early childhood. From the moment they could walk, the Sicari learned how to move with great stealth and quickness. It wasn't just because of what they did—it was how they'd survived over the centuries.

Even though she was in her mid-fifties, she was still in excellent shape, which played to her favor when it came to avoiding detection or capture in a Praetorian stronghold. Marcus had always enjoyed hiding right beneath their enemy's noses. It was a game to him. A deadly one. Particularly in this place.

But she had little say in the matter. As Marcus was the reigning Sicari Lord, she had to obey him. At least he hadn't commanded they meet at the site of Nero's Circus. It would have meant braving entrance to what was hallowed ground to so many of the Church's faithful. It would have been much more dangerous. The Praetorians were great in number at the house of the man who'd denied the Carpenter. As she hurried down the north aisle, she saw a small tour group admiring the architecture of the flying buttress on the opposite side of the church. In one of the front pews, an old woman and a child knelt on the prayer benches. Mindful of the potential threat at the altar, she quietly darted to the left and past the beautiful *Risen Christ* started by Michelangelo centuries ago.

Past the statue and the choir area behind the altar, she found the spiral staircase leading down into the crypts. Whenever she met Marcus in one of these places, *this* part of the journey was her least favorite. All the rotting death behind the walls abhorred her. The fiery cleanliness of a Sicari burial ritual was far preferable to putting a body into the ground to feed the worms.

At the end of the crypt's corridor, she paused. Nothing other than her own breathing filled the silence in the dim passage. Reassured that no one had followed her, she slid her fingers along the top edge of the stone ridge that bordered the crypt she faced. Just as Marcus's message had told her, she found the slight bump in the stone directly above the intersected P and X of the Chi-Rho symbol.

The moment she pressed the stone trigger above the Church's ancient symbol for the Carpenter, the crypt's roughly hewn façade rolled to one side with a quiet rumble. She quickly slipped through the narrow opening and tugged on the iron lever inside. The grit beneath her fingers was a reflection of how long it had been since someone had used this secret Sicari hiding place. Still, the stone slid softly back into place behind her as if time had not aged it at all.

All this intrigue and danger. Why Marcus didn't pick an open venue where the danger would be far less puzzled her. She wondered if he did it as a form of punishment for past transgressions. His or hers, she couldn't be sure. Blind, she reached to the left, her fingers fumbling to find the candle and tinderbox on the shelf. Less than a minute later, Atia used the lit candle to illuminate her way down a short corridor to a stone stairwell. She peered below and saw the faint glow of light.

Damn, he was already here. Her hand on the cold wall to steady her, she hurried down the steps. She'd hoped to be here when he arrived. She grimaced. Marcus always seemed to be one step ahead of her. It was irritating. She'd almost reached her destination when the sound of a deep male laugh echoed out into the stairwell. Just as he always had, he could easily tell what she was thinking. Disgusted with her inability to shield her thoughts from him better, she entered the small shrine and waited silently just inside the doorway.

The sole occupant of the small room knelt in front of an ancient altar to Minerva. Marcus was one of the few Sicari she knew who kept the old ways. But then Sicari Lords were trained to follow the way of justice and wisdom. And their wisdom had guided every *Prima Consul* who'd come before her. With a light touch to the icons on the *laraium*, he blew out the candle on either side of the small display and rose to his feet. Even without his monk's robes, his height would have made him an imposing figure. Pushing his hood off his head, Marcus turned to face her. It had been more than five years since their last meeting, and he'd changed. His face was still youthful, but his vivid blue eyes reflected a change in spirit.

"Not too much of a change I hope."

"Certainly not when it comes to probing my thoughts." She sent him an annoyed look.

"You never did care for that particular talent of mine," he said with a chuckle. "You're as lovely as ever."

"You need glasses."

"You'll *always* be beautiful to me, Atia."

The sincerity in his voice made her heart skip a beat, and the years faded away to when they were both younger. She frowned as the old sorrow lanced through her, and she reached up to touch her silver hair. It was impossible to go back. He changed the subject, giving her the chance to shove the painful past aside.

"I understand Ares has taken a *domina*."

"Yes, they're enjoying an extended honeymoon at the *Rennes le Chateau* estate. Emma found some interesting evidence at one of the nearby ruins."

"I see." His gaze narrowed as their eyes met. "As I recall that part of France is quite beautiful this time of year."

"Yes," she said with an abrupt nod and dragged her eyes away from his. She didn't want to remember how happy they'd been those first four years at *Rennes le Chateau*.

"Ares is an excellent fighter. He'll keep her safe."

"You say that as if . . ." She sucked in a sharp breath. "*You*. It was *you* in the alleyway the night Ares first met Emma. You were the one Ares fought that night."

"Now why would you think that?" A note of amusement drifted beneath his words.

"Because there had been no reports of a rogue Sicari anywhere in the country. The fighter appeared out of nowhere and vanished just as quickly." Atia narrowed her eyes at him. "And no Sicari would run from a fight."

"There is a difference between surrender and benevolence," he growled. "You know as well as I do Ares is no match for my skills and abilities. If I'd known the boy had planned to act as Emma Zale's protector, I wouldn't have interfered."

The indignation on his face made him all the more imposing, but she faced his anger with the same defiance she always had. The minute he leaned into her, the full power of his presence engulfed her in a storm of sensation she thought she'd long forgotten. An odd expression crossed his face as he leaned even closer.

The scent of him filled her nostrils, a clean, woodsy smell. It sent a pulse of awareness through her, and the years faded away to the first moment she'd angered him. A moment that had erupted into a night of passion that had changed everything. The memory of those moments so long ago filled her with a longing she thought she'd forgotten. She brushed them aside. She was older now, much wiser, and certainly not one to give way to impulse or passion.

"Your thoughts reveal a great deal, *mea amor*."

"Do they, Eminence?" she said in a stilted tone.

Marcus lifted her chin with one hand, a gentle smile on his firm lips. A mouth that had pleasured her so exquisitely so many years ago.

"So formal. Have you forgotten what there was between us?"

"No. The past is always with me," she said quietly. "But I thought you asked me here to discuss the *Tyet of Isis* and some new information you've uncovered."

The cerulean blue of his watchful gaze made her close herself off to him. The annoyance in his expression said her efforts to keep him out of her head had been successful. He scowled at her then uttered a soft oath and nodded sharply.

"I've received an analysis of the mutilations on the bodies of Emma's parents and her mentor. My resources believe the marks carved into the cheeks of the Zales and Russwin are symbolic to the murderer. They believe the symbol is Praetorian in origin."

"Why in Juno's name would they think it's Praetorian?"

"Because if you add two lines to the mark, it forms the *sigla*."

"The Chi-Rho," she said as she drew in a quick breath. She remembered the P and X symbol on the stone covering the entrance to this ancient temple.

It was so simple. Although her researchers had noted the similarities between the Chi-Rho symbol used by Constantine I at the Battle of Milvian and the mark left on the victims, they'd not made the connection. But then she hadn't had a forensic psychologist review the symbols, something she was now certain Marcus had done. She couldn't believe she'd made such a stupid mistake. She should have done that herself.

"But why not complete the mutilation?" she murmured and frowned. "It would signify that justice has been administered."

"I've been told the individual making the mark is most likely a fanatic who feels it would be sacrilege to mark their victims with a symbol of the Carpenter's. A symbol with deep ties to the birth of the Praetorian presence in the Church." A tic in Marcus's cheek made her realize how deeply this information concerned him. "Instead, the murderer uses the partial symbol as a way to mark the victims as heretics who are a threat to the Praetorians."

"But the Zales and Russwin weren't *Vigilavi*." Atia frowned. The *Vigilavi* were *alieni* who served the Order in different capacities. Many of them descendants of *alieni* the Sicari had saved centuries ago. She shook her head in puzzlement. "They weren't even on the Order's payroll as consultants."

"No, but they had one thing in common. They were looking for the *Tyet of Isis*, and whoever killed them was concerned they might find it."

"Praetorians are always dangerous, but a fanatical one is doubly so. I'll inform the Council of the threat and alert the guilds." She experienced a sudden rush of fear for him. "I assume you'll have Dante attempt to deal with this threat?"

"Unfortunately, I think this is one threat I will have to deal with myself." The quiet resignation threading beneath his statement made her stare up at him in fear. He didn't look away, and horror swept through her.

"You think it's him," she gasped.

"Yes." He nodded, a grim expression crossing his still handsome features.

She swayed slightly, and his strong hands gripped her shoulders. "Forgive me, *carissima*. I prayed this day would never come."

"How can you be so sure? It could be any Praetorian." She shuddered.

"No," he said firmly. "I'm convinced it's Gabriel."

"But you can't be sure it's him. It could be someone else."

"No," He shook his head. "Gregori doesn't hide the names of the Praetorian Dominus he's trained. Silvestro and Alessandro have been responsible for more deaths in my guild than I care to count. But they don't mark their victims as heretics, and they only hunt Sicari."

"It still doesn't mean it's him. We don't even know if he's alive."

"You've seen the reports. There have been almost ten Sicari killed in Rome, Venice, and Genova over the past two years. What those reports didn't explain was that all of them were murdered in the same manner as the Zales and Russwin. These warriors were all looking for the artifact, too. Those who survived the encounters long enough to give us information said their attacker had both telepathic and telekinetic abilities."

"Why wasn't this information reported to me?" she demanded.

"The men and women who died were in my personal guild. They answer to me, before anyone else. I ordered the reports be modified."

"I don't care that the *Absconditus is* your guild *or* that you're the reigning Sicari Lord. Just because the *Prima Consul* reports to you doesn't mean you can pick and choose the type of information you release to me." Her mouth tightened as she scowled at him. "The Order has *always* served at the pleasure of the Sicari Lords, but as *Prima Consul*, I'm entitled to see all information the *Absconditus* possesses when it comes to general matters of interest to the Council. It's been done like that for centuries."

"It was my intent to protect you." His voice had become stiff and stilted.

"*Protect me*," she snapped as the painful memories came rushing back. "From what? The knowledge that the *bastardi* who took our son have turned him into a killer? You tried to protect him, too, *remember?*"

The minute her words left her mouth, she regretted it. The accusation was unfounded, and they both knew it. The ashen look on Marcus's face filled her with remorse. Even the pain lashing through her was not an excuse for accusing him of failing to save their child.

"Protecting him wasn't just my sacred duty. It was my responsibility as a father," he said in a savage tone.

It was a sharp, unyielding statement, but she heard the anguish in his voice. His guilt was a tangible sensation, and her heart ached for him in spite of her bitterness. Despite everything that had transpired between them, her love for him was as strong today as it had been more than thirty years ago. She knew he'd done what he thought necessary to protect their child.

The Order had always had its spies, and someone had known she'd given birth to a Sicari Lord. Marcus had tried to protect their son by taking him away. But even that precaution had failed. The outcome would have been the same no matter where they'd tried to hide Gabriel. The Praetorians had received help from inside the Order, and if she ever found out who it was, she'd slit their throat herself. To hell with the consequences. She touched the sleeve of Marcus's robe.

"Forgive me. I spoke in anger. It was unwarranted. We both know the Praetorians had help from within the Order. They would have found Gabriel no matter what we did," she said quietly.

"I was too arrogant," he rasped. "It blinded me. Made me less vigilant."

"You are a Sicari Lord. Arrogance has always been a part of you," she murmured with a quiet smile. "But you are still human, and even you make mistakes."

"You defend me, *carissima*?"

Amazement echoed in his voice as he turned his head to look down at her. The sorrow in his vivid blue eyes made her throat tighten with tears she barely managed to hold back. *Deus*, if she allowed him to see her cry, he'd know he still had power over her. Losing Gabriel had torn them apart, and she had no doubt that what lay before them now could easily destroy them both. There was no place for emotion or sentiment between them now. It would only lead to more pain. The minute his hand touched her shoulder, self-preservation took over, and she quickly put a reasonable distance between them. There was too much pain in that touch. And longing. A wish for things to have been different.

"You've reached a decision?" she asked in a stilted tone.

"He must die."

Marcus spoke without emotion. It was just a simple statement. But its impact on her was like running into a wall. He sounded as if he was talking about someone other than their son. And that's what shattered her heart. They *were* discussing someone else. Gabriel was no longer their son. The Praetorians had taken him away when he was only two. It was unlikely he would even remember them. Silence settled between them as they contemplated what was to come. How did one kill one's own child? The question sickened her, and she turned away from Marcus. The pain was too fresh and raw.

"*It's all right, mea amor. We shall do what we must.*" Only once had he ever entered her thoughts like this. The gentle intrusion then had been to comfort her, just as it was now. The invisible caress of his hand touched the side of her face, and she trembled. A second later, she was engulfed in his strong arms and he held her quietly. "*Cry, inamorato. Cry for what we've both lost.*" The tenderness of his thoughts and the way he cradled her against him proved her undoing. The tears came hot and fast as she cried in his embrace. She was no longer *Prima Consul*, and he was no longer the reigning Sicari Lord. They were simply two people struggling with a profound grief.

Several long moments passed before her tears finally stopped. Gently she pushed herself free of his arms. Her gaze met his for a moment as her fingers pressed into her forehead. Her head hurt from all the crying.

"So after all this time you still get a headache when you cry," he said with a small smile.

"I don't cry very often." Her quiet response pulled a low chuckle from him.

"Why am I not surprised?"

The familiar strokes of his invisible fingers across her forehead felt good. In seconds, they'd eased some of her tension. He'd not lost his touch. Again the soft laugh. He'd not left her thoughts after all. She scowled at him.

"I was not reading your thoughts, Atia." He leaned into her. "I was reading your expression."

"Then stop," she bit out sharply. It was a ridiculous statement.

She knew that. But all she wanted was to finish up with their business and leave. Being here with him was affecting her in ways she'd not experienced in years. She deliberately opened up her thoughts to him, while burying her deepest emotions behind a façade he couldn't penetrate. His jaw grew tight with tension, telling her she'd succeeded in letting him see only what she wanted him to see.

"*Va bene.*" His head jerked in a sharp nod. "The incident at the Zale house cost us a considerable sum to keep quiet."

"It couldn't be helped. The house had been watched for over a week. The Praetorians shouldn't have been there. All things considered, we were lucky we only lost one man. We might have lost Emma, too, and she's a valuable resource for the Order."

"Obviously, Ares's ability to defy the rules saved her life." There was only a hint of rebuke in his voice as he referred to Ares bonding with Emma Zale without the Order's permission. The blood bond Ares had exchanged with his new wife had given her a Sicari ability, which she'd used to protect herself the night Ares and his team had searched the Zale house. Marcus would be well within his right to extract punishment from Ares in some form. His apparent lack of anger filled her with relief.

"He learned that particular trait from me, I'm afraid."

"Then I cannot punish him for what his *Prima Consul* advocates." He shook his head in amused exasperation before his expression grew somber. "The report says the only thing found was David Zale's notebook. Is there anything of use in it?

"Emma's been cross-referencing items in our databases with her father's notebook in an attempt to coordinate our search for the *Tyet of Isis*. With the clue the Order's had for some time now, and one we found in her father's notebook, I believe there's a strong chance of our success."

"And the artifacts you sent for?"

"Her observations about the coin confirm yours. It's the coin of the Sicari Lord Baldassare."

"But she saw nothing that would help us find the *Tyet of Isis*." It wasn't a question, simply a statement of frustration.

"No, Eminence," she murmured. He scowled at her use of his formal title.

"There's more?"

"The Sicari Lord coin wasn't the only object Emma read when Ares brought her to the White Cloud estate for Julian's *Rogalis*. She touched the Dagger of Cassiopeia."

"And the significance?" he snapped, his features taut with a tension she didn't understand.

"When she touched the dagger, she saw a man who looked just like Lysander Condellaire, scar and all." Her words made him send her a disgusted look.

"Are you seriously trying to suggest he's the reincarnation of Maximus?"

"I don't know what to think. But Emma's descriptions were quite vivid."

"It's a legend passed down from one *Prima Consul* to the next. Nothing more." The rigid line of his posture emphasized his tension. It was unlike him to be so resistant to the idea of reincarnation or prophecy.

"It might be simply a legend. But what if it's true? The timing *is* uncanny. Lysander leading the team here in Rome in search of the artifact. Emma's vision. What if Maximus *has* returned to claim the *Tyet of Isis*?"

"Condellaire can't be trusted." Marcus's voice was as cold and inflexible as his gaze was. "He has Praetorian blood in him."

"*Christus*, his mother was raped. Lysander didn't have a choice in who his father was, any more than Aurelia had a choice in refusing that Praetorian *bastardo*," she snapped.

"None of it changes the fact that Condellaire is half Praetorian." He glared at her. "And he's been struggling with his darker half for little more than a year. Holding it at bay—pretending nothing's wrong, or am I mistaken?"

"Lysander hasn't been keeping it in." She waved her hands in a vehement protest. "We have talked a great deal about his ordeal."

"All well and good, but will he rise to the task when lives are at stake." Marcus frowned. "I didn't interfere when you named him *Legatus* for this mission, but if he becomes unstable, Campanella is to replace him."

"Your worry is misplaced. There are few men of Lysander's

caliber among our people. He'll not fail you *or* the Order. His skills are what make him an excellent *Legatus*. You underestimate him, Marcus."

"We shall see," he said with condescension. "His telekinetic ability is strong, but his telepathic skills are unreliable and erratic. If he'd displayed his abilities sooner, perhaps he could have been trained, but now it's too late."

"He might not be a true Sicari Lord, but to suffer as he did and survive without telling those *bastardi* anything shows his heart is Sicari. He'll not betray his friends *or* the Order, even despite the horrible way he learned the truth about his parentage."

The words hung in the air like icicles as she defended Lysander. Aurelia would have been proud of her youngest boy. Lysander had become a man any woman would be proud to call her son. He'd shown his worth by surviving what few had. A Praetorian torture session. And she wouldn't let anyone, including Marcus, forget Lysander's loyalty to the Order.

"You speak as if he were your son." There was a bitter note in his voice, and she shook her head in denial.

"Lysander. Ares. Phaedra—" She caught herself as she almost said Cleo's name. "They helped fill the void in my life. You weren't there, and they needed me, just as much as I needed them. But they could never fill the hole in my heart that Gabriel's loss left inside of me."

"You know why I wasn't there," Marcus growled with anger.

"Yes, I know." The tremor in her voice made her pause as the pain of the past returned to envelop her once more. She shook her head. "Seneca needed your guidance in leading the Council, and you had to honor your promise to Aurelia."

"A promise I should never have made. I could have easily had Tito or Placido train the boy." Tiny lines fractured the skin around his lips as his mouth grew taut with tension. "I would have given it up for you. All of it."

"How could you? You were the Sicari Lord chosen to lead the *Absconditus*. You had too much honor then, *and now*, to turn your back on the Order or the promise you made."

"Honor is a cold mistress," he said bitterly.

"You did your duty. Just as I did mine. I wanted to tell Lysander the truth. All of it. Who his father really was. That he had a half-brother. But Aurelia's concern for Lysander's safety as well as Dante's became mine. Perhaps they were groundless fears, but I honored my friend's wishes, just as you did. It was important to her that you and no other Sicari Lord train Dante. She knew you. Trusted you."

"And what about my duty to you—my responsibility to find our son?" His blue eyes studied her face closely.

"Gabriel was gone. We both know you did your best. There was nothing else you could have done."

"And you. What about you, *carissima*?" He leaned toward her, his voice dropping to a rasp. "You never sent for me. Not even after that night at La Terrazza del Ninfeo."

"How could I?" she said quietly. "I knew where your duty lay. Dante needed you more than me or—the boy's safety and well-being were more important than my happiness or yours."

The words squeezed at her heart like a spiked vise. He'd never know how hard it had been not to send for him more than a dozen times. Not to tell him—she shoved the memory aside. She'd never said a word to him, because deep inside she'd hoped and prayed he would find Gabriel and bring him home. Then they might have had a chance to be the family she'd always longed for. But Marcus hadn't found Gabriel.

"But if I had walked away from it, would you have come with me?" he asked in a voice filled with emotion.

She breathed in a deep breath and released it as she considered the question. If he'd abdicated his role as reigning Sicari Lord, chaos would have erupted in the *Absconditus*. Tito and Placido had been powerful, but they'd served their time. They were too old to lead the *Absconditus* to ensure its strength and viability. And with Orlando's untimely death, Marcus had been the only one capable of leading. She'd known that when she'd blood bonded with him.

"No." She shook her head as she looked away from him. "Gabriel's disappearance made it difficult enough. If you'd abdicated, you would have come to resent me for it. Going our separate ways was for the best."

A dark note of fury exploded out of him as he spun away from her. The emotions and sheer power of his abilities sent a humming sensation through her body. Was his anger for Gabriel or what they'd meant to each other and had lost? He jerked his head to look at her over his shoulder. His expression said she'd not shielded her thoughts very well.

"Both, *carissima*. Both. I should have been more vigilant. I should have taken extra precautions. *Fotte*, none of this would have happened if I'd—"

"You give yourself too much credit for what you can and cannot control," she snapped. "Your responsibilities as a Sicari Lord would have eventually torn us apart. Gabriel's loss wouldn't have changed that. Blaming yourself is pointless. The Praetorians are the ones who turned our son into a monster. Not you."

"A monster that needs to be destroyed," he said as he turned to face her again. The hard words were like a blow to her body, and it sent a tremor through her.

"Then ask Dante to do it. Surely he's ready. Don't let your arrogance blind you to what might happen if you face Gabriel on the field of battle."

Marcus drew in a deep breath then exhaled it slowly, his eyes closing as he seemed to be absorbing her words. When he looked at her again, he gave her a brusque nod. "I shall give it thought."

The silence was tense and awkward between them, making her wish he'd never sent for her. No, it was the news he'd given her that made her wish that. Being here with him was a small taste of the Elysium Fields, despite the knowledge it wouldn't last. Suddenly eager to escape the raw emotion hanging between them, she bowed in respect to him.

"Is there anything else, Eminence?"

He didn't answer her for a long moment, and she waited in silence for him to say something. She glanced up at him, and her heart slammed into her chest at the hunger in his face.

"One day soon, Dante will assume the role of reigning Sicari Lord. When he does, I intend to come for you." The deep note of confidence in his voice made her heart skip a beat before it began to race at a frightening speed.

"I said your arrogance was expected of a Sicari Lord, but I forgot how arrogant you really are," she bit out in a sharp tone.

"Is it my arrogance you find so irritating, or is there something else that disturbs you?"

The determination and wealth of emotion in his voice sent a tremor through her. This was the Marcus she'd fallen in love with. Strong, determined, and insistent on getting his way. She was definitely in trouble if Dante became the reigning Sicari Lord. Best to ignore his high-handed declaration. Particularly when it terrified her that he meant every word. She wasn't certain she could risk giving her heart to him one more time.

"Do I have your permission to leave, Eminence?" She deliberately kept her voice neutral, her thoughts closed to him.

"Yes." He gave her an abrupt nod. "But don't mistake my words, Atia. I will come for you. Only this time I won't let anyone, or anything, make me give you up."

This time her mental control *did* slip, and the slow smile curling his mouth said her thoughts had revealed more than she cared to. Not a good thing when one was dealing with a Sicari Lord.

Chapter 7

LYSANDER strode into the small library of the Rome guild's satellite office to find Atia seated at a library table. The *Prima Consul* had sent for him a short time ago, and he'd deliberately kept her waiting out of anger. Not a prudent thing to do, but if he'd come any sooner, he might have been prone to doing her harm. In front of her, a large book lay open on the tabletop. He fought the urge to probe her thoughts and find out what she was up to. Instead, he settled on reading her body language. She was upset about something. Someone had done or said something to throw her out of her usual controlled behavior.

Good. He wanted to thank them for unsettling the *Prima Consul*. The woman deserved to have someone destroy that calm reserve of hers for what she'd done to him. He came to a halt beside the table and waited in silence for her to speak.

"You're angry with me." She didn't look up from the book as she trailed her finger across the page. When he didn't respond, she raised her head and met his gaze with exasperation. "Speak your mind, Lysander."

He clasped his hands behind his back and frowned at her. "DeLuca's presence here presents not only a grave danger to her but to the rest of the team."

"Danger is a way of life with us, Lysander. We're always looking over our shoulder on some level."

"She's too valuable an asset to the Order to toss her into this viper's nest. Her safety here is far more precarious than if she were in Chicago."

"Hmm, perhaps." Atia nodded as if weighing his words seriously before she shrugged. "But you needed a good healer, and Phaedra is best suited for the task. Marco tells me you're her partner for this mission. I can't think of anyone else better qualified to ensure she remains safe."

He drew in a deep breath then slowly released it. The woman should be grateful he had a firm grip on the monster inside him. If he were to release it . . . he swallowed hard but didn't respond to her dismissive comment. She eyed him carefully.

"The fact that you have Praetorian blood running in your veins doesn't make you any less Sicari, Lysander." The *Prima Consul* frowned as he didn't react to her words. "You're one of our best warriors. It's time you come to terms with who you are and what was done to you."

"I wasn't aware that I hadn't already done so," he said coolly. Behind his back, he tightened his grip on his wrist and his free hand clenched into a tight fist.

"Don't take me for a fool, Lysander. Many have done so to their regret." She frowned at him, but he refused to show any emotion in the face of her warning.

"I am not so unwise as to take you for a fool, *Consul*."

"*Christus*, you are far too hardheaded for your own good. You long for a woman you think you cannot have, all because of the circumstance of your birth. Are you really that uncertain of your ability to control the dark side of you?"

Atia's words hit him like a blow to the side of his head. *Merda*, was the woman that good of an intuitive? No. Cleo. He was going to have the woman's head on a platter for this. The scarred side of his face ached as the muscles tugged against the thin layer of skin. He struggled to suppress the demon inside him as he responded with an abrupt shake of his head.

"I am in complete control of my abilities."

"But *not* the emotions that came with the discovery of who you are."

"And your point being?"

"My point, you stubborn fool, is that it's time you accept that what happened that night was out of your control."

"It *was* within my control," he bit out through clenched teeth. "*I* made the decision to go into that building with only three fighters. As team leader, *I* was responsible for their safety."

"You made a leadership decision," she snapped. "And it's a miracle you survived."

"A miracle?" he rasped as his wrist ached from the way his fingers dug into his flesh. "Two fighters were tortured to death, a woman was carried off to be a brood mare for those *bastardi*, and that Praetorian son of a bitch who claimed to be my father let me live because he knew it would be a punishment far worse than death."

"No, he recognized you had your mother's heart, and not his," she said with quiet determination. "In letting you live, Nicostratus hopes you'll surrender to the darkness inside you. Why else would he tell you who he was? It's a game to him."

"This is a pointless conversation," he said without emotion.

"*Va bene.* Just remember that you are *not* your father's son." She directed that piercing gray gaze of hers at him. It was a direct command by the *Prima Consul*. "Praetorian blood might run in your veins, but your heart is all Sicari."

The reminder was of no comfort. Atia was mistaken. With each passing day, his dark blood was howling for revenge. The sinister half of him whispered constant words of encouragement, urging him to hunt Nicostratus down and retaliate. Where Praetorians were concerned, there was no Sicari code to adhere to, and his friends would be willing to go after the man with him. But Nicostratus would announce his paternal pride the minute they got within shouting distance of the man. Tension laced through him at the thought. An image of Nicostratus smiling down at him in cold amusement chilled him until he had to suppress a shiver of fear. He shoved the memory back into the hole he'd buried it in more than a year ago.

"Your message said you wanted to ask me something." He sent her a steely glare to signal the matter was finished. Frustration tightened her lips into a thin line, and she nodded.

"Yes, I wanted to know if you've had any strange dreams of late? Moments of strong déjà vu?"

Damn, was the woman half Praetorian like him? The *Prima Consul* knew he'd always been fond of ancient Roman history, but he'd never mentioned anything about his dreams. He danced around the question with an ambiguous response.

"If you're worried I'm still having nightmares related to my . . . to that night—don't."

"No, I was simply interested in knowing whether you'd been dreaming about ancient Rome."

The observation made him go rigid. What in the name of Jupiter was the woman fishing for by asking such a question? He knew better than to lie. Atia had this uncanny ability to spot a lie faster than most people could tell one. He hedged once more.

"I don't see how dreams like that would signify anything." He shrugged.

"An old legend I know of might convince you otherwise."

She resumed her perusal of the book in front of her, a frown of concentration furrowing her brow. When she didn't speak, he folded his arms across his chest and scowled at the woman. It wasn't the first time Atia had aroused his curiosity with some mysterious comment.

The woman was a master at it where he was concerned. She knew how much he enjoyed digging through history books. If there was something she wanted him to research for her, she just threw him a tidbit to pique his interest before she reeled him in. Well, he wasn't biting this time. He could play the waiting game as well as she could.

She outlasted him.

"What legend?" he growled with exasperation.

Once again, he'd allowed the woman to play him, and it pissed him off royally. She didn't look at him, but he saw her struggle to bite back a smile. Her gaze still focused on her book, she waved her hand slightly.

"It centers around Maximus and Cassiopeia."

"That's not a new story," he said with disgust. The carrot had been nothing more than a ruse. For what reason, he had *no* idea. Perhaps for no other reason than she enjoyed teasing him. She raised her head and turned those piercing gray eyes of hers on him.

"It's an old story, and few but the *Prima Consuls* know the tale. The legend says Maximus will return to find the *Tyet of Isis*."

"And what makes you think this legend is true?"

He wasn't sure where she was going with this story and he was beginning to wonder if he really wanted to know. *Christus*, he was an idiot for having even taken her bait. Her gaze still on him, Atia stood up to face him, a glint of excitement in her eye.

"A number of things have happened over the past year that make me think the legend has merit. Perhaps the most important one is what Emma saw when she touched the Dagger of Cassiopeia."

"She told me she'd read the Sicari Lord's coin, not the dagger." He shook his head slightly in puzzlement.

"She didn't say anything because she saw something that troubled her deeply."

Something about Atia's expression set off a warning signal inside his head. The *Prima Consul* had the look of someone about to spring a trap. He grimaced as he tried to form a plan that would let him leave the room without being caught in the woman's web. He couldn't. He was a sucker for a historical mystery.

And it didn't help that Atia had a way of making the most far-fetched possibility sound almost realistic. He was more than familiar with Emma and her ability. Since formally sealing her blood bond with Ares in front of the Order, she'd read a number of artifacts in the Order's possession in an effort to find the *Tyet of Isis*. Her visions had been fairly accurate, based on firsthand recorded accounts in the Order's library. Whatever Emma had seen, Atia was convinced it had everything to do with this story that Maximus would come back from the dead to find the *Tyet of Isis*.

"*Va bene*," he growled at his inability to restrain his curiosity. "I'll bite for a second time. What did Emma see?"

"She saw Maximus Caecilius Atellus, scars and all." The *Prima Consul* arched her eyebrows at him as she offered him a mysterious smile.

"How does she know it was the first Sicari Lord?"

He knew Emma's gift was an extraordinary one, but he wasn't sure he was willing to go so far as to believe she'd seen Maximus himself. Images from his own dreams pushed their way to the front of his thoughts, and he shoved them aside. They were irrelevant to the current discussion.

"She knows, because she saw him kill Cassiopeia."

"*Il Christi omnipotentia,*" he breathed. Emma's visions often included a great deal of violence, and he knew she sometimes found those images traumatic to watch. Seeing Maximus kill his wife couldn't have been an easy thing for her.

"I think it was quite troubling for her," Atia said quietly. "In fact, I think she saw a great deal more than she shared with me. However, she did tell me about an extraordinary image that might interest you."

She had his full attention, and she knew it. He clenched his teeth as he bit back his desire to ask her what else Emma had seen. Atia arched her brow at him and waited. Patiently. This time he wasn't going to give in. He glared at her, and she sent him a conciliatory smile.

"Emma said she saw you."

"Me?" He met her gaze with a frown of amazement. "Why would she see me?"

"She saw you as Maximus." The quiet announcement was all the more dramatic because Atia didn't raise her voice. He snorted with laughter as he met the *Prima Consul*'s calm gaze.

"I know Emma's gift is strong, but I find it highly doubtful it was me she really saw in her vision."

"Perhaps, but then how do you explain your dreams of ancient Rome?"

"My dreams have nothing—" *Merda*, the witch had tricked him. He glared at her smug features. "This game is over, Madame *Consul.*"

"This is far from a game." Atia quickly stood up and crossed the floor to clutch his arm. "I'm convinced it's a matter of life or death when it comes to the *Tyet of Isis.* I believe Emma saw the truth, Lysander."

"What truth?"

"I think you already know the answer to that," the *Prima Consul* said softly. "Why else would you be dreaming of ancient Rome?"

Dulcis Jesu, how in the hell had the woman known to even ask him about his dreams? He'd not told anyone about them. Like some women in the Order, the woman's strongest ability was her telekinetic power, but he knew she was intuitive as well. How she'd found out about his dreams he didn't know, and to tell the truth, he didn't care. The woman had already tricked him into admitting that he had the dreams, but it was one hell of a stretch between those dreams and what she was suggesting. And he really didn't want to contemplate what she was suggesting.

"You've been smoking crack again, haven't you?" The sarcastic comment earned him a smack on his arm.

"Damn it, this isn't a joking matter."

"I wasn't joking. I'm serious," he said harshly. He threw off her hand with a snarl of frustration. "You're playing connect the dots with clouds. You're trying to make a legend about a man dead two thousand years, my dreams, and Emma's image from the past all add up in one small package. That's not truth. That's reaching for straws."

"Then answer me this question. When you dream about Maximus, are you Maximus or are you a member of the audience watching a play. Do you *experience* the dream?"

"What difference does that make?" he snapped.

"It's the difference between a past-life experience and just a dream."

The *Prima Consul*'s comment slammed into him as he remembered the exquisite sensation he'd enjoyed when Phaedra had sucked—*no*. That wasn't Phaedra, and it sure as hell wasn't his memory of a dead woman called Cassiopeia. It was his brain longing for something he couldn't have.

"Reincarnation?" He snorted again, only this time in disgust. Shaking his head vehemently, he glared at her. "In case you've forgotten, I'm a half-breed *not* a Sicari."

"Maximus was a general in the Praetorian Guard before his enemies tried to kill him. And like you, he had both telekinetic and telepathic abilities."

"I'm *not* him, Atia." He heard the menace in his voice, but it didn't faze her. Those gray eyes of hers just studied him with curiosity before she dipped her head slightly in acceptance.

"As you wish," she said with quiet resignation as she turned away from him. "But the next time you dream about Maximus and Cassiopeia, think on what I've said here today."

He waited for her to say something else, but she didn't. She just walked back to the table where her book lay open, sat down, and resumed reading. Odds were she was disappointed in him. Uncertain, he remained where he was, half hoping she'd berate him for not believing. Her silence alone was the clincher.

Atia always shut you out when you disappointed her. Frustrated, he stalked out of the library. The setup in this Sicari facility was much smaller than in Chicago, and he took the stairs down to the next floor. What did the woman expect from him? She was asking him to believe in something he couldn't see or touch. And her suggestion that his dreams were from a past life—*Christus*—that didn't sit well with him at all.

His earlier assessment about the possibility that someone needed to verify the woman's sanity came back to haunt him. Was it possible she really *was* losing it? Whatever the *fotte* was going on, his dreams were off-limits. They were sacrosanct. Because in his dreams, Phaedra was his, and he wasn't about to share the one simple pleasure he had left with anyone.

The sound of voices floated out of the conference room as he walked down the hallway. He heard Cleo's hearty laugh, followed by a string of swear words that almost managed to make him smile. The woman had the ability to steal people's breath away with her beauty then shock them into gasping for air the minute she opened her mouth.

The moment he stepped across the conference room's threshold, everyone present grew quiet except for the soft rustle of people shifting in their seats. He didn't even have to look for Phaedra. His entire body was a divining rod pulling hard in her direction. She'd taken the seat directly to the left of his chair at the head of the conference table. His blind side. A deliberate move on her part. Most likely to avoid his gaze, given their exchange earlier.

His mood grim, he slowly walked to his chair, where a file sat on the table. The majority of the team had laptops in front of them, but he had little patience where computers were concerned. With an indiscernible flick of his fingers, the folder at his seat opened to the page he'd marked the night before. Emma's notes were extensive, but that's all they were. Notes. They were hunting for a needle in a haystack. A needle that had been missing for almost two thousand years.

When he reached the table, he looked at the file's top paper then lifted it to review the next page. It wasn't a necessary action. He'd reviewed the file extensively over the past three days. But playing with the paper served to ease the tension in him, bringing the mission front and center so he could push the rest of his emotions into the darkest reaches of his mind.

"I take it everyone has introduced themselves, and Marco has brought you up to speed on what the Order expects of us on this mission?" he asked.

Keeping his eyes on the file in front of him, he trailed his finger down the page he was looking at. Quiet acknowledgments drifted through the air from everyone seated at the table. Phaedra's voice was a soft caress against his senses despite the cool note in her voice. It was clear she didn't want to be here. The silence in the air didn't bother him, but he knew everyone was uncomfortable. Nothing more than he'd expected. Half of the team hadn't ever met until today.

"So no one has any questions." He slowly lifted his head, and his gaze slid across one face after another.

"Damn it, Lysander, of course we've got questions." Cleo's voice held a note of belligerent irritation.

Brassy and tough as nails, she spoke her mind and as always went straight to the heart of the matter without a care for what anyone thought. It was why he'd picked her for the team. She'd serve as his conscience. That and she'd hound him about Phaedra every chance she got. He suppressed a grimace.

"Then the first thing to understand is that anyone can ask a question or express a different opinion. In here we speak freely and honestly with each other." With his one-eyed gaze, he studied the faces around the table as he paused briefly. "I'll listen to anything you have to say, and I encourage you to speak up. The only thing to remember is that when I make a decision—it's final."

"*Il mio signore.*" Angelo Atellus nodded his head in his direction. "Maria and I have reviewed the clues Emma DeLuca provided us, and we've a theory we'd like to suggest."

With a nod at the man, Lysander sat down in his chair. Arms folded across his chest, he leaned back in his chair and waited for the Sicari fighter to continue. Uncertainty flashed across the man's face before he shrugged in a fashion that many natives of Italy exhibited routinely.

"We think it's quite possible we're dealing with a map of bread crumbs."

"Bread crumbs?" Cleo asked with a curious note in her voice.

"Yes. A map where our clues are like bread crumbs scattered around Rome. We just have to find a starting point." Angelo tapped the keyboard of his laptop. The computer's wireless connection allowed him to use the wall screen as his monitor. In seconds, a large map of Rome flashed onto the wall. The mouse pointer drew a yellow line along a wide, blue stripe representing the Tiber River that swung west at the north end of the city.

"If we start with our first clue, we're looking someplace along the river, about here." Angelo used his cursor to point to a spot near one of the river's bridges. "The second clue mentions Antoninus Pius's father, Hadrian. That suggests we're looking for a monument of Hadrian's. One that points toward the city wall. An educated guess says we're talking about the Aurelian walls, which were built around two-seventy A.D."

Cleo pointed toward the map. "Do you have an overlay of the ancient city that shows the walls and other monuments?"

With a grin, Angelo nodded his head. "As a matter of fact, I do. I researched some things last night, and I plotted out sites that are still accessible and not buried beneath present-day Rome."

"And if what we're looking for is under the city?" Cleo arched her eyebrows at the man.

"Let's hope that's not the case, because it will make our task a lot more difficult."

"Difficult? I think the word is we're fucked." Cleo snorted with amusement. Lysander frowned at her. He didn't want the team to be discouraged from the outset. She shrugged. "Okay, difficult."

"What about the monuments connected to Hadrian? How many are there?" Marco Campanella asked quietly. His *Primus Pilus* was asking the same questions Lysander would have asked as Ares's second-in-command. He'd made a good choice in selecting Marco as his lieutenant.

"There are at least three that I can think of off the top of my head, but I'd have to research it more to give you an accurate answer, as he also rebuilt certain monuments," Angelo said. "I think we'll need to include those as possibilities, too."

"Does anyone else think we're probably wasting our time here?" Luciano Pasquale growled. "We have a stretch of river to walk along and a couple of ancient monuments to visit. Not an auspicious beginning."

"Actually, that's not true. Angelo has given us a specific area to search." Maria Atellus shook her head as she defended her husband.

"Search for what?" Violetta Molinaro spoke up, her expression dubious.

"For anything that matches up with the clues," Phaedra answered. "Angelo, have you done any triangulations using the river as the base and one or two of the monuments attributed to Hadrian?"

Clearly in his element, the Sicari fighter nodded his head and grinned. "Absolutely. Based on my calculations, we've got a search area that's about two square miles of real estate."

"Again, what are we looking for specifically?" Violetta groused.

"I imagine we should be looking for the Sicari icon," Cleo mused quietly. "Whoever hid the *Tyet of Isis* probably used our symbol in the same way the followers of the Carpenter used the fish to recognize one another or designate a safe house."

As usual, Cleo's logic was sound. The Sicari symbol dated back before the Roman Empire to Ptolemy's time when the Guard had still been united. It made sense that the hiding place of the *Tyet of Isis* would be marked with the Order's familiar icon, a sword interlocked with a chakram. Lysander nodded at his friend.

"I think you're right, Cleo. I also believe the mark will be relatively small." He looked around at the frowns on everyone's faces. "Whoever hid the artifact wouldn't want to draw attention to the monument as a potential hiding spot, so it's doubtful it's going to be prominent."

"*Merda*, this won't be a needle in a haystack. We're hunting for microbes," Luciano said in a resigned tone.

"Not necessarily." Phaedra shook her head and frowned. "We need a cover story to avoid raising any more suspicion than necessary. Playing tourist does that while letting us photograph as much of the city as we want. We can upload the photos and let the computer search the digital images for any sign of the icon."

Admiration crossed Pasquale's face as he leaned forward, his arms resting on the table. "Smart *and* beautiful. Where have you been all my life, *cara*?"

Raw fury flowed through Lysander's veins at the other man's flirtatious manner. It didn't help matters when Phaedra laughed at the man's teasing tone. Tamping down his anger, he closed his file on the table with a sharp movement.

"Phaedra's idea seems the best one we have, unless anyone else has a better suggestion." He paused for a moment, and when no one spoke, he nodded sharply. "It seems we have a plan then. We'll cover the area Angelo's narrowed down for us in cross sections. We'll need camera equipment. Cleo, since photography is a hobby of yours, you're the lead on the shopping expedition this afternoon. Marco, have you informed everyone as to who is working with who?"

"I was about to cover that when you arrived, *il mio signore*."

"Fine," he said with a gesture for Marco to continue.

The *Primus Pilus* nodded as he picked up a small notebook and quickly read off the assignments and the sectors to cover. Beside him, Phaedra grew as still as a statue the minute her name was linked to his. Her tension was palpable, edging along his senses like the laser that had peeled his skin off one small piece at a time. He swallowed hard at the memory. In an abrupt gesture, he stood up and turned toward her. There wasn't a trace of emotion on her face, but her eyes blazed with anger. She was furious, and he knew better than to give her a chance to speak.

"I've paperwork to deal with this afternoon, so get our grid sections from Marco and study them. I'll meet you in the foyer tomorrow morning at eight thirty."

He grabbed his folder off the table and strode out of the conference room, preventing her from voicing any protests. When he reached the sanctuary of the hall, he ran his hand through his short hair in a gesture of frustration. Somehow, he was certain he'd just made a huge mistake taking Phaedra on as his partner. A mistake that might cost him more than just his sanity.

Chapter 8

THROUGH the spindles at the top of the staircase, Phaedra saw Lysander standing in the entryway waiting for her. The air vibrated with tension, and she wasn't sure which one of them was creating the uneasy sensation. Nibbling on her lip, she debated whether to try reading his emotional state.

It had never been easy to read Lysander, but since his encounter with the Praetorians, just being able to read his basic emotions had been challenging. It was as if he'd erected a brick wall, preventing her or anyone else from probing too deep. But today was different. He seemed distracted, and she had a sense of the raw emotions running deep inside him.

As she opened herself up to his feelings, the intensity of them overwhelmed her. The sheer force of it was a physical sensation and threatened to drop her to her knees. Fingers curled tightly around the banister railing, she fought to remain on her feet. An instant later, a shiver went through her at the hint of darkness emanating from him. Whatever was creating the malevolence, she knew he was worried it might consume him.

Despair scraped across her senses like sharp glass, and she cried out from the mental anguish it sent slicing through her. *Care Deus*, was this what he felt like every day? Like someone turning off a faucet, his emotions no longer flowed through her. Lysander was halfway up the staircase before she realized it, and she quickly gathered her wits. Deliberately rubbing the suede material covering her ankle, she opted to fake a twisted ankle to account for her wounded cry. The minute she saw him round the staircase's small landing, she stopped nursing her ankle and waved her hand.

"I'm fine, I just twisted my ankle," she lied as he stopped two steps down from her.

His penetrating green gaze slowly skimmed its way over her and down to her feet. Did he realize she was lying? Tension danced between them, and she caught a whisper of emotion before he tamped it down until it didn't exist. She suppressed a sigh. He was on guard again, and the opportunity to continue breaking through the wall he'd built around his emotions was gone. And at the moment, she wasn't sure she had the strength to deal with what he kept deep inside him.

"I'm surprised you didn't *break* your ankle with the spike on those boots," he snapped. "We're not going to a fashion show in Milan."

"No, but we're supposed to be acting like tourists." Irritated, she frowned. "A fact I kept in mind when I dressed. What about you? In that black leather people are going to think you're a Soprano."

What she didn't tell him was that he looked sexy as hell the way he was dressed. *Deus*, even with his horrible disfigurement, he was still splendid. Raw power emanated from him, drawing her in like a magnet. He wore a black leather jacket over a black turtleneck shirt, while soft black leather pants hugged his muscular legs. Her fingertips tingled as she remembered what it had been like to run her hands over his sinewy body. The air in her lungs disappeared as she breathed in his delicious scent.

It was the smell of soap mixed with something dark and sensual. It wrapped its way round her senses, tying her into knots. He looked every inch the seasoned warrior, and his black eye patch only heightened the sense of danger about him. He was an open invitation to be bad. And with him, she wanted to be as wicked as she could. Anything to make him respond to her.

Deus, she was insane. Subconsciously, she'd actually listened to Cleo's outrageous suggestion. It was the only explanation for the boots and the rest of her outfit. Her outfit wasn't overly provocative, but it wasn't sedate, either. The hair on the back of her neck rose and her stomach lurched at the hunger that suddenly flashed in his green gaze. The look was enough for her to know she didn't need to read his emotions to know what he was feeling. She knew desire when she saw it.

His one-eyed gaze drifted slowly upward over her blue jeans tucked into her Dal Co' originals to the jean jacket she wore over a red sweater. She suddenly realized the sweater clung just a little too snugly to her breasts because his gaze lingered there. *Care Deus*, had he just used his mental ability to caress her or were her nipples stiff just because she wanted him so badly?

She swallowed hard at the memory of the last time he'd made love to her. Their bodies had melded together perfectly as he'd stroked her with every inch of his body. Heat pooled between her legs at the thought. She wished they were in a secluded spot. She wanted the chance to seduce him. She wanted to make him see that no matter what had happened in the past, they were good together.

Their gazes locked, and the desire on his face made the scarred muscles of his cheek taut with tension. She instinctively stepped toward him, and he stiffened. Another wall rose between them, and frustration whipped through her. Damn it, the man would drive her crazy if this was the way things were going to be between them while they worked together. She drew in a sharp breath then blew it out just as harshly.

"Is this the way it's going to be then?" She glared at him. "Because if it is, I want a new partner."

"What are you talking about?" His tension was still present, but he skillfully covered it with a nonchalant demeanor.

"You know *exactly* what I mean." Her sharp words made him narrow his eye at her. "I think we need to work with other people. Ex-lovers *never* make great partners."

The Praetorians had peeled off the side of his face in jagged strips, but they'd left his beautiful mouth intact and it was now a thin line of determination.

"As I said in the conference room yesterday, I'm willing to listen to ideas, but I have the final say. I paired everyone up based on their strengths and weaknesses."

"And exactly *how* do we balance each other out?" she snapped, incensed by his calm, rational tone.

"You're a valuable asset to the team. I've no doubt the Praetorians will discover you're here, and I'm the most qualified to ensure you're protected."

His response made her mouth fall open as she stared at him with first amazement and then an anger that slowly spread through her until she was rigid with outrage. She narrowed her gaze at him and took a step down the staircase to bring her closer to him. Even when she was furious with him, her body still responded to his on a primal level. It raised her ire that much more.

"That is the most *asinine* reason I have *ever* heard in my entire life," she said with a sharp hiss. "I might be a simple healer, but I've kicked your ass in the gym before."

"One time doesn't qualify," he drawled. It was rare to see him amused, but she could have sworn she saw a flash of humor in his green eye.

"Are you laughing at me?" she asked stiffly. The fact that he seemed to think so little of her fighting skills hurt. She was a damn good fighter.

"No." He shook his head. "But my fighting skills are the best of anyone on the team. You're a valuable asset to the Order, Phaedra. I can't let anything happen to you."

She noted he didn't say that *he* didn't want anything happening to her, just his concern for the Order. She wanted to hit him. She brushed past him with a harsh noise of fury and charged down the steps to the foyer. When she reached the foot of the stairs, she stood there fuming. The man needed someone to dropkick his ass back to Chicago.

Behind her, she heard the sound of Lysander slowly descending the marble stairs. The man had made her so furious she was ready to fight a group of Praetorians single-handed. She stiffened as he walked past her and picked up an expensive-looking camera off the narrow table standing against the entryway wall. He fiddled with a couple of settings then placed the digital equipment in a carrying case.

She watched in silence as he moved toward the interior door and pushed it open. Still angry, she followed him out into the sunshine. As she stood on the stoop, the solid oak door of the safe house snapped shut behind her with a loud click.

The air was warmer than she'd expected, but her sweater and jacket were lightweight enough that she was quite comfortable. Her anger eased somewhat as the sunny day lightened her mood. Several black motorbikes were parked in front of the house, and Lysander moved to the bike farthest from the door. He stored the camera bag in the bike's lockbox, while retrieving two helmets at the same time.

Her fingers curled around the edge of the headgear he handed her as she stared at the bike. Pressing into all that black leather and male heat would amount to little more than a torture session. Tension rippled through her as she shifted her gaze from the bike to the helmet in her hand.

"Can't we just take a taxi?" she said in a tight voice.

"No." Lysander didn't look at her as he swung his leg over the bike to straddle it. "I don't want to get caught someplace without any means of escape."

"Well, do you even know where we're going?"

"I believe you're about to tell me."

The detached note in his voice said he'd already immersed himself in his *Primus Pilus* role. No. He was *Legatus* for this mission. And as *Legatus*, he was entitled to her obedience and respect. The map she'd tucked into her jean jacket pocket crackled softly as she pulled it out to look at it.

"Marco assigned us the sector adjacent to the Temple of Hadrian." Holding the map so he could see it, she pointed to the circle the *Primus Pilus* had made on the map. "We're to cover this section of the grid. There aren't a lot of ancient sites in the area, so we should be able to cover everything before mid-afternoon. I suggest we start with the temple."

"Fine." He gave her a curt nod. "What I want you to remember is that we're in the heart of Praetorian country. If you sense anything, even the slightest hint of danger, I want to know. Understood?"

The crisp words honed the sharp edge of her nerves as she watched him pull on his helmet. He was right, but she didn't like admitting it. Reluctantly, she tugged her own headgear into place as Lysander kick-started the machine. The motor running, he turned his head toward her. Unlike her helmet, the one Lysander wore had a visor that hid his entire face. With his visor down, she couldn't read his expression, but his rigid body language said he wasn't looking forward to the ride any more than she was.

She drew in a deep breath and swung her leg over the bike. The minute she settled into the bike seat, a demon inside her made her wrap her arms around him and press herself into his back. He grew hard as stone, and she smiled with satisfaction. Served him right for refusing to take a taxi. Nonetheless, it was an exquisite torment to have her arms wrapped around him again. Beneath her left arm, she felt the leather scabbard under his jacket that held his short sword. It was a silent reminder that a Sicari was rarely able to relax their guard.

Lysander shifted into gear, and with barely a glance in either direction, he roared out onto the street. The way he moved in and out of traffic made her think he was deliberately trying to unnerve her. He was doing a good job. She tightened her hold on his waist and tried to catch a glimpse of the city as he raced by it.

The one thing she wanted to do was see some of the city. The Sicari had left Rome hundreds of years ago, but it had once been home to her ancestors. She wanted to visit at least one or two historical sites while she was here. Rome might be the global headquarters for the Praetorians, but she'd be safe enough during the daylight, provided she stayed in crowded places.

There was also the stiletto she had sheathed in the side of her boot. Unlike Lysander, it was difficult for her to carry a sword during the daytime, but the blade she carried would enhance her skills in hand-to-hand combat. Horns blared in her ears as Lysander zipped past two cars to get out in front. He sailed through a stoplight that turned red just as they entered the middle of the intersection. The result was the sound of more car horns filling the air.

"*Il Christi omnipotentia*, you're going to get us killed," she shouted in the vicinity of his ear, doubting he could even hear her through his helmet, not to mention the noise of the morning traffic.

If he had heard her, he didn't give any indication, but it did seem like he'd slowed down. They moved through the city streets quickly, and she could only hope Lysander knew where they were headed. Following the car in front of them, they made a sharp right turn, and she sucked in her breath as the car came to an abrupt halt in the middle of the road without any warning. With the ease of someone who'd been riding motorcycles a long time, Lysander's quick reflexes enabled him to skillfully wheel the bike around the other vehicle. Their close call shot her blood pressure up, and she was ready to tear the other driver apart for such a stupid stunt. As they sped by the other car, she had to settle for an evil glare at the man.

Several long minutes later, they came to a stop on a narrow street. She could tell Lysander was waiting on her to get off the bike, and she quickly put several feet between her and the motorcycle. Tugging her helmet off her head, she set it down on the bike seat. Without speaking, he pulled the digital camera from the lock box at the back of the motorcycle then shoved the black nylon camera bag in with the helmets. The minute he'd secured the bike, Lysander nodded toward a bright square several hundred yards away.

"The Temple of Hadrian."

With a sweep of his hand, he gestured her to lead the way. Still annoyed with him, she walked toward the *piazza* in silence. Not that she expected her silence to annoy him, but making a scene would draw unwanted attention to them, and she knew better. As she turned the corner, a chill of excitement slid through her at the sight of the temple.

Massive columns rose upward to meet the ceiling they supported. At one time, Romans would have walked through the columns to reach the inner sanctum of the temple. Now, a modern building occupied the temple's interior with the outer stone columns serving as a façade for a financial institution.

People filled the *piazza*, and she immediately opened herself up to the emotions swirling in the air around her. After more than a minute, she released a sigh of relief. The only thing she sensed were the emotions of people worried about ordinary things. Lysander stood quietly beside her, and she could feel him watching her. She turned her head to look up at him in hopes of seeing some emotion on his face she could decipher. The expression on his face grew shuttered in an instant, and the emotion she glimpsed was gone too quickly to define. The silent look he sent her demanded a report, and she bit back the urge to reach out and probe his emotions.

"Well?"

"Nothing unusual," she said. "People worried about jobs, families, lovers . . ."

He didn't even flinch as she allowed her sentence to trail off. Disgusted with herself for thinking she could get a reaction from him, she stretched out her hand.

"Let me have the camera. I'll shoot some pictures, and you can play bodyguard."

This time she did get a reaction from him. The glare he sent her made her smile up at him sweetly as she took the camera from his hand. He didn't like the way she'd demoted him. With a frown, she tried to reacquaint herself with the basics of the camera. The class Cleo had given yesterday had been short, and this camera wasn't like the ones her friend had bought for everyone.

This one had a well-worn look to it. She didn't remember Lysander ever taking pictures. At that moment, he released a snort of irritation and leaned forward to press into her back so he could look over her shoulder. His chest brushed against her body as he pointed toward a silver button on top of the camera. His touch sent a streak of fire zipping across her skin.

"Press the silver button to take the picture. It has an automatic focus, so all you have to do is press this button to zoom in or out." He pointed to a black button near the camera's built-in handgrip.

She swallowed the knot in her throat and nodded as she placed her eye against the viewfinder and took a picture. With a quick turn of a dial, she was looking at the shot she'd just taken of the upper level of the temple. Flipping the camera's settings so she could take pictures again, she walked forward and shot several pictures of the temple's façade from different angles. Aware of Lysander always close behind her, she lowered the camera and turned her head to look at him.

"Go stand at the railing over there," she said as she bobbed her head in the direction of the fencing that kept the people from falling into a stone escarpment. "I'll take your picture. Make it look like we really are the tourists we're supposed to be playing."

Together they crossed the *piazza*, where she took several pictures of Lysander standing against the railing before she joined him and proceeded to quickly shoot one section of the stone façade after another. While she moved along the side of the building taking pictures, she noticed Lysander had stopped to study the columns. As she reached the end of the temple's sidewall, she turned the corner to continue photographing the building.

No sooner did she lose sight of Lysander than he was there again. Close at hand, ready to protect her if the occasion demanded it of him. Even if he didn't have a personal interest in her safety, she still liked knowing he was there. It wasn't that she was afraid to walk around Rome during the day, but being near him under any circumstances was better than not seeing him at all. And it gave her the opportunity—she slammed the door shut on the thought, bracing against the idea's persistent attempt to break through.

Determined not to listen to the voice in her head, she turned the camera lens toward the stone foundation of the structure and zoomed in on the exterior stones supporting the temple. The shutter release whirred softly as she systematically plotted a visual path along the stones. She tried to get as close as she could, while ensuring that the picture encompassed the largest amount of stone possible.

Yesterday when Cleo had handed out camera equipment, her friend had given everyone a photography lesson. Brief and basic, the instructions had confirmed her own observations in the team briefing earlier that morning. While they needed to zoom in when taking pictures, they had to be systematic enough to allow the computer to form a complete picture of the building.

As quickly as possible, she continued to photograph each section of the stone façade. It was one thing for a tourist to take lots of pictures, but entirely something else for someone to photograph a building inch by inch. She always shielded herself from the constant bombardment of others' emotions, and while she didn't sense anything unusual, she had no desire to arouse anyone's curiosity.

She zoomed in on another section of stone, her eye pressed to the viewfinder. The sight of a faint mark on a stone that bordered the section she was photographing made her frown. It was a shadowy indentation that didn't look like it belonged. Resisting the urge to shift the camera lens in the direction of the mark, she finished photographing the remaining sector.

Eager to get a closer look at the mark, she shifted her position along the iron fence surrounding the building until she was standing directly over the stone. The trench surrounding the structure made it difficult to get a good view of the stone. Since the mark was on one of the structure's foundation stones, the angle didn't allow for a level examination of the granite block. Even worse, the face of the stone was eroded.

Like a large portion of the temple's stonework, weather and time had damaged the large block of granite. But it still looked like someone had deliberately etched a mark into the rock. She zoomed in on the spot with the lens and clicked the shutter release button. Despite the sunlight, the shadows in the ditch prevented her from seeing the mark clearly. She turned her head toward Lysander, whose stance was one of rigid wariness.

A second later, a sudden tingling against the back of her neck made her heart skip. They were being watched. The individual was more than powerful. It was malevolent. She shuddered.

Responding to the sensations she sensed would only alert the enemy that she was aware of their presence. Dread slithered down her spine with icy persistence. He already knew. The *bastardo* knew she was aware of his presence, and it amused him. And *aroused*. Suddenly, fear swelled up inside of her, threatening to overpower her ability to think.

Run.

If she put distance between—her heart slammed in her chest as an invisible hand grasped her ankle, holding her in place. The mental touch ignited a fierce anger inside of her. It suppressed her fear, and she envisioned the last Praetorian she'd killed. It was what she'd do to this *bastardo* when he came out of hiding.

She could almost hear his mocking laughter, and she gasped as the firm pressure of unseen hands slid slowly up her legs. It was an insidious caress that sent shock rippling through her body. She tried to retreat again, but the man's invisible fingers dug painfully into her buttocks before sliding down over the back of her legs to force her legs slightly apart. A moment later fingers brushed across her inner thigh.

Trembling with horror and disgust, she tried to call for Lysander, but a firm pressure covered her mouth, preventing her from calling out. *Oh God*, this couldn't be happening. Sickened by the violating touches, she struggled to break free of her attacker's invisible grip once more. Her attempt met with a response that terrified her.

Relentless and unyielding, a firm pressure crept its way over every inch of her body until she was incapable of moving. It didn't just hold her in place. It emphasized how powerless she was to stop him. The *bastardo* was in complete control, and she'd never felt so helpless in her entire life. The man's lust flooded her senses, and she released a soft sob as unseen hands slid over her waist to lightly stroke the underside of her breasts. She whimpered at the nauseating touch.

Where was Lysander; couldn't he see something was wrong? The sensation of derisive laughter crawled across her skin in the same revolting way as her attacker's unseen hands. He could feel her terror, and he liked it. She bit back tears. The man could do whatever he wanted with her, and she couldn't stop him.

Stunned, she tried to deny what was happening to her, but the invisible stroke inching its way slowly up her inner thigh told her otherwise. Revulsion sent bile racing to her throat, and with a strength born of fear she partially broke free of her unseen assailant's grip. She turned toward Lysander and took two steps before an incredible pressure crashed into her body. Helpless again, she saw Lysander racing toward her.

He was at her side in seconds, and she immediately sensed a change in her attacker. The invisible presence suddenly seemed surprised then irritated, almost as if he'd made an unexpected discovery. Her attacker's mental hold eased slightly then tightened.

"You'll have to go through me first, you sorry fuck," Lysander snarled in a low voice.

If she didn't know better, she would have thought Lysander was actually communicating telepathically with her assailant. She choked back a cry as the invisible touch slipped off her then clutched her thigh in a merciless grip. She could almost hear the man's laughter. It said he could have easily kept her from moving, and there was the unspoken promise that he'd find her again.

Suddenly she was free and stumbling back into the *piazza* with

Lysander's arm supporting her at her waist. She staggered to a halt, but Lysander ruthlessly grabbed her arm at the elbow and hurried her forward again.

"*No,*" he growled. "We're leaving. *Now.*"

She knew better than to argue with him, and she didn't want to. A shudder ripped through her as she allowed Lysander to hurry her back to where they'd parked the motorcycle. She darted a look behind her and flinched as Lysander squeezed her elbow.

"Don't look back," he ordered sharply. "If he's watching, he'll know you're afraid."

"Afraid? He already knows I'm afraid of him. I haven't been this scared since I killed my first Praetorian," she snapped as another wave of anger swept through her. She wanted to kill the *bastardo* who had just terrorized her. "I couldn't see him, but he could damn well see me. It's the only explanation I can come up with for the vibes I was getting. The son of a bitch enjoyed what he did to me."

The memory of the way he'd touched her made her stomach start to churn. *Deus,* she'd felt so helpless. The thought of what might have happened to her if Lysander hadn't been with her only increased her nausea. The minute they reached the parked motorbike, she jerked free of Lysander's hold. Bracing herself against the wall with one hand, she threw up what was left of her breakfast. When she finished, Lysander offered her a package of tissues. She grabbed several of the white sheets and wiped her mouth.

"Since when do you carry tissues?" she rasped.

"I don't." He nodded toward the shop across the street as she looked up at him. "Thank the shopkeeper across the street."

She looked around him and saw the elderly woman standing in the doorway of a small gift shop. With a weak smile, she waved her thanks to the woman watching them with a concerned look. When she looked back at Lysander, she saw a troubled expression furrowing his brow.

The instant he realized she was watching him, his face returned to its usual stoic look. She closed her eyes as she struggled with the horror of what had just happened. A hand touched her arm, and she recoiled. Eyes flashing open, she met Lysander's unrelenting gaze.

"I know," she murmured. "We have to go."

Lysander handed her helmet to her in silence, and in less than a minute, they roared away from the historic site. Arms wrapped tightly around Lysander's waist, she didn't care where they were going. She just knew she wanted to get away from the temple. Eyes closed, she tried not to think about what had just happened.

But it was impossible. She shuddered as she remembered the way the man had touched her. It had to have been a rogue Sicari who'd assaulted her. She couldn't come up with any other explanation. Praetorians were telepaths. They didn't have telekinetic abilities. That wasn't entirely true. Her stomach lurched with a sickening sensation as she considered the whispers of her childhood. She immediately dismissed the idea. Praetorian Dominus were a myth. The man had to have been a rogue, but even they usually didn't hide like this one had.

She'd expected open confrontation, something where she could fight back. Not this type of an assault where she was helpless to do anything to save herself. Even worse had been the eerie way the *bastardo* had reacted to her terror. It was almost as if he could read her fear. That meant he had to have been close enough to see her. See how frightened she was.

Deus, there had only been one other time when she'd been that terrified—that helpless—in her entire life. She'd lied to Lysander. The night she'd killed her first Praetorian hadn't been frightening at all. Until today, nothing had surpassed the terror she'd felt the night the Praetorians had murdered her parents. She choked back her tears. She wasn't about to cry in front of Lysander two days in a row.

Moments later, the bike slowed and swerved slightly. When she opened her eyes, she saw they'd returned to the safe house. She hopped off the bike and stepped around Lysander to knock on his visor. He pushed it up to stare at her in silence.

"Why did we come back here?" she snapped in reaction to the thought he intended to leave her here. Alone. "There are at least four other monuments we need to photograph."

"We're done for the day." He draped one arm over the bike handle, his other resting on his hip as he studied her. "I think you need some breathing room."

"I'm fine." She shook her head in protest. If she went back inside, she'd be alone, and she didn't want to be alone. She didn't want him to leave her. "We need to complete our portion of the grid."

"It can wait until I get to it."

"*No*," she exclaimed vehemently. "You are not going to leave me here alone. I refuse to let that *bastardo* win, and if I go inside and hide, he wins."

He tugged the helmet off his head and ran a hand through his short, cropped hair. She could tell he was angry, but he was also uncomfortable. Obviously, he didn't know how to handle something like this, but then neither did she. Had he expected her to just retreat into the safe house like a meek little mouse? His jaw hard with tension, he shook his head.

"I don't have any intention of leaving you alone, Phaedra," he said quietly.

There was a fierce, protective quality about his demeanor that made her heart skip a beat. It made her feel safe. As if protecting her wasn't just business, but that her safety was important to him because he cared about her. She immediately crushed the hope trying to grow inside her. She was a fool to think he felt anything for her other than a sense of responsibility.

"Then stop arguing with me, and let's finish our grid," she said firmly. "I'll be fine."

She looked away from him and fought to control the sickening feeling taking root in her stomach as she remembered those few short moments of vulnerability. She knew rogue Sicari often came to hate their own kind, but this man had been different. His hatred of the Sicari had equaled the fierce hatred she'd sensed in the Praetorians she'd fought. It had been malevolent and twisted.

The chill of it still lingered on her skin. She trembled at the memory of the rogue's unseen touch sliding over her body. It had seemed to take an eternity for Lysander to reach her. All the while, she'd been powerless to stop the invasive touch of that sick *bastardo*. Was that what it had been like for Lysander when the Praetorians had tortured him? That helpless feeling?

"You need to talk about it with someone, Phaedra." There was a gentleness in his voice that steadied her nerves. "He violated you, and you can't lock it up inside of you."

"You're a good one to talk," she said sharply. "You've not bothered to talk to anyone about what happened to you."

"I talked to Atia." Stunned by his statement, she stared at him in silence. Arms resting on the motorcycle's handlebars, he shrugged. "I knew I needed to talk to someone."

You could have talked to me. She ignored the small dart of relief that he'd not talked to Cleo. Instead, she waved his words aside.

"All he did was grope me. I'll be fine." Her abrupt response made him narrow his eye.

"I could order you to stay here."

"You could, but you won't," she said in a stiff voice.

"*Christus*, and Atia calls Ares an obstinate devil." With a slight shake of his head, he released a harsh breath. "I know I'm going to regret this, but we'll continue, on one condition."

"What?"

"You're not to leave my side for one second. Understood?"

"Yes."

There wasn't any way she would admit it to him, but it was a condition she was more than happy to follow. He eyed her carefully for a moment before he nodded his head. She stepped forward to get back on the bike, and his hand shot out to catch hers in a gentle grip.

"I'll find him, Phaedra, and when I do, I'll make him pay." The harsh note in his voice made her shake her head as she stared into that vivid green eye of his.

"How in the hell do you think you can find a rogue Sicari? You're not a telepath."

"Rogue Sicari or not. I'll find him."

His emphatic statement made her swallow hard as she nodded. A second later, he released her, and she threw her leg over the leather bike seat. As she settled into the curved seat, she wrapped her arms around his waist. The man couldn't possibly think her assailant had been Praetorian, could he? No. That wasn't possible. Lysander didn't have the ability to read minds nor did he have intuitive powers like her. So how in the name of Jupiter's Stone did he think he could find her assailant?

The real problem was whether her assailant would find her, and she was convinced the son of a bitch wouldn't have any trouble finding her at all. And if his telekinetic ability was as strong as she thought it was, she wasn't going to be safe when he found her. She wrapped her arms around Lysander's waist, and a dark chill sluiced across her skin as the motorcycle rolled out into the street again. Suddenly, she wished she were back home in Chicago.

Chapter 9

THE minute she entered the safe house's foyer, she heard the laughter filtering through the narrow hall that led into the kitchen. The sweet aroma of herbs and spices filled her nostrils, causing her stomach to growl with hunger. It surprised her. She hadn't realized she was even hungry.

Lysander had offered to stop and eat several times throughout the day, but the idea of food had simply churned her stomach. The fact that she hadn't wanted anything to eat only emphasized how badly shaken she was by her encounter with the rogue Sicari. She pushed aside the dark memory, refusing to give in to the unsettling helplessness it continued to breed inside her.

Her neck tingled as Lysander came through the front door after her. No matter where she was, she always knew when he was nearby. It was like an internal radar set just to his signal. With a quick glance over her shoulder, she gestured toward the kitchen.

"Sounds and smells like dinner." She turned away from him, but his hand stopped her from moving.

"If you're not up to eating with everyone, I can have your meal sent to your rooms."

She looked at him from over her shoulder with mixed emotions. Ever since this morning, he'd been treating her with kid gloves. While she appreciated his concern for her well-being, it was wreaking havoc with her heart. The worst thing was knowing that at any minute they'd go back to the way it had been for the past year. Cold words and that callous disregard whenever she was around. She shook her head.

"I'm fine." She forced a smile to her lips. "I'm actually hungry, and it smells like you have some serious competition in the kitchen."

As she headed down the narrow corridor with Lysander behind her, she heard him mutter something under his breath. But when she glanced back at him, his features were unreadable. A moment later, she entered the bright and homey kitchen. Cleo was the first to notice their arrival and she arched her eyebrow at them.

"All hail the conquering heroes," her friend said with a laugh as they entered the spacious kitchen and adjoining dining area. "We were beginning to think we'd have to send out a search and rescue team. Run into trouble?"

"Nothing we couldn't handle." She forced a note of bravado into her voice to ward off any unwanted inquiries. "We just had a lot of pictures to take."

"You look pale, *bella*." Luciano Pasquale stared at her from across the wide expanse of counter where he was dishing out servings of cannelloni from two large casserole dishes. "Are you feeling all right?"

Her radar kicked in again as Lysander stiffened beside her. His tension was a clear sign he was still on duty as her protector. She suppressed a sigh. If only his behavior was because he cared about her. Ignoring the silent guardian at her side, she smiled at Luciano.

"Honestly? I'm weak with hunger," she said. "It smells wonderful. Who's the cook? And don't say Cleo, because I know better."

Maria Atellus, plate in one hand, pointed with the other toward Pasquale. "Luciano made it because Cleo bet him that he couldn't beat the *Legatus*'s cannelloni recipe."

Angelo Atellus lifted up a large bowl of salad over his wife's head and carried it through the wide French doors that opened out onto a large, glass-enclosed patio. Over his shoulder, he ordered his wife to bring him a plate of food and proceeded to set the silver bowl on the large table sitting under a wooden trellis covered with grape vines. From where Phae stood at the counter, she could see Atia talking with Marco, the *Primus Pilus*.

"Angelo, where's the olive oil and vinegar?" Violetta shouted over Cleo, who was chastising Luciano for having dripped sauce onto the counter.

Pasquale didn't bother to respond to her friend's exasperated comments. Instead, he gestured for her to grab a plate. "Come on, Phae, take a plate, and let me introduce you to my heavenly cooking."

"Ego's not a problem for you, is it, Luciano," she said with a laugh.

"Never, *carissima*. Nor do I let it stand in my way when I see something I want."

There was a playfulness about his arrogance that made him charming as opposed to annoying. Laughing, she reached for a plate, but Lysander beat her to the stack of yellow plates with a grapevine design encircling the edges. A plate in each hand, he stretched out over the counter and silently waited for Luciano to fill the dishes. The look on Pasquale's face went from jovial flirting to one of careful appraisal.

Lysander's tension showed in the way the scarred tissue covering his cheek was drawn tight over the bone. The black patch covering his missing eye only emphasized the menacing bearing reflected in his stance. She couldn't see his eye from where she was standing, but she was certain it would be the icy green color it always turned when he was trying to intimidate someone.

Startled by his action, she stiffened slightly as Cleo raised her eyebrows and tilted her head toward Phaedra. *Christus*, the woman was going to grill her the first chance she got. Ignoring her friend's speculative look, she accepted the plate of food Lysander handed her and headed out to the terrace.

What in Jupiter's name had that been about—protection. Lysander was thinking Luciano's attentions might make her feel threatened. She suppressed a sigh. The last thing she wanted was a Sicari bodyguard, especially if he wasn't in love with her. As she crossed the threshold out onto the patio, Atia motioned toward her.

"Come sit beside me, Phaedra."

Muscles knotting with tension, she slowly obeyed the command. Atia had called Lysander earlier, and his conversation with the *Prima Consul* had been mostly one-sided. But from the few words she'd overheard, she knew the conversation had been about her. It convinced her that Lysander had texted the Sicari leader about her attack.

Atia wouldn't mention the incident in front of anyone else, but she wasn't so sure the woman wouldn't find some pretext to drag the two of them away on some urgent matter of business to discuss what had happened. All she wanted at the moment was to eat and have a couple of glasses of wine in hopes of distancing herself from the entire affair.

Obeying the *Prima Consul*'s command, she sat next to the woman, while Lysander sat on the opposite side. She released a soft noise of aggravation. It was like someone had placed her in protective custody. The rest of the team settled into their chairs as a bottle of dark red Lambrusco made its way around the table. She poured a healthy portion into her glass, ignoring the arched look Atia sent her way.

The look irritated her. First a bodyguard, now a mother hen. She knew how much she could drink before her healing ability was diminished. A second later, she took a bite of the cannelloni on her plate. The flavor of the dish burst over her tongue in a delightful symphony of Cavallo cheese, spinach, pasta, and a tomato-based marinade. She immediately turned her head toward Lysander as she saw him take a bite of the dish.

Surprise swept across his face, before a calculating look hardened his saturnine features.

In a controlled, measured movement, he carefully laid his fork down, and his long fingers reached out to lightly stroke the stem of his wineglass. It was obvious he'd realized that Luciano was a threat to his culinary reputation.

Known for his stoic mannerism, the few times Lysander displayed any emotion was in the kitchen, and he guarded his cooking laurels jealously. He loved to cook, but now there was a new face in town when it came to skills in the kitchen. And the man was definitely not happy about it. Those who didn't know him would assume he was relaxed, but she knew different.

He was plotting Luciano's demise in the kitchen. She could see it in the hard look of his green eye and the tension in his body. The man wouldn't give up his title without a hard fight. He'd use every skill he'd learned in that cooking school in Tuscany. Across the table,

Cleo's expression was one of pained contemplation. Clearly, her friend was in a major dilemma. She'd touted Lysander's skill, and here was a dish that equaled if not surpassed her friend's ability. Luciano turned his head and grinned at Cleo.

"Well, *bella*, how is it?"

"It's delicious," Cleo said in a cautious voice. Her gaze shifted to Lysander, who met Cleo's gaze with calm acceptance.

"It's more than that, Cleo, and you know it. It's exceptional," Lysander said quietly. He lifted his glass of wine toward Luciano. "Well done. *Salute*."

Everyone around the table acknowledged the toast with enthusiasm and a chorus of compliments. Phaedra tilted her head toward Lysander.

"So what dish are you going to fix to show him up?" she murmured.

"I'm not." He turned his head toward her and met her gaze.

"Oh, please," she said as she eyed him with disbelief. "You were plotting something the minute you took a bite of that cannelloni."

He lifted his wineglass to his mouth and took a drink. When he returned it to the table, he shifted in his seat and turned toward her. One elbow on the table, he draped his other arm over the back of her chair. He was close enough to touch, and the male scent of him flooded her senses until her blood ran sluggish through her veins. *Deus*, she wanted to kiss him. Touch him—make him cry out her name with need. She swallowed hard as his eye narrowed at her.

"It amazes me that you think you can read my mind so well, but you can't read Pasquale's intentions." The unexpected observation made her frown.

"What are you talking about?"

"The man wants you."

There was a hard edge to his words, but not even that really registered as she struggled to understand why he would even notice such a thing. As she stared at him in amazement, his gaze grew shuttered. With a shake of her head, she rolled her eyes at him.

"Don't be ridiculous," she said with a sniff of disgust. "You just don't want to admit the man can match your skill in the kitchen."

"And you hate being wrong." He nodded in the direction of the other man. "He's had his eyes on you for the last few minutes, wondering whether there's anything between us."

Her heart slammed into her chest at the way Lysander's mouth thinned with what appeared to be anger. Was he upset that Luciano was flirting with her? She reached for her wineglass and took a long draught of the fruity Lambrusco. What in Jupiter's name was she thinking? The man hadn't changed overnight.

But it was impossible not to notice something *had* changed between them. She didn't know whether the incident with the rogue Sicari had something to do with his change in demeanor or whether she was simply looking at him differently. She frowned. Even if there was a small shift in the tension between them, she needed to remember the callous way he'd ended their relationship before it had even really begun.

He'd brutally said she'd been nothing more than a one-night stand to him. His cruel words had inflicted wounds that even a year later were still raw. Ironically, it had been at that moment she'd realized she was in love with him. The realization had only heightened the pain of his rejection, and her natural reaction had been to taunt him at every opportunity. He'd never retaliated—not once, and she'd always been too afraid to ask why. Afraid because loving him the way she did, she didn't want to know just how indifferent he was to her. Instead, it was easier to taunt him in an attempt to hurt him as much as she was hurting.

But she was tired of being angry. Tired of trying to get a reaction from him when she knew, deep down, nothing she did or said was going to change the way things were between them. Lysander looked at her again and arched his eyebrow at her. Praying her expression hadn't revealed her feelings, she slowly turned her head in response to Lysander's silent command.

The moment she did so, she saw Luciano watching them with a narrowed gaze. As her gaze met his, he lifted his wineglass in her direction and sent her a mischievous smile. The man's flirtatious manner was impossible to resist, and she smiled back. The minute she did so, she sensed a change in Lysander. The tension in him went up a notch.

She stiffened as the whisper of an unseen hand cradled the back of her neck in a possessive touch. It was gone so fast, she wasn't sure whether it had been real or imaginary. Had Lysander caressed her? Her heart slammed into her chest in a frantic beat at the thought. She peeked a glance in his direction. Although his arm still rested on the back of her chair, he was in the process of taking a drink of wine.

If she didn't know better, she could swear he was struggling hard to maintain that stoic calm of his. No, she was reading more into his behavior than there was. But if he'd not touched her, then—she shivered as an icy chill slid down her back. Was it possible the rogue Sicari had found her? No. She wouldn't even go there. It was crazy to think the *bastardo* was within reach of her.

The Order owned almost the entire city block surrounding the safe house, and despite its aged appearance, the complex was well fortified. The security equipment in place was the best money could buy. From steel doors at the main entrances, to iron defenses at every window and balcony, the house was almost impenetrable. She looked back at Luciano, and saw him watching her intently.

Had he been the one to touch her? *Deus*, she wasn't even sure someone had touched her. She bit her lip. The fact that she was even obsessing about it showed how edgy her encounter with that rogue son of a bitch had made her. She resented it. And she hated herself for letting the incident affect her at all. Beside her, Atia laughed. Startled, she looked at the *Prima Consul*, who waved her hand at Angelo seated opposite her.

"I can assure you, Atellus, I think I'd rather come back as a rock in the next life than explore the catacombs with you."

"But they're fascinating, Madame *Consul*." Angelo laughed as he leaned forward and wagged his finger at Atia. "Why, for all you know, the bones of the person you were in a past life might be at rest there."

"Impossible. Sicari never bury their dead. We leave this earth in a purifying blaze of fire." Atia sniffed her disdain before grinning at the man opposite her. "All my past lives have all been as a Sicari. I feel it in *my* bones. You, Angelo Atellus, are a historian who doesn't appreciate the romantic aspects of history. Dried up bones are *not* romantic."

"Not so, *il mia signora*. I think history can be quite romantic, even tragically so. For example, I find the story of Maximus and Cassiopeia *most* compelling. Here was a man who'd just lost most of his men in the Battle of Milvian Bridge. He's in retreat from Constantine I when he learns his wife is still in Rome, about to be handed over to fanatical followers of the Church." Angelo's expression was one of pensive sadness as he met Atia's gaze across the table. He made a noise that was a mix of amazement and disbelief.

"I can't imagine what Maximus must have been thinking, feeling, as he raced back to Rome only to arrive too late to save Cassiopeia. The man must have had nerves of steel to make his dagger hit its mark as the mob was burning his wife alive." Atellus reached for his wife's hand and sent her a loving glance. "I would gladly give my life for Maria, but I do not know that I would have had as steady a hand as Maximus must have."

Listening to the conversation, Phaedra remembered her dreams and felt like kicking herself. Her dreams were nothing more than a memory from a story she'd heard since childhood. Well, maybe not a story, but at least bits and pieces of the legend. She'd simply made the first Sicari Lord look like Lysander in her dreams. She was an idiot. Atia's shoulder brushed hers as the *Prima Consul* leaned forward to rest her elbows on the table. A contemplative look on her face, the older woman folded her hands and formed a steeple with her forefingers.

"I have always viewed Maximus as the standard by which all Sicari are judged. To put a dagger through his wife's heart as she was being burned alive had to have taken immense courage. He must have been an extraordinary man," the *Prima Consul* said. With a nod of agreement, Angelo folded his arms and rested them on the table as he sent the *Prima Consul* a quizzical look.

"Recently, I came across the writings of *Prima Consul* Julius Marchio from the mid-sixteenth century, which I have been reading before bed."

"Clearly a sedative if you're reading it late at night," Atia said with a laugh.

"Sometimes, but last night I read that each *Prima Consul* is tasked with watching for signs that Maximus has returned to the

Sicari." Angelo's gaze never left Atia's face as he continued. "Marchio was convinced the Sicari would never find the *Tyet of Isis* until Maximus was reborn. Have you heard of this prophecy?"

"There are a great many stories, secrets even, handed over when one takes on the mantle of consul." Her expression guarded, the *Prima Consul* shrugged. "The story Marchio refers to has been around for centuries."

"Then you don't believe the story?" Angelo frowned. "Marchio seemed convinced the story was true, and he even detailed signs to look for."

"As I said, there are many tales passed on from one consul to another. Some are more plausible than others." There was the slightest clipped note in Atia's voice as she straightened and pushed her dinner plate toward the center of the table. "Do I think it possible that Maximus and Cassiopeia will be reincarnated? Yes. I have always believed the soul's journey doesn't end with just one life."

"But what about the signs, *il mia signora*? In his writings, Marchio says an *alieni* will read the Sicari Lord's coin. Did not *Legatus* DeLuca's *domina* read the coin?"

Angelo's words brought all conversation to a halt as everyone turned toward Atia. Her expression closed off and noncommittal, the *Prima Consul* gave the man across from her an imperceptible nod.

"Yes, Emma read the coin, but it showed her nothing about the return of Maximus."

"Then perhaps we are closer to finding the *Tyet of Isis* than we realized, because there are other signs as well."

"Such as?" As a politician, Atia was excellent at keeping her thoughts well hidden, but the tension flowing from her had an almost tangible quality to it.

"Marchio says a *Primus Pilus* who is of mixed blood will find the *Tyet of Isis*."

Angelo's statement was like a thunderclap in the room, and Phaedra gasped at the possibility of someone with even an ounce of Praetorian blood finding the artifact. The thought appalled her. The shudder rippling through Atia was tangible, but her reaction was nothing compared to Lysander's as the glass of wine he held shattered.

Red wine and blood splattered the surface of the table as an oath flew from his lips. Instinct made her reach out to him, but an invisible hand encircled her wrist in a painful vise. He didn't bother to look at her as he stared at Angelo, who was gasping for air, his face white with fear as his eyes met Lysander's hard gaze.

"I have no need of the *Curavi*, Phaedra," Lysander said in an icy voice as his green eye darkened with fury. "Atellus, if you're questioning the loyalty of my *Primus Pilus*, you're questioning not only my choice for second in command, but my leadership as well, and that's something I won't allow in my guild, small that it is."

"Let him go, Lysander." Atia's voice was firm, but gentle. "He was simply repeating what he'd read."

Lysander hesitated at the *Prima Consul*'s words, then with a sharp nod, he released his grip on the other man. A second later the grip on Phaedra's wrist vanished as Lysander shoved his chair backward in a vicious movement as he stood up. Angelo inhaled several deep breaths as he recovered from Lysander's invisible chokehold.

Maria, her arm wrapped around her husband's shoulders, looked frightened, but not so much that she couldn't muster up the courage to glare at Lysander. His features were like a stone statue, cold and without emotion as he met the woman's angry look.

"I have every confidence in Marco Campanella. Anyone even *hinting* at the possibility that he's not Sicari or loyal to the Order will be challenging my authority as *Legatus*. A challenge I will *not* let go unanswered."

The quiet words carried a lethal message that said any challenge to Lysander's authority would not end favorably for the challenger. The unspoken promise was reinforced as he surveyed the faces staring up at him with a deadly calm. Satisfied he'd made his point, Lysander left the table and vanished into the kitchen. Phaedra watched him go with a sense of confusion. His reaction had been completely out of character for him. In his wake, the lighthearted mood had evaporated, leaving everyone somber and uncomfortable. Still ashen from his chastisement, Angelo turned his head toward the *Primus Pilus*.

"I ask *Indulgentia*, Campanella. It was not my intent to question either your birth or your loyalty to the Order."

"Granted." Marco frowned as he nodded sharply. "It was the implication in your statement that angered *Legatus* Condellaire. The *Legatus* is an honorable man who values the lives and reputations of everyone in his guild, even you, Atellus. It's something to keep in mind."

Angelo nodded his understanding as Cleo broke the tension by getting up from the table and collecting dirty dishes. A silent sigh of relief rippled through the group at her action, and everyone quickly followed her example in cleaning up dinner. Reaching for her plate, Phaedra jumped as Atia stayed her hand with a light touch.

"Leave it," the *Prima Consul* said quietly. "I wish to speak with you."

"What about?"

"Lysander sent me a text message about the assault. It's why I called him earlier. I wanted to know how you were feeling." The concern in Atia's voice made her nibble at her lip. The woman had been good to her and Ares since their parents had died.

"I'm fine."

"He told me you think it was a rogue Sicari. Are you sure?"

"I'm not sure what else he could be." She shrugged, dismissing the fantastical notions she'd considered earlier.

"When I talked to Lysander, he said you were quite upset."

"I'm fine now."

"Are you sure? It's unhealthy to keep it locked up inside, *piccola mia*."

"When I'm ready to talk, I will, but not until then."

"*Va bene*," Atia said with a sigh of frustration.

Grateful the woman was done questioning her, she picked up her plate along with Lysander's and retreated to the kitchen to help clean up dinner. In less than fifteen minutes, the kitchen was spotless with everyone wandering off to spend their free time as they wished. Unwilling to go to her room where she'd be left alone with her thoughts, she pulled an unopened bottle of Lambrusco from the fridge and raised it into the air with a jerk of her head to Cleo.

"Want to join me for a couple of drinks out on the patio?"

Eyebrows raised, her friend shrugged her acquiescence. "Sure."

The night air was unseasonably warm for Rome, but it was the perfect temperature for relaxing under the moonlight. The garden was softly lit with squat black garden lights placed strategically throughout the large area. She opened the wine and set the bottle on the table after filling her glass. Cleo poured a glass as well, then plopped herself down into a nearby lounge chair. Her legs swinging up onto the cushions, she sent Phaedra a curious look.

"Looks like you took my advice."

"What advice?"

"Don't play that game with me. You know exactly what advice I'm referring to."

Cleo's gaze narrowed on her. Phaedra avoided her friend's gaze by taking a drink of wine. It tasted sweet on her tongue, and she was finally beginning to feel warm, fuzzy, and relaxed.

"If you're asking me if I tried to seduce him, the answer's no."

"Then what *did* happen between the two of you?"

"Nothing." She shrugged and held the wineglass up to study it in the dim light of the patio.

"Like hell it didn't. Lysander was glued to your side ready to tear anyone apart if they came near you." Cleo snorted with a scoffing laugh. "So, out with it."

"I don't want to talk about it." She sent her friend a pleading look. "I'm feeling warm and fuzzy right now, and I want to stay that way."

"In other words, you're tipsy, and you sound like you're ready to cry." Cleo sighed. "You know drinking makes your ability weak. If someone stumbled in here bleeding like a stuck pig, they'd probably die because you wouldn't be able to do a fucking thing for them."

Her friend's comment made her wince. Cleo was right. At this point, she doubted her ability to heal at all. That rogue Sicari had managed to unsettle her more than she wanted to admit. And while drinking had numbed her to the tension making her edgy all day, she knew better than to have more than a couple of glasses of alcohol while on a mission. She set her wineglass down and rubbed her hand across her forehead. *Deus*, she was a fool. If Atia realized how out of it she was . . . not going there. She stumbled to her feet.

"Okay. I'm tipsy. But I'm going to bed."

"Do you need me to come with you?"

"I'm more than capable of getting to my own room without help."

Cleo arched her eyebrows but didn't rise from her chair. Taking a sip of wine, the Sicari fighter nodded. "*Va bene!* I hope you have a hangover tomorrow. It would serve you right."

"You're empathy is amazing, you know that?"

"You don't deserve it. You know better."

"I needed to take the edge off, okay." She saw her friend lean forward ready to ask questions, and she waved her hand. "Not tonight. I'll cry and I don't want to cry."

"Then go to bed. We'll talk in the morning."

With a nod of her head, she headed toward the kitchen. Inside the large room, she stumbled over one of the floor's stone squares and almost fell into the kitchen's wide island. Slowly, and cautiously, she made her way through the hall and then the foyer. The staircase seemed gargantuan as she stood at the foot of the steps. With a grimace, she grabbed the rail and pulled herself upward. Behind her, a soft laugh filled her ears, and fear swept through her. He'd found her. As she whipped around, she lost her balance, but strong arms were there to keep her from falling.

"You're feeling pretty good right now, aren't you?" Luciano said with a chuckle. The sight of him filled her with relief. She shook her head.

"I'm doing just fine, thank you."

She turned back around to head up the stairs when a strong arm wrapped its way around her waist. The unexpected touch made her shrink back as she tried to shove him away. Surprise and concern swept across his face, and he threw up his hands in a gesture of reassurance.

"I was just trying to help. You're in no condition to climb these stairs alone, and you know it."

With a nod, she allowed Luciano to pull her into his side and help her up the steps. As they reached the top of the stairwell and turned the corner, Luciano released her to gently guide her with one hand on her elbow. She swayed slightly and leaned into him. He smelled good, but not like Lysander. She sighed.

"You're a nice man, Pasquale."

"Ouch, *that's* an insult," he said with a soft chuckle.

"No. It's not an insult."

She stopped him and leaned into him to kiss his cheek. The moment she did, he went rigid, and she saw his gaze fix on something behind her. She turned her head and saw Lysander striding toward them. *Fotte*, he was going to read her the riot act for getting drunk. No. She was tipsy. Big difference.

"I'll take it from here, Pasquale." Lysander's voice was low and almost menacing.

He wasn't just pissed at her, he was furious. Great, another mark against her. The man would wind up hating her before this mission was over. A firm grip captured her elbow and guided her back down the hall. Looking over her shoulder, she smiled at Luciano.

"See you in the morning, Pasquale."

The man grinned at her, and with a shake of his head, he entered a room close to where he was standing. A moment later, Lysander pushed her none too gently through the door of her suite. She batted his hand away and heard him utter a small noise. Immediately, she turned around and saw the bandage on his hand. She grabbed his wrist and looked at the white bandage for a moment before looking up at him.

"Let me heal this."

"You're too drunk to heal anything."

"Not this little cut." She bobbed her head at his hand and tightened her grasp then closed her eyes.

"It's insignificant, Phaedra," he said quietly as he removed her fingers from his wrist. "I've lived through worse."

The gentleness in his voice said she wouldn't be able to heal him even if he did accept her offering. His emotional wounds weren't something she could heal, no matter how hard she tried. Those he had to tend to himself. She abruptly turned away from him to hide the fact that there were tears in her eyes. Although she wasn't sure if she was crying for him or for herself. Swaying on her feet, she shrugged off his steadying touch and removed her jacket then staggered toward her bedroom.

The *bastardo* could go fuck himself. She was the best healer in the Order, but if he wanted to be a martyr and live with pain, fine. It wasn't like she cared. *Liar.* She stumbled over her feet at the thought. *Deus,* she should have removed her boots a long time ago. The heels were the reason it was so difficult to walk straight, not the fact that her heart was breaking and she was ready to break down into tears.

She stopped and sat down on the floor and removed the offending footwear. With one hand on the chair closest to her, she pulled herself upright, and tugged her sweater up over her head. Behind her, she heard Lysander draw in a sharp breath and she turned to face him.

"What's wrong?"

"Are you planning on stripping on your way to the bedroom?"

"I don't know. It's not like you haven't seen it before," she said bitterly at the disapproving note in his voice. "Are you planning on watching?"

An odd emotion flashed across his face, but it disappeared before she could name it.

Arms folded across his chest, he shook his head. "I'm here to make sure you get into bed without knocking yourself out. You've had a tough day, and you're more than a little drunk."

"I'm tipsy. *Not* drunk," she snapped.

Maybe she was a little drunk. Could he blame her? She spun around, intent on going to her bedroom, only to stumble and fall backward. The warmth of him penetrated her flesh as he stopped her fall and swung her up into his arms. Her palm pressed into his chest, where the rapid beat of his heart thundered beneath her fingers. She sighed. He was right. She'd had a tough day, but when he held her like this, she felt safe, and nothing else mattered. The moment they entered her bedroom, tension flooded his body. Almost immediately, he set her down and nodded toward the bed.

"Into bed, Phaedra. Now."

She stared up at him. The man made her crazy. Even though he'd refused her healing touch, it didn't change the fact that he'd been there for her today. She still didn't want him to go. The truth was she didn't want to be alone. If he'd just stay with her, she'd feel safe. She stretched out her hand and pressed her fingers into his chest as she studied his stoic yet grim expression.

"Don't leave me," she whispered. "I need . . . you make me feel safe."

Tension etched his features into a tight mask, and he inhaled a deep breath. "Let me get Cleo to come stay with you."

"*No.* Forget I asked." Determined not to let him know how helpless she was feeling at the moment, she turned away from him and stumbled toward the bed. "Just go."

She fumbled with the snap and zipper of her jeans before hobbling her way out of the pants. Behind her, Lysander made a choked noise before the warmth of his large hand settled on her shoulder.

Chapter 10

THE minute he touched her, Lysander knew he was on thin ice. *Il Christi omnipotentia*. He'd never seen her this fragile before. He swallowed hard as she turned her head to look at him over her shoulder. The minute her gaze met his, her eyes grew watery. At that moment, he knew he'd lost the battle to leave her.

"I'll stay until you fall asleep," he murmured as he brushed a teardrop off her cheek.

A quiet sob passed her lips before she spun around completely and pressed her warmth into him. The bliss and torment that flooded his body at having her in his arms again was enough to drive him crazy. And it wasn't just desire that made him tug her body snug against his. His arms wrapped around her, the silky warmth of her skin heating his fingertips. Resting his chin on the top of her head, he waited for her crying to stop. He was going to kill the *bastardo* that had assaulted her. Her sobs finally ebbing away, she tipped her head back to look up at him.

"I feel safer with you here."

The fact that she trusted him so completely, despite his brutal rejection a year ago, was enough to make him feel as though someone were gutting him with a sword. It was humbling in so many ways.

"He can't get to you here, Phaedra."

"Realistically, I know that," she whispered. "I just don't think I can forget."

"You won't forget, but the fear will ease."

The minute she reached up to lightly touch the scars on his face, he stiffened. She blinked the tears off her long lashes as she gently traced her fingers over the grotesque side of his face.

"Were you afraid?"

The softly spoken question startled him, and he swallowed hard. Atia hadn't even dared to ask him that, nor had he allowed himself to remember what those terrible hours had been like before Cleo was hovering over him. A shudder went through him as the memories engulfed him with a savage fury. His jaw locked with a painful tension, he nodded.

"Yes," he ground out between clenched teeth.

Afraid? *Merda*, he'd been terrified, consumed with rage and guilt at how helpless he was as he listened to Dominic's agonizing shrieks or felt the terror vibrating off Marta. Even now, he could feel the rope biting into his wrists as he tried to free himself. The drug the Praetorians had given him had suppressed his abilities, but it hadn't eliminated the pain. The deaths of his friends would always be on his conscience despite everyone telling him he couldn't have known they were entering a Praetorian stronghold.

"Lysander?"

The one-word question pulled him away from the dark memories as Phaedra's hand cupped the scarred side of his face. Suddenly he realized he was trembling. As his gaze focused on her sweet features, he saw a gentle acceptance there that invited him to tell her everything. He immediately closed himself off to the possibility of revealing his inner torment. The last thing he needed was to let this woman inside his head, because if he did, he'd wind up showing her things he couldn't bear for her to know. He caught her hand and gently pulled it away from his face.

"You need to sleep." He nodded toward the bed. "You'll feel better when you wake up."

She nodded and allowed him to guide her toward the bed like a docile lamb. The only problem was she didn't look like a lamb. He didn't think he'd ever seen a woman look so damn tempting in his entire life. The wisps of red material covering her rounded buttocks and crossing her back tested his willpower like nothing else he'd ever experienced. A little off balance, she swayed slightly as she tugged her hair out of its braid until it tumbled across her soft shoulders. He buried the urge to pull her into his arms.

She slipped under the covers and curled up into a fetal position in the bed. The forlorn look about her made his heart ache, and his protective instincts went into overdrive. He'd keep her safe even if it meant giving his life for hers. He'd never tell her, but she was the most valuable thing in his life.

He stretched out his hand and mentally pulled one of the room's chairs closer to the bed. The quiet scraping noise made her jerk upright in the bed. He immediately regretted not picking up the furniture to move it closer to the bedside. When she saw him settle into the chair, she slowly lay back down and closed her eyes. As he sat there watching her, he was struck again by how vulnerable she seemed.

A soft sigh eased out of her, and in a couple of minutes, she was asleep. His elbow resting on the arm of the chair, he rubbed the edge of his unscarred jaw as he watched her. He hadn't lost just three team members in that Chicago warehouse last year. He'd lost Phaedra and the life he might have had with her.

The thought made his muscles grow hard with tension. He might have lost Phaedra, but he wasn't about to let anyone hurt her. She thought a rogue Sicari had attacked her this morning, but she was wrong. The *bastardo* had to have been a Praetorian. Lysander had seen glimpses of the man, dressed as a clergyman, praying at a Church altar.

Worse, he'd seen the man standing by as men wearing the Praetorian emblem on their shoulders slaughtered an entire family. Sicari were merciful when they killed, and they didn't kill children. Not only that, but the Praetorian could do more than just read minds. He had telekinetic abilities, too, and it made him uneasy.

His gut twisted as he remembered how the Praetorian had taunted him in his head while the son of a bitch had continued to touch Phaedra. Despite raising a mental shield against the man's probing thoughts, the *bastardo* had seen how much Phaedra meant to him. It had amused the Praetorian, and he'd gloated in detail as to what he was going to do to Phaedra the minute he was alone with her. The anger inside him still burned hot and fiery.

He'd have to kill the man. Not for revenge, even though he wanted that really bad. But this wasn't about retaliation. It was about protecting Phaedra and other Sicari. Most of all, it was about justice. The Sicari Code didn't allow revenge killings, but it did allow him to protect the interests of the Order.

The problem was, this *bastardo*'s skills equaled his own. Perhaps even surpassed his? And he'd seen enough of the man's thoughts to know that the sorry fuck would play as nasty as he could. It wasn't going to be a fair fight, and the Praetorian would use his feelings for Phaedra against him. He knew it was probably a mistake to go after the man without backup. But how in the hell was he supposed to explain he'd read the Praetorian's mind or mentally challenged the bastard to a fight? It had been agonizing to watch her trying to fight off the man's invisible touch. The idea of any man caressing Phaedra was maddening. But to see someone touch her against her will made him feel helpless—and he'd had more than his share of not having control over things. The memory lashed at him with the sting of a whip.

He crushed the dark memories and tried to remember every detail he could that he might be able to use against the Praetorian. There were only a few hours for him to form a strategy before his appointment with Phaedra's attacker. When he'd challenged the man, the Praetorian had filled his head with mocking laughter before finally agreeing. It hadn't been one of his more lucid moments, but there hadn't been much else he could do. He'd just have to find a way to beat the bastard.

He leaned forward in his chair and clasped his hands behind his head. Like Phaedra, he'd thought a rogue Sicari was her attacker, and he'd automatically reached out with his thoughts to see if he could discover where the man was hiding. He'd been as surprised as the Praetorian to learn they could read each other's thoughts.

He'd never run into a Praetorian like this one before. The man didn't just have telepathic abilities. He had telekinetic powers as well. It worried him that the Praetorian might be stronger than him. One more reason why he might not survive to see the sunrise.

The strength of the man's abilities had been surprising. That the sick bastard had effortlessly tormented Phaedra while taunting him at the same time said the Praetorian had been toying with them. The man probably could have brought both of them to their knees.

It's what made him think that maybe the legends were true. As a kid growing up in Atia's house, he'd overheard plenty of conversations and thoughts that others hadn't. Ones he probably shouldn't have heard. Sicari Lords were legend among the Sicari, but he also remembered the mutterings about the Praetorian Dominus, whose abilities were similar to that of a Sicari Lord. Everything he'd ever heard, he'd taken with a grain of salt, and until today, he'd always discounted the possibility of a Dominus. Now he wasn't so sure.

Phaedra made a soft noise and began to writhe on the bed. A moment later, he sprang to his feet as she screamed and shot upright in bed. He reached her in two quick strides and sank down onto the bed then pulled her into his arms. She was shaking so badly her teeth were chattering. He didn't say anything, he just held her. As her trembling slowly subsided, she raised her head off his chest to look up at him.

"Better?" He eyed her carefully as she raked her fingers through her hair and nodded. "Then back into bed."

"You'll stay?"

"I'm not going anywhere for the moment."

She slipped back under the covers and turned her back to him. Quietly, he returned to his chair and waited for her to fall asleep again. Every minute or two, she'd turn over in bed in an effort to achieve a more comfortable position. After about fifteen minutes, she sat up and sent him a pleading look.

"I know it's a lot to ask . . . considering the way things are between us, but would you mind holding me until I go to sleep?" The request made him go still as a statue, and she immediately cringed with embarrassment. She waved her hand in dismissal. "It's okay. Never mind."

Frozen in his chair, he watched her fall back onto the mattress and turn her back to him. *Christus*, he needed to have his head examined for what he was about to do. Despite the warning going off in the back of his mind, he removed his boots and went to join her on the bed. She jerked her head to look over her shoulder as his weight shifted the mattress, and the gratitude in her beautiful brown eyes swelled his heart.

Cautiously, he stretched out beside her and pulled her backside into his chest. The minute his arms wrapped around her, it was as if she'd never left his side. Her warmth pushed its way through his clothing until it penetrated his skin. Holding her like this was like walking into a burning building. There was no way he was going to come out unscathed.

She didn't speak, and for that, he was thankful. Her tension reverberated through him for several long minutes until she slowly relaxed. The minute she drifted off to sleep, he was able to relax himself. *Merda*, and he'd had the balls to think Atia was using questionable judgment in bringing Phaedra here. What the fuck was he doing? For more than a year, he'd managed to keep his distance from her, and in forty-eight hours, every bit of that wall he'd built between them was on the verge of collapse. He closed his eye.

Deus, he was tired. Today had been a mental drain unlike any in recent memory. Phaedra's attacker, her insistence on continuing with their task, fear for her safety, Pasquale's obvious attraction to her—all of it had come to a head when Angelo had started talking about that ridiculous journal of *Consul* Julius.

The man had been dead more than two hundred years, and he didn't want to hear some nonsense about a prophecy. He knew his reaction to the man's discussion with Atia had made him look like a madman. Perhaps he was. He'd been hiding his mixed blood for more than a year now, and tonight's dinner conversation had unnerved him.

The sound of Phaedra's soft breathing reminded him of her immediate response to his breaking the wineglass he'd been holding. She'd not hesitated to reach out to him. Her selfless act had terrified him more than anything else could. The Praetorian side of him had been feeding his anger, and he'd instinctively known he wouldn't be able to keep her from discovering his secret if she'd touched him. The darkness had been too close to the surface.

It had been an uncharacteristic response from him, and while regrettable, it had reinforced the fact that as *Legatus* he wouldn't tolerate disloyalty or disobedience. He frowned as he acknowledged one of the driving forces behind his reaction to Angelo's conversation.

Technically, he was still a *Primus Pilus*. When he'd accepted this mission, he'd gotten Atia's promise that he could return to Chicago as Ares's First Spear. And the fact that he was a half-breed Praetorian hunting for the *Tyet of Isis* made him uneasy about *Consul* Julius's prophecy. He'd never really believed in prophecies or past lives, but tonight's dinner conversation had pulled everything together in a way that made him desperately wish he'd never accepted this assignment.

Accept? He snorted softly at the notion. Atia had literally forced this mission on him. She'd been insistent to the point of threatening him with a demotion if he refused. Staring up at the ceiling, he remembered the dreams he'd been having for so long. He didn't like it, but it was far too easy to recall how the woman in his dreams had called him Maximus.

He groaned at the thought, and Phaedra shifted beside him at the sound. Afraid he might wake her, he bit the inside of his cheek. Now that she was asleep, maybe the best thing to do would be to catch a few hours' rest in his own room before he went searching for the enemy.

The soft floral scent of Phaedra's hair filled his nostrils. Maybe he could hold her just a little longer. There was no harm in that. Actually, it was crazy to stay here. It would only sharpen the pain of leaving her. Yawning, he ignored the thought. He just wasn't ready to let her go. It was the last thing he remembered as he drifted off to sleep. That and the softness of the woman curled up against him.

SHE was still damp from her bath and smelled of blue lotus. The intense floral fragrance was an intoxicating smell. It didn't surprise him that his cock hardened at the sight of her. She was beautiful. He stretched out his hand to her as she approached the bed. The sight of her mischievous smile drew a low growl from him as she slipped her small hand into his. It obviously amused her to see him aroused. He grimaced and she laughed.

"Just a few more weeks, mea amor.*" Cassiopeia pressed her palm to her large belly. "I miss loving you just as much as you do me."*

He gently tugged her down onto the bed. She uttered a soft grunt of discomfort as she laid down and rolled onto her side to face him. His touch tender, he brushed a strand of silky black hair out of her eyes. There was a glow about her that lit her up from the inside. He'd never seen her more beautiful, and it made him ache for her.

The babe was due soon, but it had been six long weeks since he'd last lain with her. He missed her. Although she'd satisfied him with her mouth whenever she sensed his need, it wasn't the same as burying himself inside her. Still, he wasn't about to risk the life of his son.

She'd even suggested he use one of the slave girls, but it had been easy to read her thoughts and know she wanted him to refuse. It had been easy to say no. Not so much because she wanted him to, but because he wanted no other woman but her. His hand stroked her rounded stomach, and he chuckled as the child inside her kicked hard.

"He's strong, isn't he?" He laughed at her annoyed frown.

"You laugh because you're not the one carrying this restless little one," she said in a nettled voice. "And how can you be so certain he isn't a she?"

"Because my wife is dutiful and obedient." He caught her hand in his and kissed her fingers before grinning at her. "She wouldn't think of bearing me anything but sons."

"Now, you are acting like the skilled, confident general who expects all to go according to his plan and no other." The mischief in her statement made him chuckle.

"You exaggerate the skills of a simple soldier, mea amor.*"*

"Never. Maximus Caecilius Atellus, adopted son of Gaius Quinctilia Atellus, is Rome's greatest general," she said with confidence. "After all, as his wife, I know it to be true."

"A wife who, like any good legionnaire, will do her duty and produce a healthy son for her lord and dominus.*" He laughed loudly as she poked him in his shoulder at his teasing.*

"So if you're so certain I shall bear you a son, what do you propose we call him?"

"Demetri." The name came to him without hesitation.

"Demetri? But that's a Greek name. Why not something like Augustus or Tiberius?"

"I wish to honor the man who brought us together."

"But Octavian was the one who introduced us when he brought you to meet my father."

"Yes, but it was a tribune by the name of Demetri Septimius who pointed you out to me when we were at the Colosseum to see the chariot races. You were the most beautiful creature I'd ever seen." His soft words brought a smile of joy to her face as she touched his cheek. There was no need to say anything more. He knew she could easily read his heart.

"Then Demetri it shall be," she whispered. A somber expression crossed her beautiful features as she raised her hand to study the long scar on her palm. "Do you think he will have your ability? I never received any special power from our bonding."

"Perhaps not, but your blood will run through our son's veins. That is a special power of its own design." He rolled onto his back and looked up at the fresco on the ceiling. "And I confess I'm not sure I want him to. My abilities are more often a curse than an asset."

"It's not a curse, mea cor. It makes you stronger than your enemies."

"You"—he turned his head and wrapped his arm around her shoulders to pull her close to him as he smiled down at her—"are prejudiced."

"Yes, I am. But that is because I love you so much." The deep emotion in her voice made him tighten his embrace.

"And I you, mea dulcis," he murmured as she yawned and closed her eyes.

Moments later, he heard Cass's soft breathing as she fell asleep. She was all he needed in life, and the thought frightened him. If something were to happen to her and the babe—he pushed the thought from his head and kissed her brow. He wouldn't beg trouble. He'd make an offering to Vesta tomorrow asking protection for

Cass and their child. He yawned. Vesta had always answered all of his prayers. His last thought as he fell asleep was that he had no need to believe the goddess would do otherwise now.

HER touch made him stir as her mouth brushed against his. Delicious and enticing, the tip of her tongue laced against his lips, teasing him to open his mouth and give her entry. Still half asleep, he didn't resist. It was a kiss of temptation, and he groaned softly as her tongue danced with his. She tasted sweet and far too tempting. The scent of her swept across his senses until his body was hard with need.

Deus, he'd missed her. His fingers glided down a silky smooth arm to the wrist he'd held so tightly with his telekinetic ability earlier. With a gentle twist of her arm, she freed herself from his grasp and reached up to touch the demonic side of his face. He stiffened at the caress, but she deepened their kiss and pressed her body into his with an insistence he wasn't capable of rejecting.

He grew rock hard, aching for the heat of her. Need barreled through him as he rolled her onto her back without breaking their kiss. Crushing his mouth against hers, he demanded a response that matched his. She answered his summons with a passion that made him hotter than he'd ever thought possible. Desire whipped through him, tugging at every cell in his body.

He wanted to touch her everywhere, bury himself inside her until he couldn't tell where he ended and she began. A blinding need engulfed him, making him slide his mouth off hers and down the side of her neck to her shoulder. Nipping at her skin, he heard her suck in a sharp breath of pleasure as his thumb circled a hard nipple beneath satiny material.

Eager to reach the taut bud, he caught the narrow strap of her bra with his teeth and dragged it off her shoulder until the cup of the lingerie released the plump breast it cradled. He restrained himself from taking her in his mouth the instant she was free. He wanted some sign from her that her blood was running as hot as his was. Slowly, he brushed his mouth across her skin, waiting for her to plead with him to suckle her.

"Please." Her whisper was hoarse with desire. "Please don't tease me."

"Am I teasing you, *carissima*?" He edged his tongue close to the darkened skin near her nipple then blew lightly against her wet skin. Another mewl whispered out of her.

"You know you are. For the love of *Deus*, Lysander, please."

The soft cry sent satisfaction sailing through him. She wanted him as badly as he wanted her. He answered her plea, gently nibbling on the tip of her until her hands cradled the back of his head and urged him to take her into his mouth completely. He obliged, savoring the incredibly sweet taste of her against his tongue.

With each stroke of his tongue, she writhed against him, her hips thrusting up against his erection in a silent demand for the ultimate pleasure. The scent of her desire drifted up to tease his nose, and still suckling her, he slid his hand down to the wisp of material that barely covered her. His fingers slid under the maroon slip of fabric to the core of her.

Heat greeted his fingers as he parted her velvety folds and touched the small flesh of her sex. A low cry of pleasure escaped her the moment his thumb rubbed across the sensitive nub. *Christus*, he wanted her. Suddenly, she pushed up against him until he obediently rolled onto his back. She followed him, straddling him until the seat of her was rocking back and forth across his cock.

The action shot a needy blast of desire through him, his body taut with a need to explode inside her. Her hands made short work of removing her bra, and he sucked in a quick breath at the beauty of her breasts. The moment she bent over him, he instinctively stretched out his hand to touch the silky black curtain that brushed the sides of her cheeks.

Cool air brushed his stomach as she pushed his knit sweater upward to give her mouth access to his waist and then his chest. All the while her mouth caressed him, her hips continued to rock over him, teasing his cock until it was ready to break through the leather pants he wore. Blind to everything around him, he visualized pulling her up over his chest as his hands shoved at his pants. In that instance, her sharp cry filled the air, and he saw a look of panic flash in her wide eyes. Fuck, his telekinetic touch had brought back the trauma she'd endured only hours ago.

"*Merda*. I must be out of my mind," he rasped. His words were an understatement, and he knew it.

"Don't, Lysander. It's not your fault. You just startled me, that's all."

He ignored the pleading note in her voice. *Christus*, he should never have let it get this far. No. His first mistake was getting into bed with her. As gently as he could, he pushed her off him. She was simply reacting to what had happened to her at Hadrian's temple. By initiating the sex, it was a way for her to be in control. Something she'd not had when that Praetorian *bastardo* had touched her.

"No," he growled as he sat up. "This should never have happened. You put your trust in me to keep you safe, and I took advantage of that trust."

"*Deus*, will you listen to yourself. You're like some martyr unwilling to accept the fact that what just happened had nothing to do with that asshole."

"No." He jerked his arm out of her grasp and got off the bed. His hand grabbed a boot and tugged it onto his foot. "You're the one unable to face the truth, Phaedra. You had no control over what he forced you to endure. Now you're compensating."

He pulled the other boot over his foot then stood up and headed toward the door. He didn't believe for one minute that she wasn't trying to regain some sense of control over her body. Over her mind, even her soul. And even if his mental caress might have just startled her, the moment had been sobering enough to bring him to his senses. He couldn't believe how close he'd come to giving in to his need for her.

Behind him, he heard her scrambling off the bed. Fuck, if she stopped him now, he was going to have to hurt her. Something he *desperately* didn't want to do. She caught up with him before he was halfway across the room and gripped his arm with a strength that surprised him.

He flinched as he sensed the anger flowing through her fingers into his body. He recognized that anger. It was the same kind of fury that was with him every day, and he wasn't sure it would ever leave him. He hoped for her sake that she would find a way to let her rage go.

"I'm not compensating for what happened to me. I'm not about to give that son of a bitch that much satisfaction. You're using what happened to me as an excuse."

"An excuse for what?"

"You're running away from me—from what happened between us just now." Her words were a dash of icy water in his face.

"I don't know what the hell you're talking about," he said in a cold voice.

"Yes, you do. Just now, when you were touching me—you felt something."

There was a confidence in her words that made another portion of the wall he'd built between them crumble. It sent a bolt of fear streaking through him. He avoided her gaze and shook his head.

"No, what happened here was you waking me up and reminding me that I haven't been laid in a while." His tone was intentionally cruel as he pulled free of her grip and started toward the door.

"You *porco*," she said fiercely. "You turn around and say that to my face."

Coming to an abrupt halt, he steeled himself for what he was about to do. Slowly, he turned to face her, prepared to deny any culpability in the matter. It was a mistake to turn around. She faced him in nothing but that slip of silk that mimicked underwear, and she was exquisite in her anger.

Fingers splayed across her rounded lush hips, she looked like a vestal virgin ready to defend the temple from the entire Praetorian army. His heart sank and he cleared his throat in an attempt to say the words he needed to say. He failed. A look of triumph lit up her face, and in two strides, she threw herself at him and tugged his head down to meet her demanding kiss.

The taste and scent of her made it impossible to push her away, and he yielded to her for a brief moment. It was a kiss of desperation on his part as much as hers, and he knew the stakes were high if he allowed her to bend him to her will. As much as he wanted her this very minute, he also knew her motivations weren't anything more than a need to recover some of herself from what had happened to her.

Trauma was driving her need, and even if it weren't, he wouldn't head down that path with her. The end results would be disastrous, and he refused to take advantage of her desire to make this morning's incident insignificant, when it was just the opposite. She had to find a way to deal with what had happened in some other way, no matter how much he wanted to carry her back to her bed and spend the night sliding into the slick, velvety heat of her. His hands gripped her upper arms and gently pushed her away from him.

"No, Phaedra. It's not going to happen."

"For the love of god, Lysander. This isn't about what happened this morning. I need you," she whispered in a husky voice that danced its way across every one of his senses.

The look she sent him stretched his nerves thin as wire. *Christus*, the woman was determined to get her way. Usually, his discipline enabled him to remain in complete control where she was concerned. But tonight . . . tonight, she was testing him as he never had been before. He wanted to give in to the plea in her voice. Offer the solace she needed, the assurance that she'd be okay.

Even if he tried to explain it to her, she wouldn't believe him, but he understood what she needed better than anyone else. Witnessing her assault had been one of the hardest things he'd ever endured. Just as hard as the torture he'd barely survived at the hands of Nicostratus. And he recognized the helpless feeling in her.

That sense of having no power and the frantic need to find a way to regain that sense of control. He knew what being out of control meant. It was the difference between keeping the demon inside him locked up or unleashing it to wreak havoc in his life and those he loved. It was the difference between salvation and the death of his soul. The demon nudged at him. She had no idea what was at stake, but somehow he needed to make her understand that what she was asking wasn't possible.

"Trust me, Phaedra." He shook his head as she protested with a sharp exclamation. "I know what I'm talking about. You're trying to take back control, and this isn't the way to do it."

"Damn it," she snapped. "I know the difference between what that *bastardo* did to me this morning and how I feel when you touch me. I'm not the one running scared here."

The demon chuckled with glee as his anger escalated. He drew in a sharp hiss of air at her accusation. Whether it was because she'd hit so close to home or that she was beginning to wear down his resistance, he didn't know, but it infuriated him. His hand snaked around the nape of her neck and roughly tugged her toward him. Surprised, her eyes widened as she met his gaze.

"Scared? Look at this face, Phaedra. Is this the face of a man who doesn't know what fear is?" He leaned into her and from his scalp to his jaw, the twisted flesh was there for her to see in all its glory. "Wake up and take a hard look at yourself in the mirror, *cara*. *You're* the one running scared here."

"Lysander, I didn't—"

"No excuses." The minute her hand touched his demonic profile, he shoved her from him. "Fucking me isn't going to erase what happened this morning, Phaedra. You proved that the minute I caressed you with my ability. You screamed. And if anyone understands what you're going through, it's me."

Her dark brown gaze met his, and he recognized the pain in her eyes. It made him want to give in to her need, but he couldn't. Deliberately, he turned away from her. She uttered a soft protest, but he ruthlessly crushed his desire to heed her cry. Instead, he walked out of the room.

Chapter 11

LYSANDER'S tread was light as he walked down the dark alley near the Temple of Hadrian. The moon was waning in the sky, and while there was the occasional beam of light illuminating his way, his hunting ground was predominantly in the dark.

He wasn't even sure Phaedra's attacker had even heard the mental challenge he'd issued as they left the temple yesterday morning. No, he was sure the Praetorian had heard him, he just wasn't sure he was going to show up when and where he was supposed to. But logic said it was more important to find Phaedra's attacker before the sick bastard found her.

Atia would be livid that he was doing this on his own, but lately, the darkness inside him had been difficult to control. The best way to deal with it was to let it loose in open combat, and the man he was looking for would give him the opportunity to let off a little steam before he exploded under the wrong circumstances.

The *Prima Consul* would have to settle for him having told Marco where he was going. His *Primus Pilus* hadn't been happy about Lysander going off to parts unknown, but his First Spear had agreed to wait two hours before he came looking for him. Provided his cell phone didn't get damaged, Marco would be able to use the GPS module to find him. It probably wasn't one of his brightest moves, but protecting Phaedra was all that mattered.

His body grew taut at the memory of touching her, holding her in his arms again. He should never have allowed himself to touch her. Hell, he should have left that damn bedroom the minute he put her to bed. He drew in a deep breath and blew it out again. He'd done nothing but complicate things tonight. *Merda*, he'd done more than that. He'd put himself at risk for her learning the truth. If she thought he was hiding something from her, the woman wouldn't give up until she figured out what his secret was. Then where would he be?

The sound of a door opening made him dart to one side of the alley. His back pressed against the wall, he saw a young man step into the dark side street, before turning to lock the door he'd closed behind him. There was nothing in the stranger's thoughts that even hinted at a Praetorian connection. Moments later, the man rode off on a scooter, leaving him alone in the alley once more.

As the dark lane grew quiet again, his thoughts returned to Phaedra and the earlier event at the temple. The raw anger he'd felt then surged through him once more. A cat cried out in the dark behind him, and his body grew taut like a tightly coiled spring. *Christus*, he was thinking too much. But it was difficult not to. Was it possible the myths were true? Maybe, but if so, how? How could a Praetorian Dominus just appear out of nowhere like this? Someone should have at least reported something.

It would be easy for a Dominus to hide within the Church, and even from the Praetorians themselves. Still, the possibility of a Dominus was extraordinary, given the Praetorian culture itself. While the Praetorians used the Church to serve their own agenda in eradicating the Sicari, they did so under certain constraints. The devotional vows and other codes within the Church made it difficult for them to openly ensure their lineage didn't die. Their lifestyle prohibited them from acknowledging any children they sired, and only males could enter the priesthood. Whether their contempt for women was deeply rooted in their culture or they were worried about inbreeding, they killed their female offspring at birth.

It was a probable explanation for why they seemed to be fewer in number in the last century. Without female progeny to carry on their line, the Praetorians needed women for breeding purposes. It was why younger Sicari women were never tortured. They were breeding stock to the Praetorians. The few Sicari women who'd escaped had told horror stories about their lives among the Praetorians. An image of Marta flitted through his head, and his gut churned. Phaedra wasn't valuable to the Praetorians simply for her remarkable gift. The bastards would see her as breeding stock with the added plus of having a valuable skill she might pass on to a male child.

Phaedra's ability was so strong that if she were to bear a child by a Praetorian, the child could easily have the abilities of a Sicari Lord. But raised as a Praetorian, the child would be trained as a Dominus. Taught to hate the Sicari. The idea of Phaedra being used in such a way hardened his muscles as he continued to walk through the shadows. The proverbial saying, over his dead body, took on new meaning where she was concerned.

Stretching out his senses, he blocked out the mundane and listened for the whisper of Praetorian thoughts. Nothing. Did he really think it would be that easy? His telepathic skills weren't always reliable, and if the Praetorian was stronger than him, the man could be easily hiding his thoughts. He rolled his shoulders slightly, the weight of his sword pressing into his back. It was fashioned in the style used by his ancestors, who'd been generals under the likes of Julius Caesar, Augustus, and Marcus Aurelius.

The sword gave him a sense of security. Particularly when security for a Sicari on one of Rome's dark streets was an illusion. The only protection he had was the sword on his back and his abilities. His friends would call him insane for being out here alone in Praetorian territory. Marco had certainly used the word, and a few others. Atia wouldn't call him insane. She'd simply chew him a new ass and then some for violating the rules.

All Sicari were required to work in teams of two or more no matter where they were. But what no one understood was that he'd not been alone last year. He'd had a team of skilled Sicari with him last year in Chicago, and he'd led all of them into a trap. In his arrogance, he'd ignored several signs that something wasn't right. He'd made the wrong choice, and it had cost three fighters their lives, leaving him the sole survivor. And the only reason he'd survived was because the man torturing him had discovered who he was.

Nicostratus had taken great pleasure in skinning him. His hand touched the mutilated skin on his face. Logically, he knew it would have been impossible to resist reacting to the pain. But knowing he'd surrendered and begged for relief was something he'd never forget. To be stripped of power, dignity, even his humanity—he grunted with a fierce, deep emotion at the thought.

His pain had served as a natural barrier against Nicostratus learning any key strategic information. But he'd fought desperately to keep that shield up by thinking about those he loved. When the *bastardo* had read his thoughts about his mother, that's when the true torture had begun. The son of a bitch had laughed at him.

Nicostratus had found the emotional torture he inflicted far more amusing than the physical. Atia was wrong. His father wasn't expecting him to come after him. Nicostratus had known full well he'd likely become an outcast if his parentage became common knowledge. It had happened to others in the distant past. He'd be no different.

The scum had taken greater pleasure in tormenting him emotionally than inflicting physical pain. It had been the primary reason the *bastardo* had ended the physical torture. His father had taken enormous pleasure walking away from him alive. The man had done so with the belief that the internal devastation he'd caused would be a worse torture.

The Praetorian fuck had been right. It would have been far better to deal with the physical agony of torture and eventual death than the mental anguish he'd dealt with for the last year. It was why tonight he had nothing to lose, because he'd already lost everything. Holding Phaedra tonight, coming close to making her his again, hadn't helped things. If he survived, she was going to keep on asking questions. With a growl, he shoved his thoughts into the recesses of his mind. Focused. He had to stay focused and find Phaedra's attacker. He needed to make sure the Praetorian didn't get near her again.

The whisper of a laugh brushed the edge of his senses. Muscles tight with tension, he immediately looked upward. Praetorians were notorious for dropping off a rooftop to surprise their enemy. Seeing nothing, he peered into the darkness, looking in every direction. Once more, the laugh sounded in his head. This time it was louder.

"Show yourself, you sorry *stronzo*," he muttered.

"*As you wish.*"

The man's words echoed in his head with an ease that was

unsettling. He'd known the Praetorian's skills equaled his, but there was something completely different about this bastard. Maybe he'd made a mistake in not bringing Marco as backup.

"Of that I've no doubt, Unmentionable," his opponent's thoughts echoed in his head. The Praetorian was obviously amused. *"You're the type to always rush in where even angels fear to tread."*

A tall figure stepped out of a doorway into the alleyway. Lysander instinctively threw up a shield against the man's mental invasion and focused his attention on the Praetorian moving slowly toward him. There was just enough light to see that the man wore the hooded garb of a warrior monk. The *bastardo* looked like one of the fanatics the Church had employed during the Middle Ages to eliminate those posing as a threat to the Church's authority.

"Go *fuck* yourself." Lysander reached for his sword, but an invisible hand stopped him.

"Come now, don't be so hasty in your wish to die. I propose we settle this dispute honorably."

"Praetorians have no honor." He strained to mentally undo the tight grip on his wrist as he watched the man walk toward him at a nonchalant, deliberate pace.

"Ah, but I'm not just any Praetorian. I do have some honor."

"Bullshit. If you had any honor, you wouldn't have violated the woman I was with today."

"Ah, yes, Phaedra." The Praetorian's thoughts revealed just how much the man was aroused by her. *"Phaedra is special. I can't think of any woman better qualified to bear my sons."*

Fury blazed through him. The man wasn't going to get anywhere near her. With a thrust of his hand, he visualized the Praetorian flying backward. Immediately the man's grip on him was broken. The man stumbled back several feet, and he easily sensed the other man's amazement.

"Again you surprise me, Unmentionable. You're stronger than I expected."

"There's more where that came from." He pulled his sword out of its scabbard and he gestured with his fingers for the other fighter to come forward.

"I see." For the first time, he heard the man's actual voice.

Pleasant and low, it revealed none of the malice he could sense in the Praetorian's head.

The man suddenly broke into a hard run, the monk's cloak he wore streaming out behind him as he lunged forward. In the low light, Lysander saw the flash of steel in the Praetorian's hand, and with a calm that surprised even him, he braced himself for the first blow. When less than three feet existed between them, the other fighter suddenly launched himself into the air and used the building as a springboard to send himself vaulting over Lysander's head.

The Praetorian's unexpected move surprised him, and he almost had a sword cleaving him open from the back of his skull downward because he'd been caught off guard. He quickly visualized the Praetorian's sword missing him, and he heard his opponent utter a soft oath as the sword glanced off his shoulder without leaving a scratch. Without hesitating, Lysander whirled around and dragged the tip of his sword across the man's midsection in one quick stroke.

Lysander caught a faint mineral scent in the air. He'd drawn first blood. It was little more than a scratch, but the Praetorian's anger was instantaneous. So the *bastardo* wasn't so confident anymore. He could hear the furious oaths flying through the man's head. He curled his lips back in a malicious smile of satisfaction.

"My apologies," he sneered. "My sword slipped. I trust you're still able to continue?"

With a low roar of anger, the Praetorian thrust out his hand, and in an instant, Lysander was on his knees, gasping for air. His sword fell to the street with a clang as he instinctively clawed at the invisible fingers wrapped around his throat. The unseen hand around his throat squeezed harder, the air in his lungs slowly disappearing. Somewhere in the back of his mind, a voice shouted at him that he couldn't pry invisible fingers off his neck. He had to do something else to break free of the Praetorian.

Feverishly, his fingers scrabbled across the cobblestone for the leather grip of his sword. Struggling for air, he tried to see his attacker through his blurred vision. The other fighter stood in a relaxed stance, sword at his side and a smile of contempt on his face. His air almost gone, Lysander slowly visualized the Praetorian stabbing his blade into his foot.

Seconds later, his opponent cried out in pain, and he was free. He scrambled backward to huddle against the wall, desperately dragging deep breaths of air into his lungs. The rage emanating from the other fighter said there was no more time to recover. One hand pressed into the stone formation, he pushed himself to his feet and staggered to one side of the Praetorian.

His breathing still ragged, he swung his sword in a low, sweeping arc at his opponent's thigh. He missed. An instant later, he had to swing his sword upward to block the Praetorian's blade. Sparks flew off steel, and he dropped his guard as he fought to stabilize his footing. An instant later, the Praetorian's sword sliced into the fleshy part of his upper arm. Grunting with pain, he staggered back in a sideways motion, his sword falling from his hand.

Too late, he realized the movement put his enemy on his blind side. The sound of a sword slicing through the air forced him to drop to the cobblestones. Using the last of his reserves, he broke his fall with a cushion of unseen energy then rolled over onto his back. Directly above him, the Praetorian flipped his sword in an expert move and drove it downward.

Clapping his hands together, Lysander trapped the Praetorian's blade between his palms, barely keeping the sword from piercing his chest. Although his telekinetic ability was drained, he could still read the Praetorian's thoughts. The man's jubilant mood infuriated him. The son of a bitch needed to learn not to count his chickens before they hatched. He wasn't about to call it quits yet. With the cold steel of his enemy's sword still between his hands, he used all his strength to twist the weapon out of the man's hands. It flew through the air until it hit the street with a loud clatter.

The Praetorian's dark growl of anger became a roar of pain as Lysander simultaneously kicked his leg upward and jammed his foot into the bastard's crotch. One hand clutching his groin, the man sank to his knees and drew in a hiss of air before he met Lysander's gaze.

"Enough of these games, Unmentionable," he snarled. "Time to die."

Once more, an invisible hand wrapped itself around his throat. Choking and gasping beneath the pressure around his neck, Lysander's hand reached out to his side in a desperate search for his sword.

Still nursing his groin, the Praetorian sent him a cold smile as he tightened his grip around Lysander's neck.

"Good-bye, Unmentionable. I'm certain your woman will be an unbelievably good fuck."

Not even the man's taunt was enough to help him free himself of the grip on his neck. Unable to breathe, he fought not to pass out as his fingers scrabbled desperately across damp cobblestones. Where the hell was his sword? The pressure at his throat increased again. Dizzy from lack of air, he slowly sank into a darkness where Phaedra raced toward him with a welcoming smile.

HE caught her up in his arms, his mouth seeking hers in a deep kiss. Deus, she tasted like the Elysium Fields, warm and sweet. He'd missed her more than he'd ever thought it possible to miss someone. It had been more than two months since he'd felt her warming his body. His battlefield tent was comfortable enough, but without her curled into his side, the nights were always cold no matter the time of year. He was tired of war.

Weary of being away from her so much. The minute he could convince Maxentius to free him of his duties, he was going to take her to the farm her father had given them. There they'd live out the rest of their days in peace. Lifting his head, he stared down into her eyes with a sense of dread. It was easy to see the fear in her gaze.

"What's happened?"

"Nothing." Her forced smile said she was lying. "I'm simply happy to see you. I hate it when you're gone for such a long time."

"While I'm delighted you missed me," he said as he allowed her to help him remove his leather armor. "We both know that's not why you're frowning."

"It's of no consequence. As a general's wife, I should know that worry is a fruitless effort." Her soft sigh illustrated that whatever was troubling her clearly had her even more worried than usual.

"I'm relieved to hear you do worry about me," he teased with a quiet laugh.

The remark made her wince, and he frowned. There was an air of vulnerability about her that bothered him. It was unusual.

Cassiopeia was fearless. So much so, that it troubled him at times. She had stood up to more senators than he cared to admit. She'd even cut Maxentius down to size on more than one occasion, which fortunately for both of them had amused the emperor. When she turned her head away, he caught her chin and forced her to look at him as he arched his eyebrow at her.

"Tell me what's troubling you."

"It's Octavian," she whispered. "I . . . he came to visit me."

"Octavian?" He shook his head in puzzlement. "He's an old friend. Why would his visit bother you?"

"That's what I thought . . ." Her voice faded into silence.

"Damno ut abyssus, Cass. Tell me what's wrong."

"He said you were a fool to serve Maxentius," she said in a rush. "He said Constantine will execute the Praetorian Guard when he takes Rome."

Her fear was tangible as she quickly wrapped her arms around his waist to burrow deep into his chest. The heat of her penetrated his tunic as he kissed the top of her head. Dulcis matris Deus, he knew Octavian had been unhappy with the way Maxentius had been running the campaign against Constantine, but the Praetorian Guard had pledged their loyalty to the emperor. Surely, his old friend hadn't broken that oath.

"The Guard will never throw their support to Constantine. Octavian's talking treason."

She lifted her head, and the fear on her face aroused his anger. Not only was the man talking like a traitor, the figlio di puttana had frightened Cass. Anger sliced through him. Eyes wide in her face, she pressed her palm against his heart.

"He knows where Maxentius keeps the Tyet of Isis."

The words made his blood slide cold and sluggish through his veins. If Constantine acquired the Tyet of Isis, Alexander the Great's potion would give the usurper the ability to create his own Praetorian Guard. The possible ramifications of Octavian's traitorous intent made his blood pound with fear. The man had to be stopped.

"What else did he say?" he asked quietly, and she looked away from him. "Cass?"

"*He said Constantine will ride triumphant into Rome in thirty days' time because he'll use the* Tyet of Isis *to become a Praetorian.*"

"*Fotte,*" he rasped. "*He's not just declaring treason against the emperor, he's betraying his oath to the Guard.*"

"*What are you going to do?*"

"*I'm going to hunt the* bastardo *down and slit his throat,*" he growled. *She blanched at his harsh words, and he caressed her cheek. "It will be all right,* mea amor. *I'll convince Maxentius to let me have the box for safekeeping. He knows he can trust me, although if he knew you were aware of it as well, he might not be so trusting.*"

"*I'm scared, Maximus,*" she said in a husky voice. "*I love you so much. If I were to lose you, I wouldn't want to live.*"

WITH each word, her voice grew fainter, and he railed against the knowledge that he was losing her. He called to her, but she was little more than a wraith in his arms. Raw fury roared through him. Phaedra was lost to him again. What had he done to anger the fates? The world suddenly rushed by him, past and present merging into a steady stream of blurred images until, with a choking noise, he was back in the present struggling for air.

In the next instant, he was free, and the Praetorian was lying flat on his back with a stunned look on his face. Dragging in huge gulps of air, Lysander's fingers found the steel of his blade, and his hand wrapped around the grip of his sword. What the hell had happened? He hadn't broken the Praetorian's stranglehold on him. Still gasping, he saw a dark figure emerge from the darkness. The sight of the man's monk's robe made him release a quiet groan.

"*Christus.* Not another one," he rasped as the man came to a halt a few feet away.

"I can assure you, Condellaire, I am *not* the enemy," the stranger snapped without even looking down at him. *Merda,* the man knew his name.

The Praetorian had scrambled to his feet and was staring at the newcomer with an expression of suspicion, which quickly changed to loathing. With a flick of his wrist, the Praetorian called his weapon to him, the sword flying up from the ground and into his hand. In response, the stranger showed the sword he carried beneath his long flowing cloak. With a slight bow, the Praetorian shook his head.

"You'll forgive me, Eminence, if I put off this long overdue meeting. I wish to give your execution my full attention."

"Confidence is good, but too much of it offers one the opportunity to misstep."

Lysander stiffened at the title the Praetorian had used. That was the honorary title one used with a Sicari Lord. For a Praetorian to use it even with a Sicari Lord was unthinkable. To their enemy, the Sicari were unmentionables. Pagans who threatened their holy order. Why would the Praetorian be so deferential? As quietly as he could, his fingers wrapped around his sword. The movement triggered nerve endings that reminded him how bad his arm hurt. He grunted. His arm wasn't the only thing that hurt. The inside of his throat was on fire, and his neck throbbed from where the Praetorian had used his mental strength to brutally choke him. He was lucky the bastard hadn't actually crushed his windpipe. Hell, he was lucky the stranger had come along. He didn't understand how, but the man had managed to stop the Praetorian from killing him. The physical and mental strain he'd exerted had left him exhausted, but sword in hand, he managed to lurch to his feet to watch the small drama unfolding before him.

"I was warned about your penchant for sage wisdom." The sarcasm in the Praetorian's voice made the other man stiffen with what appeared to be anger.

It was impossible to be certain because the man's manner was so restrained and dignified. He couldn't even read the man's thoughts. In fact, now that he thought about it, he'd not received any thoughts from the man at all. The only individual he knew of with that type of ability and control was a Sicari Lord. It was difficult to believe he was staring at a legend he'd only known through childhood stories. But with each passing second, he was growing more convinced this man actually was a Sicari Lord.

"Do not mistake wisdom as a sign that I'm a doddering old fool.

I'm well prepared to do what I must." The Sicari Lord's voice was quiet, yet authoritative.

"Then prepare well, Eminence," the Praetorian snapped viciously. "Because the next time we meet, you'll die by my hand."

"I am at your disposal, my son." The Sicari Lord bowed slightly in what was almost a courtly gesture.

With a sharp sound of disgust, the Praetorian whirled around and vanished into the darkness. Frustration lashed through Lysander, and he glared at the Sicari Lord.

"*What the fuck!* You're just going to let him go like that? The son of a bitch threatened my healer, and if I don't stop him, he's going to come after her."

The Sicari Lord didn't answer. Instead, he raised his hand, and two fighters emerged from the darkness. One of them a woman, she stepped forward and bent her head as the man whispered something to her. She nodded then stepped away and remained silent. The Sicari Lord turned to face him when he'd finished speaking to the woman. He pushed his hood back to show his face and arched an eyebrow at him.

There was something vaguely familiar about the man, but Lysander couldn't place where he'd seen him before. The faintest whisper of the answer echoed in the back of his mind, but he couldn't hear it clearly. At that precise instant, the Sicari Lord narrowed his gaze at him. For some reason, he could have sworn the man was disappointed in him, but he couldn't figure out why.

"You had a vision of Maximus and Cassiopeia." It wasn't a question. It was a simple, calmly spoken statement.

"I don't know what you're talking about." Lysander shook his head and met the man's gaze steadily. A faint hint of a smile touched the man's lips.

"It is said that Maximus loved Cassiopeia so much he killed her to save her."

"I know the story," he said with irritation. "But I fail to see what it has to do with me."

"So you don't remember the vision."

The man's question was simply another statement. The Sicari

Lord was testing him. But for the life of him, he didn't know why. He chose not to answer. The last thing he'd do was share his innermost desires, no matter what shape they took. He'd been dying. It was natural that the one person he loved above all others would fill his thoughts as that Praetorian *bastardo* choked the life out of him. The Sicari Lord tilted his head slightly in a contemplative manner.

"You were willing to give your life for Phaedra. Is that because she's a Sicari or do you have some other reason to protect her?"

"She's a valuable member of my team. What other reason would I need to protect her?" he said through clenched teeth. Hell. Was the man probing his thoughts without permission?

"There is always the possibility that you're simply waiting for the opportunity to turn her over to your brethren."

For a moment, he couldn't believe what he'd just heard. *Merda*, the man knew he had Praetorian blood. The bastard had definitely probed his thoughts without permission. Did he think his rank and position gave him the right to violate a Sicari's thoughts and probe deep beneath the surface?

"I am *not* a traitor to the Sicari." Ramrod straight, he eyed the man with furious contempt.

"Nor was Maximus to the Praetorian Guard, and yet Octavian painted him a traitor." The Sicari Lord studied him for a moment then gave him an abrupt nod. "We shall see."

"Instead of talking history to me, we should be going after that Praetorian son of a bitch."

"He's more concerned with destroying me now than he is with finding Phaedra," the man replied.

"*Merda*," he snapped with disgust. "How do you know that?"

"Because he knows who I am." The Sicari Lord bent his head, his mood somber, almost bleak. A moment later, the man sent him an intent look. "The vision you had, have you had them before?"

"You tell me. You're the one who's probed my thoughts already," he growled.

"Your thoughts were easy to hear without probing." The Sicari Lord sent him a harsh look that was a silent reprimand. "I repeat. Have you had these visions before?"

His internal debate wasn't going his way at all. This was a Sicari

Lord, and as a Sicari, he owed obedience to the man. On top of that, something about the man said he wasn't the type of man who let rules stand in the way of him gaining information. Deep inside of him, he identified with the Sicari Lord. If the means justified it, he broke the rules, too. And the idea of *this* man probing his thoughts was far less appealing than sharing the fact that he'd been dreaming for some time. He released a noise of anger.

"Yes."

"I'm certain you can expand on that." Amusement in his voice, the man tucked his sword away under his cloak without looking away from Lysander.

"I've been dreaming about Maximus since I was a kid," he ground out between clenched teeth.

"That long." The statement sounded more like the man was thinking out loud, and the way the Sicari Lord rubbed his chin only reinforced the notion that he was expecting something more from him. The man studied him intently. "I'm curious. Do I look familiar to you?"

"What the hell kind of question is that?" He avoided a direct answer. This entire conversation was making him edgy.

"A straightforward one, I thought. So I shall ask again. Do I look familiar to you?"

"No." Instinct made him throw up a mental block to ensure the Sicari Lord didn't discover his lie. The man frowned, and again Lysander felt as though the man was disappointed in him.

"I see. And Phaedra? Has she mentioned any dreams?"

"Not to me, she hasn't." Growing more irritated by the minute, he glared at the man.

"But then you keep her at a distance, don't you?" The Sicari Lord nodded as if suddenly having an epiphany. "In the days ahead, Condellaire, you must never question your instincts. Don't think. Act. It will save your life and that of the woman who is a part of your destiny."

Deus, the man wasn't just a Sicari Lord, he was crazy. He needed a shovel to dig his way out of the crap this guy was handing him. The man facing him chuckled softly.

"I'm certain my sanity seems in question, but I assure you I'm quite sane. Things will reveal themselves in time," the Sicari Lord said. "In the meantime, Cornelia will take you back to the safe house. When you arrive, tell the *Prima Consul* that Marcus has found the boy. As for me, or my people, you are to say nothing. Secrecy is the greatest weapon I, and those who serve me, have against the Praetorians. Do I have your word?"

"What, you're going to trust a half-breed's word?" He sneered, still smarting at the way the Sicari Lord had questioned his loyalty to the Order.

"I have no choice." The man sent him a look that said he expected a response.

"You have my word."

"*Bene.* However, if I discover you've broken your word, I'll hunt you down and slit your throat." The words were simple, matter-of-fact, but a deadly note ran beneath them. It wasn't a threat, merely a fact.

"Understood, Eminence."

Lysander bowed his head, and when he straightened, the Sicari Lord had already vanished into the night, taking one of his bodyguards with him. The woman called Cornelia moved to stand at his side, pulling a small Mag light from her pocket in the black leather jacket she wore. She quickly examined the wound on his arm and shrugged.

"You'll live. Come." With a sharp gesture, she indicated he was to follow her.

Wearily, he slid his sword back into the scabbard on his back and hurried after her. In silence, they moved quickly down the alley and wound their way through several dark streets toward the more populated sections. As he followed the Sicari woman, it was impossible not to reflect on the events of the past hour. If he weren't the *Legatus*, he'd most likely be whipped for doing something as stupid as going after the Praetorian without a partner. He grimaced. Actually, Atia was within her rights to order his punishment.

If it hadn't been for the Sicari Lord's arrival, the *Prima Consul* wouldn't have had the opportunity to even make such a decision. Ahead of him, the Sicari fighter moved quickly, yet with a stealth that amazed him. It was obvious the woman had received special training. Like the Sicari Lord, the woman revealed nothing to his senses. His skills were extensive, but hers clearly surpassed his by a large margin. *Particularly when he failed to use his head*. He winced. A fine example he was setting for his team. Something Atia would take great pleasure in pointing out.

They'd gone several blocks when she stopped in front of a sleek Italian sports car. Even though he was exhausted and in pain, he eyed the black vehicle with appreciation. It was a thing of beauty. He was learning Cornelia was a woman of few words as she nodded at him to get in. In less than a minute, they were in the compact vehicle with the engine revved up as the Sicari woman tooled the car through the dark streets. As they emerged from the quieter areas and encountered slightly heavier traffic, she darted the sports car in and out of the other vehicles with the skill of a stunt driver.

She didn't ask for directions, and it was obvious she knew where she was going. Just as they'd done on foot through the dark alleyways, they maintained their silence in the car. And even if he'd been in the mood for conversation, something told him Cornelia wouldn't be interested in talking. He closed his eyes and rested his head back on the car's low headrest until the car's rumbling became the soft purr of an idling engine.

"The safe house, *Legatus*."

With a nod, he got out of the car, and the minute he'd closed the door, the woman threw the car into gear and drove off without a backward glance. Weary to the bone, he blew out a harsh breath then entered the safe house. Less than a minute later, he was past the security door locks and was standing in the foyer. Usually, the house was dimly lit this time of the morning, but the glare of lights made him grimace. Marco had raised the alarm. A rush of footsteps made him brace himself as the sound of excited voices echoed out of the narrow hallway leading into the kitchen. Everyone was awake. Marcus didn't seem to understand that the words *come looking for him* weren't quite the same thing as rousing the entire household. He'd talk to his *Primus Pilus* about that later. Hoping to avoid questions until he could talk to Atia alone, he quickly strode toward the staircase. He'd only climbed two steps when the *Prima Consul* appeared in the entryway followed by the rest of his team, including Phaedra. Too late. He averted his gaze from her and steeled himself for Atia's inquisition.

"Where have you been? Marco says you wouldn't tell him where you were going." The *Prima Consul*'s tone wasn't a question. It was an order that said she'd only tolerate a straightforward answer. He hesitated for a fraction of a second before he turned to face her.

"I went looking for that Praetorian we discussed."

When he'd sent Atia a text message after Phaedra's assault, he'd made sure to let the *Prima Consul* know he was certain they were dealing with a Praetorian. Between his text message, and their short phone call afterward, the *Prima Consul* knew Phaedra's assailant wasn't just a telepath, but possessed telekinetic skills as well. And while she'd not given him a direct order not to hunt the bastard down, Atia had made it clear he was to avoid the man.

"*Fotte,*" Atia said with a sharp gasp of horror as she stared at him. "Have you lost your mind?"

He didn't know what surprised him most, the language that was out of character for her, or the distinct fear echoing in the *Prima Consul*'s voice. But it was the way her face had drained of color that worried him the most. He ignored the rest of the team spilling out into the foyer and hurried to her side. Atia brushed off his solicitous hand, her gaze focusing on his arm and then his throat.

"You're injured. Phaedra." The *Prima Consul*'s voice rang out crisply.

It was a sharp command, and Phaedra, along with Cleo, pushed her way to the front of the small group gathered in the hall. Both women gasped when they saw him, but when Phaedra rushed toward him, it caught him off guard. He immediately retreated several feet, only to find his back pressed into the spindles of the staircase.

"*Mea Deus,* what happened to you?" Phaedra whispered as her hand lightly brushed across his throat.

Her touch was electric, but he didn't want the pity he could hear in her voice. In a sharp move, he grabbed her wrist and jerked her hand away from his skin before releasing his grip on her. Even that touch had enough of a charge that it made him wish he hadn't used up all his telekinetic ability just so he could push her away without touching her. Struggling to maintain his composure, he ignored Phaedra and looked at the *Prima Consul*.

"I have a message for you, Madame *Consul*. I was instructed to tell you that Marcus has found the boy, and he'll do what he must to resolve the matter."

Gut instinct had told him Atia would find the message unsettling, but the last thing he'd expected from the *Prima Consul* was for her to faint. Despite the way his body protested, he leaped forward and caught her before she hit the floor. The deep cut on his arm sent a shrieking message of protest through his shoulder as he lifted the older woman up into his arms.

Stunned by her mother's reaction, Cleo took longer to respond than he did. Seconds later, pandemonium broke out in the entryway as everyone reacted to Atia's collapse. More than half a dozen questions pelted him from all directions, and everyone was pushing forward, trying to offer assistance.

"*Enough*," he roared. The noise stopped abruptly. "Campanella. Secure the house. The rest of you go back to bed. There's nothing more to see here."

He turned toward the stairs then paused. "Phaedra. Come with me. The *Prima Consul* may need you."

"I'm coming, too," Cleo exclaimed, a worried note in her voice.

As he reached the second floor and strode down the hall, Atia stirred in his arms. He turned his head slightly to look at her. Although she was still pale, her expression had regained that regal look that said she was the one in charge.

"I'm quite capable of walking, Lysander." The command in her voice was one he knew better than to ignore. He stopped just short of her door and immediately set the *Prima Consul* on her feet.

"Damn it, Mother. Why do you have to be so stubborn? You just passed out." The irritation in Cleo's voice layered the worry that ran deeper.

"I'm feeling much better," Atia said quietly as she slowly walked the last few steps to her room. "But I do think I'll lie down."

"I'll come with you to make sure you don't pass out again. We don't need a martyr on our hands." Cleo sent him a look of angry disgust. "We've already got enough of those in here as it is."

Atia didn't object to Cleo's gentle bullying. Instead, she gave her daughter a nod of acquiescence. The two women entered Atia's room, but the *Prima Consul* stopped Cleo from closing the door. Her expression unyielding, she looked directly at him.

"You are to let Phaedra see to your wounds."

"I have a scratch on my arm, nothing more."

"A scratch that would require stitches if a healer was unavailable." The *Prima Consul* arched her eyebrow in an autocratic manner. "Phaedra."

"I'll see to his injuries," Phaedra said quietly, a determined look on her face.

As Atia slowly closed her door, he caught the sly gleam in the woman's eyes. *Merda*, the woman was interfering where she shouldn't. Furious, he turned his head and saw Phaedra studying him with an amused expression on her beautiful features.

"Let's get this over with," he growled.

"My pleasure." The sultry note in her voice tightened every muscle in his body. "It would be best to do this in your room so you can rest afterward."

Christus, they'd already been down this road earlier. He didn't need a repeat. The memory of holding her in his arms knotted his muscles with tension. With a growl of frustration, he sent her an abrupt nod then headed toward the staircase and up to the third floor. His place was definitely better than hers. At least he could retreat to his bedroom and lock the door behind him.

When he entered his small apartment, he headed straight for the couch. At least here, the torment of having her so close would be a little less painful. He wasn't sure he could keep her from seeing deep beneath the surface when it came to his thoughts. But he needed every ounce of concentration he had to hide the monster inside him. It was going to be bad enough watching her take on the pain of his injury.

The idea of her sensing the monster inside him shot a bolt of panic through him. *Deus*, maybe he should just let her see him for what he was. He crushed the thought with one blow. No, he refused to cause her any pain. He knew how much she hated the Praetorians for what they'd done to her parents. He'd find a way to hide his secret from her. The thought of being the catalyst for bringing her past to the surface—hurting her—was the last thing he wanted.

The scent of her filled his senses as she brushed past him. Sweet. Oh so sweet. Like a tangy fruit, fresh and ripe for the picking. He suppressed a groan as she sank down onto the sofa beside him. *Il Christi omnipotentia*, he didn't think he could do this. He could only hope he'd buried his secret deep enough. Touching her would be like entering the Elysium Fields one more time, all the while knowing that in mere seconds someone would throw him back into hell. She turned toward him, and he knew it was too late.

Chapter 12

ATIA stared at her daughter standing at the foot of her bed. Cleo's expression wavered between worry and irritation. She suppressed a sigh. It was understandable that Cleo would be confused by her behavior.

"Do stop acting like I'm on the verge of death, *cara*. I fainted."

"Something you've never done before in your life, Mother."

"I'm simply feeling the stress of the search. I know we're close to finding the artifact, but I'm afraid the Praetorians aren't far behind us."

"I could maybe buy that story, if it wasn't for the fact that you fainted. Stress didn't have a fucking thing to do with your swooning." Cleo emphasized the word "swooning" in a somewhat sarcastic fashion. "That message scared the piss out of you."

"Must you use such language?"

"If memory serves, not more than fifteen minutes ago, you said *fotte*."

"Touché," she muttered with irritation at having her transgression thrown back in her face.

"So who's Marcus, and who's the boy?"

Cleo folded her arms across her chest and eyed Atia closely. How like her father she was—strong, determined, and so sure of herself. Although they were often at odds with one another, it did nothing to dampen the love she felt for Cleo. She was proud of her daughter. Atia waved her hand in denial and shrugged, her brain working fast to form a plausible answer.

"Marcus is someone I knew a long time ago. I was startled to hear his name."

"Did he know Father?" Cleo's expression was one of curious speculation.

"Yes, he did, as a matter of fact." It was always best to tell the truth as much as possible.

"And the child?"

"So many questions." She frowned. "There are *some* things only the *Prima Consul* is privy to. You know that."

"I get that," Cleo said with a disgusted look. "But I've never seen you react like that to *anything* before. Are you in some sort of trouble?"

"Your imagination is *far* too vivid, *carissima*. It startled me to hear from Marcus." She forced a smile to her lips.

"*Obviously*. I can't remember the last time you said *fotte*. In fact, I can't remember you ever saying it until tonight. That's two firsts in the space of five minutes."

"All right. I think we've now established the fact that I said the word," Atia snapped. "Might we move on to a different subject? Perhaps the topic of sleep? Something we've both had little of tonight. Lysander isn't in need of rescue, and I would like a little more sleep."

She knew that wasn't going to happen. There was no possible way she'd be able to sleep now. Now that Marcus had found Gabriel. She winced, and Cleo sent her a suspicious look.

"Why do I think you're up to something?"

"I am *not* up to anything. I simply want to rest." Exasperated, she sent her daughter a stern look. "And unless I'm mistaken you were still up when Marco woke up the house."

"I couldn't sleep." Cleo's gaze shifted away from hers. It made her heart ache for her daughter.

"Again? He's not worth losing sleep over, *carissima*."

"I wasn't losing sleep over Michael."

"Why don't I believe you?"

"Because you're my mother, and you're terrified I won't ever blood bond with anyone."

"Don't be ridiculous." She sniffed indignantly. "I don't care whether you exchange a blood bond with someone or not. Your happiness is all that matters to me."

"I *am* happy. You just don't want to accept that I'm not ready for any type of commitment."

"And it's the why that concerns me."

"There is no *why*, Mother. I'm doing what men have been doing for centuries. I'm playing the field and making up for lost time on behalf of the female sex."

Atia closed her eyes at Cleo's flip, yet stubborn, denial. She knew just how much her daughter had loved Michael Giordano, and when the *bastardo* had betrayed her . . . the thought made her wince. Cleo had never tolerated people who lied to her.

A shiver skated down her back. What would she do if she ever learned her mother had been lying to her since she was a baby? *Deus*, she should have told her the truth years ago. What good would it have done? Her eyes flew open as Cleo touched her shoulder then leaned over to kiss her cheek.

"Get some rest, okay?" Cleo said as she headed out of the room. With the door open, she paused. "I love you, *Mamma*."

"I love you, too, *carissima*."

The love in her daughter's eyes made Atia's heart ache as she watched the bedroom door close behind Cleo. Tired, she pinched the bridge of her nose as she picked up her cell phone off the nightstand. With a tap of the screen, the phone displayed a colorful wallpaper and the time. Six fifteen. It would be dawn soon. She stared at the screen of the phone until it dimmed.

Restless, she stood up and paced the floor. She knew she needed to go back to bed, but the idea of lying down to do nothing more than toss and turn was far from appealing. Palatine Hill. It had been more than ten years since she'd last visited La Terrazza del Ninfeo. She'd gone there to think before she accepted the mantle of *Prima Consul*. There was a peaceful serenity about the crumbling aviary that always soothed her senses. It helped her think.

She released a derisive laugh at the bittersweet sensation drifting through her. No. It wasn't the only reason she was always compelled to visit La Terrazza del Ninfeo whenever she could. She uttered a sharp noise of self-disgust. Ridiculous. She went because she enjoyed its beauty. She silenced the laughter in her head as if she were swatting a fly.

The ruins were in the middle of one of the most popular tourist spots in Rome, which made it relatively safe, but in the early-morning hours, it was still dangerous. Ignacio wouldn't be happy that she wanted to go out at such an early hour, particularly not after the excitement with Lysander.

The need to escape the confines of her room exploded inside her, and with a curse, she reached for her cell phone. The man could always send one of the other fighters with her if he didn't want to go. He wouldn't. She quickly punched a text message into the phone then pressed the send button.

In the last several hours, a distinct chill had settled over the city. It had cooled her room enough for her to know she'd need more than just the sweater she wore. She quickly retrieved a lightweight jacket from the closet then headed downstairs. When she reached the foyer, she waited impatiently for Ignacio to join her.

She grimaced as she remembered how frantic Ignacio had been the other day when she'd eluded him to meet with Marcus. She'd tried to explain without revealing any secrets, but it hadn't prevented the man from reading her the riot act. A sigh broke past her lips.

Ignacio Firmani was a good man. He'd been good to her *and* Cleo. The man doted on Cleo now, just as he had when she was a baby. Over time, he'd become such a part of their lives that when she took the rite of ascension into the office of *Prima Consul*, it had been natural to ask him to act as her *Celeris* and head of security. Ignacio had said yes and nothing else. Just yes.

A disgruntled growl echoing above her head made her look up to see her *Celeris* coming down the steps with a dark expression on his craggy features. Clearly unhappy about the early-morning hour, Ignacio came to a halt in front of her and bowed slightly.

"You have need of me, *il mia signora*."

"I want to see the sunrise from La Terrazza del Ninfeo."

"The sunrise."

It was a statement, but she heard the question in the sardonic note in his voice as he nodded at her with a jerk of his head. Even if his voice had been emotionless, she would have known what he was thinking. Aware that he had to be tired, she shook her head.

"Never mind. We're both tired, and you need your rest," she murmured.

She shouldn't have called him. She should have called Benedict or Tony.

"I'm not that damn old," he muttered as he eyed her closely before turning away to head toward the rear of the house. "And I won't get much rest knowing you're running around Rome without me."

"At least I called you this time and didn't take off on my own, *vecchio amico*," she said in a placating tone as she followed him. The moment the words were out of her mouth, he came to an abrupt halt and whirled around to lean into her with a dark expression.

"And the next time you do something so idiotic, I'm going to keep you under lock and key."

"Don't be ridiculous," she said with an exasperated smile. "You can't lock up the *Prima Consul*."

"I wouldn't," he snapped. "I'd be locking up Atia Vorenus, a stubborn woman who's too blind to see what's right in front of her."

Startled by his behavior, she swallowed hard as his eyes narrowed at her. There was a flash of fire in his dark eyes that surprised her even more. Beneath the calm, there was a passion in him she'd not seen until now. Or had she deliberately refused to see it? Either way, she didn't know how to react to it.

"I am *not* stubborn." She latched onto the safest portion of his statement.

"I see." He closed the distance between them even more until there was only an inch or two between them. "So the fact that you refuse to acknowledge the second portion of my comment is not being stubborn."

"I . . . I am most definitely not blind either," she snapped. "I see quite well, thank you very much."

"Do you?"

His hand caught her chin, and he forced her to look him directly in the eye. There was a fiery light in his brown eyes that made her throat constrict slightly as he glared at her. He'd never touched her in such an intimate fashion before. It was a possessive touch, and it shifted the balance between them.

Deep down she'd always wondered if he cared for her, but not once in the more than twenty years she'd known him had he strayed from their platonic relationship. And he'd certainly never touched her like this. Caught off guard by his unusual behavior, her eyes widened as he drew closer then stopped just inches away from her mouth. *Care Deus*, was the man about to kiss her? She'd no sooner allowed the thought to enter her head, than his hand curled around her neck and he tugged her into him to capture her mouth in a hard kiss.

She was so surprised she froze, unable to think. The minute his tongue teased her mouth open, she shuddered. It was a hot caress, and although he simply tempted her with his mouth, the kiss said he wanted to do much more. The fiery touch of his lips against hers sent a signal from her brain that she'd missed being kissed—being touched. The thought made her instinctively respond to his caress, her mouth moving against his.

It had been such a long time since she'd thought herself desirable, and his hot touch made her feel just like that—desired. It had been even longer since a man had kissed her with a passion that said he wanted to caress every inch of her. The last time—she shuddered and jerked away from him with a gasp. *Matris Deus*, what was she doing? She was blood bonded to Marcus. Almost as if he could read her thoughts, his eyes narrowed as he studied her with a fierce look, his breathing ragged. In a slow, seductive move, his thumb slowly brushed across her lower lip.

"My patience is coming to an end, *carissima*. One day soon you'll have to choose between a ghost and me," he growled fiercely. "I've waited far too long as it is."

Stunned by his words, she watched him wheel sharply on his heel and stalk away from her. Dazed by what had just transpired between the two of them, she followed him through the kitchen and along the narrow corridor that led to the garage. Suddenly the steady, comfortable relationship she'd enjoyed with Ignacio had been turned upside down. It made her feel uncertain and on edge.

It was as if she was being unfaithful to Marcus. She flinched.

How could she be unfaithful to a man she'd not lived with for more than twenty-five years? The simplicity of the answer made her bite back tears. Because she'd never stopped loving him. Her heart convulsed with pain at the thought. Wasn't life supposed to become less complicated the older one got?

The silence between her and Ignacio didn't ease as they entered the garage that was large enough to easily hold five or six cars. At the moment, there were only two. Both of them Land Rovers. One vehicle beeped as Ignacio pressed a button on his key. His walk indicated a restrained anger that increased the sharp tension between them.

When he jerked open the car door, he didn't even bother to look at her as she climbed into the Land Rover. The door slammed shut with a fury that made her jump. *Deus*, she'd seen him angry before, but not like this. This display of emotion was so unlike him. He didn't say a word. He simply drove out of the garage with a ferocity that made her wrap her fingers around the hand grip just above her head.

The diplomat in her went to work trying to figure out the best way to handle the awkward situation she found herself in with Ignacio. As he drove through the relatively empty streets of the city, she stared out at the dark buildings and occasional all-night café. Was he thinking of resigning as her *Celeris*?

The thought of him doing so dismayed her. He'd been her friend since Cleo had been just a toddler, and he was one of the few people she trusted in the Order. Ignacio always seemed to have the pulse of the Council, and she'd come to rely on him for not only information, but as a sounding board. There were far too many politicians on the Council quick to service their own needs before the Order itself.

Losing Ignacio meant her ability to govern would be weakened. A fact a number of Council members would look to capitalize on. The crest of Palatine Hill rose in front of them, but she was no closer to a solution when they reached their destination than she had been when they left the safe house. As the car came to a halt, she quickly reached for the door handle. A firm hand prevented her from exiting the car. Her gaze fell to the strong fingers curled around her arm before she looked up to meet his harsh look.

"A few days ago, you vanished into the heart of the city without benefit of protection. This morning, you would have come here alone if I'd forbidden you to leave the house." He glared at her as she opened her mouth to protest. "Don't. I know you too well. As *Prima Consul* of the Sicari Order, you're taking unacceptable risks. If the Praetorians captured you, do you really think you will be able to keep from telling them all your secrets?"

She swallowed hard at his question. Should she tell him that she'd not been in that much danger at the Santa Maria sopra Minerva? No. While she trusted Ignacio, there was no need for him to know about the Sicari Lords. They were not invincible, and they operated the *Absconditus* in secret to protect the younger Sicari Lords they trained. Children like Gabriel. Her breath caught in her throat as she closed herself to the pain the memory of Gabriel brought her.

"You're right," she said stiffly. "I shall take greater care not to make you or the others worry about my safety while we're in Rome."

"*Fotte*, I'm not saying this as your *Celeris*. I'm saying this as a man who cares for you—deeply."

The intensity in his voice made her wince. *Deus*, this was becoming far too complicated. She wanted the comfortable familiarity she'd grown used to where he was concerned. She averted her head and nodded, unwilling to say anything. The tension between them was far too volatile. A moment later, he uttered a soft growl of frustration and released her. A horde of Praetorians on her heels couldn't have made her move faster to get out of the Land Rover.

She heard Ignacio leave the vehicle as well and jumped at the way he slammed the car door. It was something he wouldn't have normally done. Sound always drew attention. She swallowed her immediate impulse to chastise him. Instead, she circled the back of the car and headed up the footpath leading to La Terrazza del Ninfeo. The fact that most of Palatine Hill was closed to the public for excavation work made it a little more difficult to achieve her goal, but she always kept a set of archeological credentials in the car.

Even with the trail still cloaked in the waning shadows of the night, she had no trouble navigating the dirt path that led up to the aviaries. Rainaldi had designed the two buildings in the seventeenth century for a member of the Farnese family, and it was one of her favorite spots in all Rome. Whenever she visited here, it calmed her—gave her a sense of peace that was not always easy to come by in her role as *Prima Consul*. The quiet, particularly at this time of the morning, was something she cherished.

Behind her, she heard Ignacio's footsteps fade as he stepped off the path to stand guard. The sky had lightened considerably, and she quickly circled the light, coral-colored aviaries to drink in the view. The crisp air she breathed in had a mildness to it that said spring would be early this year.

She moved to sit on a stone bench that overlooked the city. Already she could feel some of her stress ease as the solitude enveloped her. A thin line of yellow edged its way along the horizon illuminating the city with soft hues of yellow, rose, and mauve. As the line thickened, she frowned. What was she going to do about Ignacio? The man had literally declared himself in the car. Something told her he wasn't about to let her evade the subject, no matter how hard she tried. And it *was* a subject she wanted to avoid.

She couldn't explain to him that the man he thought was a ghost from her past was still alive. And that she was still bonded to him. Would Marcus be willing to break their blood bond? If their most recent meeting were anything to go on, she was certain he'd strongly object to doing so. Then there was the question of whether *she* wanted to be done with it.

With a frown, she forced herself to watch the sunrise over the city. She'd come here to find some peace. For a long time, she did nothing but watch as the sun slowly crept its way upward to paint cream and pink hues on the façades of Rome's ancient monuments.

Color spilled across the crumbling Coliseum, the Pantheon, and other monuments on Capitoline Hill. The view was stunning and she was so lost in the beauty of it that she didn't know he was there until her neck tingled with that familiar frisson. Only Marcus could evoke that type of sensation in her. She sprang to her feet and turned around to see him standing a few feet away. His cerulean eyes were unreadable as his gaze met hers.

"I thought you might come here," he said quietly.

In the early-morning light, he was magnificent. The silver in his dark hair seemed more predominant today than when they'd met in the crypt. But it didn't detract from his features; if anything, it made him more handsome. He'd discarded his monk's cloak for a dark blue sweater and matching pants, and he wore his sword in a scabbard slung over his back. The well-toned muscles beneath his clothing belonged to that of a younger man, a clear indication he was in excellent physical condition. She drew in a sharp breath.

The man wasn't just magnificent. He was devastating. Perhaps more so than when they'd first met all those years ago. Despite the several feet between them, he set off a heat in her that no man had ever been able to duplicate. She swallowed hard as she fought to keep her heart beating at a slow, easy pace. She failed. Why was he here? Had he—her heart slammed into her chest.

"Gabriel?" she whispered.

"No, *carissima*. Nothing's changed." He moved quickly to skirt the bench and take her hands into his. "I came because I knew my message would upset you. I would have remained silent except for the fact that you were angry the last time I kept something from you."

A mirthless laugh escaped her. *Now* the man decided to listen to her. She didn't resist as he gently forced her to sit down on the bench. He'd come because he was worried about her. It made her feel cherished. She frowned. How had he known where she was?

"How did you find me?" It annoyed her to hear the breathless note in her voice. He smiled almost as if he'd read her mind, but she knew it was the expression on her face that gave her away.

"I remembered how you always enjoyed the sunrise from this vantage point when you needed solitude," he said as he released one of her hands.

The fact that he remembered made her heart swell with a happiness she didn't want to feel. She was grateful he didn't mention the last time the two of them had been here. It was a wonderful memory, but if Marcus were ever to learn the truth—she refused to even consider the possibility. As she studied his face, his solemn expression troubled her.

"What are you going to do . . . about Gabriel?"

"He's no longer Gabriel, *cara*." He kept her hand in his as he turned to stare out at the vista in front of them. "He almost killed Condellaire."

"*Dear God.* Those were Gabriel's fingerprints on Lysander's neck?" she gasped.

"Yes. If I'd arrived just a few minutes later . . ." There was a note of concern in his voice that frightened her. She'd already lost her son. She wouldn't lose Marcus, too.

"You *must* send for Dante."

"The boy's not ready."

"He's been your pupil since he was five. Are you telling me that you've been able to teach him nothing?" Her scornful words were deliberately meant to prick his ego, and as he stiffened beside her, she knew she'd succeeded.

"Your point is well taken, but then Gabriel is my responsibility, not Dante's. My son's actions reflect on me."

The inflexible note in his voice angered her. Were all Sicari males this stubborn or had she simply had the misfortune to know only obstinate ones? When she grabbed his arm hard, he turned his head to look at her.

"I've already lost one—my son—do you expect me to mourn you as well?" she snapped.

A small smile tipped the corners of his mouth, and he carried her hand to his lips. He lightly kissed the tips of her fingers, his breath filling the pores of her skin with heat. The fiery warmth sank down to the cellular level, where it created a chain reaction of sensation that sped like lightning through her body.

"That's the second time this week you've expressed concern for my well-being. Perhaps winning your heart again won't be as difficult as I first thought." His eyes met hers as he gently turned her palm upward and kissed the scar in the center. The tenderness in the touch reminded her of so many other similar moments, and she struggled hard to keep breathing.

"It's natural for me to be concerned about the father of my . . . son," she whispered.

"Is that the only reason, *inamorato?*"

He slid his mouth to the inside of her wrist. The caress sent a stream of fire racing up her arm until it crashed into her shoulder and spread rapidly into the rest of her body. A knot formed in her throat as she struggled to think of something coherent to say. For the love of Jupiter. She was the *Prima Consul*. One would think she could string two words together into some semblance of a sentence.

"Of course, it's the only reason." Relief swept through her at the matter-of-fact sound of her voice. With a quick breath, she pulled free of his touch and slid back along the bench to put distance between them.

"I see," he said with a frown as he pinned her with that striking blue gaze of his.

When she didn't flinch beneath his hard gaze, his jaw became a sharp line of granite. He looked away from her and stared out at the city slowly coming to life before their eyes. She studied his profile for a long moment before she followed his lead and looked at Rome spread out before them in her faded, but still beautiful, glory.

The man's behavior was thoroughly confusing, and she found it unsettling. It meant she wasn't in control. He was. But then he'd always been in control where she was concerned. It had been one of the reasons she'd fallen in love with him. A tremor shot through her as she noted that the sun was more than halfway over the horizon. In a few more moments, the sunrise would be complete. It seemed more like an ending than a beginning.

"So you still tug on your ear when you're nervous or worried about something." His observation made her start as she realized she'd been rubbing her ear between her fingers. She hastily dropped her hand as her eyes met his amused ones. "You've always been good at closing your thoughts off to me, *carissima*, but whenever you tugged at your ear, I knew you were upset or trying to hide something from me."

His amusement said he was teasing her, and her heartbeat increased several more notches. She didn't want him to tease her. He was dangerous when he flirted with her. And while a part of her enjoyed his flirtatious manner, another part of her was sending loud protests and warnings to her brain.

"Naturally you'd choose to remember something less than flattering," she muttered in a disgruntled tone.

"On you, I always found it *bellissima*."

His voice was a gentle stroke against her senses, and she fought to keep herself from trembling. Why couldn't Ignacio make her feel like this? As if she were on the edge of something wonderful and exciting. She quickly discarded the thought. Where Marcus was concerned, she didn't want to feel anything at all. But she did, and she hated herself for not being able to walk away from him, as he'd always walked away from her.

The minute the thought entered her head, she winced. That was unfair of her. Duty and responsibility were a part of them both. There had been no other choice—for either of them. They should never have blood bonded. It had only brought them heartache. It was time to let each other go. Time to stop dreaming of what might have been.

"If you wish to be freed from our blood bond, I would not object," she said quietly.

A dark look crossed his handsome features, and in the blink of an eye, he was on his feet. Blue eyes glittering with anger, he didn't even flick a finger as he used his skills to drag her to her feet and jerk her into his arms. Startled by his response, she stared up at him in astonishment.

Deus, he'd always made her feel petite whenever he towered over her like this. And she was not petite. Palms splayed across his hard chest, she could feel his heart pounding at a pace that was surprising, and her mouth went dry at the possessive look that blazed in his eyes.

"Are you telling me there's someone else?" he rasped.

The question was a warning to take care as to how she answered, and a small thrill skittered down her spine at the realization that he might actually be jealous. Without thinking, she breathed in his scent. Sharp and crisp like the air. It aroused in her an emotion no other man would ever be able to evoke in her.

The instant she admitted the truth, she realized she would have to hurt a dear friend. The one man who'd been with her whenever she had need of a strong shoulder to lean on. Ignacio's image slipped into her head, and she heard Marcus suck in a harsh, angry breath. Immediately, the answer she'd been ready to give died in her throat as she saw the rage darkening his eyes.

Chapter 13

"WHO is he?"

The second he uttered the command, he knew he didn't want to hear her answer. If she'd betrayed their blood bond, he'd have the right to kill her, but he knew he could never take her life. No matter what she did or how terribly she betrayed him, he wouldn't harm a hair on her head. Her hands pushed against his shoulders as she arched away from him.

"There isn't anyone." Despite the sincerity in her voice, he still doubted.

"Don't lie to me, Atia," he growled.

"I am not lying." Her voice wavered as she stared up at him, before she glared at him with a familiar defiance. "And even if there were someone, you don't have the right to ask the question."

"The blood bond gives me the right."

He tightened his embrace as his dark rasp echoed between them. It was a sound of desperation and he knew it. He was losing her. Now, after all these years of waiting. All these years of training Dante to take on the mantle of reigning Sicari Lord, he was losing her. He shuddered.

"We both know the blood bond is meaningless at this point."

Her sharp words were a whip cracking the air, flaying his heart open. The woman knew precisely how to extract the most blood from him. *Christus*, she was the only person, short of their son, he would willingly fall on his sword for. He shook his head.

"It has never been meaningless to me. You've been in my thoughts and heart each day we've been apart." His fingers gripped her chin as he forced her to look at him directly. "I told you I would have given it up for you. I almost did that last night we were together as lovers. Here in this very place. You'll never know how close I was to going to Tito to abdicate my title."

She blanched, her gray eyes widening until she looked as young as she had the first time he'd laid eyes on her. He watched her mouth move as if she were struggling for words, and he gave in to the urge he'd been suppressing since he'd first seen her the other day. Swiftly, before she could protest, he captured her mouth beneath his.

Her tremor reverberated its way into him, filling him with warm satisfaction. She wasn't as resistant to him as she pretended. The years separating them vanished as she slowly opened herself up to him and responded to his kiss. His tongue swept its way into her mouth as he teased a response from her that made him grow hard with desire.

His hands gripped her hips to pull her closer, lifting her up slightly until his erection pressed intimately into the apex of her thighs. A small gasp escaped her at the touch, which he swallowed as he deepened their kiss. His mouth slid off her lips and across her cheek. Praise Jupiter that he was being given another chance with her. He nibbled at her ear.

"Tell me you want me, *mea amor.*

"I . . ." She drew in a sudden, sharp hiss of air and pushed against him in an attempt to escape his embrace. "Damn you, Marcus Vorenus. I won't let you sweet-talk me into doing what *you* want this time."

"You can deny it all you want, but you've missed me as much as I have you, *carissima.*" His heart twisted violently in his chest at the way she was trying to dismiss him. Them.

"As always, you think quite highly of yourself," she snapped, but he saw a flash of emotion in her gray eyes. It gave him hope.

"No. I merely mean to claim what is mine."

"*Claim me.*"

Her exclamation was a quiet shout of anger grating across his senses. He knew she hated it when he was autocratic, but at the moment, he was out of options. If there was another man trying to take her from him, he wasn't going to let her go without a fight. The expression on her face grew haughty and mutinous.

A sudden whisper echoed in his head and grew stronger. The *Celeris* was on his way. He could deal with the man. He wasn't about to leave until he heard her say she still cared for him.

"I seem to recall telling you that I *would* come for you." He sent her an arrogant look that said she should have known he'd keep his word.

"That is so like you—arrogantly *assuming* I'd be more than happy to welcome you back with open arms."

"Don't lie to me, or yourself, Atia. There was no divide between us the night we made love here." He grabbed her hand with its long scar across the palm and he stroked it with his finger. The spot on his hand buzzed in response.

"That night was a mistake," she breathed, and panic lashed across her face.

He frowned. Something was wrong. But he was out of time. Without turning around, he threw up an invisible wall between the *Celeris* and him. He heard the bodyguard grunt as he slammed into the obstacle. Slowly, he turned to face the man. The *Celeris* stood with his head bent, his hand covering his nose.

There was something familiar about him. The moment the man looked up to meet his gaze it was like a violent electrical shock to his system. This was the man he'd seen in Atia's thoughts. Rational thought left him as his sword flew out of his scabbard and the invisible shield between him and the other man fell. Before he could move, Atia was standing between him and the *Celeris*.

"Stand aside, Atia." He saw her flinch before her expression revealed she was digging in her heels.

"Stop this now, Marcus. Ignacio is sworn to protect me."

Atia's voice was sharp as she sent him a look that said she'd fight him herself if it came down to it. It infuriated him, but at the same time it made him love her that much more for her loyalty. Behind her, the *Celeris* growled.

"You *know* this man? How?" The man's tone was far too possessive for Marcus's liking.

"Yes." She didn't look at the man. "It's complicated."

"Hardly complicated at all, *carissima*." Marcus growled as he watched the other man's thoughts lining up bits and pieces of information in an attempt to understand what she was saying.

"We're through here," she said tightly. "Ignacio and I are leaving."

"This is *him*, isn't it?" The contempt in the *Celeris*'s voice made him automatically reach out with his thoughts to wrap his fingers around the man's neck as the man continued to speak. "This son of a bitch is Cleo's father? This is what I've been competing with all these years? Not a dead man's ghost, but a deadbeat father?"

His ability to choke the man vanished. The man's words could have been a sword gutting him, and he wouldn't have been any less stunned. He couldn't move. Couldn't think. All he could do was stare at the *Celeris*, who was studying him with a look of scorn.

Somewhere in the back of his mind, he knew that at any other time such a look would have earned the *bastardo* a run through the gauntlet, simply for disrespecting a Sicari Lord. His gaze shifted to Atia, who was watching him with an expression of fear and anguish.

"A daughter? I have a daughter?" His voice was hoarse. Almost a whisper. Atia's eyes were wide in her face, a haunted look in their gray depths. She looked away and it enraged him. "*Answer me.*"

"Yes." It was a simple word, but its effect was devastating. She'd betrayed him. She'd kept his child from him. After Gabriel, how could she do something like that?

"You didn't tell him?" Suddenly, the *Celeris* was almost sympathetic. He didn't want the man's compassion.

"*Leave us.*" The command in his voice made Ignacio jerk his gaze toward him, an intractable look on his face. Clearly the man wasn't about to go anywhere without orders from Atia. Not bothering to look at her, Marcus ground out his second order. "Tell him."

"Ignacio, please go." The apologetic note in her voice fueled the anger flaring up inside of him.

"No, Atia. *Tell him.*" He bit out between clenched teeth. "*All of it.*"

When she didn't speak, he turned his gaze on her. His jaw tightened. She'd said there wasn't anyone else, and yet she seemed particularly fond of her *Celeris*. It had been easy enough for her to betray him when it came to hiding his daughter from him. Why should he think she hadn't betrayed their blood bond? *Deus*, help her if she had. Her lovely mouth moved slightly as if she were fighting to speak. He narrowed his gaze at her.

"Ignacio, it's . . . he isn't just Cleo's father. We're blood bonded."

The instant she stepped toward the *Celeris*, he reached out with his thoughts and jerked her to a halt. *Christus*, she'd actually started to go to the other man. She turned her head with a pleading look on her face.

"Marcus . . . please."

"Address. Me. Properly," he snarled.

"Eminence."

He didn't give her an opportunity to continue as he turned his head back to the *Celeris*. Satisfaction went spinning through his blood at the man's thunderstruck expression.

"*Go.*" He held the other man's gaze with a cold glare, but the *Celeris* didn't move.

When the *bastardo* suddenly looked toward Atia, his jaw tightened painfully with anger. With a mental grip that instantly had the man gasping for air, he slowly began to choke the bodyguard.

"Marcus—"

"Show respect, Madame *Consul*." He saw the color drain from her face as he increased his mental chokehold on her *Celeris*.

"Eminence, please. He's sworn his life to protect me, just as I swore an allegiance to you." Her gaze didn't waver from his as she pleaded with him.

"An oath you've betrayed."

"For the love of God, Marcus. I've not betrayed you."

His invisible grasp compressed the other man's throat a little bit more. There was something in her voice that reassured him she was telling the truth. At least she'd not betrayed their blood bond. But their daughter . . . that was another matter altogether. He dragged his gaze from her to the man whose life he held in his hand. With a snarl of fury, he flicked his wrist and sent the *Celeris* tumbling backward to the ground. He strode forward to tower over the man. A small amount of respect for the man slipped its way through his anger as the bodyguard didn't cringe, despite the quickly forming bruises on his throat.

"I won't tell you a second time. Leave us."

With a nod, the man staggered to his feet and walked back down the hill. Behind him, Marcus could almost hear the panicked thud of Atia's heartbeat. She had good cause to be afraid. Slowly, he turned around to face her.

"Does she know?"

"That her father is a Sicari Lord? No." Atia's voice was breathless as she shook her head.

"Why didn't you tell me?" The harsh question made her wince. He didn't care. She'd kept his daughter from him.

"I was afraid."

"Of what?" he snarled. "That I'd take her from you?"

"Yes." Her quiet response was the same as if she'd slapped him. His head jerked backward in response as he stared at her in disbelief. She looked away from him. "I was afraid you'd take her and I'd lose her just like I lost Gabriel."

"*Il Christi omnipotentia*," he rasped. "You *do* blame me for Gabriel."

"*No*," she exclaimed vehemently. "Nothing could have prevented what happened with Gabriel. But the thought of losing another child . . . losing a part of you . . . it was more than I could bear."

"Did you really think I would take her from you?" The moment he asked the question, he knew the answer. He would have done everything in his power to protect the child.

"You know you would have," she said fiercely. "Don't deny it. If the Praetorians had known she was your daughter, they would have come after her for her bloodline alone. And if they'd known she was *your* child . . ."

"You should have told me," he rasped, ignoring her unfinished sentence.

She was right. If the Praetorians had known he had a daughter, they would have done everything they could to find her. The Praetorian Collegium would have seen Cleo as an opportunity to breed.

The girl would have endured a hellish life. He spun away from Atia to stare out at Rome now fully illuminated by the morning sun. A daughter. He had a grown daughter he'd never met. While they'd both lost Gabriel, he'd lost more. He'd lost the joy of knowing his daughter—watching her grow up. The light touch of Atia's hand on his arm made him jump, but he refused to look at her.

"She was safer with me, *caro*. No one knew you were the father." The validity of her statement did nothing to ease his anger or pain.

"Does she know who her father is? That I'm even alive?" His jaw hardened as he waited for the blow he knew was still to come.

"I didn't correct her when she assumed you were dead. It was easier—"

"Easier for whom? You or her?" It was impossible to keep the bitterness from his voice.

"For her. It has never been easy for me. Every second she was out of my sight, I was terrified something would happen to her. Even when—when she learned how to defend herself, I worried. That will never change."

He didn't say anything. Nothing either of them said would give him back the past. And at the moment, he didn't care how Atia felt. Not once since she'd become *Prima Consul* had she even tried to tell him about their daughter.

"Your *Celeris* called her Cleo."

"Yes, it's short for Cleopatra," Atia said with a catch in her voice. "I remembered it was your mother's name. I wanted her to have as much of you as she could."

"I want to meet her."

He heard her draw in a sharp breath, and she quickly stepped away from him. When he turned his head to look at her, the fear on her face didn't even make him hesitate. She'd made her choice, now he'd made his. He wanted to know his daughter.

"I need time," she said with a flutter of her hands.

"You've had plenty of time. Why should you need more?"

"You don't know her, Marcus—"

"No. I don't." He ground out the words, his anger rising to the top once more. "But I'm going to rectify that."

"You don't understand . . . she's going to hate me."

"But I *do* understand, *carissima*. I understand all too well why she might hate you."

"It will be more than that if I can't explain my reasons. It will be as if I'm dead to her. I need time to make her see I only wanted to keep her safe." Her beseeching gaze met his. "Please, Marcus, please. Give me a week or two to find a way to break this to her gently."

He turned away from her. She didn't deserve to have her request granted, and yet he knew he would agree. Deep down, he knew that if he'd been in her position, he would have done the same thing. He couldn't fault her for her determination to keep their daughter safe. But it would take time for him to forgive her for not telling him about Cleo sooner.

Her betrayal wasn't something he could easily forgive, and forgetting what she'd done would be impossible. But there was something to be said for delaying the meeting. He needed time to digest the fact that he was a father again. It was a pleasant thought. It felt good to think of himself as a father after such a long time. His decision made, he faced her once more. The anguish on her face tore at his heart, but he resisted the urge to comfort her.

"You have two weeks." His jaw went hard with tension as tears filled her eyes. *Il Christi omnipotentia*, he'd never been able to handle her tears. "Two weeks and no more. I *will* meet my daughter, Atia, and that's a promise."

She nodded her head before she turned and headed down the hill. Pain lashed at him as he watched her go. *Christus*, he was a dumb *bastardo*. Even now, when he knew she'd been lying to him all these years, he still found it hard to let her leave him. He was a fool to love her, and an even bigger fool for wanting to keep her with him.

Chapter 14

THE minute Phaedra stepped past Lysander to sit on the couch, the scent of him brushed across her senses. She didn't think there was a single nerve in her body that wasn't in a state of high alert as she struggled with a mixture of emotions. She'd been furious when he'd left her bedroom an hour or so after midnight. Furious, hurt, but most of all stunned.

One minute he'd been on the verge of making love to her and the next he was rejecting her all over again. All because she'd cried out in surprise when he'd caressed her with his mind. Reluctantly, she conceded his invisible touch had frightened her for a brief moment. She'd needed only an instant to recognize the stroke of Lysander's thoughts on her skin, but that fleeting moment of delay had broken the fragile chain of connection between them.

It had given him an excuse to put distance between them. But she refused to believe the only reason she'd instigated their kiss was her need to take control. She'd gone to sleep feeling safe and had awoken to the sound of his heart beating beneath her cheek. Kissing him hadn't been about control. She'd done it because she loved him. Because she'd missed him and wanted to feel his touch again.

Instead of grasping his hands, she leaned forward to gently examine the wound in his arm then the bruises on his neck. It wasn't uncommon for a healer to study a wound before the *Curavi*. It helped them to focus their energy on the worst wound first, but he stiffened at her touch nonetheless. Serious injuries were always healed up to a point where the patient's body could easily continue the healing process without undue stress and pain on the part of the healer or patient. For her, examining Lysander's wounds was simply the need for a brief moment to settle her nerves.

Although his injuries tonight were inconsequential compared to his horrific injuries last year, he had to be uncomfortable. Her gaze shifted downward to his throat. The dark bruises on his neck still made her stomach churn. The impressions were clearly from someone's fingers. Whoever had choked him had to have had great strength to leave these kinds of bruises, particularly when Lysander was so strong himself.

She was certain his throat had to be hurting almost as much as the nasty gash on his upper arm. *Deus*, was he really going to let her perform the *Curavi* on him? The last time he'd really needed her touch, he'd refused. She drew in a deep breath at the memory. Her gaze met his, and she frowned slightly. If she didn't know better, she could have sworn there was a look of panic in that beautiful, deep green eye of his.

She dismissed the idea. What could possibly have him worried? If anyone should be worried, it was her. The pain he'd experienced was only part of what she'd feel during his healing. There was a strong chance she'd receive impressions and images from him, and not necessarily from whatever had happened to him tonight.

It wasn't unusual for a healer to see or experience the emotions of their patients. It was the worst part of being able to cure people. Training had taught her the discipline to shield the emotional impact during the empathic process, but when people were in pain, their emotions and thoughts were often intense. It made for an intimate connection she didn't enjoy. Physical pain always went away, but what her mind registered during the *Curavi* could sometimes linger for hours. It made for a draining experience.

Tonight it could be worse than anything she'd ever experienced before because it was Lysander she'd be healing. The fact that they'd been intimate could easily make the connection that much stronger. What if everything he'd been saying about their relationship was true? If she saw that in his thoughts—she refused to believe it. She couldn't. He wanted her, his kisses had said that much. He might have used what had happened to her earlier today as an excuse not to make love to her, but it didn't change the emotions he'd revealed when he touched her.

"Can we get on with this?"

His dark growl made her jerk her gaze up to his face. The expression on his angelic profile was hard and unyielding. She flinched as he arched his eyebrow at her. The look on his face didn't help ease her tension. It said he wanted her out of his apartment sooner than later. Where was the man who'd kissed her so passionately just a few short hours ago?

Suddenly she wasn't so certain of anything where he was concerned. For once, she hoped he succeeded in keeping her from reading his emotions. Because the thought of learning something she didn't want to know terrified her. She swallowed hard, and with palms up, she offered him her hands.

"With your permission, I must touch you to heal your injuries."

The traditional opening of the healing ritual made him flinch, and she fought hard not to read anything into his reaction. He gave her a sharp jerk of his head that indicated his eagerness to be done with the whole affair, and slowly he put his hands in hers. Without a second thought, she automatically shielded herself from a barrage of his emotions. The powerful pulse of energy suddenly flowing between them was a clear indicator of his heightened emotions. The raw intensity of it was stronger than anything she'd ever experienced as a healer.

She wasn't sure if it was her emotional connection to him or if his Sicari abilities were stronger than anyone she'd healed before. Not even Ares's strength had felt this powerful. Or was it the memory of these large rough hands of his gliding across her body, his fingers stroking her into a frenzy of need. The thought flushed her skin with heat. With determination, she cleared her mind of everything and closed her eyes to concentrate on nothing but healing him.

Slowly, her mind grew still as she focused on the task at hand. The moment she pictured his injuries in her head, a familiar rush of warmth stirred in her blood. It took more than a minute for the healing heat to reach her hands and flow into Lysander's body. The first sign the *Curavi* was working was the sting that erupted in her arm. The sensation expanded in strength until it was as if the sword that had stabbed him was piercing her own flesh.

Sharp and slicing, the intensity of the pain made her gasp, while nausea washed over her. She didn't have to open her eyes to know that a steady stream of blood was flowing down her arm. The smell of it assaulted her senses, and she choked back a cry as the image of a dark figure fluttered through her head. Her training made her push the vision aside. She didn't want to see the bastard that had hurt him. It was hard enough knowing he could have been killed.

Determination swept through her, and she made herself narrow her focus of concentration until she saw only his injuries. Slowly, the pain in her arm ebbed away, and a different type of throbbing pelted her body. Fire streaked down the inside of her throat as she felt her windpipe slowly collapsing beneath the pressure. Again, the dark image came at her.

Like a bat with enlarged wings, it beat at her mental shield with persistent fury. Something deep inside her recognized the darkness. It had touched her before. She flinched as the pain in her throat increased. There was something about this injury that was different. This hadn't been a physical assault. Someone with extraordinary telekinetic abilities had tried to kill Lysander. Another image emerged to battle the darker one. Bright and welcoming, the vision drew her to it. She heard Lysander growl something beneath his breath, but she clutched at his hands to keep him from breaking the healing bond between them.

The crushing pain around her neck increased, and it became difficult to breathe. Air disappeared from her lungs at a fast rate, and then suddenly she was free. Somewhere in the distance, someone called out to her. She turned toward the sound and stared in disbelief as she saw a woman who could have been her twin, racing forward.

Confused, she looked down at her hands and saw they were that of a man. Quickly looking herself over, she recognized a familiar Roman military uniform, right down to the personalized bracers on her arms. Maximus. She looked up again only to see the woman slowly fade away into a fine mist.

"Goddamn it, Phaedra, wake up *now*."

The sharp command was a dull roar in her ears as strong fingers bit into her arms and shook her like a rag doll. Suddenly, her lungs were able to draw in air again, and she gasped loudly. Still choking, she clawed at her throat only to have a strong hand stop her.

"Easy, *carissima*. It'll pass."

Somewhere in the back of her mind, she realized she was reclined in Lysander's arms. *Deus*, her head hurt. She touched her temple and winced before her eyes fluttered open to meet Lysander's gaze. There was a stark look of desperation on his face. It twisted the scarred side of his face into a horrifying mask that made her fear he might be in pain from the way the skin stretched so tightly over his facial muscles.

Her head still throbbing, she pushed herself away from him and sat upright on the couch. As she stared at him, an image flitted its way through the back of her mind like a hummingbird. She reached for it, but it was an elusive thought determined to avoid capture.

"Are you all right?" With a frown, she leaned forward to examine his arm. She ignored the woozy sensation the movement caused, while still rubbing her forehead. "What happened?"

"What happened?" he rasped harshly. "*Christus*, you were supposed to heal me, *dolce cuore*, not try to take a ride across the Styx."

The endearment was the only thing in his reply that sank into her brain. It warmed her as she felt her body continuing to heal from the injuries she'd pulled out of his body and into hers. Her throat still ached, but she could tell it wouldn't be long before the pain was gone completely. Exhausted and disoriented, she rested her head on the back of the couch and closed her eyes.

Christus, she hadn't felt this out of it since her first healing. She frowned. What in Jupiter's name had she done to make her feel this bad? One second she'd been healing Lysander's throat and then the next she'd been transported to ancient Rome where she'd found herself in Maximus's body. She drew in a sharp breath.

Deus, she was an idiot. She'd passed out from the lack of oxygen. She'd failed to break the *Curavi*. Even a novice knew how to recognize when it was time to break the connection between patient and healer. The connection between them should have been broken the moment her air started to disappear.

It had been a grievous error on her part not to realize she needed to pull back from the healing. She could have died. Perhaps she had. Why else would she have experienced being in Maximus's body and seen herself running toward her. Him. *She'd* been running toward Maximus, only she'd *been* Maximus.

Hell, the whole damn thing was so confusing. The memory of her Roman general made her draw in a sharp breath. Had it been her dream? Either her dreams had somehow found their way into the healing process or what she'd seen were images from Lysander. But why would the scene she'd witnessed during the *Curavi* be so similar to hers?

Unless he'd—*care Deus*, he'd been dying. That's what had connected the images to the healing. Someone had almost killed him until something had happened to bring him back from the brink. Her heart skipped a beat as she remembered how it had felt to be on the edge of death. His near death. They weren't her dreams she'd seen. The images had to have come from his mind not hers. She shot upright, only to have the room spin dizzily around her. Nauseated, she flopped backward.

"Damn it, Phaedra, lie still." The concern in his voice softened the harsh command.

She turned her head toward him. He looked as tired as she felt. Without thinking, she reached out and brushed her fingers over the side of his scarred face. He immediately jerked away from the touch.

"How long have you been dreaming about the Sicari Lord and his wife?"

Her question hovered between them as an impassive expression settled over his features. Even though his face was devoid of emotion, she knew he was calculating how much she might have seen during the *Curavi*. His hesitation made her think he'd been dreaming about the ancient Roman couple for a long time. Perhaps even longer than her.

"Does it matter?" he asked.

"It does when I've been dreaming about them, too." Her words didn't even make him flinch. Instead, he stood up with a growl rumbling deep in his chest.

"You're not in any condition to go back to your room right now, and to be honest, I'm too damn tired to carry you there. So you'll have to sleep here on the couch. I'll get you a blanket."

Her mouth fell open in amazement as he calmly changed the subject and walked away from her. The minute he disappeared into the bedroom, she regained her wits and struggled to her feet. If he thought she was going to let him just walk away from her and this discussion, he'd better think twice. There was a reason for her dreams *and* his. Because she was certain he was having similar visions. They had to be connected. But how and why? The dizziness forced her back down onto the cushions of the sofa.

"Hell," she exclaimed fiercely. Determined to go after him, she braced herself on the arm of the couch and got to her feet one more time.

"Goddamn it, you little fool." His voice was harsh with fury. "What the fuck do you think you're doing?"

"Isn't it obvious? I'm trying to follow you."

"Of all the pig-headed women," he growled.

He dropped what he was carrying onto the coffee table in front of the couch then gently shoved her back onto the sofa. He knelt beside her to swing her legs up onto the cushions and adjusted the pillow he'd brought under head. With her settled on the couch, he reached for the damp cloth on the table behind him then turned to stare down at the blood-soaked sleeve on her arm. The expression on his face illustrated his indecision as to how to go about cleaning her arm without her having to take her shirt off. He growled softly and thrust the washcloth toward her.

"Here," he rasped as he sprang to his feet.

His movements fast and jerky, he snapped open the blanket he'd gotten from the bedroom. The soft coverlet fell over her legs up to her waist, warming her almost immediately. She grabbed his hand as he started to retreat.

"Lysander, please. We need to talk about this."

"*No*—we don't." He glared down at her.

"Give me one good reason why not."

"It means nothing." The sharpness of his voice made her flinch and she shook her head.

"You're wrong. Your dreams and mine do mean something. I just don't know what yet."

"Go to sleep, Phaedra."

With a weary shake of his head, he headed toward his bedroom. Frustrated that she didn't have the strength to follow him, she hit the couch with her fist. And he called her stubborn. Using all her strength, she pushed herself up to look at him over the back of the couch.

"You're a stubborn jackass, you know that."

Her shout bounced off the bedroom door as he closed it behind him. With a fierce noise of disgust, she tugged her shirt off. The effort made her dizzy again, forcing her to fall back onto the pillow he'd brought with the blanket. The man could try the patience of a saint.

Quickly cleaning the dried blood off her arm, she tossed the damp cloth onto the table then pulled the blanket up to her chin. She inhaled a deep breath before releasing it completely, and stared up at the ceiling. He'd almost died. Her heart skipped a beat at the thought. The idea that something that horrible had almost happened to him was enough to send chills through her.

Could he have fought the rogue Sicari? Had he gone after that creep? He'd said he'd find the man. No, he couldn't have done that. He wouldn't have known where to find him. She winced as her headache seemed to intensify. She needed to rest. When she woke up, she'd drill him on where he'd been, and she'd make damn sure that he'd answer her.

The one thing she knew for certain, he'd been crazy to go out on his own. He'd broken the Order's rule that Sicari were not to walk the streets of Rome at night without a partner. Normally, it was a punishable offense, but it was doubtful Atia would do anything about it. The message Lysander had given the *Prima Consul* had left the woman so shaken she probably wouldn't even remember to admonish him.

Deus, she was tired. When she woke up, she was going to have it out with Lysander. All of it. She no longer believed what he'd told her in the hospital. The man cared about her. She was ninety-nine percent sure of it. She grimaced. It was that one percent that had her

worried. She closed her eyes as a yawn tugged her mouth open. She'd
deal with all. . . she yawned again. . . of it when she woke up. She'd
find a way . . . to get him to open up to her. Her brain was too. . .
fuzzy. . . to think about it now. It was her last coherent thought.

*THE shouts and screams out in the street reverberated off the walls
of the atrium, and she shivered. Four days. The crowd had been
massed outside the door for four days, shouting for her to come out
and repent her heresy as a follower of Vesta, Jupiter, and Juno. She
almost spat on the floor at the notion. The baby kicked, and her
hand touched her stomach with a sinking heart.*

*Dulcis Jupiter, she should have tried to flee the city for her aunt's
home in Civitavecchia the moment the shouts outside the house
had begun four days ago. Somehow she was certain Octavian was
behind the unruly crowd outside her door. But leaving the house
would have been a sign of cowardice, and she was not a coward.
Even if she'd tried to run, the babe would have slowed her down,
and that meant putting Demetri's life in danger.*

*Soft laughter caught her ear, and she turned to see Demetri
peeping out at her from behind one of the columns supporting the
roof, a flower floating in the air in front of him. The sight made
her shiver. If Octavian were to see Demetri now—she refused to
consider that possibility. Why hadn't she listened to Sevilia? Her
friend had left Rome more than a week ago. She should have sent
Demetri with her to the country. But then she'd never thought that
Maximus would be anything less than victorious. Never believed
that Constantine would have a vision that would rally his men to
an unexpected victory. She moved past the impluvium to grab the
flower and swept her son up in her arms.*

*"What have I told you about using your ability where others
might see, mea delicia." She kissed his cheek and pressed her face
into his neck. She was terrified for him.*

*"I heard the men shouting. Why are they calling for Papa?" The
innocent question made her raise her head to look down at him.
Praise Jupiter that the child didn't understand they weren't calling for
Maximus. No, the cry was for her, Maximus's whore. The heretic.*

"*They're angry, dulcis cor. I think they'll go away soon.*"

Adela suddenly appeared from the back of the house. "Forgive me, Domina. *I turned my back—*"

"*It's all right, Adela. I know how good he is at escaping.*" *She handed her son to the woman and tickled Demetri in his side.* "*Aren't you,* mea delicia?"

"*Shall I put him to bed,* Domina?"

"*No, let him play for now, but in the garden. Not here in the* atrium." *She leaned forward to kiss her son's brow. His pudgy hands caught her face, and he looked up at her with a serious expression.*

"*When the people go away, will you be happy again, Mother?*"

"*Yes,* mea cor," *she said as she suddenly realized she no longer had a choice where Demetri's safety was concerned. She looked over his head at Adela.* "*Send Posca to me.*"

Adela bobbed her head as she led Demetri away. Cassiopeia watched them leave, her son looking back over his shoulder to grin at her. She smiled and blew him a kiss, but it did little to ease the terrible ache in her heart. It was possible she might never see her son again after today.

The shouts from the street had dimmed somewhat, but they continued to fray on her nerves, and she paced the tiled floor in an effort to ease her anxiety. In a restless gesture, she nibbled at the tip of her thumb as she considered all the options open to her. If she tried to leave the house with Demetri, whoever was watching the back of the house would alert the mob. But if Posca carried Demetri out in secret, the two of them might easily go unnoticed.

Perhaps in the dead of night Posca could take her and Demetri out of the city. Even then, discovery was likely, and what would happen when Maximus came for her? The mob would either kill or sell the slaves, leaving him with no way to find them. No. The wife of General Maximus Caecilius Atellus wouldn't show fear in the face of this mob or its instigator. She wouldn't flee. She would make her husband proud of her. She'd wait here for Maximus, while Posca took Demetri to her aunt's house in Civitavecchia.

Maximus would come for her. She only hoped it would be soon. Footsteps sounded behind her, and she turned to see Posca running toward her. Short of Adela and Tevy, Maximus's tribune, Posca was the only other person she trusted without question. Maximus had rescued the man from certain death in the Colosseum and had earned a trusted servant for life. The sheer bulk of the man had made Maximus choose him as a bodyguard for her and Demetri. As the man came to a halt, he bowed slightly then stood at attention in front of her.

"Yes, Domina?"

"It will be dark soon. Can you get Demetri out of the house without anyone seeing you?"

"It will be difficult, but I will see you and the boy reach safety outside the city walls."

"You will only have Demetri to worry about." *She waved her hand in an abrupt fashion as the cries outside swelled to an almost fevered pitch. A knot lodged in her throat at the sound.*

"But, Domina, I cannot protect you, and the boy, if you don't come with me," *the tall man protested fiercely.*

"We both know you will not escape detection if you leave with the two of us. You yourself said you've seen Octavian's men near the rear of the house." *She shook her head vehemently.* "No. You must see to Demetri's safety first. By the time you have given him into the care of my aunt, Maximus will have come for me. We will join you in Civitavecchia."

She knew it was unlikely Maximus would reach her before the mob breached the front door. Posca knew it as well. She could see it in his face.

"I must insist, Domina. I gave my word to the general that I would protect you and the boy at all cost. I will find a way to get both you and the child to safety." *Posca's voice was harsh with frustration as he tried to change her mind. She raised her hand to stop the man's objections.*

"Maximus will know you had no other choice but to leave me behind. I want to ensure Demetri is safely away from all this madness."

"But, Domina—" *The bodyguard glowered at her as she interrupted him.*

"I'm with child," *she exclaimed with a catch in her voice.* "I would only slow you down."

The man's face paled at her words. He muttered something violent under his breath before he shook his head.

"If you do not come with me, it is not only you, but the babe as well, that you put into jeopardy."

"And you know what they will do to Demetri if we're caught," she said with a sharp hiss of anger. "I will not have my son sold into slavery."

"Then let me find a safe place in the city for the boy. I'll return for you, then the three of us will go to Civitavecchia."

"I can't risk someone I don't know protecting my son, Posca. He will go with you. I will be well enough until Maximus comes for me. And he will come." Her hand trembled as she waved the man away. "Now go. Quickly."

With a final grunt of frustration, the man bowed and hurried away to do as ordered. Left alone to her thoughts, the shouts outside the house were like razors biting across her skin. Maybe she should let Posca take her away with Demetri. No, they'd be watching the house, and it would be easier for the bodyguard to sneak Demetri out past the spies than if she were to go with them as well. And she would slow them down. The stress of the journey could easily cause her to lose this child as well. She'd miscarried their last child, and she would do nothing to risk the life of this baby.

The baby kicked her again, and she smiled as she touched her gently rounded belly. She'd not yet told Maximus about the child, but already she knew it was a boy. He'd be pleased. A loud boom echoed past the main entryway into the atrium. The cries outside intensified, and slaves came racing into the atrium from all directions.

The sound came again, and her heart slammed into her chest. They were trying to break the door down. Demetri. She raced toward his bedroom only to meet Posca carrying a large sack on his back with Demetri inside. Her son grinned at her, and tears blurred her vision as she pressed her mouth to the boy's forehead.

"You're about to have a wonderful adventure, mea delicia, *and I want you to do exactly as Posca says, do you understand?" She waited for him to nod his head, but instead he put his finger against his mouth to indicate silence. With a smile, she touched his cheek. "That's right,* mea cor, *you must be very quiet."*

A mischievous smile on his face, he ducked back underneath the flap of the sack. The pounding on the front door increased, and she grabbed Posca's arm.

"Go. Go now," she said fiercely.

"Come with me, Domina."

"No, it's Demetri you must save now. I shall wait here for Maximus or your return." The instant she spoke, she knew she'd never see either Posca or her son again. Her heart splintered into a thousand tiny shards, and she clasped her hands together in a tight grip not to pull Demetri from the sack over Posca's shoulder. "Go."

"I will protect the boy with my life."

His expression grim, the servant bowed his head in her direction then moved with great speed toward the back of the house. As the front door to the house cracked behind her, she watched Posca disappear carrying Demetri over his shoulder. When they were out of sight, she turned and moved to stand in front of the impluvium. It wouldn't be long now.

More slaves came from different areas of the house, clearly frightened. She quietly reassured them and ordered them to go about their tasks. Adela remained with her, and she knew better than to tell her to go. The freedwoman wouldn't listen. She was loyal to a fault. The booming noise increased, and with each loud crash, the door groaned its protest.

Minutes later a violent crack split the air around her, and the door gave way to a mad rush of people. The house slaves who had disobeyed her orders scurried for safety the moment the door crashed inward. Alone in the middle of the atrium, except for Adela, she faced the angry horde that stormed into the house. Determined not to show any sign of fear, she managed to maintain her composure as the mob entered her home. The shouts and cries slowly died away as she faced them in silence.

Dulcis Jupiter give her the strength not to yield to the terror spreading through her limbs. She wanted to run, but she wouldn't. She was the daughter of Gaius Quinctilia Atellus and the wife of Maximus Caecilius Atellus, one of Rome's greatest generals. She wasn't about to let these filthy fanatics know that inside she was shaking like a lamb knowing it was about to be slaughtered.

Suddenly, the crowd parted, and her heart slammed into her chest. Octavian. The man wore a cruel smile, his demeanor one of supreme confidence. The tribune helmet he carried was quickly handed off to the young officer with him before he bowed in front of her.

"As beautiful as ever, Cassiopeia."

"To what do I owe this . . . pleasure?" She paused for just long enough for him to know she was insulting him.

"Your husband has failed Maxentius. Their armies have been defeated. Constantine is on his way into Rome as we speak."

"Maximus." Swaying on her feet in shock, she barely breathed the word, but it was enough for Octavian to chuckle.

"He's not been found yet, but when he is, his life will be forfeit."

His words made her draw in a breath of relief. He wasn't lying to her. If Maximus were dead, Octavian would have gloated. She stiffened her spine and met the Praetorian's gaze with disdain.

"Maximus will kill you if you do anything to harm me or our son."

"I'm grieved to hear you think I would harm you, mea dulcis. You know I've always cared for you, Cassiopeia," he said softly. For a brief moment, she thought she heard a note of sincerity in his voice. It was gone before she could be sure.

"Then why are you here?" A second later, his hand gripped her waist, his fingers digging deep into her side. The painful grasp tugged an unwilling gasp from her.

"But for your protection, of course, mea karus. In fact, you need not worry your pretty little head about anything. Despite the fact that you're a heretic in the eyes of the Church, I've no doubt you will find it easy to repent your heresy to save your son."

The thought of Posca having just left made her flinch. Octavian saw her expression, and his gaze narrowed with assessment. Without hesitating, she threw up a mental barrier around her thoughts. It was something Maximus had taught her in the event a moment such as this came. Neither of them had ever believed it would happen. Deliberately, she filled her thoughts with images of Maximus destroying Octavian to help her forget her son's departure.

Octavian's grip on her arm tightened as he realized she was hiding something. With a jerk, she pulled free of his grasp to stand rigid in front of him. She refused to show any sign of weakness in front of this *bastardo*. And she needed to keep her wits about her to ensure the man didn't suspect that Demetri was no longer in the house. All Posca needed was a short time to get far enough away from the house to escape Octavian's men.

"Do not threaten me, traitor." She stiffened as he cupped her breast, his thumb running across her nipple in an insolent gesture. Revulsion shuddered through her at the vile touch.

"You have only to sleep in my bed, and I'll let you live."

"Pig." She didn't think twice as she spit in his face. Her punishment was a brutal slap that dropped her to her knees.

"You just signed your death warrant, *mea karus*. You know far too much about the *Tyet of Isis*, and clearly you cannot be trusted," Octavian snarled. "Take her."

Someone dragged her to her feet and pushed her roughly toward the door. Behind her, Adela released a scream of grief, which was cut short a moment later. Cassiopeia didn't have to look back to know the woman who'd been her confidante and protector for years was dead.

Maximus.

She knew he was dead, otherwise he would have been here before Octavian. He would have come for her if he could. What she didn't understand was why she still felt him. It was as if she could feel his warmth, his touch. Hope whispered through her, and she raised her head to search the crowd lining the street. Was he here? Was it part of a plan to rescue her?

The sensation slowly ebbed from her, and her heart grew numb. He was dead and so was her heart. Inside, the baby kicked her, and a tear rolled down her cheek. She fought to keep the tears at bay. She and the babe would meet Maximus in the Elysium Fields. Then, when it was time, their son would join them. But for now, Demetri would be safe from the likes of Octavian and his fanatical followers of the new church.

A sharp jab from behind forced her to walk faster, and this time she couldn't hold back the tears. Everything she'd ever loved had *been ripped from her simply because of a small box with a secret inside. It would destroy the Praetorian Guard. Once Octavian had the* Tyet of Isis, *he would control who lived and died. The balance of power had been broken as Maximus feared and their lives lost because of one man's craving for power.*

THE sound of a car blaring its horn jerked Phaedra out of the dream as late-morning traffic echoed in the street outside the room. Fear flooded her senses, and she clutched at the blanket as she came to grips with the fact that she wasn't in ancient Rome. Relief slid through her as she recognized Lysander's suite in the Rome safe house.

She closed her eyes again and drew in a deep breath as the emotions the dream had aroused in her swept through her again. *Deus*, to have to say good-bye to one's child like Cassiopeia had was inconceivable. And to be pregnant, knowing she was going to die. She shuddered. The Sicari Lord's wife had more courage than she could ever have. The memory of Octavian made her frown.

Nowhere in the stories she'd heard had there been any mention of the man. Maybe Lysander was right. Maybe these dreams were little more than her imagination running wild. Maybe Octavian was nothing more than an outlet for that dark image she'd seen while healing Lysander last night. She went rigid with shock.

There had been something so familiar about the darkness at the time she'd been healing Lysander. But it wasn't until just now that she recognized the venomous presence. Her fists hit the sofa cushions. The rogue Sicari. The fighter who'd tried to kill Lysander had been the rogue Sicari. She was certain of it. She shivered.

It was the same malevolent presence she'd experienced at the Temple of Hadrian, and it explained Octavian's role in her dream. The same darkness had possessed him as well. Octavian had to be a representation of the man who'd tried to kill Lysander last night.

Last night she'd been convinced that Lysander couldn't have found the rogue Sicari, but every instinct in her body said that somehow he'd done just that. But how? With a grimace, she threw off the blanket and jumped up from the couch. Lysander had kept his word. He'd gone after the man because of her. Her heart skipped a beat. He'd gone after that son of a bitch because of *her*, not just because the man was a threat to the Order.

Lysander had gone out to defend her honor. The act of a man who cared. She drew in a sharp breath of hope before the reality of what had happened hit her. *Deus*, he'd gone after that *bastardo* without backup. In the process of defending her honor, he'd almost gotten himself killed last night, the dumb *bacciagalupe*. The man needed someone to rip him a new one, and at the moment, Cleo wasn't here, but she was more than happy to fill in for her friend.

Angry that he'd succumbed to the ridiculous notion of chivalry, she stalked across the room and charged into his bedroom.

"You went—"

At almost the same second she burst into the room, Lysander bolted out of the bathroom in nothing more than a towel. He didn't need any more than that as she went flying backward to hit the wall. She hung there for a brief instant before she slid downward and landed in a heap on the floor. Stunned, she gave her head a sharp shake as if doing so would help her make her less groggy.

"Goddamn it, Phaedra, what the hell's the matter with you, busting in here like that. I could have killed you," he rasped.

One knee resting on the hardwood floor, he knelt down to help her sit up and lean back against the wall. His mental blow still had her feeling wobbly, and she closed her eyes for a moment. The minute she pulled in a deep breath, his scent washed over her. Fresh, raw, wholesome male. Whatever soap he used, it had a spicy smell that made her want to lean forward, press her nose into his skin, and just breathe. *Deus*, he smelled wonderful.

"Phaedra, open your eyes," he snapped. "Look at me."

"Stop yelling." She glared at him as she rubbed her head with her hand. "I'm not deaf."

"*Christus*, you made me think . . . *don't* do that again. Understood?" Whatever he'd really wanted to say, he managed to hold it back. She nodded her obedience.

It was about all she could do at the moment, since her body was slowly coming alive as her senses were attuned to his frequency at every level. She drank in another breath of him, and her heart skidded along at a fast pace. Slowly, she allowed herself the pleasure of letting her gaze drift downward across strong, muscular shoulders to toned, well-sculpted arms. Deus, he was gorgeous.

His chest rose and fell at a quick pace that indicated his heightened state of emotion. She tentatively reached out with her senses, and her heart skipped a beat at the wild mixture of emotions churning inside him. They rolled off him at a dizzy pace. There was the concern for her safety and a primal need to protect. That primal urge sent a thrill through her. Then there were the soft tendrils of an emotion she was almost too frightened to identify. A sudden rush of delicious heat streaked through her veins, and in the blink of an eye, she knew the truth.

He did care.

For whatever reason, he was hiding it, but he cared about her. Afraid to look at him just on the off chance her senses were misfiring, she dropped her gaze lower to the sight of a bent leg where the skimpy towel he was wearing parted and draped the sides of his thigh. His leg was a thing of beauty. Taut, sinewy muscles bulged slightly against the skin. There was a long scar that ran diagonally across the lower part of his thigh.

One more reminder that he'd suffered by refusing the *Curavi*. Tentatively, she reached out and ran one finger along the fine, white line. The harsh breath he sucked in pulled her gaze back to his face. The naked desire she saw there made her shudder, and her hand moved from his leg to his mouth. It had always been the most beautiful thing about him, and she was so glad that Praetorian monster hadn't destroyed it.

Suddenly, a strong hand gripped her wrist, and in less than a second, he'd pulled her to her feet. Stark need tightened his features, but he released her and turned away. A wave of fury crashed over her, and she drew in a sharp hiss of air. The son of a bitch didn't have the courage to love her, even though she knew he wanted to.

Every fiber in the man's body was drawn to her, and he didn't have the guts to admit it. A growl rumbled out of him as he slowly turned to face her. Her gaze flitted from the horrible disfigurement of his demonic side to his angelic profile, which was drawn up hard with anger. She glared at him.

"What?" she said angrily.

He didn't answer her. Instead, he stepped back into her, his fingers slipping between her breasts to the fragile strip of material holding her bra cups together. The touch made her gasp, and she was suddenly aware of the cool air on her shoulders. She'd been so determined to chew him out that she'd forgotten she wasn't wearing a shirt.

The heat of his fingers pressed against her skin, and with a sharp tug, his fingers broke the bra, the cups sliding off her breasts to expose her completely. Her immediate reaction was to cover herself. She'd been expecting him to pull her toward him, not undress her.

At least not yet.

She reached out with her senses and caught the faintest whisper of something dark. It was a part of him, and yet she could tell he fought it constantly. Surprised by it, she retreated from him until her back was against the wall. A savage look tightened his ravaged profile, and his unmarred side reflected an emotion she couldn't describe.

Invisible hands caught her wrists and pulled them up over her head to pin them to the wall. She drew in a quick breath of surprise but didn't take her eyes off his face. The terrible emotion he was struggling with wouldn't win, she was certain of it. He would never hurt her. His features darkened, and he moved forward to brush his mouth over her shoulder. A primitive noise rumbled out of him.

"Is this what you want, Phaedra? A half man, half monster?"

With a turn of his head, he gave her a magnified view of his horribly scarred face. There was no eye patch to hide the eyelid sealed shut over the indentation where his eye had once been. From his scalp to his jaw, the twisted flesh was there for her to see in all its glory. His marred flesh broke her heart, not because of what he looked like, but because of the bleak note in his voice. His pain was deep. So far down, she wondered if her love was strong enough to help heal his spirit. *Deus*, she wanted to kill the Praetorian devil that had tried to destroy him.

"Do you really think I'd be here if I didn't want to be?" She tried to break free of her invisible restraints but failed.

"I don't know what the hell to believe."

There was a quiet desperation in his voice that said he was standing on the edge of a great precipice. It made her long to hold him. Reassure him that if he fell, she'd fall with him because he was all she wanted. With renewed determination, she strained to free herself from his mental grip.

"Kiss me and I'll show you what to believe," she said in a voice that challenged him to listen to his heart and nothing else.

Chapter 15

THE woman had him on the brink of breaking every rule he'd ever made where she was concerned. He bowed his head to keep from looking at her, feverishly trying to clear his head so he could think straight. That blatant look of desire on her face was enough to pull him off the edge into an abyss from which he wouldn't be able to return.

How in the hell had he gotten himself into this predicament? Right. Her charging into his bedroom like a Praetorian on the loose. The sound of his door crashing open had thrown him into reactionary mode. He'd learned never to question. It was a quick way to die. Or worse.

It wasn't until he'd seen Phaedra flying backward and hitting the wall that he realized his mistake. An error that could have easily killed the one person who meant the most to him. Then he'd tried to walk away from her—away from those brown eyes glowing with an invitation he desperately wanted to accept but knew he couldn't. But it wasn't her eyes that had made him turn around. It had been her thoughts. He'd not meant to read her mind, but his resistance where she was concerned had been almost nonexistent.

He'd been so busy trying not to make love to her right here on the floor, he'd barely noticed that he was reading her thoughts until the word "coward" sounded in his head. He'd almost shouted his denial at her unspoken allegation, but stopped himself just in time. The fact that he'd come so close to exposing his secret infuriated him. He'd almost lost control. The next time he might not be so lucky.

Now she was asking him to believe that she really wanted to be here with him. *Merda,* he didn't have any trouble believing that at all. No, his biggest problem was that he was teetering on the edge of giving way to her demand. She was so fucking determined, and he was fast losing the battle against her persistence. Especially when she smelled so goddamned good. *Christus,* what was she wearing?

Nothing from the waist up, his brain answered, even though he'd really been trying to identify her sweet scent. He lifted his head slightly to study her breasts. They were full and lush. Seeing them locked away in that damn bra had driven him to rip the thing off her. He'd always been a breast man, but Phaedra's made him hard just looking at her.

His mouth watered at the thought of swirling his tongue around the tip of her, and he heard her gasp then watched in fascination as she arched her body forward. *Merda.* With her hands pinned above her by his mental hold, she was the most tempting creature he'd ever seen in his life.

"Please, Lysander, touch me. Touch me with your hands, so I know this is real."

Soft and husky, her voice stroked him, enticed him into doing what he knew he shouldn't. He leaned forward and caressed one breast with his mouth and the other with his hand. As his tongue swirled around a hard nipple, his thumb rubbed against the other. She tasted as good as she smelled.

He heard her moan with pleasure, and it drove him to work his mouth up to her shoulder and then the nape of her neck. With every caress, one more brick in his wall crumbled into dust. Deep inside he heard the roar of warning, but he ignored it. Just another moment, a few more seconds of denial.

That's all he needed. To touch her like this, breathe in the scent of her. He was going to Tartarus for this, but holding her again was worth the price he'd eventually pay. His mouth grazed its way along her jaw, and he deliberately took his time as a whimper echoed out of her. *Deus,* he loved the way she responded to him.

Loved the way she quivered against him. She abruptly turned her head, and her lips brushed across his. The explosion of desire her kiss ignited slugged its way into every cell in his body. Pleasure and need mixed with darker emotions he didn't want to face. Her teeth tugged gently at his lower lip, and he automatically deepened the kiss and swept his tongue into her delicious mouth.

In the next instant, he was drowning in a bloodred haze of passion as her tongue swirled with his. *Christus*, he wanted her. Needed her. Right now, right here. His body was hard, and the urgency driving him had him making short work of her jeans, shoving them downward as her feet slipped out of one leg and then the other.

The towel whipped off him, and then it was nothing but hot skin, just like the last time. Desire blinded him to everything but the urgent need to slide into her hot folds and stay buried there. There wasn't time for seduction. He'd been without her for too long. He just wanted to sink into her silky depths and drown himself in the sensation.

His hands cupped her buttocks and he lifted her up until his cock found the sleek creamy center of her. With a low cry of satisfaction, he rocked inside her, his body on fire at the way she clutched at him. It was like having a velvet vise around him growing tighter every second only to release him for a tantalizing moment before her body renewed the process.

He released his mental hold on her wrists and she immediately wrapped her arms around his neck to arch away from him, making it easier for him to thrust up into her. Beneath his mouth, her silky skin tasted like peaches. Hot, sweet peaches. He'd missed her so damned much. It was as if he'd been starving and hadn't realized the extent of his hunger until this moment. He couldn't get enough of her. He'd gone without her for so long, and now he was like a starving man unable to keep from satisfying his hunger. And she felt so damned good wrapped around his cock. With each surge into her tight core, her body responded with tiny spasms that rippled over his erection, hard and fast. He shuddered. Fuck, he was ready to come right now.

"*Inamorato*, I can't . . ." He choked back a shout as he throbbed violently inside of her.

A sob of pleasure parted her lips, and she fell forward to bury her face in his neck as her body clenched with savage intensity around him. It made him deaf and blind to everything but the way her body was loving his. Slowly, he edged his way down off the cliff he'd been standing on and carried her to the bed.

He was going to have to deal with reality soon, but he wanted to put if off as long as possible. Gently laying her on the bed, he dropped down next to her onto his back and closed his eye. What the hell had he been thinking? This was exactly what he'd been trying to avoid for the past year. And he didn't even have an escape route. *Merda*. What kind of excuse was he going to be able to use to keep her at a distance now? She sure as hell wasn't about to let him get away with saying he'd been in need of a good fuck. That had been his excuse a year ago.

But what had happened just now had been anything *but* a good fuck. If there had even been the tiniest piece of him that hadn't loved her before, it was gone. She didn't know it, praise the gods, but she owned him now. Body and soul. The mattress shifted slightly and a warm hand slid across his chest.

It was a gentle touch, but the warmth of it conveyed an emotion he didn't want to name. *Christus*, he was a doomed man. He didn't have to open his eye to see her shift her body upward so she could lean over him. It was easy to see her in his mind as her dark curtain of hair brushed over his shoulder and she lowered her head to kiss him. It was a featherlight touch, but it was enough for him to ache for her all over again.

In the next instant, he sucked in a harsh breath as her mouth touched the thin scars that crisscrossed his flesh where his eye had once been. There was little sensitivity left in his disfigured face, but he could imagine what he didn't feel. A shudder went through him as her mouth touched his cheek, caressing every inch of his scarred tissue. Something wet rolled down the side of his neck, and he suddenly realized she was crying. He rolled her onto her back to stare down at her, his fingers wiping away the tears shimmering on her skin.

"Don't, *carissima*."

"But you wouldn't let me touch you," she whispered. The sharp edge of pain in her voice said how deep his rejection had hurt her. "You wouldn't let me heal you."

"I didn't want to see you suffer as I had." He choked out the half-truth.

"And at the hospital?"

The accusation in her words slashed at him. He'd known she'd been hurt, but something in her voice said she'd been more devastated than he'd realized. He didn't want to consider what that meant, because it would explain her recent determination to make him admit that he cared for her. Make him say he still wanted her. One of them she'd just proved, and he wasn't sure how long the thread he was hanging from would keep him from admitting the second part.

He rolled away from her and sat up on the edge of the bed. Deep in the back of his mind, he'd known this topic would come up, but he sure as hell hadn't expected it to be this morning. He couldn't look at her because she'd know if he was lying to her. And no matter how many truths he offered up, he *would* have to lie.

"*Christus*, I didn't want anything to do with anyone." Especially her. Truth.

"I understand that, but you didn't even let me try to heal you. I might have been able . . ."

"What? Give me back my eye?" He refused to look over his shoulder at her. "Even if that had been possible—and I doubt seriously it would have been—do you really think I'd want my eye back at the expense of seeing you experience that kind of pain?" he growled. Truth.

"But it would have been my choice." Her lips placed a gentle kiss on his shoulder as he felt her come up on her knees and press into his back.

"No healer has ever tried anything like that before. It might have killed you for all we know. I wasn't about to let that happen." Truth.

"You don't know that. Even *I* don't know the extent of my ability." She started to knead his shoulders. Had she sensed the tension in him? Hell, yes. She was an intuitive healer.

"I don't know why we're even discussing the goddamn thing. It's over and done with."

"No, it's not. Whatever happened that night, there's something dark and ugly eating you from the inside out."

The words sliced through him with the sharpness of a Praetorian blade. There was a certainty in her voice that made his heart slam into the wall of his chest. She was saying she'd sensed the Praetorian side of him. *Il Christi omnipotentia*, why hadn't that son of a bitch just killed him that night? At least she'd never have to know about the monster inside of him.

"I don't know what the hell you're talking about." Lie.

"I know better. I sensed it at the hospital and over the past year I've felt it. I was just too blind to understand what I was sensing in you. Worse, I can sense it in you now. It's as if—you asshole!"

Her sharp gasp surprised him, and the hard fist slamming into his shoulder made him twist his head in her direction. Those gorgeous brown eyes glared at him with a fierceness he'd seen her reserve just for Praetorians. His gut lurched the minute he saw the fury on her face.

"You made me forget why I came in here in the first place! You went after that bastard who assaulted me, didn't you?"

The expectation of a completely different accusation left him unprepared for this charge. Caught off guard, he shook his head slightly as he tried to come up with an answer. Frustration glittering in her eyes, she planted her hands against his shoulder and gave him a hard push. He just stared at her, his brain scrambling to recover his wits.

"Don't you dare lie to me, Lysander Condellaire," she snapped. "You went after him. *Didn't you?*"

"It was necessary," he growled as he tried to keep his expression neutral.

"Have you lost your mind?" Her question was almost a shout.

"No." Another lie. He'd lost his sanity the minute he'd made love to her moments ago.

He calmly stood up and stepped away from the bed. The towel he'd dropped earlier flew across the room and into his hands. He wrapped it around his hips and tucked it into place as he deliberately kept his back to her. Behind him, Phaedra released a sharp noise of fury.

"No?" she bit out in a fierce tone. "What in the hell made you think you could find the guy? And on top of that, you went after him alone. *Christus*, you know better—"

The sound of her horrified gasp made his heart stop before it crashed into his chest. Fuck, this time she really had figured it out. She'd realized that his telepathic ability had allowed him to track the man. He slowly turned to face her, prepared for the disgust and hatred he knew would be sculpted on her beautiful features. As his gaze met hers, the air left his lungs at the look of horror and fear on her beautiful face.

Il Christi omnipotentia, he'd known she'd hate him, but it had never occurred to him that she might be afraid of him. He took a step forward, his heart like a stone in his chest at the way she was staring at him. Her hate he could deal with, but he couldn't bear to have her be afraid of him. He'd rather suffer again at the hands of that Praetorian bastard who was his father than have her afraid of him.

Before he could take another step forward, she scrambled off the bed and leaped toward him. He didn't give her the opportunity to slug him. Instead, he caught her wrists in his hands then forced her arms behind her back. The action pressed her soft breasts into his chest, and he tried to stifle the heat barreling down into his groin and the beginnings of an erection.

"I can—"

"Explain? Explain why you have a death wish?"

Her furious response knocked the wind out of him. His secret was still safe. The relief made him sag slightly, and she wiggled against him. It only made his cock expand and grow. God help him. The woman was going to be the death of him in more ways than one.

"I don't have a death wish," he rasped as he stared down at her mouth.

He'd always thought she was beautiful, but when she was angry, she had a sultry fire about her that made him ache for her.

"I don't believe you," she said sharply. "I can think of at least a half dozen times in the past year when you and Cleo encountered Praetorians only to hear her say you didn't hesitate to take on two or three of them all by yourself. Actually, 'went berserk' was the phrase she commonly used."

"It wasn't like that," he snarled.

"Then what was it?"

The demand showed she expected an answer, but he hesitated. What was he supposed to tell her? Deep inside, he *had* wanted to die. Had he deliberately thrown himself into combats where he might die? No. That meant he wouldn't have been able to keep her safe. He might not have any other reason to live, but watching over her was reason enough. He met her gaze and swallowed hard. *Christus*, he was slowly weaving a fragile web of half-truths that were so close to lies that pretty soon, he wasn't sure he'd be able to tell the difference.

"I was angry. Killing those *bastardi* was like killing the man who tortured me." He paused, his breathing suddenly shallow as he realized how much he wanted his Praetorian father dead. "But more importantly, I knew that every Praetorian I killed might be the one that had murdered your parents. I wanted retribution for *both* of us."

"*Dulcis matris Deus.* Thank you," she breathed the words as though they were a prayer of rejoicing. Arms still pinned behind her, she pressed her face into his chest, her mouth tenderly caressing his skin. "I *knew* you were lying to me when you sent me away that day in the hospital."

He shook his head as she raised her head to look up at him. Just the look on her face said his confession had pushed him into territory he'd not been willing to visit. He'd revealed far too much in the last half hour, more than he had in a year. He needed to repair the damage. Fast.

"Phaedra—"

"Don't deny it. You're crazy about me." The confident note in her voice told him she wasn't going to give up until he gave in.

Where she was concerned, he'd lost the battle. But was it a battle he really needed to fight? The odds of being discovered grew less every day. He'd known he was Praetorian for an entire year now, and no one was the wiser. Why shouldn't he grasp a small acre in the

Elysium Fields? Didn't they deserve a little bit of happiness for the high price they'd both paid over the last twelve months?

Perhaps his best strategy was to simply not admit anything. Just let the cards fall where they may and see what hand he was dealt. She'd be his and he could just live in the moment and not think about the future. It was a dangerous path to take, but she wasn't going to let him walk away from her again without a fight. He'd make the most of what time he had with her, whether it was for hours or years. He released his grip on her wrists, and she immediately wrapped her arms around his neck.

"I'm not going to deny anything," he said with a sigh of defeat. An expression of disappointment flashed across her face before she grimaced.

"Okay. Not exactly the confession I was hoping for, but it's a start," she said in an optimistic tone as a smile of exasperation brightened her face. "You're the most hardheaded man I know."

The comment struck him as incredibly funny, given he was sporting the mother of all hard-ons, and the female penchant for thinking a man's brain was between his legs. He couldn't help it, but a loud laugh escaped him. Startled, she stared up at him in surprise, her hands sliding down to rest against his chest.

"Hardheaded?" His hands caught her by the hips and tugged her into him as he smiled down at her. "I suppose you're right."

"That's not what I meant, and you know it," she gasped, a rosy color filling her cheeks. His smile widened.

"Disappointed?"

Despite the wicked glint of humor in his eye, she could still sense the bleakness deep inside him. It worried her, but she didn't probe. She'd gotten him to confess that he cared for her. Well, not exactly, but close enough. Everything else would have to come in small increments. One step at a time. She pressed into him, her hands lightly stroking the strong angles of his shoulders and chest.

"No. But I will be if you don't make love to me again," she murmured.

He bent his head toward her, and the moment his mouth brushed over hers, she gave a sharp tug to the towel around his waist. It fell to the floor, giving her the ability to stroke him. He was thick and hard in her palm. *Deus*, he was beautiful.

She wanted to memorize every inch of him with her hand. Her fingernail scraped gently along the ridge that ran from the base of him to the spot where the ridge ended just beneath the cap of his glorious erection. The touch made him shudder, and she experienced a sense of triumph.

He was hers. She'd finally broken through the wall he'd built around himself. Her hand curled around him, and she slowly caressed up and down the rigid length of him. The touch made him deepen their kiss, and the moment his tongue touched hers, an explosion of sensation raced through every inch of her body.

His hand cradled her neck as he explored the heat of her mouth in a hard, demanding kiss. There was something wild and unrestrained about the way his tongue danced with hers. He didn't give so much as he took. But she was more than willing to give him whatever he wanted. She'd missed him so much over the past year that the last hour seemed like a dream.

What scared her the most was that he might try to rebuild that wall between them. Her hand squeezed gently over his erection, and it dragged a deep groan out of him. The sound made her tighten her grip. His response was to rock against her palm in a clear sign of pleasure. He broke their kiss to slide his mouth across her cheek until his teeth tugged on her earlobe.

"You have a wicked hand, *carissima*." The raspy sound of his voice in her ear sent a shiver racing down her back. "But as much as I like what you're doing to me, I want more."

"More?" she asked with a sudden, quick move of her hand up and down his hard length.

The action tugged a sharp breath from him, and she smiled as she leaned forward to kiss his solid chest. The tension in him had made his entire body hard, and she loved that her touch had the power to affect him that way.

"Yes, more, *inamorato*," he murmured in a husky, seductive voice that reverberated off her skin to create a tingling sensation. "I want to touch every part of you. Caress you until you're begging me to stop."

"I don't ever want you to stop touching me."

"Be careful what you wish for, *carissima*."

There was a whisper of amusement in his voice as he picked her up and carried her the few feet back to the bed. He laid her down but didn't follow her. Instead, he stood looking down at her, a sinful smile curving that beautiful mouth of his. The mischievous glint in his eye had barely registered before a gentle touch brushed across her skin. Feathery light, it danced its way over every inch of her. It was as if his mouth were everywhere on her body all at once. It created a frisson of pleasure that made her tremble as the pressure of the caresses increased.

"*Oh God,*" she moaned as her body arched upward into the tiny, invisible touches.

"I take it you like this."

Desire and amusement echoed in his husky voice as he slowly sank down onto the bed beside her. He leaned into her slightly, and his sexy smile lulled her into thinking he was about to kiss her. He didn't.

Suddenly, the sensation of a wet tongue swirling around both nipples at the same time made her gasp as the same wet heat touched her between her legs. A thousand unseen fingers explored her body, touching, caressing, and teasing her into a state of exquisite arousal. She could have sworn his teeth were gently abrading her nipples when those invisible teeth were replaced by the sensation of his mouth suckling both breasts simultaneously. It drew a sharp gasp of pleasure from her.

Christus, she'd never experienced anything so erotic in her entire life. It created a craving inside her that intensified with each indiscernible kiss or stroke of his hand. She wanted him. Needed him. Her gaze flew to his, and she saw his jaw tighten as he watched the way she was responding to his touch. His expression was one of rapt concentration as he used his ability to pleasure her. With each unseen caress, he teased her body up to the point of a climax before he withdrew for a brief moment only to begin all over again.

Each peak his invisible caress carried her to, she was certain it would be the one that took her over the edge into a state of bliss. And every time he denied her, she willingly gave herself up to his mercy one more time. Her breathing ragged, she whimpered with need, her body wanting—demanding—satisfaction. She stretched out her hand to him, but he shook his head.

"Not yet, *inamorato*," he rasped.

The invisible kisses rippling over her skin intensified while her areoles grew more sensitive with each unseen nip of his teeth. It was enough to drive her mad. Where one sensation ended, another began. She moaned and she could hear the intense need in the sound.

"Please, *caro*. I *need* you."

"No," he growled.

A hot sensation drifted over her inner thigh again, stealing her breath away. An instant later, she cried out as the invisible stroke of his tongue swirled its way around her sex then dove into her wet core. It created a rush of liquid heat between her thighs, and she bucked up against the unseen touch. It was a pleasurable torture that sent her over the edge. Her senses on fire, she dug her fingers into the bed sheets as she sobbed from the wicked sweetness of his lovemaking.

"Please *carino, now.*"

With her next breath, the solid weight of him settled pleasantly onto her. He smelled spicy hot and all male. Hers to hold and caress. His mouth crushed hers, and she clung to him as the tip of his erection pressed against her sex. Lord, the man was hell-bent on driving her insane with need. A soft whisper echoed in her head. It was so faint she wasn't even certain she'd heard it. It was almost as if she'd heard him say "I love you."

Hope blossomed inside her. Had he whispered the words or had she—every thought fled from her head as he thrust into her, filling her completely. With each stroke of his body, he branded her his, and she cried out as her body clutched at him in a frantic effort to sustain the pleasure. But it was impossible to hold back the feverish response she could feel building inside her.

Faster and faster, he thrust into her until her orgasm sent wild shudders skimming their way into every fiber of her being. Her body rippled over his erection, clinging to him, throbbing against him. With a shout, he slammed into her one more time, his body arching away from her as she watched him shudder violently over her. His face was taut with pleasure for several seconds, his body jerking against hers, before he slowly relaxed against her. Tenderly, her gaze caressed his face as her love for him filled her insides with warmth that was intensified by the waves of sensation ebbing away like a gentle tide.

"*Deus*, where did you learn how to do that?" she whispered.

"You're the first woman to inspire me to do it."

The tenderness in his voice sent her heart soaring. It was a testament to how he felt about her without committing himself. She closed her eyes. One step at a time. It was a creed she needed to remember. He'd been through twenty different levels of hell, and there was so much he was still holding inside him. He just wasn't ready to tell her how he felt. The memory of the whisper made her sigh. Had she really heard him say it? She frowned as it suddenly occurred to her it had been a thought sighing softly in her head, not soft words in her ear.

She immediately dismissed the notion. She hadn't heard him say a thing. It had been her imagination and nothing more. And even if she'd heard something in her head, it had to have been wishful thinking on her part. Sicari warriors didn't have the ability to read minds or enter the thoughts of others unless they were a Sicari Lord. And she was *certain* he wasn't a Sicari Lord. If he were, it wouldn't make sense for him to hide the fact.

His head slowly dropped until his forehead pressed against hers. At this moment, he reminded her so much of her Roman general except for the terrible scars. Even the way his body melded with hers was a reminder of the man who came to her in her dreams. Strong hard arms, a solid warmth against her skin, a powerfully sculpted chest, and that deliciously sensual line of his lips.

If he'd died last night . . . She shuddered. It was the fact that she'd almost lost him that had made her so angry—so scared.

"You almost died," she whispered. He lifted his head and stared down at her with a frown.

"What?" The tension in him had returned, but his expression revealed nothing but puzzlement.

"When I performed the *Curavi*. I saw how you almost died. Experienced it. How that *bastardo* almost succeeded in choking you to death. It's how I know you've been dreaming about Maximus and Cassiopeia. I saw a small bit of the vision you had."

"*Fotte*, not *that* again." He blew out a harsh breath as he quickly withdrew from her to lie on his back beside her.

"Can we please just talk about it?" she asked as she turned her head toward him. He kept his gaze focused on the ceiling.

"There isn't anything to talk about. They're just dreams. I don't know why you and Atia are trying to read something into them."

"Atia knows about your dreams?" She inhaled a sharp breath as she came up on one elbow to stare down at him. "You told *Atia*?"

The way his expression quickly closed him off to her was alarming. It reminded her of all the times he'd kept his distance from her, and she couldn't bear for him to retreat now. But she also knew they needed to find out why they were both dreaming about a couple who'd played such an important role in Sicari history.

"I told you I'd been talking to Atia. The woman tricked me into telling her about them," he growled. "And just like I told her, I'm telling you, the dreams mean *nothing*."

"But what if they do?"

"Drop it, Phaedra."

"I can't. I know they mean something, and I'm worried about the consequences if we ignore them."

She pressed her palm against his chest, the beat of his heart reverberating against her fingertips. *Deus*, his heartbeat was like a revved-up car engine. The man knew exactly what she was talking about but wasn't willing to admit it. He released the growl rumbling in his chest.

"Consequences? From a dream?"

"What if these dreams are part of that prophecy Angelo was talking about at dinner last night?"

"If you're talking that past-life crap, forget it. I'm not Maximus reborn."

"Then maybe you're Cassiopeia reincarnated," she teased in an effort to lighten the mood between them.

"Is that your way of asking me for a repeat performance to prove your theory wrong?"

Despite the small smile curving his lips, the harsh note underlying his words made her hesitate. Okay, so threatening his manhood, even in jest, hadn't been a good move, but she knew humor had the ability to heal. If she could make him laugh, maybe he'd come to realize these dreams were important.

And she wanted to hear him laugh like he had a few minutes ago. It had been a glorious sound. He'd laughed that way that one night they'd spent together before everything had changed. She shook her head as she met his intense gaze.

"No. I wouldn't *ask* you to repeat that incredible technique of yours. I'd *demand* it," she said with a mischievous smile. "I'm just saying that you and Cassiopeia have a great deal in common. In my dreams, she's incredibly stubborn, determined, fearless, and loving."

She leaned into him to kiss the scarred tissue of his face and forehead. He immediately stiffened, and the tension in him throbbed its way into her as she followed each descriptive word with a kiss. Something inside her made her stress the last word.

The green eye staring at her darkened with an emotion she couldn't decipher. And suddenly she knew in her heart he loved her, and that he was Maximus. He was the man she'd loved and lost in ancient Rome, and she refused to give him up again. He was her Roman general in every way but one—those terrible scars on his face. He jerked his head away from her.

"*Goddamn it.*" The oath passed his lips as he glared at her. "Let it go, Phaedra."

"I can't."

"Why the hell not?" he ground out between clenched teeth.

It was a valid question and she knew she was revealing her heart if she told him the truth. What if she was wrong about him and how he felt? No. She knew he loved her.

"Because in my dreams . . ."

"What?" He eyed her carefully, as if he somehow knew what her revelation was going to be. She flinched then met his gaze steadily.

"Because in my dreams, you're Maximus . . . with one exception. You don't have *any* scars."

Her words hung between them as he stared at her with a stoic expression for a long moment. Then without a word, he turned his head away from her. It wasn't the response she'd expected. For a moment, fear slid across her skin, but it was gone as quickly as it came as he looked at her again.

"Even if—and I *stress* the word 'if'—if all this were true, what the hell do you suggest we do about it?"

"I don't know. But if you'd admit that it might be true, maybe we could figure it out together."

"Together?"

The way he said the word made her swallow the knot rising in her throat. His hard body grew even harder, and she saw a glint of something she didn't like in his eye. Determined not to give in to fear, she scowled at him.

"Yes, together. You and me. And don't tell me that what just happened here was a roll in the hay, either. I bought it the first time, I won't buy it again."

The minute he winced at her words, she knew he'd lied at the hospital. The relief and joy streaking through her veins made her weak for a moment. He'd been protecting her from something all along. Cleo had been right. He'd always had her back. How could she have missed that? *Deus*, she'd misjudged him. Whatever he was hiding from her, she didn't care. All that mattered was keeping him from going back into that shell he'd been hiding in for the past year.

"What do you want from me, Phaedra?" There was a note of frustration in his voice that said she was beginning to tread in dangerous waters.

"Let me into your life. Don't shut me out like you did a year ago. I don't care why you did it. I just care about how we go forward."

He quickly slid away from her and off the bed. The closet door flew open with a loud crash as black pants flew off a hanger and into his hands. Shoulder blades hard with tension, he tugged the soft leather over his sinewy legs. She blew out a harsh breath of frustration. She'd pushed him too far. What had those bastards done to him that he was so afraid of sharing with her? Frightened, she scrambled off the bed to stand directly behind him. She could tell he knew she was there just from the way the muscles in his back bunched up in taut knots.

"Damn it, Lysander Condellaire, talk to me. Don't walk away from me."

"We've a job to do. Get dressed." The sharp command left her reeling.

"Just like that? We're back to where we started before you made love to me?"

He became a statue at the question, his back a symmetrical line of tense beauty that DaVinci would have loved to have sculpted. His head dropped down toward his chest as he shook his head.

"*Il Christi omnipotentia*, woman, give me some breathing room." There was a desperate note in his voice and it made her ache for him.

"If I give you breathing room, you'll come up with a reason to run away from me again," she whispered, her voice cracking with fear as she struggled to hold back tears.

The silence in the room was a ship's anchor on her shoulders as she waited for him to say something. Anything. When he slowly turned around, her heart lodged in her throat. He looked trapped. *Merda*. She'd pushed him into a corner. If they had a chance together at all, he'd have to come to her. As much as she wanted to, she couldn't push the issue with him.

She whirled away from him and went searching for her clothes. She quickly found her jeans and underwear. The bra was useless. She suppressed the memory of how it got ripped. Her T-shirt was in the sitting room and would have to suffice until she got to her room.

With a sharp tug, she pulled her jeans on, eager to leave. The heat of him suddenly pressed into her back, and his strong hands settled on the curve of her shoulders. The gentle touch sent a tremor blasting through her. *Deus*, the power this man had over her was so strong, she knew she was willing to do anything for him.

"I'm not running, *inamorato*." A shiver skated down her back as the warmth of his breath fanned across her bare back. "The other day you said we needed ground rules. I agree. I'm just not sure what they are yet."

Relief spread through her, and she turned around to wrap her arms around his bare waist. Pressing one cheek into his chest, she swallowed the knot in her throat as he held her close. This time the silence between them was comforting, and she squeezed back tears for the tenderness she could feel in his embrace. He'd taken the first step. She couldn't ask him for more than that.

He'd endured so much at the hands of the Praetorians. What she'd gone through yesterday was nothing compared to what he'd suffered. But it allowed her to understand his need for order and an ability to control what happened in his life. Yesterday she'd been helpless to stop what happened to her, and he'd been just as helpless a year ago. She'd been pushing so hard, she'd lost sight of the fact that he still had a lot of healing to do.

That desperate look on his face a few minutes ago had been a vivid reminder of what the Praetorians had stolen from him—from her. She hated them for it. The intensity of the emotion washed over her like a powerful wave of fire. Every single one of the *bastardi* deserved to die. They'd stolen her childhood when they'd slaughtered her parents, and she hated them for it.

As far as she was concerned, there wasn't a Praetorian alive who deserved mercy. They'd never shown mercy to any Sicari. And somehow, she'd find a way to make as many of them pay as she could. The strong muscles beneath her hands suddenly grew hard and rigid, and she lifted her head to see a bleak expression flash across his face. She drew in a sharp breath, and a sliver of fear snaked its way through her.

"What's wrong?"

"Nothing." He shook his head before he gave her a quick kiss and released her. "I thought I heard someone knocking on the apartment door."

As he turned away from her, she could have sworn she saw another look of despair twist the scarred tissue of his profile. But when she touched his arm, he turned his head to smile at her, his eyebrows arched in a silent question. Before she could speak, she heard a loud knock on the sitting room door followed by a shout of greeting. Lysander's rueful expression matched her own sense of awkwardness.

"*Fotte,*" she exclaimed with a small groan. "Cleo."

Chapter 16

LYSANDER summoned a black T-shirt from the closet with an imperceptible wave of his hand then pulled it over his head. With a light touch of reassurance to Phaedra's cheek, he stepped around her and headed for the door.

It was a fact. He was certifiable. He'd had the opportunity to just let her go, and instead he'd gone to her. Told her they'd figure out how to go forward from here. He drew in a deep breath and released it as he moved from the bedroom into the sitting room.

"You need to learn how to knock."

"I did. I always knock," Cleo said with exasperation. "You don't complain when I crash your place in Chicago."

Whenever Cleo had a fight with her mother, she had a habit of dropping in unexpectedly. He didn't mind. The two women were always at loggerheads, even if they adored each other. They were too much alike. He frowned.

"Yeah, well this isn't Chicago where you have the run of the apartment."

Cleo moved toward the couch and held up Phaedra's shirt for inspection. She didn't look at him. Instead, she slowly studied the tousled blanket and pillow on the sofa.

"I was looking for Phaedra, but I think I've found her." Although his friend's voice was neutral, he knew better.

"She was exhausted last night, so I made her sleep on the couch."

It was the truth, but for some reason, it didn't come out that way. His jaw locked with tension as the woman he viewed as a sister studied him intently. The assessment in her gaze raised his level of discomfort several notches.

"Right. So where is she now?"

Merda. He stood there for a moment unsure what to say. Was this how a deer in the headlights felt? He didn't like the feeling at all. When he didn't answer, Cleo sent a pointed look in the direction of the bedroom.

"Is she here?" There was just a hint of amusement in her voice.

"Exactly what is it you want, Cleo?" he ground out between clenched teeth.

"For you to be happy."

The sincerity in her quiet response didn't surprise him. It was the kind of wish any sister might have for a brother. But the usual layer of sisterly razzing was missing, and it took him aback. Cleo generally covered her deeper feelings with good-natured teasing and rarely showed the affection she felt for him. But the earnestness in her voice showed how much value she placed on their friendship.

Aside from Ignacio, he was the only other male figure in her life. The two of them had always been close, and they'd always looked out for each other. As his gaze met hers, he was suddenly aware how uncomfortable she was at showing her true emotions. She looked away from him as a grimace tugged at her features.

"So can I talk to her or do you just want to deliver the message?"

"Lysander, hand me my shirt please." Phaedra's voice floated out of the bedroom like a bumblebee hell-bent on stinging him.

A broad smile curved Cleo's mouth, and when he uttered an oath beneath his breath, she laughed. Heat immediately flooded his face until the scarred tissue on his face was tingling with fire. He swallowed the tight knot rising in his throat and hurried forward to snatch Phaedra's shirt out of his friend's hand. Cleo held on to it for just a fraction too long, and he glared at her.

She immediately released it and raised her hands in playful surrender. In less than five seconds, he was across the room and thrusting the shirt through the narrow opening between the doorjamb and the bedroom door. In the next instant, his skin was ablaze as the moist warmth of Phaedra's mouth enveloped his forefinger and her tongue swirled its way around the tip.

The image of her doing the same thing to his cock made him cough to cover up a surprised yelp as he yanked his hand away from the hot touch. *Il Christi omnipotentia*. The minute he turned back to face Cleo, his cheeks heated up again at her arched look of amusement. Fuck. He couldn't remember the last time he'd felt this awkward. Unable to think of what to say, he just stood there. A second later, Phaedra emerged from the bedroom, her gaze flitting from him to where Cleo was standing.

"Okay, you've found me. What's so important?"

"Irini cut her hand on the meat slicer, and it looks like it'll take eight to ten stitches to fix her up unless you're up to offering the *Curavi* to her."

Sympathy flitted across Phaedra's face at the questioning look on Cleo's face. She sent Lysander a quick glance before she nodded her head. "I'll come right now."

"Good," Cleo said with a smile and turned to leave the room. The suite's main door halfway open, she stopped to look over her shoulder, a deadpan expression on her face. "By the way, Ares and Emma arrived about an hour ago. I'm sure they'll be glad to hear the two of you are getting along so well."

"Cleo Vorenus," he snarled, but his friend was gone before he could finish saying her name. "Goddamn it! The woman's going to announce to the whole world that you spent the night here."

He started to pace the floor, his hand rubbing the back of his neck. The whole idea of being with Phaedra was still so new to him. He hadn't even considered the notion of everyone knowing the two of them were in a relationship. Especially when he still wasn't sure he was making the right decision to be with her. *Christus*, he didn't like being this uncertain about something.

Up until this morning, everything had been cut and dried. Now all that had changed and he wasn't sure of anything at all. He blew out a breath and turned to see Phaedra with her hand on the doorknob. With a frown, he immediately visualized his hand on the wooden door to hold it shut as he strode toward her.

"Now who's walking out on who?" he snapped.

"I'm not walking out. Irini needs my help."

She didn't look at him, but the rigid stance of her body said she was angry. He stretched out his hand to brush his fingers across her cheek, only to have her flinch and shrink away from his touch. *Damn it*, she wasn't angry. She was hurt. The fact that he'd not been happy about Cleo knowing she'd been here all night had sent her the wrong message. But then he was having a hard enough time adjusting to what had happened over the last hour or more. He was scaling a rocky versant without safety gear, and he wasn't sure he should even be climbing the mountain.

"Phaedra . . . this isn't easy for me," he rasped. She turned her head and the sight of her blinking back tears was worse than that Praetorian *bastardo* trying to kill him last night.

"It's not supposed to be easy, Lysander. Loving someone always involves risk. It's not about ground rules, it's about whether or not you're going to take that leap of faith to be with me. It's not like I'm asking for the blood bond."

The minute he jerked away from her, regret slammed into him. The color drained from her face, and she bit down on her lower lip. The tormented expression in her beautiful brown eyes made him want to sweep her in his arms, but he couldn't. How could he have been so *stupido*? Of course, she'd eventually want the blood bond.

Fear tightened his limbs like petrified wood. *That* was one place he wasn't willing to go. Sex was one thing. It didn't hold the same type of consequences or commitment the blood bond did. The transference of abilities between Sicari before a blood bond was sealed was extremely rare. It might happen once every couple of hundred years. And while the Sicari gene structure acted as a natural barrier to sexual diseases, the blood bond was a whole new ball game.

It wasn't just a lifelong commitment. If they performed the blood bond, the odds of her gaining one of his abilities multiplied exponentially depending on the strength of her own powers. Phaedra's intuitive nature was strong enough that the minute his blood mixed with hers the evolution of her ability was pretty much a certain thing. And, he sure as hell wasn't going to mix his tainted blood with hers. He refused to make her into something that had caused her so much pain in her life. Praetorian. Pain flashed in her eyes when he didn't answer her and she shook her head.

"I can't begin to imagine what those *figlio di puttanas* did to you that night, but I know it changed you. Whatever this darkness is you're carrying around inside you, it's coming between you and the one person who cares the most about you. Me."

"There are some things I'll never talk about, Phaedra. And if that's what you're looking for from me, then it's not going to happen," he bit out.

"I wasn't asking you to spill your guts," she snapped back in a furious tone. "I'm just trying to figure which way to turn. First, you tell me you're trying to come up with some *ground rules* between us, but that comment about Cleo sends a completely different message."

"*Fotte.* Cleo caught me off guard, that's all. Hell, I'm still trying to get adjusted to this *us being together* thing, let alone sharing it with anyone else. It wasn't something I was ready for."

"Then the real question is, are you ready for me?" There was a desperation in her voice that tugged at him. *Christus*, the slope of this mountain he was on was getting more slippery by the moment.

"No. The question is whether you're prepared to handle damaged goods," he muttered. And he was damaged goods. She deserved better. He wasn't being totally honest with her. Instead, he was being selfish and deceitful when it came to being with her. A gentle hand touched the horrifically scarred side of his face. The emotion he saw shining in her eyes was frightening enough to make him want to run as far and as fast as he could from her. He was digging his own grave, and sooner or later, she was going to send him tumbling into the pit and bury him.

"I don't think you're damaged goods. I think you're the most beautiful, courageous man I've ever known."

The soft words made him close his eyes against the love and pain they aroused in him. He was neither of those things, but her belief in him gave birth to a hope that he might live up to her expectations. At that moment, he knew he'd crossed a burning bridge. There wasn't any going back. He'd have to take his chances with her. The longer he kept his secret the less chance there was of getting caught.

The blood bond. What about the blood bond? The inner voice in his head mocked him. He pushed the thought aside. He'd deal with that when the time came. *And if she discovers the truth?* He swallowed the knot in his throat and pulled her into his arms. Later. He'd come up with a plan later. He loved her, and at the moment, that was all that mattered to him. Everything else could wait until he had time to come up with a decent plan of action.

"Suggestions on what we say when Cleo blabs to everyone she can?" he asked with a wry twist of his lips.

"We just smile and act like it's the most natural thing in the world," she said as she pulled his head down to hers for a gentle kiss. "It's the truth, isn't it?" There it was again, that note of fear in her voice. He nodded.

"The natural part is one thing. Smiling? That's a different issue altogether." He arched his eyebrows at her. It was true. He'd always been rather serious, but since that night in that warehouse, he'd been stoic to the point of being an automaton.

"Then save your smiles for me," she murmured huskily. "They make me feel like I'm the only woman you see in the room."

You're the only woman I'll ever see. Loving you makes me whole. The thought drifted out of him, and the minute he saw her frown, he panicked. *Merda*, he'd done it again. Maybe this wasn't going to work after all. He forced a smile to his lips and faked an expression of curiosity.

"What?" He kept the question simple, hoping and praying she'd dismiss it as her imagination. Her gaze searched his face for a moment before she shook her head.

"Nothing. I just . . . well, for a second there, I thought I heard you say something."

"Is that your way of fishing for a compliment?"

"Maybe." She laughed. "But I'll go fishing later. Right now, I need to get down to the kitchen and take care of Irini's cut. I'll see you in a little bit?"

"Yes. I'm going to have Marco assemble the team for an update on yesterday's progress after I talk with Ares and Emma. I think the two of them have some new information that might be useful."

"All right," she said with a smile. Then with a light kiss, she was gone.

He stood there for a moment contemplating how he'd just sealed his fate where she was concerned. There was no going back now. With a growl of disgust, he wheeled about and forced himself to focus his attention on the task at hand. The sooner they found the *Tyet of Isis*, the sooner they could go back to Chicago. After a quick call to Marco, he finished dressing and headed downstairs to the library. It was a favorite haunt of Atia's no matter which facility, and he fully expected her to be holding court with Emma and Ares in the room.

But she wasn't anywhere in sight when he entered the small study. The sight of Ares and Emma bent over a book on the library table filled him with pleasure. He was delighted that his friend had found Emma. Ares had blamed himself for the death of a loved one long enough. It was time he found some happiness in his life. And from the look on his friend's face, it was obvious he was happy. He cleared his throat to quietly announce his arrival, and the two of them immediately looked up from the book they were studying.

Broad smiles on their faces, they hurried forward to greet him. He grasped Ares's forearm with his hand in the manner the Sicari had greeted one another since the days of the Roman Empire. As he turned to greet Emma, he stiffened when she moved forward to hug him enthusiastically, but the tension in his body gave way as he hugged her back. In the short time they'd known each other, she'd become a friend. Ares had chosen well. Emma was no longer an *alieni*, she was Sicari. He stepped back and looked at Ares.

"I expected to see Atia in here," he said with a frown of puzzlement. "Did someone let her know you'd arrived?"

"Your *Primus Pilus* is looking for her now, but Ignacio is gone, too. Campanella can't reach him on the cell phone, but that could just mean they're not in the car." Ares shrugged slightly, his manner indicating he wasn't unduly concerned as yet. "She probably wanted to see the sunrise from some spot over the city. You know how she likes to do that at the White Cloud estate."

"*Il Christi omnipotentia*," he exclaimed harshly. "This isn't the

Michigan estate. It's Rome. She can't just ignore the fact that there's a Praetorian Dominus in the city."

"What?" Ares's sharp, one-word question emphasized his sudden change of mood.

"A Praetorian Dominus?" Emma's face revealed her confusion.

"The Praetorian equivalent of a Sicari Lord," Ares said in a grim voice. He didn't look away from Lysander as he reached for his wife's hand in a silent gesture of reassurance. "What makes you think there's a Praetorian Dominus in Rome."

"Because I fought one last night," Lysander said grimly. "The bastard would have killed me if I'd not had help."

"How?"

At Ares's query, he shook his head.

"A Sicari Lord saved him," Atia declared from the library doorway. The three of them jerked around to see the *Prima Consul* entering the room with a pinched expression on her face. Atia's arrival had saved him from lying to his friend about the Sicari Lord, but he sure as hell hadn't expected her to know a Sicari Lord had saved him. On the heels of that thought was the realization that Atia always knew everything.

That had always amazed him about her. But this was the first time he'd ever thought of her as anything less than indomitable. He frowned. She looked exhausted—drained—like she'd been in a vehemently contentious policy discussion with an angry group of senators. He'd never seen her look so unnerved before. Worse, there was a look in her eyes that signaled fear.

Even from the first day he'd come to live with her, he'd *never* seen her afraid of anything. Despite his irritation at the way she manipulated people and situations, he still cared about her, and seeing her like this worried him. He took a step toward her, but she waved him away in a silent command not to question her.

"The presence of the Praetorian Dominus simply makes our task harder, but not impossible." The firm note of strength in Atia's voice lessened the air of uneasiness about her. "I've already alerted those in charge of our headquarters in Genova and the Council as well."

"How do you know the individual who intervened was a Sicari Lord?" Ares asked as he stared intently at the *Prima Consul*.

"Because the man who sent a message with Lysander last night is a Sicari Lord I've known for more than thirty years." There was a slight crack in her voice that said this man was closer to her than she was admitting.

"And all this time you didn't bother to tell anyone that he existed?" This time Ares's voice was a sharp condemnation.

"It's for their protection as well as ours," she snapped. "Sicari Lords aren't invincible. Their abilities are simply stronger than ours and take longer to fade, but if outnumbered, they can die just like any of us. They've been betrayed in the past, and their existence is known only to a few."

"Their? You said their," Ares snapped. "Are you saying there's more than just one?"

"Yes."

While his friend was clearly stunned, Atia's response didn't surprise Lysander. The fact that the Sicari Lord who'd come to his rescue hadn't been alone had made him wonder if those with him had the same skills. It made sense. He glanced at Ares before returning his attention to the *Prima Consul*. With a gesture that signaled regret, Atia's hand brushed across her chin as she released a quiet sigh.

"I'm breaking every rule there is by telling any of you this, but you know how fond I am of breaking rules." She glanced in his direction before returning her gaze to Ares. "Lysander already knew of the Sicari Lord's existence because of his encounter with the Praetorian Dominus. And now I'm entrusting you and Emma with this secret."

Both Ares and Emma nodded their silent agreement not to betray the *Prima Consul*'s trust. Then Ares asked the question Lysander had been wanting to ask since last night.

"Can we expect their help if we have need of it?"

"I can't say. The *Prima Consul* is at the beck and call of the reigning Sicari Lord. He sends for me when he wants, but my ability to contact him is extremely limited."

Atia's resignation indicated she was holding nothing back. While he wouldn't refuse help from the Sicari Lord, Lysander wasn't going to count on his assistance, either. The Praetorian Dominus had definitely shifted the balance, making their mission all the more dangerous. The thought of losing another Sicari on his watch twisted his stomach into knots. No. He refused to lose anyone on his team, even if he had to take a sword instead of them. His gaze moved from Atia to Ares.

"Then we'll operate under the assumption that we're on our own as far as this Praetorian Dominus is concerned," he said quietly. "Instead of two to a team, we only go out in groups of three or more."

"Agreed," Ares said with a nod. "Where do you want to start next?"

The question was his friend's way of saying he had no intention of trying to lead this mission. He appreciated the gesture of support. For the first time since Atia had made him *Legatus*, he realized he wanted to succeed at this assignment.

"I've asked Marco to assemble everyone in the conference room on the hour. We need to take a look at what ground we've covered so far. It'll help bring you and Emma up to speed on our progress, and I want to know what the two of you found in France."

"Well, that sounds like a plan to me." Emma smiled at him with a hint of mischief in her eyes. "In the meantime, why don't you tell me where I can find my sister-in-law?"

The question sent heat flushing up his neck as Ares folded his arms and sent him an inquisitive look that said Cleo had been talking. *Christus*, he was going to throttle the woman. Beside him, Atia cleared her throat. He turned his head in her direction and was relieved to see her composure had returned.

"I believe Phaedra is in the kitchen performing the *Curavi*. One of the *Vigilavi* cut her hand."

Emma nodded, and after getting directions to the kitchen, she left the library. A slight smile on her face, the *Prima Consul* arched an eyebrow at Ares.

"Marriage suits you."

"I agree," Ares said with a nod of his head.

The cryptic answer was more of a habit when it came to answering Atia. They both knew it was better to say little than too much. The *Prima Consul* had a memory like a steel trap, and she would often pull something out of thin air to either drill home a point or to gently mock someone.

"And her ability?" This time the question was a command.

"Her technique still needs refinement, but she's becoming quite adept." Ares's expression was one of pride in his wife's achievements.

"I'm pleased to hear it," Atia replied. "Now then, I'm sure you want to see your sister, and I have a couple of items I wish to review with Lysander. Please close the door on your way out."

It was a dismissal, and he was just as startled by her crisp words as Ares. He sent her a quick glance and saw the distraught mood she'd displayed earlier had returned. With a slight bow in her direction, Ares headed for the door. As he passed by, Ares arched his eyebrows and bobbed his head in Atia's direction. Lysander could only offer up a small shrug in response. Whatever was bothering the woman, he was certain she was about to share it with him.

He was even more certain he wasn't going to like what she had to say. As the library door closed with a soft thud, he turned toward Atia and waited. She didn't look at him. Instead, she crossed the floor to stand at the window overlooking the interior courtyard of the Sicari satellite facility. She didn't speak for several minutes, and he found the silence uncomfortable. What the hell had he done that was so terrible she couldn't speak?

"I need your help, Lysander." Desperation filled her quiet words, and he recognized the all-too-familiar emotion. This wasn't about him after all. At least he didn't think it was.

"You know my sword is always yours to command."

"Of that I had no doubt. You and Ares have always been loyal, and I am deeply grateful." Atia didn't look at him. "But it's not your sword I have need of. It's your ability to counsel Cleo that I need."

"Cleo?" He frowned and shook his head in puzzlement. "What's wrong with Cleo?"

"At the moment, nothing. But there's something I have to tell her, and she's going to need to talk to someone. I want that person to be you." Desperation and pain echoed in Atia's words as she continued to look out the window. "The two of you are as close as natural-born siblings. She respects your opinion, and it's why you're the only one I can turn to."

"What makes you think Cleo isn't going to want to talk to you?"

"Because I've lied to her."

He drew in a sharp breath. Cleo had her idiosyncrasies, but the one thing she couldn't tolerate was when someone lied to her. It infuriated her, and true to her Italian roots, she stubbornly refused to even acknowledge the person's existence afterward. In only one or two rare cases had he ever seen her relent. She'd rather someone confess their sins up front than lie about it. Maybe Atia's lie was fairly harmless, but from the look on her face, he knew otherwise.

"What did you lie to her about?"

"Her father."

"I thought her father was dead." Puzzled, he frowned at her.

"No, I simply let her and everyone else believe that," Atia whispered as she turned to face him. "Her father is very much alive and well."

For a moment, he wasn't sure he'd heard her correctly. Cleo's father was alive? Why would Atia hide something like that from her daughter?

"Why did you keep it a secret?" he asked.

"Because I was trying to protect her. Marcus and I were no longer together by the time I learned I was pregnant with Cleo. I'd already lost one . . . I knew that if anyone found out she was Marcus's daughter she'd be in danger."

"Are we talking about the same Marcus the Sicari Lord was referring to last night?"

"The Sicari Lord you met last night *was* Marcus."

He stiffened as he met Atia's anguished look. What the hell was she saying? That Cleo was the daughter of a Sicari Lord? *Merda*, Cleo was an exceptional fighter, but his friend's abilities were pretty much nonexistent. On occasion, she could sense danger, but even that talent was random and sporadic at best.

"But Cleo doesn't have the abilities of a Sicari Lord."

"Not every child does. It's like most genetic traits. Sometimes a child might look like their parents and other times they don't. Cleo never exhibited any sign of special abilities like her father or her . . . but she's very much like him in other ways."

The slight stumble in her response made him study her carefully, but she averted her gaze. She wasn't telling him everything, but he didn't have the right to press her for anything more than she was willing to share.

"So after all these years, why tell her the truth now?"

"Because he wants to see her."

"Are you telling me that after all this time he's suddenly taken an interest in her?" he snapped.

Sicari Lord or not, the *bastardo* didn't have the right to just waltz back into Cleo's life like this, expecting her to welcome him back with open arms. The *Vigilavi* he knew on the Chicago police force had harsh words for deadbeat dads, and he was certain they'd have a few choice words for Marcus, Sicari Lord or not. Atia pressed her fingertips to her temples and closed her eyes as if she were in pain.

"He didn't even know about her until this morning," she whispered.

Guilt and remorse riddled her response. For whatever reason, she'd chosen not to tell the man about Cleo, but he could tell she was paying a heavy price for it now. He reached up to rub the back of his neck. This was one hell of a mess, and his friend was going to have her mother's head for it.

Merda, this was something Cleo might never forgive her mother for. His gaze met Atia's, and he realized she was thinking the same thing. A soft noise broke from her as she turned away from him. *Christus*, what was he supposed to do now? He sure as hell couldn't reassure her that everything was going to be all right.

"Do you want me to be there when you tell her?"

"No. I have to do this myself. But thank you." Atia straightened her spine and dragged in a deep breath but didn't turn around. "Go. I believe you have a briefing in a few minutes."

"Is there anything I can do for you?"

He didn't like seeing her like this. There was an aura of defeat about her that reminded him that she wasn't just *Prima Consul*, she was a woman who had limits, just like everyone else.

"Go, Lysander. I'll be fine." The command was unmistakable, but he heard the quiver in her voice. She was in pain, and he didn't know how to help her. "*Now*."

Without another word, he left her alone.

Chapter 17

GABRIEL Russo stared at the marble chess set in front of him. He was losing. The fact pissed him off so much he wanted to kill the next person who entered the room. Glaring at the board, he carefully studied the pieces left.

"I believe it's your move, Gabriel."

He looked up at the man sitting across from him as Nicostratus's voice rose upward to echo quietly against the cathedral ceiling. The library was one of his adoptive father's favorite rooms. He wasn't sure if it was the enormous room's intimidating effect on anyone who entered or if Nicostratus simply enjoyed the intricately carved mahogany woodwork that lined the walls and bookshelves in the room.

Carvings that even by his measure of hate for the Sicari seemed a bit extreme. During childhood, this room had always made him uneasy with its frightening depictions of heretics being tortured for their sins. Nicostratus was watching him with his usual detached amusement that irritated him a lot more than he cared to admit. A thin veneer of contempt had always lain beneath his father's affection for him. If one could call it affection. It had always made him feel he was unworthy of the name Russo.

"I'm thinking," he said between clenched teeth. Across from him, Nicostratus sighed heavily.

"Either make a move or forfeit the game, Gabriel."

Without touching his king, Gabriel turned it on its side to signal his acceptance of defeat. A chuckle rumbled in Nicostratus's chest. It wasn't a pleasant sound. But then his father had always enjoyed reminding him that he was not a true Praetorian despite his abilities or his loyalty. Maybe he should show his father exactly how powerful he was. The thought made him bite down on the inside of his cheek. He should feel gratitude, not anger toward his father.

Nicostratus was the reason he was still alive. The man had rescued him from his real father. Taken him before Marcus Vorenus, the Sicari Lord, could sacrifice him to his pagan gods. He owed his adoptive father his life. And the *bastardo* never let him forget it. Nicostratus arched an eyebrow at him and glanced down at the chess piece on its side.

"You were distracted during our game." The unspoken question behind the statement was one he knew he was required to answer.

"I encountered an unusual Sicari couple last week at Hadrian's temple. They've been on my mind of late."

"I imagine they're part of that small contingent of Sicari who are searching for the *Tyet of Isis*. That pagan whore who gave birth to you is with them."

There was a note of sadistic amusement in Nicostratus's voice. He ignored it. That and the slight twinge that came at the mere mention of his mother. Growing up, he'd always harbored a secret wish that he could hear from her lips why she would let his birth father sacrifice him in one of the Sicari's heretic rituals.

He'd not outgrown that secret wish. Even after all these years, he still wanted to know why. The tentacles of Nicostratus's thoughts slowly slid into his head. He easily held the man's probing at bay, biting back a satisfied smile as he sensed his father's angry frustration. The older man withdrew from his head as a cruel smile curled his lips.

"Interesting, you've enhanced and strengthened control of your telepathic ability over the last several months."

"You've taught me well . . . Father," he said quietly as he watched Nicostratus realign the chess pieces on the board.

Nicostratus winced at the paternal reference. Gabriel tried to ignore the pain it caused him, but he couldn't. It was like the tip of that unmentionable's sword grazing across his stomach again. The heretic was the first fighter outside the brotherhood to lay a blade on him, but that humiliation was nothing compared to the lack of approval by the man who'd raised him.

He locked his jaw in a deliberate effort to keep his expression neutral. The last thing he wanted was for Nicostratus to know how much he needed the man's blessing. One day he'd find a way to make the man proud of him, and then there'd be no doubt about his loyalty to the Praetorian brotherhood.

"Tell me, Gabriel, what was so unusual about this couple you met?" Clearly uninterested in whatever response he received, Nicostratus finished righting the chess set then stood up and carried it back to the library shelf where it had been kept since Gabriel was a boy.

"The woman is a healer."

"That's not unusual among Sicari females." The bored sneer in the man's voice made him grit his teeth.

"This one is special." The quiet conviction in his voice made his father turn toward him with an expression of curiosity on his face.

"Special? How?"

"Her ability is the strongest I've ever come across. While probing her mind, I saw how she brought the Zale woman back from the brink of death. I believe she is quite valuable."

"Are you referring to the incident with Granby in Chicago?"

"Yes." He ignored the unspoken criticism he heard in his father's question. It had been a mistake to hire Granby. His mistake. And he was still paying for it months later.

"You have a name?"

The question made him nod as he reached into his robe pocket for a slip of paper. It seemed almost sacrilegious to give heretics names. He knew he was an exception among his brother Praetorians when it came to his fastidious avoidance of speaking the name of any unmentionable. Giving them names always made him feel unclean. He handed the paper to his father, who took it from him with a sigh of exasperation.

"Phaedra DeLuca. That name has a familiar ring." His father frowned then shook his head in agreement. "Perhaps you're correct. A woman with that kind of ability would most assuredly breed several strong healers."

"Normally we would have to wait until she bears a child to have something to motivate her to heal. But I believe we can motivate her from the moment we bring her to the basilica."

"Exactly what do you have in mind?" For the first time ever, there was a hint of something in the man's voice that made him think he'd finally earned a small bit of approval. He shrugged off the thought.

"The unmentionable she was with. He means a great deal to her."

"How does that help us?" The approval vanished.

"She loves the fighter. I believe she's willing to do anything to protect him."

"Hmm, possibly. But we have a limited supply of *Potior* for keeping the warrior sedated. We can't afford to waste what we have simply in an effort to force the female to heal our wounded."

"Then perhaps we should breed the two of them. Their offspring could strengthen the foundation of the Praetorian brotherhood."

"What makes you think we need a heretic Sicari fighter and his whore to strengthen our bloodline?"

The contempt in Nicostratus's voice filled him with resentment as he stood up to face the man who'd raised him. The note of disgust in his father's voice was a reminder that his blood was Sicari as well. Would the man feel the same way about the Sicari warrior? He bit the inside of his cheek as the answer pounded through his head. He looked his adoptive father in the eye.

"Their offspring would be your grandchildren. The Sicari warrior is your *bastardo* son."

The stunned look on his adoptive father's face tugged a bitter smile to Gabriel's lips as he watched the older man's expression evolve into something akin to pleasure. The man actually seemed pleased by the announcement. He should have known it would be that way.

"So Lysander Condellaire has come to the place of his conception." The way his father said the unmentionable's name sickened him.

"Shall I arrange for their capture?"

"But of course," Nicostratus said with a pleased smile. "Well done, my son. Well done."

The unexpected praise sent a jolt of pleasure sailing through him as he bowed his head toward the man who'd raised him. As he straightened, he realized that Nicostratus wasn't even looking at him. He grew rigid with anger. His father wasn't pleased with him. The son of a bitch was pleased that the unmentionable was here in Rome.

A dark fury snarled its way into his limbs as he wheeled about on his heel and strode out of the library. He'd see that unmentionable dead first before he'd bring that piece of shit within spitting distance of the church. All these years, he'd always done everything his father had asked, and not once had the man given any indication that he was proud of him. And now, after all this time, this fuck had the balls to take pride in the actions of an unmentionable over him.

The door to the library thudded closed behind him, and he stood there dragging in deep gulps of air as he struggled to keep from going back into that room to kill the bastard outright. It would be a stupid thing to do. One didn't kill a Patriarch of the Collegium without consequences. They'd send Alessandro, or worse, Silvestro, after him.

He was strong enough to beat Alessandro, but Silvestro was by far the most powerful of all the Praetorian Dominus. He didn't stand a chance against him. Death was an inevitable fact of life, but *exsilium* was far worse. He wasn't about to risk his soul for Nicostratus Russo. The Collegium and the Church were his life. Without them, he was nothing.

Footsteps whispered across the stone floor of the priory's main hall, their owner headed in his direction. James. The boy had been fucking one of the women in the Sicari installation for weeks now, which meant they had access to Phaedra DeLuca. The young man came into view, and he walked toward his novitiate. Wrapping his arm around James's shoulders, he turned him around so they headed back in the direction the young man had just come from.

"Well?"

"The *Vigilavi* would never willingly betray those they serve, Your Grace, but Irini's mind is like an open book. Everything she knows is information we can use to monitor the movements of the Sicari."

"Good, good. I'm quite pleased with your work, James."

Filled with glee at the thought of having access to the inner sanctum of the Sicari facility, he decided he would allow James open access to the bitch his father had brought into the seraglio over a year ago. The woman had given birth to a female child three months ago, and it was time they bred her again.

"Irini knows nothing about the *Tyet of Isis*. But she's overheard the Sicari discussing a number of monuments in the lower Forum area. I believe they're focusing their search in that vicinity."

"Excellent. I have another task for you. I want to know whatever this Irini of yours knows about Phaedra DeLuca."

"As you wish, sir. I'm seeing Irini again tonight."

The seemingly innocent comment gave him pause, and he eyed the younger man closely. James had been seeing quite a bit of the woman of late. It would be a shame if the boy had succumbed to temptation. It was against Praetorian law to form attachments with a woman. Sex for pleasure's sake or procreation was encouraged, but anything else meant severe consequences.

He would hate to have to kill James just when the boy was proving so useful. When the young man looked at him, there was a hint of awe in James's face that wiped away his suspicion. The boy was a devout pupil. The idea of James feeling anything for this Irini woman was clearly misplaced.

"Then let's hope this female of yours provides us with useful information. The Patriarch has taken a special interest in your efforts, and I would like to give him a positive report of your progress by the end of the week."

"Thank you, sir. Oh, I almost forgot. There was one small thing. It was barely a memory, but Irini heard someone mentioning the Circus Maxentius. Perhaps we should have it watched?"

"Hmm, no. I doubt it's of any importance."

The minute he said no, something inside him revolted. He frowned as they continued walking along the stone corridor of the Collegium's basilica. Perhaps he'd been too hasty in his dismissal of the minute piece of information. The unmentionables *had* been visiting a great many of the old monuments.

"I imagine you're correct, sir." James bobbed his head in agreement. "As I said, it was a small thing."

"But then good things come in small packages, don't they,

James?" He smiled at his novitiate. "I think your suggestion to watch the Circus Maxentius is an excellent one. Have one of the younger novices keep an eye on it, but only at night. The unmentionables will want to explore the ruins unencumbered by tourists or police."

"Yes, sir."

"Now then, I have a surprise for you. Your work has been exceptional to date, and I believe you're entitled to a reward. I intend to give you access to the unmentionable in the seraglio."

"The bitch that tries to kill every Praetorian who comes near her?"

The excitement in the boy's voice made him smile. There wasn't a single Praetorian in the Rome Collegium who hadn't wanted to be the first to fuck the unmentionable and emerge without receiving a scratch or bite. To date, not one Praetorian had succeeded in using the female and emerging unscathed. She was a wildcat.

He'd contemplated putting his own prick between her legs a number of times, but the idea of soiling himself in such a way repulsed him. James, however, seemed eager to take on the challenge. Clearly, his young protégé was hoping to be the first to tame the bitch. The boy was enthusiastic enough that he might actually succeed where others failed.

In a way, he admired the unmentionable's refusal to give in to her fate. But the child would no doubt change things now. The females allowed their connection to their infants to control them. No doubt, the female would willingly roll over for James the minute he offered her a chance to see the child.

Would the unmentionable healer be like that? Would she fight him just as fiercely? He was certain she would. The thought excited him. He would be the first to have her, and no one else would touch her until he was finished with her. There was something about Phaedra DeLuca that called to him. It wasn't just her skills he wanted.

He remembered the way she'd shuddered beneath his mental touch. It had made him rock hard touching her the way he had. She was a prize he wanted badly. Like the rook in a chess game, he was eager to capture her. The only thing standing in his way was a knight and a king. The knight he could finish off easily.

He'd almost succeeded the other night, except for the interference of the king of all unmentionables. Marcus Vorenus. His muscles knotted under his robe. The time had come for Vorenus to pay for his crimes. The crime of sacrificing a small boy. He would make the *bastardo* pay for what he'd done.

Chapter 18

TIBER RIVER, ITALY
OCTOBER 28, 312 A.D.

THE screams of dying men filled his ears as he wheeled his horse about on its haunches and raced along the rear line of the Praetorians he commanded. His men were being slaughtered, and with their backs to the Tiber River, there were few options to choose from when it came to saving them.

Damn Maxentius to Tartarus for destroying the Pontis Milvian. He'd told the bastard they'd need the bridge if something went wrong. But the incompetent fool had been so confident of a victory he'd refused to listen. The emperor had ordered the stone bridge destroyed, and next to the remains, he'd built a flimsy wooden structure that was unlikely to hold up under the weight of the men, let alone the ration wagons.

As he raced toward the nearest cohort, an image of Cass filled his head. Jupiter's Stone, she was going to be a widow despite his promises to her. No. He wasn't ready to give up that easily. He wasn't going to leave Cass or Demetri to the likes of that traitor, Octavian. He tugged on the reins and the animal carrying him slid to a halt at the rear of the first company in the cohort.

"Retreat," he shouted as his prefect turned toward him. A split second later, the man sank to his knees with an arrow jutting out of his throat. The soft whistle accompanying the deadly shaft said there were more on the way. Cak. "Testudo. Now."

The minute he roared the command, the men threw up their

shields and moved quickly into formation, their armor creating a tortoiselike shell to protect them. The whistling sound grew louder, and he growled with anger at the arrows flying toward his men. Just before the projectiles reached him, he threw up an invisible shield to block the arrows from touching him or his horse. In front of him, several missiles found targets through cracks in the turtlelike formation, filling the air with more screams of pain, but most of the men had survived.

"Where's the centurion?" The din of the ongoing battle was so loud he wasn't sure any of the men had heard his shout. A soldier pushed his way out of the small company to slam a fist against his chest before flinging his arm outward in a salute.

"The centurion is dead, Legatus."

"Not any more he's not. You're promoted to the rank of centurion," he roared. "Now get these men down to the riverbank and get across the Tiber the best way you can. Regroup at the Porta Flaminia."

He didn't wait for the man to answer as he urged his horse forward to the next small company. At each group of soldiers, he ordered retreat. The air was thick with dust and smoke the closer he got to the bridge. Constantine had closed the gap between his army and Maxentius's Second Legion, positioning catapults within striking distance of the front line.

Flaming missiles from the massive weapons sent men scattering like roaches exposed to light as the deadly balls of fire fell from the sky. With the line broken, it was impossible to hold off the advancing army. The fighting had not yet reached the river, and he saw two of his tribunes directing the retreat across the makeshift structure that barely passed for a bridge.

Men staggered their way across the less-than-sturdy planks, while horses, some with riders, swam against the strong current in their effort to reach the opposite shore. Carefully, he negotiated his way through the carnage to where his tribunes were shouting orders in first one direction and then another. Quinton was the first to see him.

"Cak, what are you still doing here! You said you were going to cross more than an hour ago."

"I was detained. How many have crossed?"

"Two cohorts."

"Two," he exclaimed as his gut twisted. Less than a thousand men out of almost fifty thousand.

"Maximus, you must cross the river now. The Praetorian Guard won't follow anyone but you. And you need to ensure the Tyet of Isis doesn't fall into Octavian's traitorous hands."

"Maxentius—"

"The emperor is dead," Quinton shouted, his horse rearing up as a ball of fire hit the ground near the bridge. "The battle is lost. You must go now. Crispian and I shall meet you at the Porta Flaminia as planned."

He hesitated and looked over his shoulder at the chaos behind him. The cohorts he'd ordered to fall back and cross the river were doing just as he'd instructed. But in all the chaos that reigned, he doubted many of them would survive the crossing. With a sharp nod at the tribune, he steered his horse down the riverbank and into the water. The Tyet of Isis was the last thing he was worried about at the moment. Praise the gods he'd managed to convince Maxentius to let him hide the precious box. At least it was safe for the moment.

Another fireball shot through the air to land directly on the rickety bridge. The sickly smell of burning flesh and death clung to him like sweat. Steeling himself to look back in Quinton's direction, he saw his young tribune struggling to bring his horse under control. He started to go back when another fireball landed directly on top of his friend.

His gut twisted at the horrific sight. It was too late for his friend. The only thing he could do was continue toward the south bank and retreat to the Porta Flaminia. From there he'd be able to take stock of what was left of Maxentius's army and what sort of terms he could secure for the men. Shrieks of agony and terror filled the air as he urged his stallion into deeper water. All around him, men struggled to swim their way to the opposite shore amidst a growing number of bodies in the water.

Although tired, his large horse carried him safely to the south bank of the river. Here the chaos was muted. Whether out of years *of habit or orders, the men who'd survived the crossing had fallen into rows of four men across as they trudged their way along the Via Flaminia back to Rome.*

The road that led to Cass and Demetri. They were his sanctuary from all this death and destruction. Vesta help him if anything happened to either of them. A shout off to his left made him turn his head, and he saw Crispian riding toward him. The man saluted as he pulled his horse to a halt then grasped his arm in greeting.

"Praise the gods you're still alive. When I saw Quinton fall, I was certain you had joined him in the Elysium Fields."

"I am apparently harder to kill than most." They were words he'd repeated to Cass time and again, but he never intended to say them to her again.

This was his last battle. He was through. It wasn't just the defeat they'd suffered here, it was the unnecessary carnage. Most importantly, it was Octavian's betrayal. The traitor had broken rank and taken one cohort of the Praetorian Guard and thousands of other soldiers with him to join Constantine's ranks. The son of a bitch had pitted brother against brother today. And he'd not rest until Octavian was dead.

Another shout filled the air, and he turned his head to see Tevy riding toward him. An icy chill slithered down his back. He'd left the tribune in Rome to monitor the mood of the Senate and ensure the safety of his family. The fact that he was here meant only one thing. Something bad had happened. The man brought his horse to a skidding halt, his expression grim.

"The mood of the city is unstable, and I fear the domina and the child are in grave danger, il mio signore."

His most trusted tribune's words made him colder than the October waters of the Tiber had. Hands already stiff from the chilly river crossing, he went rigid as he considered the ramifications of what had happened. Crispian, his horse fidgeting until he forced the animal to walk in a tight circle, jerked his head in the direction of Rome.

"If your family is in danger, then mine and the others are as well. We both know what will happen to the children if Octavian finds them first."

"He will not let them live," Maximus whispered to himself.

Demetri and the other children had the blood of Praetorian sires flowing through their veins. Praetorian fathers who'd taken the potion Alexander had brought back from India. If they'd inherited any abilities from their fathers, they would be a threat to Octavian and Constantine. Already his own son was showing great strength when it came to moving objects and reading minds. He knew Crispian's children had displayed similar qualities.

"We must get them out of Rome," Crispian said grimly.

His tribune was right. The children had to be protected at all costs. He met Crispian's worried gaze and nodded.

"How many families do you think are still in the city?"

"At least twenty, I cannot say for certain." The tribune's features were dark with worry.

"Take what's left of the cavalry. Get as many of the families as you can out of Rome and head for Civitavecchia. Take only what you can carry. My wife's aunt has an estate there. You'll find sanctuary there until you're able to move northward to Tevy's estate in Genova."

"What about you?" Crispian asked in a sharp tone. *"You're the strongest of us all, except for Octavian. We cannot afford to lose you."*

"No. We cannot afford to lose the children." He ignored the way every part of him was shouting for him to go in Crispian's stead, but his duty was here. *"I will lead the men back to Rome. We should reach the Porta Flaminia in less than three hours. Once there, I'll negotiate . . . terms of surrender."*

Both men stared at him in grim acknowledgment of their defeat. It was the first time in all the years they'd known each other that they'd suffered such a blow. Still Crispian hesitated.

"Come with us. Constantine will grant the men immunity. The officers are the threat, especially those of us who've drunk the potion."

"My duty lies here. Now go." He sent his old friend a look that told the man it was a command.

With an abrupt nod, Crispian immediately urged his horse into a gallop. As the tribune rode away, Tevy waited in silence for his orders.

"Take four men from my personal guard with you back to Rome." Maximus pointed toward a small contingent of soldiers a short distance away. "I want my wife and son out of the city as quickly as possible. You know Octavian will go after them first."

"If necessary, I will give my life to save them." His friend's heartfelt words created a knot in Maximus's throat.

"You are a loyal friend, Tevy."

"We have known each other for many years. I do not believe destiny is finished with us yet." With a sharp salute, Tevy rode away to do as he'd been ordered.

As Maximus watched his friend ride off, he prayed that Vesta granted him the wish to see Cassiopeia and their son again. He turned to face the Tiber River. On the north side of the water, the fighting had pushed many soldiers into the river. With no place to run, they were being cut down like animals. Resolve locked his jaw into place. There was nothing he could do for those poor bastards. But as for the men on the south bank, he could get them safely back to Rome.

With a loud cry, he dug his heels into the sides of his horse and began the task of reorganizing what was left of Maxentius's army. It was an arduous job. More than two-thirds of his Praetorians had either defected or were dead. It forced him to rely on the centurions to get the companies into order. It took almost four hours to reach the Porta Flaminia, and when they arrived, a small contingent of men bearing the symbol Constantine had carried into battle greeted them.

The sight of the banner, with its P and X intertwined on the white cloth, fluttering in the breeze, made his gut clinch with resignation. He should have done as Crispian said. He should have returned to Rome for Cass. Instead, he'd sealed his fate as a prisoner that Constantine would eventually put to death. One of the new emperor's representatives rode out to meet him, and he pulled his horse up short, waiting for the rider to reach him.

"Legatus Maximus Caecilius Atellus?"

He answered the question with a nod and waited for the man to continue. With the traditional Roman salute, the soldier handed him a scroll of parchment.

"*Emperor Constantine extends his greetings and wishes to assure you there will be no repercussions for any supporters of Maxentius. He asks that you meet with Legatus Octavian to discuss the disbandment of the Praetorian Guard.*"

His fingers curled around the scroll, crushing it. Empathy swept across the soldier's face, but the man said nothing. Aware he needed to respond, he offered the man an abrupt nod.

"I accept the . . . Emperor Constantine's offer." He swallowed the fury rising inside him at the thought of having to report to a traitor. "Where might I find Legatus Octavian?"

"He's dealing with some unrest in the city. Several of the more fanatical Church followers are threatening to burn several citizens at the stake."

"I thought you said there would be no repercussions," he snarled. "I hardly call burning someone at the stake a display of benevolence."

"The mob's actions are not condoned by the emperor," the man said stiffly. "Legatus Octavian has gone to stop the slaughter."

The words were like icy water streaming through his blood. The man didn't know Octavian was a fanatic follower of the Nazarene. He wouldn't hesitate to burn heretics who refused to convert to his way of thinking. The man hadn't gone to stop the mob, he'd gone to watch. A sudden image of Cass filled his head, and for a moment, he could have sworn he'd heard her call out his name.

The sound had been so real, he found himself surveying the landscape in hopes that she was somewhere close by. When he didn't see her, his mind closed around the fact that Octavian wanted the Tyet of Isis, and he'd do anything to get it. He stopped himself. Not even Octavian had the colei to murder a senator's daughter. He ignored the voice inside him that said otherwise.

"Then perhaps I might return home and make myself presentable for the Legatus."

"Of course." Once again, understanding flashed across the man's face as he nodded. "We'll see that your men are fed and the wounded cared for."

There was a sympathetic note in the young man's voice that indicated his sincerity. It made it that much harder to accept the man's *offer. Hate he could deal with, but not this quiet concern from the enemy. He swallowed hard, and with a few instructions to the lead centurion, he nudged his horse forward. The Porta Flaminia grew closer, and he'd almost reached the gate when a familiar figure rode out of the city at breakneck speed. Tevy. His heart stopped as he acknowledged the fact that Cass and Demetri weren't with the tribune. He sagged in the saddle. They were gone, and he'd never felt so alone in his life.*

LYSANDER shot upright in bed with a shout. His heart pounded like a freight train in his chest as he gasped for air. Almost immediately, a pair of soft arms wrapped their way around his shoulders and waist as Phaedra pressed her warmth into his side. She wasn't gone. She was here with him. He hadn't lost her. Her hand stroked the back of his neck as she pressed her lips against his bare shoulder.

It was a tender touch that made him realize what Maximus had lost. A shudder rippled through him. The battle he'd just seen was haunting in its sharp clarity and vivid imagery. He understood death, although he'd never seen anything on this grand a scale before. It had been so real he could still smell the stench of it.

It had sickened him then just as much as it did now. The thought made him stiffen. It was a Freudian slip—nothing more. But the battle wasn't the most horrifying part of the dream. He'd seen, felt, what Maximus had experienced when his tribune had rode out of the Flaminia Gate to meet him. The man's wife and son were dead.

"Hush, *carino*, shhh. It was just a bad dream." Her voice soothed him, but it didn't lessen the ache deep inside.

"He lost them," he whispered.

"What are you talking about, *caro*? Who lost who?"

"Maximus. I saw him when he received the news that Cassiopeia and Demetri were dead."

He gently broke free of her embrace and fell backward into the pillows. His eye closed, he saw the image of Tevy riding out toward Maximus. The memory of that last moment in his dream filled him with the same despair he'd experienced just before he'd woken up.

It echoed the sense of hopelessness he'd experienced the night Nicostratus had told him he was a half-breed.

If there was anything about Maximus that resonated in him,
it was that despair. The knowledge that things would never be the
same no matter what he did to atone for his choices. If Phaedra were
ever to learn his secret, she wouldn't just hate him for his tainted
blood. She'd hate him for hiding the fact from her. For making love
to her without telling her what he really was. It might not have been
a conscious choice the first time, but every time he made love to her,
he was making a choice.

For the past week and a half, he'd awakened every morning to
her nestled in his arms. He'd still not figured out what sort of ground
rules to set for their relationship. Instead, they'd simply fallen into
a comfortable, yet open-ended routine. Once they'd finished their
cataloging of monuments for the day, they'd come back to the installation, have dinner, and come back to his apartment for some quiet
time together.

She hadn't pressed him for a commitment, but he knew she would
eventually. The farther down the road the better. He needed time to
come up with a solution that would allow them a permanent relationship without the blood bond. That wasn't going to be easy to do.
Phaedra wouldn't understand his refusal to seal their relationship.
She shifted her body to lie on her side, her head propped up with her
hand, while her other hand rested on the spot where his heart was
still pounding at a quick pace.

"You said Demetri was dead." Her soft observation made him
turn his head toward her.

"Yes." He shrugged slightly. "Demetri was their son."

"How do you know that?"

The question pulled every muscle in his body taut like a wire.
He knew she still believed their dreams were interconnected, but
she'd not pressed him on the matter in several days. It seemed the
topic was officially off hiatus. Just looking at her face, he knew she'd
recognized the name Demetri. He just didn't want to know *how* she
knew the name. Her gaze narrowed on him, that lovely mouth of
hers tight with determination. He shrugged as he tried to come up

with an answer that would satisfy her and yet save him from the trap he knew lay just up ahead.

"I must have heard it somewhere."

He wasn't about to confess that this wasn't the first time he'd remembered the name. The first time had been the dream he'd had of Pha—Cassiopeia being pregnant. The images from that dream came flooding back, and he clenched his jaw. He wasn't going there.

"Where did you hear it?" Her persistence made him grimace.

"*Merda*, I don't remember," he growled.

"Of course you don't," she snapped. "That's because none of the stories we've heard ever mentioned a son or a Demetri."

"*Christus*, woman, it was just a dream. I must have heard the name somewhere and my head just threw it in for the hell of it. It doesn't mean a goddamned thing."

"Yes, it does," she said with a flash of triumph in her brown eyes. "Because in the last dream I had, I saw Maximus and Cassiopeia's son, Demetri. So tell me why our dreams mean nothing if we *both* know they had a son called Demetri?"

Okay, he hadn't seen that one coming. He immediately backpedaled and tried to come up with a response. *Il Christi omnipotentia*, the woman was relentless in her determination to make him admit a connection between the two of them and the ancient Roman couple. A small voice in the back of his head challenged him to listen to her. He squashed the idea just like he would an irritating gnat.

The ramification of believing he was Maximus to her Cassiopeia was the one place he didn't want to go. It was one thing to think reincarnation plausible, but it was something entirely different to believe his dreams were an instant replay of a past life. Dreams where he relived another life's joys, sorrows . . . mistakes.

"They're dreams, Phaedra, nothing more."

"Then how can we be dreaming about moments that aren't included in all the stories about Maximus and Cassiopeia we've heard since we were kids?"

"Such as?" he grounded out.

"Such as the fact that they had a child named Demetri."

"That's stretching it a bit thin, don't you think, *carissima*?" He released a harsh breath of exasperation. "Why are you so dead set on these dreams meaning something?"

"Because if we are Maximus and Cassiopeia, I don't want us to wind up the same way they did—one of us . . . dead and the other one left alone." Her words sent a chill down his back.

He remembered the despair Maximus had felt in his dream. Had her dreams created similar emotions in her? It would explain the fear he'd heard just now in her voice. What if he bought into her idea that they had once lived together as husband and wife in ancient Rome? It would mean he'd have to accept the possibility that he'd once lived as Maximus Caecilius Atellus. A man revered by the Sicari.

That reason right there was why he couldn't believe. Maximus's blood had been pure—untouched by the madness and the hate that flowed in the veins of the Praetorians. By the circumstance of his birth, Lysander's blood was tainted, and he wasn't even worthy of thinking he could have been Maximus. He reached out to caress her cheek.

"You're worrying about nothing, *inamorato*," he said. She turned her face into his hand, her lips grazing his palm.

"Am I? I wish I could believe that," she whispered as she met his gaze. "It's kind of hard not to worry when you hide things from me."

"What are you talking about?"

His heart skidded to a halt before it kicked into high gear. Did she know about his plan to visit the Circus Maxentius tonight with Ares and Pasquale? No, he'd been careful not to let anything slip. He studied her face closely. What he saw in her eyes scared the hell out of him. She shook her head.

"You shut me out for more than a year after that night in the warehouse. You're still shutting me out about what happened." Her whisper resounded with a pain and sorrow that ate away at his heart. But she'd just helped him figure out one of the ground rules.

"Ground rule number one. We aren't going to discuss that night. Ever," he bit out.

"*Deus*, you're a stubborn devil. You'll talk to Atia about it, but not me." Again the note of hurt in her voice. He forced himself to ignore it.

"It's over, Phaedra. It's in the past."

"No." she exclaimed in a low, fierce voice. "It's not over. You're still paying the price for what they did to you, and so am I. It doesn't matter that you've talked to Atia. It's a wall between us, and it says you don't trust me."

"*Il Christi omnipotentia*, that's not true."

"Yes it is," she snapped as she rolled away from him to stare up at the ceiling. "I hate those Praetorian *bastardi* for what they did to you. I hate them for killing my parents. Every single one of them deserves to die. No quarter given. I want *all* of them dead."

He turned toward her to see tears of pain and anger well up in her eyes. The sight sent ice sluicing through his veins. How in the hell could he ever tell her the truth? He'd made the right decision to reject her a year ago. And he'd made a grievous error to let himself believe they might have a chance now.

She was right. His secret was standing between them. It always would. She'd suffered too much at the hands of the Praetorians. There wasn't a chance in Tartarus that she'd be able to love a half-breed like him. She rolled into him, her warmth heating his skin as her lips brushed against his chest.

"I lost you that night in Englewood, Lysander. And now that I have you back, I don't think I can bear losing you again."

The heartfelt words flayed at his conscience like a whip. If she ever found out the truth . . . *Christus*, their relationship was based on nothing but lies. Except one. He loved her. That was the truth.

The alarm on his watch pierced the quiet between them, and he turned his head toward the timepiece sitting on the nightstand. He needed to meet Ares. The relief sailing through him at the thought of escaping was followed by guilt. He was running, and he wasn't proud of himself for it. But leaving her right now would give him time to try to find a solution to the problem. The minute the notion slipped into his head, he immediately knew there was only one answer. Telling her the truth. Something that would destroy them both.

In a quick move, he rolled her onto her back and kissed her. She sighed beneath him, and he lifted his head to look into her beautiful brown eyes. Instinctively he knew this happiness wouldn't last, but at this moment in time, he was the luckiest man alive. He kissed her again, then got out of bed and proceeded to dress.

"Where do you think you're going? I haven't had my way with you yet tonight," she teased lightly as her fingertips trailed their way across his bare shoulder and down his back. It was a tempting touch that appealed not only to his base needs, but the inner piece of him that adored her. He resisted the urge.

"I told Ares I'd meet him in the library."

"At this hour?"

"It's not that late." He glanced over his shoulder at her and smiled. "Take a nap."

"I'm not sleepy. When will you be back?"

"I'm not sure. That depends on Ares. But I'll be sure to wake you." He forced himself to keep his voice lighthearted, satisfied that he'd kept his answer vague enough not to arouse her curiosity.

He didn't want her figuring out that he and Ares were going to the Circus Maxentius tonight without her or Emma. Her gaze narrowed suspiciously on him, but she didn't question him as he finished dressing. With one last kiss, he left the bedroom and headed out of the small suite. The house was quiet as he made his way down to the library, which was opposite the installation's main conference room. That room was dark in contrast to the muted lighting inside the library. One light illuminated the room, and it was on the library table.

Seated at the table the *Prima Consul* generally used, Ares was bent over a book. Opposite him, Luciano Pasquale stood leaning against one of the room's bookcases. Ares looked up with a slight frown.

"Any problems?"

"No. She didn't suspect a thing," Lysander replied.

"Good. Take a look at this."

Ares gestured for him and Pasquale to join him at the library table. As they reached the table, he turned the book in front of him around so the two men could read it.

"What am I missing?" Pasquale frowned as he studied the book.

"When Angelo reported finding the four Sicari symbols out at the Circus Maxentius, it seemed odd there were so many in one place when we've only found one at each of the other locations. The fact that the first Sicari Lord was one of Maxentius's generals makes the four icons seem like a blind alley. But tell me what you make of this."

Ares tapped at the left page of the open book in front of them. Frowning, Lysander stared at the diagram his friend had pointed to. He traced his finger over the drawing of the monument's exterior walls.

"According to Angelo, the Sicari symbols were found at the two front towers," Ares said as he pointed to different locations on the diagram. "And in between the rear of the circus and the imperial box, here and here."

"If you draw lines from point to point, it forms a square," Pasquale said quietly.

"Right, and if we draw diagonal lines from point to point—" Ares arched his eyebrow as the other man interrupted him.

"X marks the spot," Pasquale said with excitement.

"*Christus*, it's more than that," Lysander exclaimed with quiet exhilaration as he looked up from the drawing to meet Ares's triumphant gaze. "That X is centered directly over the *spina*, right where the obelisk would have been."

"*Spina?* Obelisk?" Pasquale looked at the two of them with a puzzled frown.

"The *spina* is the barrier that the chariots had to race around." Lysander pointed toward the stone construction that divided the center of the circus. "There were all types of ornaments sitting on top of it, but the tallest one was the obelisk at the end of the *spina*."

"An obelisk, my beautiful wife pointed out earlier, that was dedicated to the goddess Isis." Ares grinned with elation. Struggling to restrain his own excitement, Lysander grinned back at his friend.

"I take it this means we're doing some excavation work tonight," Pasquale said. Slapping the other fighter's back with his hand, Lysander nodded.

"Absolutely." He turned back to face Ares. "Emma's going to have your head if we find something."

"Don't remind me." His friend grimaced. "But we both know it's too dangerous for her *or* Phaedra to go with us to the circus. We'll make them see that when we get back."

Beside him, Pasquale tensed and cleared his throat. "Looks like you're going to have to do your explaining now."

He looked at the Sicari fighter to see him nodding toward the library door. Whirling around, he saw Emma walking into the room followed by Phaedra. His heart dropped like a stone. Both women were dressed for a night mission, and while Emma didn't carry a sword, Phaedra wore her weapon in a scabbard on her back. The anger on their faces was evident as Emma headed straight for her husband.

"You must think I'm a half-wit," she snapped as she stopped in front of Ares. "I told you the obelisk was the center point of those four icons, and you casually brushed it off. But you knew I was right, and you planned this little trip out to the Circus Maxentius without me. Did you really think I wouldn't find out what you were up to?"

"Not until it was over," Ares bit out as he glared at his wife.

"And you thought you could just sweet-talk me into not being angry afterward?"

"No," his friend exclaimed before he grimaced. "All right, yes. But, *Christus*, Emma, it's too dangerous. Do you remember the last nighttime mission I took you on? If something happened—"

Ares didn't get a chance to finish before he landed hard on the floor with a loud thud, his feet kicked out from under him by a strong, invisible force. "Damn it, Emma."

"How many times do I have to show you that I can take care of myself, at least well enough so I can run away if I need to? You need me now, just like you did in Chicago, and you know it."

As his friend was picking himself up from the floor, Phaedra tapped Lysander on the shoulder. He immediately assumed a stoic expression as he turned to face her. Her brown-eyed gaze met his with about as much warmth as an ice storm. *Great, it was his turn.*

"So what's your excuse, Condellaire? And it had better be good," she said in a calm manner that belied the anger he saw flashing in her eyes.

A quick glance in Ares's direction showed his friend rubbing the top of his head in a plain effort to figure out a way to placate his wife for not inviting her along for the ride. Caught up in the same quandary as his friend, he reached for the first thing that came into his head.

"As *Legatus*, it's my job to select the best-qualified team members for specific assignments. I didn't choose you for this particular task." He winced at her expression. Not a good choice of words, particularly when he wasn't even sure he was worthy of his title.

"And what makes you better qualified than me to go to the Circus Maxentius in the middle of the night?" That serene note in her voice was beginning to make him uneasy. It didn't matter. As *Legatus*, he was well within his right to select who went on what missions.

"My fighting skills are superior to yours, and you know it, Phaedra."

"So my fighting skills aren't good enough for you to include me on a reconnaissance that happens to be pretty much in the heart of Praetorian territory, correct?"

It was easy to tell by the sound of her voice that she wasn't going to forgive him easily for his decision. It didn't matter. This wasn't Chicago where the Praetorians had a minor presence. This was Rome. Home base for the *bastardi* and in a deserted ruin no less—it was a hell of a lot more dangerous.

The last thing he wanted was to see something happen to her. He knew Ares felt the same way about Emma's safety. It's why his friend had agreed they wouldn't tell either of the women what they were planning.

"Yes," he said firmly as he answered her question. He knew he was right. Her fighting skills weren't even half as strong as her healing ability. The second the thought shot into his head, he knew he was doomed and he suppressed a groan.

"Right." She stepped around him to stare at first Pasquale and then Ares. "Tell me, which one of you is the healer on this mission?"

Christus, he was an idiot. He'd walked right into that one. Phaedra slowly turned back to him, her indignant expression making him feel like an ass. Hell, he'd known she'd be pissed, but like Ares, he'd figured she wouldn't find out until after the fact. He winced at her expression. Pissed was an understatement.

"Emma, let's leave the boys to their little soiree out to the Circus

Maxentius. That *is* where you're going, isn't it?" Her fiery gaze seared its way into him.

It was a statement, not a question because both women knew exactly where they were going. She headed for the door. Her back straight and rigid with anger. The next words out of her mouth horrified him.

"Emma, I think we should follow up on that Colosseum idea you had. I'm sure Cleo and Violetta wouldn't mind some fun tonight."

"I think you're right," Emma said fiercely as she made to follow her sister-in-law.

Ares didn't let his wife get far, and he heard Emma utter an oath behind him as he watched Phaedra heading toward the exit. Furious at the way Phaedra was trying to manipulate him, he waved his hand and the library door slammed shut. In the next instant, he envisioned his hand on her arm and dragged her back to him. When she was close enough, his hands bit into soft flesh as he forced her to face him.

"You're not going anywhere without me," he rasped.

"I'm glad to hear you've come to your senses about taking Emma and me with you to the circus," she purred.

"You're not—"

"Of course, we could always go rogue for a few hours." She sent him a defiant look.

"Damn it, Phaedra," Ares snapped. "Use your head."

"I am using my head, Ares. The problem is the two of you aren't using yours." She continued to glare at Lysander as she answered her brother. "You need a healer on this mission. You need Emma's archeological expertise in case you come across something *you* can't figure out, brother dear. So what's it going to be? Do we go with you or should the two of us girls plan our own little party?"

"Goddamn it, woman," Lysander growled.

She had him over a barrel, and she knew it. There wasn't any doubt in his mind that she'd do exactly what she said, and Emma would follow. As for Cleo, the woman would find it more than amusing to go rogue for a few hours the minute she heard what had happened. It wouldn't matter to Cleo what penalty she'd have to pay for doing so. And knowing Atia's sense of humor, the *Prima Consul* would find it amusing that the women had balked at the reason he and Ares had for refusing to take the two with them. It was unlikely Atia would impose even a small punishment on any of the women if they disobeyed orders to stay in the installation.

"*Merda,*" he snarled as he turned to Ares. "Suggestions?"

His friend's expression was one of furious resignation. Ares glared at his wife then his sister. "They don't leave us much choice. And I'd rather have Emma with me than worry about her traipsing around the city in the middle of the night all by herself."

"You say that as if you're the only one who worries," Emma said sharply. "Has it ever occurred to you that *I* might spend my nights worrying about *you*?"

Ares grimaced at the accusatory note in his wife's voice and released a harsh sigh. Like Ares, Lysander was growing resigned to the fact that they had little choice but to let the women come with them. He sent Phaedra a hard look before turning to Pasquale.

"Get Cleo. She'll balance out the strength of the team," he said to the other warrior. "Meet us in the garage. We'll take the Land Rovers."

The Sicari fighter nodded and hurried from the room. With the other man gone, he looked at first Emma and then Phaedra. "The two of you are going to do exactly as you're told or I'm going to see to it that Atia sends both of you to the White Cloud estate until Ares and I are done here in Rome. You got that?"

"I think we can manage that, can't we, Emma?" Phaedra said as honey dripped off every one of her words.

It set his nerves on edge, and not in a good way. If she could get this furious with him about being left out of an expedition, it was clear the minute she learned his secret her reaction would be explosive.

Chapter 11

THE cold silence filling the Land Rover made Phaedra extremely uncomfortable. She knew the two men in the front seat were furious with her and Emma, but it couldn't be helped. The idea of Lysander and her brother going out on a mission without a healer terrified her. There were a hell of a lot more Praetorians here than there were back home in Chicago.

A fact she wondered if Lysander was aware of at a subconscious level. Cleo had been right about Lysander taking more risks over the past year when it came to his fighting Praetorians. She'd gone into the Order's database and reviewed the past year's reports on missions where he'd encountered Praetorians. She was certain it was because of what had happened to him, and the thought of him taking on more risk without a healer close enough to keep him alive was terrifying. She jumped as Emma touched her arm. As she met her sister-in-law's somber gaze, Emma nodded toward the two men in the front seat.

"They'll get over it," her sister-in-law whispered with a slight smile.

She nodded. Yes, but at what cost to the precious ground she'd gained with Lysander. He was still skittish about their relationship. While everyone in the installation knew they were involved, he kept his distance from her emotionally when they were in front of others. It made her believe he didn't want to openly acknowledge they were a couple, and it stung.

Then he'd do something like he did tonight. He'd been protecting her again. She didn't like the way he'd tried to do it, but his motivation warmed her heart. There was a comforting sensation to being treated like a prized possession he needed to protect. It irritated the hell out of her, but she couldn't deny that there was a part of her that liked his authoritative manner. It made up for some of the distance he maintained with her in front of others. It showed he cared, and that's what mattered the most to her.

Lysander suddenly doused the lights of the car and slowly drove about another half-mile farther down the deserted roadway before he pulled off the pavement and proceeded to back the car into a large expanse of foliage until vegetation partially engulfed the vehicle. As he shut off the engine, he shifted in his seat to look at her and Emma.

"Don't forget what I said," he said in a terse tone. "I'll have Atia send you back to White Cloud so fast it'll make your heads spin if you step out of line tonight. *Capicse?*"

Beside her, Emma nodded, and she did the same. The look he gave her seemed particularly harsh compared to the look he'd given Emma. How long would it take him to get over being angry with her? At least as long as it took for them to get out of the Circus Maxentius without incident. Fear for her safety was driving his anger, just as her fear for him drove her to insist on coming with him. He was nervous about the possibility of running into Praetorians, and she understood that.

It wasn't exactly something she was hoping for, but she sure as hell wouldn't mind killing one or two of the *bastardi* for all the pain they'd caused the two of them. With a grunt of irritation, Lysander looked at Ares and jerked his head toward a high wall across the street.

"Let's do this." His sharp command made her wince as he got out of the car.

She slipped out of the backseat of the vehicle and closed the door with a quiet thud. In the darkness, the black Land Rover blended in with the foliage, concealing the vehicle to the point that it would go unnoticed by passing cars. Directly beside them, Luciano had parked in the same way, and she saw Cleo getting out of the second Land Rover's front seat. Cleo sent her a conspiratorial wink as her friend took in Lysander's grim expression.

Overhead, clouds drifted across the moon, affording them just enough light to see without making them obvious targets when they had to cross the ground between them and the circus wall. With everyone gathered around him, Lysander nodded toward the stone fence.

"Okay, we've got a mixture of brush and open ground to cover before we reach the circus wall. Phaedra? Anything?" He looked at her in a clear indication he wanted to know if she sensed any Praetorian presence. When she shook her head, he gave her a sharp nod. "All right, let's move fast and stay alert."

No one questioned his orders as the team quickly crossed the two-lane highway and headed toward the stone façade that had once housed thousands of spectators. It took several minutes of a steady jog to reach the wall surrounding the ruins. Lysander motioned for Luciano to go over the wall first, and then Cleo. While it would have been easier to move farther down the length of the structure to find an opening in the crumbling wall, she knew it would waste precious time. As the two fighters vanished over the wall, he turned his head toward his shoulder.

"Cleo, Pasquale. Status?" Lysander's voice echoed softly in her ear through the surveillance gear she wore just like everyone else.

"All clear," Cleo said in a soft voice.

At the confirmation, Lysander nodded at Ares and Emma. Less than thirty seconds later, Ares used his telekinetic ability to effortlessly lift Emma up over his head until her hands grabbed at the top of the surface. As her sister-in-law disappeared over the stone barrier, Lysander turned to her.

The harsh expression he'd been wearing in the car hadn't softened as he gestured for her to step into the saddle stirrup he made of his hands. She suppressed a sigh of resignation. If the man thought to make her regret her decision to force his hand in bringing her with him, he was mistaken. She wasn't going to let him out of her sight if she could help it.

She stepped forward, and with a small hop into the makeshift step he offered her, she allowed him to propel her upward to the top of the wall. In seconds, she landed on the opposite side, with Lysander and Ares following her in short order.

Stretched out before them was the wide expanse that had once served as a track for chariot races. In the middle were the remains of what had been the *spina*. Emma looked at Lysander and nodded in the direction of the barrier that ran down the middle of the huge, oval track.

"The obelisk would have been at that end, closest to the imperial box," she said quietly as she surveyed what was left of the *spina*. "There's not much left in the way of a good foundation, but hopefully the *Tyet of Isis* is still here."

"Phaedra." Lysander didn't look at her, but her entire body vibrated when he spoke her name. He didn't have to ask the question for her to know he wanted a confirmation of her earlier assessment of any Praetorian presence.

"Nothing. If there's a Praetorian anywhere nearby, they're exceptional at disguising their whereabouts."

She saw him go rigid at her response, and she frowned. It was almost as if he were expecting trouble. He nodded sharply.

"Pasquale, you're to help Emma with that folding shovel of yours. The rest of us will stand guard."

Not needing a direct order, the team moved quickly along the remains of the stone divider running down the middle of the circus. The length of the barrier was almost a quarter of a mile long, and as they reached the end, she was marveling at the engineering that had to have gone into the immense complex.

The clouds parted slightly as they reached the end of the stone divide. Emma knelt on the ground and illuminated the stones in front of her with a small penlight. Over the next hour, Emma examined every inch of the ruins at her feet. Occasionally, she'd mutter to herself as she studied the stone foundation. The sudden sound of her sharp inhale made the entire team turn in her direction.

"Give me the shovel." With a sharp gesture at Pasquale, she extended her hand for the tool. Luciano unfolded the small spade and handed it to her. Ares took a couple of steps closer to her.

"You found something, *inamorato*?" Phaedra could hear the excitement in her brother's voice as he leaned down slightly over his wife.

"It's a metal plate of some sort directly beneath this stone." Emma said as she gently scraped away at the dirt surrounding the granite.

"Wouldn't someone have seen it before now?" Pasquale's cynicism matched Phaedra's.

"No. It was covered with the mud they used for mortar." Emma worked carefully to scoop away dirt from under the stone as she continued her explanation. "Whoever put it here had to have dug under the original marble that encased the *spina* and shoved it under the stone. It might just be a marker or something the engineers used, too. I won't be sure until I can look at it."

The excitement in the group resonated across Phaedra's senses. She knew everyone was hoping they were going to find the *Tyet of Isis*, but under that exhilaration was a tension that made her nervous as hell. There was a familiarity to it she didn't like. She slowly turned to study the large, open expanse they were in. Nothing seemed out of place or odd, but the sensation that something was wrong grew inside her. In that instant, Lysander was beside her.

"What is it?"

"I'm not sure. It just doesn't feel right."

He didn't wait for further details. He simply dipped his head toward the mike he wore on his shoulder. "Emma, we don't have time to be cautious here. Dig fast."

As she turned back toward her brother and sister-in-law, Phaedra caught a glimpse of movement at one of the main towers that stood at one end of the circus. Her nerve endings screamed a warning, and she automatically drew her sword. The minute she did so, the soft whisper of other swords leaving their leather casings echoed in her ears.

She took a couple of steps toward the tower as the clouds parted so the moon could illuminate the landscape. The shadowy figure moving near the tower made her suck in her breath with relief. A cow. *Il Christi omnipotentia*, it was just a cow. All around her, she could sense the relief, and she was certain it was Cleo whose amusement was filtering through the group's sudden release of tension. Behind her, she heard her sister-in-law's exclamation of triumph and turned back toward her at the same time as the rest of the small party.

"Got it," Emma said with a strong note of satisfaction. Her fingers gently brushed across the dirt-encrusted metal as Ares's hand caught his wife's elbow and pulled her to her feet.

"You can look at it later," he said gruffly. Despite the brusque note of concern in his voice, there was a hint of pride as well.

Lysander nodded at Ares's statement. "Okay, we got what we came for, so let's move."

"And what if it *isn't* what we came for? At least let me figure out what I'm holding." The moonlight illuminated Emma's stubborn expression as she glared up at Ares. The minute she saw her brother hesitate, Phaedra nodded.

"She's right. If it's not what we came for, we'll have to do this all over again. We're here, let's finish it." She met Lysander's hard gaze steadily. They both knew Emma was right, but she could tell he didn't want to admit it.

"*Va bene,*" he snapped with a note of disgust in his voice. "Quickly. The longer we stay here, the greater our chances of running into trouble."

Emma hadn't waited for his approval and had already pulled a small brush from the backpack she carried. She thrust her penlight into her husband's hand and forced him to hold it so the light shone on the metal plate's encrusted surface.

"Damn it, it's all in Latin. Give me a tablet of hieroglyphs, and I can rattle it off like the alphabet," Emma sighed with disgust as she looked up at her husband. "Latin never held any interest for me, until I met you, *mio amor.*"

"Let me try," Ares murmured. He directed a steady beam of light down at the piece of metal as he studied the artifact Emma tilted in his direction. "The *Tyet of Isis* . . . Octavian . . . center of all that is Sicari."

Phaedra jumped the instant her brother said Octavian's name. Without thinking, she jerked her head in Lysander's direction. Did he recognize the name, too? A flash of indefinable emotion flitted across his face before he assumed the stoic look he'd perfected. It didn't matter how much he tried to hide it, she was certain he'd recognized Octavian's name and its significance.

"Who the fuck is Octavian?" Cleo asked in an irritated manner.

"*Christus*, this clue isn't any clearer than the ones we already have."

"Octavian is the Praetorian who betrayed Maxentius at the Battle of Milvian Bridge," Lysander murmured then stiffened as if suddenly realizing he'd spoken out loud.

"How do you know that?" Ares frowned as he stared at his friend in surprise, and the question made Lysander's scarred cheek muscles grow taut across his cheekbone.

"Something I read somewhere, I think." Lysander shrugged, and Phaedra was certain he made it a point not to look in her direction as he turned to Emma. "Are you satisfied this is what we came for?"

"Yes. It might not be what we were hoping to find, but it tells us we're on the right track," her sister-in-law said as Lysander nodded then glanced around at the team.

"All right, everyone. We're done here. Let's move." He sheathed his sword and waited for the others to follow suit. "Pasquale. Take point."

Like a well-oiled machine, they all turned and headed back the way they'd come. The distance between them and the wall closed rapidly as the group maintained a steady jog. Beside him, Lysander could sense Phaedra's gaze on him every few seconds. Up until he'd heard Octavian's name, his anger at the way she'd wrangled her way onto this expedition had been at a steady boil. But the instant he heard Ares read the plate, resignation, and more than a hint of panic, had replaced his anger.

The minute she got him alone, she was going to force him to admit that their dreams were interconnected. And at the moment, he didn't have a leg to stand on when it came to arguing *against* her logic. When he'd heard Octavian's name, it had been like having someone kick him in the teeth. He'd known exactly who the *bastardo* was and what he'd done to Maximus's men at that last battle.

Vivid images of Quinton being struck down by a fireball from a catapult and dead bodies floating in the Tiber River swept through his head until a chill slid down his back. They were dreams, nothing more. He knew it was a tired argument, and Phaedra wasn't about to let him dodge the bullet this time. And he sure as hell wasn't going to like admitting it either.

They were about twenty yards away from the stone façade that had once been the support for stadium seating when he heard the whisperings in his head. He abruptly came to a halt, forcing Cleo, who was behind him, to bump into him before coming to a stop as well. In a fluid motion, he pulled his sword out of its scabbard as he dipped his head toward his shoulder mike.

"We've got company." His sharp statement brought the entire group to a halt. Weapons drawn, the team formed a circle, their backs to each other with Emma in the center. Phaedra flanked him, and without taking his eyes off the wall in front of him, he tilted his body toward her. "Phaedra?"

He already knew the answer but was hoping he was wrong. There were five Praetorians on the opposite side of the wall. One of them was the piece of shit who'd assaulted Phaedra.

"He's here." Her voice didn't crack, although he could tell by the tension in her body she was frightened.

"*Who's here?*" Ares's words were like a whip cracking in the earpiece.

"*Tell him, Unmentionable.*" The Praetorian Dominus's thoughts echoed strongly in his head. "*And tell your lovely bitch that fucking her is something I'm looking forward to.*"

"*Enough, Gabriel.*" The familiar voice echoing in his head was like someone dropping him into an icy lake. Nicostratus. He went rigid as he struggled with the fear that rose up into his throat. "*Ah, I see you recognize me, my son.*"

"You are *not* my father, you sorry fuck," he snarled, refusing to give in to his terror.

"Lysander?"

Christus, he'd responded to Nicostratus out loud. How was he going to explain that? He heard the fear and bewilderment in Phaedra's voice as her hand reached out to touch his arm. The control he usually had over his telepathic ability vanished as he caught the first stirrings of horror swirling in her head. *Dulcis matris Deus*, even the tentative touch of her hand revealed her awakening realization of what he was.

The knowledge sliced into his gut with a sickening twist. To think he'd actually allowed himself to believe they stood a chance at happiness together. He drew in a sharp breath as his heart clenched painfully. The sensation couldn't have been more agonizing if someone had ripped the organ out of his chest. Not even the torture he'd endured at Nicostratus's hands had been this painful.

"Then Gabriel was right. The bitch must be quite special if you value her so highly."

Nicostratus's thoughts filtered their way into his head as two figures dressed in flowing hooded capes vaulted their way off the top of the wall in front of them. His father and the Praetorian Dominus. A moment later, three more figures followed. Fuck. Lysander grunted with angry frustration. He should have known something would go wrong tonight. He should have locked Phaedra in a closet before coming here. How in the hell was he going to keep her safe?

"You won't, Unmentionable. Have you forgotten how easily I defeated you the last time?" The Praetorian's sneer was meant to infuriate him, and he fought to keep himself from rushing forward to confront the *bastardo*.

"You still lost, didn't you?" Satisfaction rolled through him as he could read the fury in the Praetorian Dominus's mind at being reminded he'd lost to a Sicari Lord.

"There will be no avoiding justice tonight, heretic. Tonight I shall leave my mark on you, just as I have on so many others."

Lysander threw up a mental shield as the man's thoughts swarmed in his head. He was wasting his energy using his telepathy this way, and he needed all the strength he had to keep this *bastardo* out of his head. If he didn't, the Dominus would be able to easily counter any maneuver Lysander made in his effort to defeat the Praetorian. And it was going to take a hell of a lot more than brute strength.

"Defeat me?" Gabriel's mocking laughter echoed in his head. *"You truly are delusional, Unmentionable. You cannot defeat me, heretic. For your insolence, I think I'll fuck your woman slowly while forcing you to watch."*

"I told you once, and I'll tell you again, you're going to have to

go through me to get to her," Lysander snapped as he fought to fortify his mental defenses. He grimaced. It was the second time he'd
responded to Gabriel and Nicostratus out loud, and he was sealing
his fate every time he verbally answered the taunts in his head.

"Who the fuck are you talking to?" Ares bit out without looking
away from the approaching threat.

"I believe the question you should be asking my son is which
one of us is he talking to." Nicostratus's voice carried across the last
fifteen feet that separated the two adversarial parties. It was a bomb
obliterating what was left of his world.

"Son?" Pasquale spat out the word as if he'd just tasted something unpleasant.

"Yes, *my* son," Nicostratus said.

Il Christi omnipotentia, was that a note of pride in the *bastardo*'s
voice? The man's quiet laughter dragged him back into that dark pit,
while the mutilated side of his face twisted and pulled until his face
was on fire again like it had been the night Nicostratus had tortured
him. All around him, his friends muttered their disbelief.

"What the hell is he talking about, Lysander?" Ares's question
was tight with disbelief and anger. He ignored the question.

"I. Am. Sicari." He enunciated each word in an effort to believe
the statement was true. Inside he knew it was a lie.

"Oh, but we both know differently, don't we, my boy?" In the
darkness, Nicostratus's voice rumbled across the circus field like
thunder. "Show them the birthmark. The one we *both* have."

"*Christus*, is he telling the truth, Lysander?" Cleo's words
reflected her shocked horror.

He didn't want to answer the question, but he wasn't about to
lie either. His silence was no less damning. He didn't even have to
probe his friends' minds to know what they were thinking. Their
thoughts found him. Whispers of shock, disbelief, and horror, even
a trace of fear, crashed into him. Distrust followed, and the sensation scraped across his nerve endings until his entire body ached.

He'd always known the moment of truth would be hard, he'd
just never realized how agonizing it would be. Beside him, Phaedra's
reaction was the worst. Her shock and horror he understood, but it
was her fear that almost brought him to his knees. Her reaction said

it more clearly than any words could. He'd lost her. Only this time it was forever.

He pushed the pain deep. He couldn't save her if he was distracted. And *she* was why Gabriel and Nicostratus had come. They'd come for Phaedra. His jaw tightened at the thought. Over his dead body.

"With pleasure, Unmentionable."

He shut out Gabriel's sneer. With a discipline he'd sharpened since the night his father had tortured him, he closed off his thoughts to everything but the task at hand. With pinpoint precision, he visualized the Praetorian Dominus crashing to the ground from a vicious right hook.

His invisible blow sent Gabriel flying backward, and before the Praetorian hit the ground with a thud, he charged the man. As Gabriel sprang to his feet, Lysander flipped his sword so the tip was pointing behind him. Darting past the Praetorian, he dragged his blade across Gabriel's arm. The Praetorian Dominus shouted with rage.

"I seem to recall I drew first blood the last time, too, Praetorian," Lysander said grimly as he spun around to face the man.

Behind Gabriel, he could see Ares fighting Nicostratus, while the rest of his friends were dealing with the remaining Praetorians. Friends? He had no friends anymore. The lapse of concentration cost him dearly as an invisible pulse of energy slammed into him like a baseball bat.

The blow sucked the wind out of his lungs and sent him to his knees. Quickly, he cleared his head of everything but the man striding toward him, allowing Gabriel to think he was too stunned with pain to move. That part wasn't hard to imagine. The *bastardo* had packed one hell of a punch in that mental blow. As the Praetorian Dominus's boots came into view, Lysander allowed his senses to visualize the precise moment Gabriel lifted his sword.

Before the man could strike, he jammed the hilt of his sword up into the man's balls. The Praetorian Dominus howled with pain and sank to one knee. Immediately, Lysander rolled to the right and was on his feet to send his blade flying toward Gabriel's thigh. His sword barely grazed the man through his cloak, as the Praetorian Dominus still had the wherewithal to wave his free hand and knock the blade aside.

"Perhaps I underestimated you, Unmentionable. In some ways, you fight just like a Praetorian. And if you think to impress your father, you shall fail." Gabriel's words were like fuel on a fire.

"I'm not trying to impress anyone, you *figlio di puttana*. I just want you dead," he spat out fiercely.

"As I you, so prepare yourself, Unmentionable. You've not long to wait."

In the next instant, Gabriel sprang to his feet, and with a rounded cartwheel, the man whipped his body through the air, his cloak hitting Lysander in the face—blinding him. A moment later, a sharp blade sliced into his shoulder, the tip of the sword just missing his neck. Pain lashed at him, and he grunted at the way his shoulder ached. Ignoring the pain, he whirled around, only to wind up flat on his back as another of Gabriel's mental blows knocked him off his feet. In response, he visualized his boot slamming into the Praetorian Dominus's jaw.

The mental foot action sent Gabriel's head snapping backward, while giving Lysander the opportunity to get back onto his feet. He'd barely managed to regain his own footing as Gabriel straightened and glared at him with hate twisting his features. *Christus*, the man's recovery was amazing. Didn't this guy feel pain?

"Pain is a relative term, Unmentionable." Gabriel's voice was cold and brittle as he read Lysander's thoughts. "But for you, it holds no meaning because your life is at an end."

A hard weight pressed into his entire body, forcing him to his knees. His mental reserves were beginning to weaken, but his only option was to push back against Gabriel's hold on him. The Praetorian Dominus increased the weight bearing down on him, and despite managing to rise to his feet, Lysander still couldn't break the man's hold over him.

With a grunt, he deepened his concentration and threw more of his telekinetic strength into fighting back. The intensity of his focus made it impossible to see Gabriel's sword flying through the air at him until it was too late. He tried desperately to shift his focus and block the sword, but his reserves were almost nonexistent. Resolved to his fate, he closed his eyes and shut out Gabriel's gloating thoughts as he waited for the sword to slam into his chest.

In that moment, steel clanged against steel as another sword blocked Gabriel's, sending it spiraling away from Lysander. The Praetorian Dominus uttered a noise of fury as Lysander opened his eyes to see Nicostratus lowering his sword. Stunned, he stared at his biological father.

"We're done here, Gabriel. We've lost this round."

"No," the Praetorian Dominus exclaimed with vehemence. "I want him dead."

"Not tonight." Nicostratus glared at the other man. After a long moment, Gabriel whirled away and ran toward the wall. Nicostratus turned his head toward Lysander. "You didn't disappoint, my boy. You're everything I could ever hope for in a son."

"Get away from me, you sick *bastardo*."

Lysander swung at the man as rage welled up inside him. Nicostratus easily dodged the blow then dragged his blade across Lysander's chest. A moment later, the Praetorian was retreating toward the wall surrounding the circus. Fire streaked through Lysander as he swayed on his feet, unable to move. He heard someone behind him, and he froze. There was still the matter of his Praetorian blood to deal with. Without looking at the person behind him, he went down on his knees and bent his head.

"Whoever you are, make it quick," he said with a tap to the back of his neck.

"Get up, you *bastardo*." Cleo's hand bit into his shoulder wound as she dragged him to his feet. "You've got a fucking lot of explaining to do before I put you out of your misery."

The pain in his shoulder made his stomach churn as Cleo released him and stepped back away from him. *Christus*, she'd deliberately gripped his injured shoulder. He couldn't blame her. She was furious with him. The fact that she was even talking to him was amazing, because in her book, he'd lied. He had no doubt everyone else would feel the same way. He slowly staggered to his feet, his entire body on fire as nerve endings signaled pain. Slowly he turned toward the small group staring at him. Their cold expressions, with the exception of Emma's sympathetic one, hurt worse than the wounds setting his body on fire.

"Phaedra will have to perform the *Curavi* at the safe house. It's too dangerous to stay here. Let's move," Ares said coldly and turned away to head back to where they'd parked the cars.

One by one, the rest of the team turned and followed Ares. Phaedra was the last to move. Her face devoid of emotion, she turned her back to him and followed her brother. In that moment, Lysander hated Cleo for not killing him.

Chapter 20

LYSANDER was Praetorian. The enemy.

Somewhere deep in the back of Phaedra's mind, a small voice denied the words, arguing that he wasn't the enemy. She silenced the protest with an anger born of renewed grief. He was the son of a Praetorian. But more horrifying than that, his Praetorian *bastardo* of a father had murdered her parents. The reality of it was repugnant. Lysander's father was the butcher who'd killed her parents.

Fear rushed through her blood as she remembered how the Praetorian's voice had echoed across the Circus Maxentius. Like his face, she had never forgotten the monster's voice. Even now, after all these years, she remembered that cruel voice taunting her and Ares as the *bastardo* had stood over her mother's mutilated body. The terrifying memory flashed in front of her eyes. The priest's closet. Her mother's screams. The peephole she'd peered through to see her mother's murderer. Lysander's father.

Her stomach churned as she fought not to throw up. She was in love with the son of the man who'd butchered her parents. Lysander hadn't just betrayed her by hiding the truth. He'd made her betray the memory of her parents. Her heart shattered. The pain of it lancing through her with an agony that surpassed the injury on her leg.

She should have sensed the evil in him. How had he been able to keep it from her? No, she'd sensed it. She'd seen that darkness in him. The memory of that day on the stairs flitted through her head. His emotions had been dark. Riddled with despair. At the time, she'd been convinced his emotional state was the result of the torture session he'd endured. Now she knew differently. She'd simply mistaken it for what it really was—his Praetorian blood.

Her heart twisted inside her chest. She couldn't believe that. Didn't want to believe it. There had to be some other explanation. She'd seen his despair, the tortured nature of the beast inside him. She was certain of it. It hadn't been his attempt to deceive her. No. She would have seen any duplicity on his part. *Just like she'd seen the truth that he was Praetorian?*

How could she be sure he hadn't been deceiving her? He was a telepath. He could have known she was at the top of the stairs reading his emotions. It would have been so easy for him to deceive her. He was Praetorian. It was what the *bastardi* did. That and work toward their goal to exterminate the Sicari.

A shudder rippled through her as her thoughts came full circle. Lysander's father had butchered her parents. The thought made her numb. Everything in her world had collapsed on her in the blink of an eye. Phaedra fought back the tears as she stared out the backseat window of the Land Rover. She hadn't felt this lost since the weeks and months after her parents were murdered. And seeing their killer tonight had pulled all of her grief back to the surface. Her hand trembled as she wiped a tear off her cheek. She was grateful Lysander was driving the other vehicle. Being in the same car with him right now would have been unbearable. It had amazed her that Cleo had chosen to go with him.

Beside her, Pasquale drew in a sharp breath of pain as Ares hit a bump on their way back to the safe house. *Deus*, she'd been so wrapped up in her own misery, she'd forgotten that Luciano and Ares were both injured. Her brother had minor cuts and bruises that Violetta or the *Vigilavi* doctor could heal.

But she remembered how Luciano had been forced to lean on Ares to make it back to the car. Lysander had been hurt, too. In the moonlight, she'd seen his shirt splayed open to reveal a chest wound, and his shoulder had been wet and glistening with blood, but she'd known his injuries were minor. He hadn't been hurt badly, and she'd found herself offering up a small prayer of gratitude that he'd survived. Even despite learning his terrible secret, she'd been relieved he would be okay.

She turned toward the man next to her at the same time Emma turned around in her seat. The fact that her sister-in-law had escaped their encounter with the Praetorians without a scrape was a small miracle. But it wouldn't stop Ares from giving them hell for quite some time to come.

"Are you all right, Luciano?" Emma's voice held a breathless note that indicated her heightened state of adrenaline as a result of the battle they'd all survived. It was Emma's first, and if Ares had any say in the matter, Phaedra was sure her sister-in-law wouldn't be seeing action any time in the near future.

"I'll be fine," Luciano said through clenched teeth. "Just a slight twinge over that last bump."

"Let me see," Phaedra said in a calm voice.

She scooted across the middle of the seat, ignoring the pain in her leg. The Praetorian *bastardo* she'd taken out had managed to leave a long, nasty cut from her hip to midthigh. It would be at least another hour before it healed properly. Unlike those she healed, it took her body a lot longer to recuperate from any injuries. And if she healed anyone while she was injured, it took even longer for her own wounds to heal.

When she was close enough to examine Luciano's wound, she pulled her penlight out of her pocket and illuminated his thigh. She bit back a gasp. The cut was almost to the bone. He was lucky. Any closer and the blade would have severed a main artery, causing him to bleed out on the field. He was fortunate in more ways than one, because she'd never healed anyone bleeding from a primary arterial vein, and she wasn't sure whether she could. Still this cut was almost as bad, and it needed healing now. Without hesitating, she extended her hands to him.

"With your permission, I must touch you to heal you."

In the front seat, Ares released a harsh curse. "Damn it, Phaedra, wait until we get to the safe house. I've already called to have a doctor meet us at the house."

"Whether I do it here or at the safe house is a moot point. Violetta doesn't have the ability to heal a wound like this. I don't even know if she'll be able to heal your cuts. And then there's Cleo and . . ."

She didn't dare say Lysander's name. Not yet, the pain of his betrayal was still too raw. With every beat of her heart, the physical sensation of his lie sent a throbbing pain into every part of her. It was an ache she didn't think she would ever recover from. She forced herself to focus on Luciano and repeated the traditional saying of the *Curavi*.

"I can wait, *carissima*."

"*Christus*, will you just accept the damn *Curavi*," she exclaimed.

Luciano studied her carefully for a moment then gave her an abrupt nod as he placed his hands in hers. She immediately closed her eyes and as always the familiar warmth of healing rushed through her body into her hands. The pain when it came was agonizing. She shuddered as she felt the deep cut on Luciano's leg form on her own leg. She was grateful his wound wasn't on the same leg as her own injury. It would have hurt far worse.

For several long minutes, she clung to Luciano's hands, accepting the pain he'd endured as penance for loving a Praetorian. The enemy. The *bastardi* responsible for the death of her parents and countless others. The pain in her leg slowly eased, and she released her grip on Luciano's hands before she leaned back against the car seat. Drained, she kept her eyes closed, wanting to do nothing but curl up in her bed and go to sleep. The sleep of the dead where she didn't have to feel anything.

She must have dozed off, because the sound of a car door opening made her jerk upright. Still groggy as a result of healing Luciano, she clung to the car door as she got out of the vehicle. The second Land Rover wheeled into the parking space beside them, and she averted her gaze as Lysander and Cleo got out of the vehicle.

Her hand pressed into the side of the car, she shuffled forward. Out of the corner of her eye, she saw Lysander stepping into plain view, while Cleo joined him. How could her friend have anything to do with him? He'd betrayed Cleo, too. Unable to stop herself, she turned her head toward Lysander. His face was like a marble statue, pale and without expression.

A sudden urge to go to him swept through her. She wanted answers. Wanted to understand why he hadn't told her. She swayed slightly as she braced herself on the car's tailgate. She saw Lysander take a step forward as a strong pair of arms lifted her up off her feet. Startled, she looked up at Luciano's grim profile and immediately found herself longing for Lysander. Her gaze drifted back to Lysander, and she saw his stoic expression dissolve into one of fury as Luciano sent him a cold glare.

Cleo grasped Lysander's arm and held him back as Luciano carried her into the house. Drained of energy and emotion, all Phaedra wanted was to crawl into her bed and sleep. In sleep, she could forget everything. The moment they were inside, there was a flurry of activity. The *Vigilavi* who worked in the house were already prepared to tend to the wounded who couldn't receive the *Curavi*. As Luciano carried her through the hall toward the main stairs, Atia met them coming down the steps. Clearly surprised, a flash of fear swept across her features.

"Lysander?"

"The Praetorian is with Cleo," Luciano said with outraged disgust.

"*Deus*. How many know?" Atia's question made Phaedra stiffen in Luciano's arms as she stared at the woman in horror.

"You knew?"

"I've known since he was a baby that he's half-Praetorian. Lysander didn't find out until Nicostratus tortured him. He's struggled with the knowledge ever since."

Atia's words made her sick. Lysander hadn't just talked with the *Prima Consul* about his torture session. He'd shared who he was with Atia. Not her. She moaned softly. How could he possibly love her if he didn't trust her to tell her the truth? Closing her eyes, she sagged against Luciano's shoulder.

"I want to go to my room. *Now*." At her command, Luciano moved up the staircase, and in less than a minute, they were at the door of her small suite. "I can make it from here."

"Are you sure?" he asked as he set her on her feet.

"Yes, thank you." She opened the door of her apartment and paused as Luciano touched her shoulder.

"If you need anything, *carissima*, you know where to find me."

"Thanks, but I'll be fine."

She pushed the door open, and out of the corner of her eye, she saw a flash of movement. Turning her head, her heart crashed into her chest at the sight of Lysander coming down the hall. She had no stomach for a confrontation with him now or later. Quickly entering her suite, she slammed the door closed. Her fingers brushed over the lock without flipping the bolt.

If he really wanted in, all he had to do was pick the lock with his thoughts. Still feeling sluggish, she made her way into her bedroom and tumbled onto the mattress. Curled up on top of the sheets, she dragged a pillow into her chest and clung to it as if it were a lifeline. One by one, the tears came. They soaked the pillow as she sobbed herself to sleep.

"MAXIMUS."

She shot upright off the bed in the room where Octavian's slaves had imprisoned her. It was just a dream. She lay down again and stared up at the ceiling. This morning when Octavian had stormed into the house, she'd never imagined that the man would take her prisoner. When Maximus returned home, he wouldn't know where to find her. The sound of the bedroom door opening made her sit up.

The manner in which Octavian entered the room, as if he had the right to, angered her. She was the daughter of Gaius Quinctilia Atellus, not some whore he could walk in on when it suited him. The glare she sent in his direction didn't seem to faze him, or if it did, he ignored it. In fact, he arched his eyebrows as if he knew exactly what she was thinking. As she'd done earlier, she shielded her thoughts as Maximus had taught her. She'd become quite good at it, and Maximus had been convinced he'd transferred some of his ability to her as the result of their blood bond. Her stomach lurched as Octavian sat down on the edge of the bed.

"Beautiful," he murmured as his hand stretched out to brush across her cheek. She shrank away from him, and the feral smile on his handsome features sent a shiver down her spine. "I have news."

Fear coated her skin in ice, but she refused to give him the satisfaction of knowing he'd made her think the worst. Instead, she arched her eyebrow at him in contempt. His mouth thinned with anger.

"*Your husband is dead.*" *Octavian's words hit her like a thun-derbolt. She shook her head in denial.*

"*Liar. If Maximus were dead, it would please you to show me his head.*" *The thought of such a thing horrified her, but she knew it was true.*

"*My dear Cassiopeia, I am not a cruel man. I would never force you to endure such a thing.*" *Octavian's words were smooth and oily.* "*You'll see him soon enough when you're found guilty of heresy.*"

"*Not even you would dare to execute the daughter of Gaius Quinctilia Atellus. Constantine would ban you from his court.*"

"*Ahh, but I have no intention of executing you,* mea dulcis. *I will simply explain that I was too late to prevent the mob from extract-ing their misguided justice.*" *His words made her cheeks grow cold as the blood drained from her face, and he chuckled.*

She turned her head away as a wave of hopelessness washed over her. If Maximus were alive—no, he was alive. She could feel it. And when he learned where she was, he'd risk his life to rescue her. The knowledge made her heart skip a beat. If he tried to do that, he'd certainly die. No, she had to find a way to escape and reach him first.

"*You're far too quiet,* mea mellis. *What are you planning in that pretty head of yours?*"

"*Nothing,*" she said as a whisper of a thought not her own brushed through her head. She met his gaze with a surreal sense of calm.

"*If you're thinking you can escape, Cassiopeia, don't. The Prae-torians guarding the house are loyal to me, and the household slaves know the harsh consequences of betrayal.*"

"*Would you be any less suspicious if I were to calmly accept you as my jailor?*"

"*No.*" *He smiled. It frightened her because his gaze remained flat as a reptile's gaze.* "*At least you've not lost your spirit. It's one of the things that always excited me about you.*"

"*And you disgust me.*" *She met his gaze with a look of scorn. Her reward for her defiance was the anger that flashed across his face before he leaned toward her.*

"At least you understand it's impossible to elude the hand of justice." Octavian's mouth was so close she couldn't help but turn her head away from him. His fingers captured her chin, forcing her to look at him. "You're a heretic, Cassiopeia. And you will be punished, just like your husband and the boy."

Her heart stopped at his words. Care Deus, if he found Demetri—no, she refused to believe that Posca would fail her and Maximus. He would keep Demetri safe. A flutter of movement inside her belly heightened her fear. The baby. If Octavian discovered she was pregnant with Maximus's child—he would kill her immediately. He wouldn't risk her escaping and bearing a child that might one day be his downfall. Again, the whisper echoed in her head. This time it was stronger, deeper. It convinced her that Octavian was attempting to read her mind. She immediately forced herself to block off her thoughts with images of Maximus finding her. They gave her courage. She would find a way to escape.

A look of fascination on his face, Octavian's thumb brushed over her mouth. "What was it you saw in Maximus that you never saw in me? I could have given you everything he gave you and more."

"I didn't love you."

"Instead you loved a traitor."

"Maximus isn't a traitor. You're the one who's betrayed the oath of the Praetorian Guard. You're the one who wants the Tyet of Isis to further your own ambitions, not to protect it."

"And I was not so weak that I shared all of its secrets with a woman."

"Maximus has never been weak."

"No? You bent him to your will." Octavian's hand caressed the side of her neck, and she shivered at the vile touch. "He betrayed his oath to the Guard by telling you about the Tyet of Isis."

"That's not true. I learned of the box when I blood bonded with Maximus," she exclaimed.

The moment she spoke, Octavian stiffened and slowly pulled away from her. The look on his face said she'd made a mistake. Many in the Guard frowned upon the blood bond. It meant the woman might acquire a special power, and in Rome, a woman with power was a threat. Especially if she acquired all the powers of *the man she blood bonded with. Octavian grabbed her hands and turned them palms up. She winced at the way his fingers bit into her hands as he stared at the long scar on her left palm.*

"The secret of the Tyet of Isis *is sacred to the Guard. He knows that. It's why we don't share a blood bond with a woman." His disgust evident, he narrowed his gaze at her. "What ability did your traitorous husband give you when he bonded with you?"*

"Nothing. I have never been able to move objects or read minds." If she'd received any ability from Maximus, it was her talent for shielding her thoughts. She'd had no need of it with Maximus, but she was grateful for his instruction now.

"And the box? Where is it?"

"I don't know," she lied.

"It will go easier for you if you simply cooperate." The whisper in her head became a harsh probe as he glared at her.

"Maximus didn't tell me where he hid it."

"You lie badly, mea mellis." *She gasped as his words slithered through her head, while his hand glided down to her breasts. Fear struck at her core as he shared a glimpse of what he intended to do to her before he killed her. Frantically, she tried to strengthen the wall of inane thoughts she'd placed around her secrets. His mocking laughter filled her head. "Mea care, Cassiopeia. My abilities are far more powerful than those of Maximus."*

His mind probed deeper, and she struggled to push his thoughts out of her head. The minute invisible fingers pulled the hem of her gown upward, her control slipped. Maximus had incredible powers but he'd never used his abilities to force her to do anything. Frantically, she tried to push the garment back down while keeping Octavian from probing deeper. She failed, and a moment later a strong force shoved her backward onto the bed.

"I'm not your traitorous husband, *mea dulcis.* And it's important you understand you can hide nothing from me. Not even the Tyet—ahh, so it's in the Temple of Vesta. Thank you, *mea mellis.*"

"Get out of my head, you bastardo."

Anger roared through her blood as she pushed back against his mental probe. A moment later, she knew he was no longer in her head. Whether it was because he'd withdrawn on his own or she'd managed to push him out, she didn't know. As she stared up at his face, rage darkened his features. The sudden knock on the door followed by the entry of a Praetorian Guardsman shot a bolt of relief through her.

"General Maximus and his troops arrived outside the city gates less than an hour ago. He accepted the emperor's terms of surrender." The guard's words made her heart leap with joy. Maximus had come for her as she knew he would.

"Where is he now?" Octavian snapped.

"He entered the city shortly after surrendering what was left of his legions."

"Cak." The single word of fury echoed through the chamber, and the Guardsman reached for his throat as an invisible force slowly squeezed the air from his lungs. A second later, the soldier was free of the unseen grasp. Octavian glared at the man dragging in deep breaths of air. "He'll search for his bitch first. Send a small contingent of men to Maximus's house to arrest him if he's there. I'll take several of the men to the Temple of Vesta in the event he goes there first."

The Praetorian nodded his head as he stood upright, and his fist hit his chest before his arm flew outward in a salute. As the Guard headed toward the door, Octavian quickly ordered him to halt and rubbed his chin in contemplation.

"If you find Maximus, kill him." The words made her gasp in fear. Octavian shot her an amused glance before meeting the soldier's eyes. "But before you do, tell the traitor that his wife . . . and unborn child . . . are to be burned at the stake for heresy."

This time her gasp was one of horror. The bastardo *knew about the baby. A wave of intense fear swept over her. She didn't want to die. She wanted to live. Wanted her baby to live. Octavian turned back to her and smiled. It was the smile of death, and she cried out for Maximus.*

PHAEDRA jerked awake as someone's hand touched her arm. With a cry, she rolled away from the touch to come up in a crouch on the opposite side of her bed. The nightmare of Cassiopeia at Octavian's mercy still vivid in her head, she blinked the sleep from her eyes to see Cleo watching her with concern.

"What are you doing here?" she asked in a hoarse voice.

"Mother gave me instructions to watch over you for a few hours. You were crying out in your sleep, so I thought it best to wake you."

She relaxed slightly and leaned back against the headboard. Her hands shoving her hair out of her eyes, she stared at her friend. Cleo had spared Lysander's life at the Circus Maxentius, and she wasn't sure why. Cleo rarely gave anyone a second chance, but Phaedra was glad she'd given Lysander one. She winced.

What was she thinking? The man had hidden the truth from her. From all of them. And the worst of it was, a small part of her had known. All of the little moments when he'd always seemed to know what she was thinking. She'd put it down to a special connection between them, but now she saw it for what it was.

He'd been reading her mind all this time. It was a violation. He wasn't any better than that son-of-a-bitch Praetorian called Gabriel. The knowledge sent a fiery pain through her blood until it seared every inch of her body with pain. He'd betrayed her. Betrayed them all.

"Okay, I know you're angry, but he's got a good explanation." Cleo's words echoed softly in the room. She shook her head.

"Explanation?" She released a hiss of air from between her teeth. "There is no explanation. How much damage has he done spying on us?"

"What the fuck is wrong with you?" Cleo snapped. "Do you hear what you're saying? How can you love the guy if you're going to talk about him like that? Lysander isn't a spy. He's not even a full-blood Praetorian."

"No, he's just the son of the Praetorian *bastardo* who killed my parents." The viciousness of her angry words made Cleo jerk with surprise.

"*Il Christi omnipotentia*. Are you sure?"

"I won't ever forget seeing that bastard's face through the peephole of that priest's closet my mother shoved Ares and me into."

"But you can't blame Lysander for the circumstances of his

birth." The horror on Cleo's face ebbed as she stretched out her hand, but Phaedra jerked away as her friend shook her head.

"I don't blame him for what his father did. But he lied to me."

"About what? The fact he's half-Praetorian?"

"Yes," she bit out harshly. "He could have told me, and he didn't."

Lysander hadn't even given her the chance to accept him for what he was. She closed her eyes for a brief moment. What would she have done if he had told her before this? The question frightened her because deep in her heart she didn't like the answer. Her reaction wouldn't have been any different than it had been last night.

But he hadn't given her a chance, either. He hadn't trusted her with his secret. She had no doubt that her love for him would have helped her overcome the shock of the truth. But now she was dealing with more than just the truth. She was dealing with who his father was and the fact that Lysander hadn't trusted her. That above everything else hurt the most.

"He won't come to you. You'll have to go to him." Cleo's comment made her jump.

"What makes you think I want to see him?" Her question was icy, but she knew she wanted to see him despite what had happened.

"Because I know you've got questions."

"Questions he should have tried to answer before this."

"If you love him, you'll at least listen to what he has to say."

"Don't you dare preach to me about love! You know what betrayal feels like, and this *is* a betrayal." She ignored the way Cleo's face went white. Her friend knew better. "Lysander didn't tell me the truth. Instead, he made me believe we were going to be happy together. Forgive me if I can't find it in my heart to easily forgive that."

The silence between them was sharp and discordant. With a sharp nod of her head, Cleo stood up and headed toward the door. She paused in the doorway.

"The *Prima Consul* has called for a briefing at oh-nine-hundred in the ready room. Make sure you're there."

As Cleo walked out of the bedroom, Phaedra watched her leave with a heavy heart. The disappointment in her friend's eyes wasn't something she enjoyed seeing, but at the same time, the fact that Cleo had forgiven Lysander so easily amazed her. Her friend's words echoed in her head again. *If you love him, you'll at least listen to what he has to say.* She did love him. But she wasn't ready to listen to his explanations, and she just couldn't trust him.

No, the truth was, she didn't trust herself. Could she look at him on a daily basis without remembering the fact that his Praetorian father had butchered her parents? It didn't make her feel good to ask the question. If she really loved him, she should be able to see beyond his blood. But it was still so raw and painful. Especially when it came to the memory of her parents. In some ways, loving him felt like she was betraying her parents.

She closed her eyes, only to have Nicostratus's gloating features enter her head. A shudder rippled down her spine. The Praetorian was a monster that wouldn't stay in the closet. It was bad enough to know the man had killed her parents, but to see him in her dreams as Cassiopeia's tormentor was just as horrifying. Nicostratus was a dead ringer for Octavian, and he was just as evil now as he had been in ancient Rome. His renewed presence last night made her realize there were no coincidences in all that had happened over the last several weeks.

Each dream was following a loose timeline of the events leading up to Cassiopeia's death by Maximus's hand. While there were only similarities between her dreams and the present, the characters involved made her think a climax would happen in the near future. A climax that would revolve around her, Lysander, and Nicostratus.

As Octavian, the Praetorian had been responsible for destroying Cassiopeia and Maximus in ancient Rome, and the man was about to do it again. Nicostratus might not be aware of it, but the monster had already driven a wedge between her and Lysander. Seeing Nicostratus in her dreams had left her feeling just as helpless and scared as Cassiopeia. It was a sensation she didn't like. A deep longing to have Lysander's arms around her sank its way deep into her bones until she ached.

What was she going to do if she couldn't find a way to come to terms with all that had happened? She blinked back tears. It was as if a part of her were missing. She knew it was Lysander. He made her whole. The knowledge only increased the ache in her body, telling her there was no right or wrong choice, only the acceptance of things she couldn't control.

Chapter 21

THE conference room was quiet as individuals and small groups filed into the room. Even the *Vigilavi* staffing the facility had been ordered to attend the briefing. That could mean only one thing. Atia had already informed the Council about last night's events, which meant word would spread fast about Lysander and everything that had happened last night. Atia wanted to keep gossip and innuendos at a minimum. She watched the *Celeris* adjusting the webcam. Generally, the *Prima Consul* addressed the Order only on special days celebrated by the Sicari. Today wasn't one of those days, which meant Atia was going to share the news of what happened last night, personally.

Did that mean the Council had reacted badly to the news? Cato. If anyone was going to cause any trouble, it would be him and his small band of weasels. Phaedra frowned. The man was petty and vindictive. If he could make trouble for Atia, he would, simply because he'd lost the *Prima Consul* title to her. Had he perhaps pushed her into a corner where Lysander was concerned? Maybe the Council had insisted she remove Lysander from duty altogether until a hearing could be convened.

When she'd first entered the room, she'd automatically looked for Lysander, but his absence didn't surprise her. As her gaze continued to scan the faces in the room, she suddenly realized Ares wasn't in the conference room. Neither was Emma for that matter. The sight of Cleo coming through the door made her tense. They'd parted badly earlier, and she wasn't quite sure what to expect. Relief sailed through her as Cleo offered her a half smile and headed straight for the chair next to her.

"You okay?" Cleo leaned toward her. "I know I was a little rough on you. I'm sorry."

"It's all right. I'm just . . . it's just a little more complicated than you think."

"I know, but you'll work it out with him," Cleo said with a quiet smile. "The two of you belong together."

Phaedra shook her head as a frisson skimmed across her skin with the softness of a piece of silk. It was a familiar sensation, and her heart plummeted downward before it began to pound rapidly in her chest. Her gaze darted to the conference room doorway where first Ares, Emma, and then Lysander entered the room followed by the *Prima Consul*. While her sister-in-law stood near the door, the other three moved toward the head of the conference table.

As much as she hated to admit it, the sight of Lysander made her long for the comfort of his embrace. She thought he might scan the crowded room for her, but he didn't. The black eye patch he wore only emphasized his emotionless features.

It was as if someone had placed a leather patch on a bust of cold, hard marble. But it was the tight line of his jaw that said he wasn't as calm and collected as he appeared. The fact that her heart ached for him, even after he'd lied to her, told her how much she loved him. She loved him so much.

But did she love him enough?

The moment Atia took center stage, Ares and Lysander moved to flank the *Prima Consul*. It was a clear show of solidarity on Ares's part. Her brother had obviously come to terms with Lysander's Praetorian heritage. Did Ares even know that Lysander's father had murdered their parents? It was possible her brother hadn't seen the Praetorian's face as clearly as she had.

Either way, Ares was holding Lysander blameless for his mixed blood. So what did that say about her own ability to forgive? A sliver of regret etched its way into her heart, but she ignored it. Lysander had lied to her, and that wasn't something she could forgive easily. He'd hurt her not so much with the lie as with his inability to trust her. The *Prima Consul* arched her eyebrow at the *Celeris* monitoring a laptop at the far end of the conference table, and when he nodded, Atia stared in the direction of the webcam.

"Greetings. I know this is an unusual occurrence, but I wanted to prevent rumors and misinformation from making their way through the organization. What I share with you today is information I shared with the Order's Council just a few hours ago. Last night, *Legatus* Lysander Condellaire and his team found a valuable artifact that has brought us one step closer to finding the *Tyet of Isis*."

Atia's declaration caused the entire room to stir with excitement, and she raised her hand for silence. "In addition to this new discovery, there were other revelations brought to light last night. Revelations the Council is now aware of and which I will share with you now. For some time now, there have been ritualistic executions of Sicari, *Vigilavi*, and others connected to the search for the *Tyet of Isis*. All of those executed have borne an unusual mark we now know is an incomplete version of the Chi-Rho, and it is the work of a Praetorian Dominus."

As the *Prima Consul* paused to allow time for her words to sink in, Phaedra sensed the mood of the small gathering change from excitement to serious misgiving. She imagined the reaction was the same at other installations watching Atia's address. As the group shifted restlessly in their seats, Phaedra turned her attention to Emma, who was standing just inside the door of the conference room. Emma's parents and mentor had all been victims of the ritualistic murders. Even Emma had been a target, but Ares had chosen to protect her and had fallen in love as a result. A small part of her envied her brother's happiness. Atia's voice interrupted her train of thought.

"The warriors who fought the Dominus last night now know what we're up against and will be better prepared the next time they encounter this newest threat to our existence."

The *Prima Consul* paused to look at Lysander's emotionless expression before her unrelenting gaze of authority swept across the faces of men and women in the conference room to return her attention to the webcam. The imperial look of confidence on Atia's face said she dared anyone to question her on whatever decision she was about to announce.

"Last night also revealed something I and only one or two other individuals have known for a long time. *Legatus* Condellaire's father is Praetorian." Everyone stirred at the news, but Atia's hard look of disapproval made the occupants of the room quickly grow quiet. "Up until the Praetorians tortured the *Legatus* last year, he had always believed his father had died fighting our enemy."

The *Prima Consul* turned her head toward Lysander with an expression of regret and pain. Atia was a politician, but Phaedra was certain the woman's emotions were genuine, not simply a display for her audience. The woman truly felt anguish for what Lysander was going through. Atia cleared her throat to resume her address to the Sicari in the room and those watching.

"The circumstances of his birth were kept from *Legatus* Condellaire out of respect to his mother and her traumatic sexual assault. A year ago, when the Praetorians tortured the *Legatus*, his biological father was his interrogator. The Praetorian recognized *Legatus* Condellaire, torturing him physically and emotionally with the knowledge. The man who did this is Patriarch of the Praetorian Collegium."

Another gasp flew through the room, and emotion constricted Phaedra's throat as Atia's words sank in. Slowly, she absorbed the *Prima Consul*'s words. *Dear God*, the man who was now Patriarch, and second only to Monsignor in the hierarchy of the Collegium, had raped Lysander's mother. She'd been concentrating so hard on the fact that Lysander's father had murdered her parents, she'd not really considered what his mother must have suffered at Nicostratus's hands. Only a woman of strong mental reserves could have chosen to keep a child from such a horrendous act of violation.

Her gaze flew to Lysander's expressionless features. He appeared unaffected by Atia's announcement, but she knew better. The muscles of his scarred face were taut, making the tic in his cheek more noticeable. Her fingertips tingled with the need to touch him, soothe his pain. *Christus*, he had to be in a living hell right now hearing Atia share his secret shame.

And she was convinced he was ashamed. If he hadn't been, he would have told her the truth. Told someone. She flinched. He had told someone. He'd told Atia. He'd entrusted the *Prima Consul* with his secret, not her. Instead, he'd pushed her away. It wasn't the first time she'd acknowledged the fact, but it cut deeper this time. He'd shut her out, and the pain of it pounded its way through her bloodstream until every one of her nerve endings screamed a protest.

As she studied him, she saw him stiffen. His gaze briefly scanned her face before he resumed his stare at the wall. Was he reading her mind right now? Without thinking, she reached out with her senses to find him amid all the other emotions that were flooding the room. It was like moving through a crowded square of people to reach him.

When she did, it was as if she'd reached sanctuary, despite the pain she sensed in him. It didn't surprise her that his emotions were so open to her. With all his energy focused on maintaining his impassive expression, he had nothing left with which to lock down the emotions running rampant behind his mask. The darkness of his feelings washed over her in a violent wave of fury, despair, and shame.

He was ashamed of who he was. No. What he believed himself to be. He didn't believe he was Sicari. *Deus*, no wonder he'd kept his distance from her over the past year. She swallowed hard as she realized how difficult it must have been for him. What would have happened if she had pushed back sooner? Demanding an answer as to why he'd rejected her. Would he have told her his secret? She didn't have to probe his senses any deeper to know the answer was no.

He wouldn't have told her. He still would have kept it from her. The realization was an emotional slap in the face. She struggled to accept his inability to trust her. It was one thing to accept that he wasn't responsible for his father's sins, but trust was essential to a relationship. How could she trust him not to keep other secrets from her? And without trust, they didn't stand a chance in hell.

"I have every confidence in *Legatus* Condellaire, and I am convinced he and his team will be successful in their mission to find the *Tyet of Isis. Longior vivere ordinis Sicari.*" As Atia formally closed her address, Phaedra murmured the words, "Long Live the Order of the Sicari." The phrase that ended all official Council events was second nature to her, and it took her a moment to realize she'd missed the last part of the *Prima Consul*'s speech. Suddenly overwhelmed by a desire to cry like she had last night, she ducked her head in an attempt to regain her composure.

"That will be all until the team briefing at one o'clock." Lysander's voice was brittle, and she didn't look at him as she stood up to leave the room with everyone else. As she tried to slip out of the room unnoticed, he stepped into her path. "Phaedra, I'd like to see you in the study."

"Can it wait?" She stiffened. *Deus*, she didn't think she was up to this. She barely glanced at him, unwilling to reveal how devastated she was feeling.

"No."

That was it. No compromise, just a refusal. With a sharp nod, she brushed past him and headed toward the study. *Fine. Maybe it is best to get this over with.* Less than a minute later, she entered the empty study. She didn't have to turn around to know when Lysander entered the room. Her body reacted to him like a sonar device gone crazy. At the sound of the door closing, she turned to face him, waiting for him to speak. The tension between them was like taut piano wire ready to break the minute the wrong key was struck.

His jawline hard and inflexible, he folded his arms across his chest. They stared at each other for a long moment as she waited for him to speak. The emotion penetrating the silence between them only heightened the tension in the room. He was the one who'd asked for this little meeting. Why didn't he say what it was he wanted to say so she could get out of here? Being alone with him made her feel vulnerable. If this was an intimidation tactic, it was working.

"Say something," he rasped.

"What?" She stared at him in amazement.

"Say something," he repeated himself. "Yell at me, rant, whatever you want, but just say something."

"There isn't anything to say." No. There was a lot to say, she just wasn't prepared to go down that road just now. The pain was too fresh to expose herself to more misery.

"*Fotte.*"

He took a step toward her in an explosive movement. Startled, she leaped backward in surprise, and a bit of fear too, if she was honest. He *was* half-Praetorian. The thought made her heart ache.

That was unfair of her. He'd never given her reason to think he'd harm her. His features became a carved sculpture of anguish, and he immediately turned away from her. "*Christus*, I didn't mean to scare you like that."

"You didn't frighten me." Her fierce bravado was a lie. She *had* been scared, and she despised herself for it. She knew he would never hurt her. He faced her again, and she could see from his expression that he knew she was lying.

"I want to explain—"

"Don't." She raised her hand.

There wasn't any explanation he could give her that would ease the anger and pain she was feeling right now. To keep something this important from her showed his lack of trust, and without his willingness to believe she wouldn't betray him, they had nothing. She knew he was in pain, but so was she, and she wasn't ready to forgive him everything just yet.

"Damn it, I need to make you—"

"*Understand?* I understand everything completely."

"Do you? I doubt it."

"Let me see if I can clarify it for you." She glared at him in hurt frustration. "You lied to me."

"I *never* lied to you." His mouth thinned with anger as he stood rigid in front of her.

"It's called the sin of omission. The Praetorians know it well. You could have told me. *Should* have told me who you really are, but you didn't. That's lying in my book."

"Who I really am?" The bitterness in his voice made her wince. "You know who I am, Phaedra. I'm the same man today that I was yesterday before you knew about my Praetorian blood."

"No. I don't know you at all. How could I *possibly* know you when you didn't trust me enough to tell me your darkest secret," she said fiercely. "A secret you entrusted to Atia without any problem at all."

"*Il Christi omnipotentia*, it wasn't like that."

"Yes, it *was* like that. So why don't you just drop this charade of you caring about what I think and leave me alone?"

She *didn't* want him to leave her alone. She wanted him to take her in his arms and tell her he was sorry for not trusting her. She wanted to hear him say he loved her. She wanted so much and was terrified he'd never tell her what she needed to hear. With a bowed head, he looked away from her until his demonic profile was all she could see.

"I can't do that."

"Sure you can," she sneered. "You managed to do it without any trouble once before, what's so different this time?"

"It's different because who I am is out in the open now." His entire body was knotted with tension as she fired back at him.

"So because everyone else knows now, that makes it okay? Well guess what. It doesn't. And you want to know why? Because I had to hear it from that Praetorian *bastardo* instead of you? Even worse than that, you trusted Atia enough to tell *her*. You trusted her, but not me, and you should have."

"Can you really blame me for not saying anything?" he rasped as he faced her again, anger darkening the angelic half of his face. "Look how you reacted last night."

She cringed inwardly at his accusation. "Last night our lives were at stake. Did you expect me to have a conversation with you while that *bastardo* was announcing to the world you were his son?"

"No. But afterward—"

"Afterward, I was too busy dealing with the fact that your father—"

"He's *not* my father," he growled with a ferocity that made her jump, but she didn't back down.

"That *bastardo* isn't just *any* Praetorian. Your father is the same monster who butchered my parents."

The sharp declaration was like a thunderclap in the room, and Lysander recoiled from her so quickly she thought he was going to bolt out of the room. There wasn't a drop of color in his face, and his features had hardened into a stone façade of horror. The scarred tissue layering his cheekbone was stretched so tight, she knew it had to hurt.

Even if she'd not been able to see his features, she would have known how appalled and shocked he was by her words. His senses were exploding with a fury that alarmed her. Her gaze pinned to his face, she swallowed hard as one turbulent emotion after another rolled off him. The pain that accompanied his horror squeezed at her heart. Close on the heels of those two powerful waves of emotion was intense shame.

Shame that he was related to Nicostratus and a stark fear that he might be like that Praetorian *bastardo*. Her heart ached for him, and despite all the anger and pain his betrayal had caused her, she wanted to ease his suffering. She took a step forward only to find herself fighting to remain standing as the tangible impact of his rage buffeted the space and silence between them.

It was dark and unmerciful in its intensity. Worse, it mimicked the hatred she'd sensed in Gabriel, and it frightened her. Not because she feared him, but because she was frightened for him. His rage was for Nicostratus, and she knew without any doubt that he intended to kill the man who'd sired him.

His green-colored gaze met hers, and the tormented anguish she saw there was the only emotion reflected in his expression. But she could still feel the powerful rage locked up inside him that was for the Praetorian Patriarch. She didn't even have to ask the question. The next time he met his father, he'd do whatever it took to kill the man. He shook his head slightly, almost as if in denial, but he didn't question the validity of her accusation.

"Does Ares know?"

"I don't know."

"He needs to be told." There was a finality and hopelessness to his voice that alarmed her. He nodded his head as if coming to a decision. "I'll reassign you to a new partner immediately."

The harsh rasp of his voice scraped across her senses with the sharpness of a finely honed blade. He was cutting her out of his life completely. The conflicted emotion sweeping through her made her shudder. *Deus*, how could she walk away from him? She loved him so much. It wasn't his Praetorian blood that bothered her. The blood in his veins might not be pure, but his heart was what mattered. He was Sicari. And no one, not even her, could question his loyalty to the Order.

It was his lack of trust that stung. Even now, he was showing he didn't trust her to protect his back when they were working together. It infuriated her. She deserved better than that from him. And if he thought he could avoid her anger by giving her a new partner, he needed to have his head examined. They needed to work this out—together. It was the only way either of them would be able to come to terms with themselves and each other.

"I don't want a new partner," she said with quiet determination.

"As *Legatus*, I make the assignments. You don't have a choice."

"And if you insist on reassigning me, I'll demand *Dux Provocare*." Challenging his ability to command probably wasn't the smartest move she'd ever made. And facing him in a sword fight was idiotic, but there weren't that many options open to her. She could only hope her intuition was right where he was concerned.

"You aren't that foolish," he said in low voice that was dark with fury.

"No?" She sent him a look of disgust and stalked toward the door. "Watch me."

She took a step forward and he called her bluff. Invisible hands dragged her toward him until there was only an inch between the two of them. On some deeper level, she recognized his spicy scent and breathed it in. She met his gaze defiantly. If he expected her to cower, he was in for a rude awakening. A growl of anger rumbled deep in his chest.

"Damn it, Phaedra. Use your head. You're in a hell of a lot more danger with me as a partner than if you're working with someone else."

"And exactly how do you figure that?"

"Because I'm going to be the Praetorian Dominus's target every time we meet. He's got it in for me, and eventually, he's going to win. I can't let you be with me when that happens, because I know what Gabriel's intentions are."

"His intentions?" She sniffed with irritation. "He wants me as a brood mare. Tell me something I *don't* know. Like what *your* intentions are."

Surprise made him release his mental hold on her as he straightened upright in a rigid fashion and put some distance between them. "My intentions?"

"We've been lovers for more than two weeks now. Exactly what does that mean to you?" She sent up a small fervent prayer as she waited for him to tell her what she wanted to hear.

"If that's your way of asking for the blood bond, it's not going to happen." His sharp reply sliced at her, and she struck back.

"So you're just like that Praetorian Dominus *bastardo*. Is that it?"

"What the fuck is that supposed to mean?" The angry words had the same force of a whip cracking in the air.

"Well, obviously you've just been using me for pleasure. Or maybe I've got it all wrong and there's some other reason we've been sharing the same bed."

"*Il Christi omnipotentia*. You know better."

"Do I? You were the one to bring up Gabriel and his intentions. Exactly what am I supposed to think?"

"I am *not* him." This time his voice echoed with a fury that vibrated the air between them.

"You're right. You aren't him. But at least that monster is honest about what he wants. You, on the other hand, lied to me. Made me believe . . . believe there was more to us than you ever intended."

"I've already explained why I didn't tell you."

"My reaction. Right. And that tells me you thought I would betray you to the Order if you told me your secret."

His expression became unreadable, and his neck muscles bunched tight with tension as he stared at her in silence. The only indication he was under any kind of strain was his ragged breathing. It made her think he might be in pain. Were his wounds from last night hurting him? She knew he'd refused the *Curavi* Violetta had offered him last night, and Phaedra was convinced it was a form of penance. She took a step toward him, and she saw his throat bob as he shook his head hard. *Deus*, he wasn't going to give way at all.

"I told you why I didn't tell you. If you're looking for something more than that . . . I don't have it to give." It was a rejection. Plain and simple. It made her sag under the weight of it.

"Then there's nothing more to say." With as much dignity as she could muster, she walked past him and headed toward the study door. Her hand on the doorknob, she looked at him over her shoulder. "Remember what I said. If you try to reassign me, I'll call *Dux Provocare*. And *this time*, I'm not bluffing."

Not waiting for his response, she simply opened the door and left the room. The moment she was in the hall with the door closed quietly behind her, she bit back a cry at the pain assaulting every cell of her body. The force of it was almost crippling in its intensity. Stumbling forward, she made her way upstairs. Stubborn man. How could she forgive him if he didn't want forgiveness? He cared about her, but he'd rejected her as neatly as he might have sliced open a Praetorian. She stopped in the upper hallway and stared at the door in front her. Ares and Emma's door. She hesitated before knocking. What was she going to say to him? She didn't know, but somehow she'd find a way to tell him. She rapped lightly on the door with her knuckles.

"You looking for me or Emma?" Her brother's quiet question behind her startled her, and she jerked around to see Ares headed toward her with a somber expression on his face. She nodded.

"I was looking for you. I need to talk to you."

"Come on in," he said as he ushered her into the suite. "Emma's in the library with Atia studying the artifact we found last night."

"Oh." It wasn't exactly the response she meant to make, and Ares quirked his eyebrow at her.

"Okay, something's bugging you. Out with it."

"Can we sit down?"

He frowned and gestured toward the couch. She sank down on the cushions and stared at the bowl of red roses centered on the coffee table. Leaning forward, she absently stroked the velvety petals. The scent of the flowers reminded her how soft and feminine her mother had always smelled when she'd hugged her good night. She closed her eyes at the memory. It wasn't fair that that *bastardo* was still alive and her parents were dead.

"What's wrong, Phaedra?" Ares never called her by her full name unless he was really worried about her.

"How often do you think about Mom and Dad?" Her question was met by silence, and she turned her head to see Ares staring up into space. As if realizing she was watching him, he shrugged slightly.

"Not as often as I used to. They're always there in the back of my mind, but it's not every day. More like I'll see something that reminds me of them."

She looked back at the flowers, suddenly uncertain as to whether she should tell him what she knew. Did he really need to know?

What if he hadn't seen anything? It might affect his friendship with Lysander, and right now Lysander needed every friend he could get.

"Phaedra, if this is about Lysander's father and Mom, I already know." The harsh, unforgiving note in his voice wasn't directed at her, but it troubled her just the same.

"How?"

"I knew the minute I heard Nicostratus's voice. It's not something you forget. I just didn't realize you knew who he was. I thought maybe you'd managed to block that whole night out of your head." His words sent relief spilling through her. He already knew. She didn't have to tell him.

"I've never forgotten his face or his voice."

"I should never have let you get close to that peephole."

"You were in shock. You didn't even realize I was looking until it was too late. I wanted to see Mom one last time. Just not like that."

Her stomach lurched as she allowed the memories to swell over her. Eyes closed, a tear forced its way out from behind her eyelid and rolled down her cheek. Ares's hand squeezed hers for a brief moment, and the brotherly love in the gesture warmed her heart.

"And Lysander?" she asked quietly. "How do you feel about him?"

"Do you mean the fact that he has Praetorian blood?"

She shrugged. "Not so much that, but the fact that his father . . . it doesn't bother you?"

"Lysander didn't have anything to do with Mom and Dad's death. It's not his fault that bastard raped his mother." He eyed her carefully. "I got the impression that the two of you were pretty close. He didn't tell you?"

"No," she said as she averted her gaze from her brother's curious look. "He didn't trust me with his secret. And a relationship requires trust. We don't have that."

"You need to cut the guy some slack, Phae. He's been living with this for a year, now. It had to be hard, trying to reconcile himself to who his real father is, losing the father figure he had growing up."

"But he could have told me. Instead, he sent me away that night in Genova."

"*Christus*, Phaedra, the guy went through one hell of a torture session. Two of his men died, and Marta was taken. On top of that, he was dealing with the fear of discovery and how people would react." Ares shook his head in disgust. "Look how all of us reacted last night, and this morning. Can you blame the guy for not trusting anyone with his secret?"

She winced. Ares was right. She was angry because he hadn't trusted her, not because he was part Praetorian. And her reaction last night had simply proven he'd been right not to trust her. It was a painful truth.

"Lysander might have Praetorian blood, but he's Sicari through and through. And that's all you need to know."

As she met her brother's dark gaze, she nodded. She loved Lysander. Just like Ares had said, Lysander was still the same man. He hadn't changed, but everyone else had, including her. She'd failed him. She'd always accused him of running, and yet she'd been running like mad since last night. Now she had to find a way to make him see that. Make him trust her. She didn't know how she was going to do that, but she'd find a way.

Chapter 22

MAXIMUS *watched his tribune race toward him with a sickening sensation in his gut. The mere fact that Tevy was alone told him the worst. Cassiopeia and Demetri were gone. Slumping forward in his saddle, he closed his eyes against the pain. An image of Cassiopeia fluttered through his head, her sultry smile tempting him as her hand beckoned him to come to her.*

Grief tore at him like the rabid dogs would soon tear at the rotting flesh of the men he'd left behind at the Tiber River. His hands clutched at his horse's mane to prevent himself from wheeling the animal around and charging back toward Constantine's guardsmen. As much as he wanted to die at this moment, there was something more important he had to do. Octavian had to be dealt with.

The grief inside him slowly melted into a raw fury that slid hot and fiery through his veins. He would tear Octavian's heart out with his bare hands for the bastard's treachery. Resolved to destroy the man who'd taken everything from him, he straightened in his saddle and waited for Tevy to reach him. As his tribune's horse slid to a stop, he noted the animal was foaming at the mouth, a sign that Tevy had ridden the mare hard.

"Where are they?" he asked, fully expecting his tribune to tell him his wife and son were at home being prepared for their funeral.

"The neighbors say your man, Posca, smuggled the boy out of

*the house just before Octavian and his men arrived. The domina
was taken to Octavian's house." Tevy's words pierced his grief with
a ray of hope. They were alive. Renewed energy strengthened him
as a plan of action formed in his mind.*

*"Posca will keep Demetri safe until we find them. We'll recover
the Tyet of Isis after Cassiopeia is safe and Octavian is dead."*

*"The domina is no longer at Octavian's home." Tevy averted his
gaze as he continud. "He's had her taken to the Saepta Julia. I had
your men follow them, while I came to find you."*

"Saepta Julia?" He frowned.

*"He intends to . . ." Tevy, his expression grim, blanched. "He
intends to turn her over to the Nazarene's fanatics."*

*His tribune's statement sent ice sluicing over Maximus's skin. If
Octavian gave Cassiopeia to the Church, they'd kill her. The fanatics despised Rome's religion and traditions. In the back of his mind,
he heard a soft whisper. Cassiopeia. Eager to touch her, even if
only with his mind, he reached out for her with his thoughts. As his
mind touched hers, the panic raging inside her was overwhelming.
The images flowing between them only heightened his fear for her.
Octavian climbing a makeshift podium. Bundles of wood forming
a pyre. As best he could with the threadbare contact he'd achieved,
he reassured her that he was coming for her. Her panic eased and as
the thread between them unraveled, her courage made him proud.
He snapped his head in Tevy's direction.*

"Pull Titus and Vidal from the ranks. We'll need them."

"They'll—"

"Get them, now."

*He didn't wait for Tevy to obey the order. He simply tugged at
the reins of his horse and sent the animal off at a gallop toward
the mounted soldiers Constantine had posted outside the Flaminia
gate. He returned moments later with two horses for the two soldiers Tevy had pulled from the ranks.*

*"I don't care who tells you to stop," he said grimly as he met the
gazes of the three men watching him. "You stop for nothing until I
tell you to. We ride to the Saepta Julia. Tevy, if something happens
to me, you know what to do."*

Maximus urged his horse into a gallop and raced toward the

Porta Flaminia. In minutes, they were inside the city, but the crowded streets slowed their progress. Desperate to reach Cassiopeia, he shouted for people to make way. They did, but far more slowly than his soldiers would have.

Their snail's pace created a terror inside him he'd never experienced before on the battlefield. What if he didn't reach her in time? He fought back the fear and pushed his horse forward. He would reach her. He wouldn't let anything or anyone stop him. As they drew closer to the Saepta Julia, the crowd thickened and became impassable by horse. He could see the dome of the Pantheon, and he remembered the alleyway he had used when he'd moved the Tyet of Isis from the Temple of Vesta. He glanced over his shoulder.

"Vidal. Stay with the horses," he snapped. "Tevy, Titus. Rally to me."

He was off his horse in one swift move to aggressively push his way through the crowd toward an alleyway flowing into the Via Flaminia. With Tevy and Titus on his heels, he made his way around the back of the Pantheon to the alleyway he'd visited only a few days ago. Here the crowd flowed steadily into the square, but there was less traffic.

It made it easier to move forward, and the closer he came to the square at the Saepta Julia, the easier it was to hear brief snippets of one person talking followed by the roar of the crowd. Focusing his thoughts, he reached out to touch Cassiopeia's mind. He found her easily, which told him she was very close to him. As he continued down the alley, the crowd thickened again, and her fear grew stronger.

"I know you can hear my thoughts, *mea amor*. I'm here. Listen to me carefully, *mea kara*. I need you to show me exactly what you see. All of it."

Her fear rushed at him like a wild animal frantic to flee a threat. One hand braced against a building wall, he fought to remain on his feet in the face of her terror. By the gods, he was going to have Octavian's head for what the bastard was doing. Once more, he pushed through her terror to reach the part of her mind he could reason with.

"Cassiopeia, enough. Listen to me."

Even when talking to her directly, he'd never been so harsh, but it caught her attention and her fear eased somewhat. Relief slowed his heart rate, and he rubbed the leather of his arm bracers across his forehead to keep the sweat out of his eyes.

"I'm here, *mea amor*. Now concentrate. Let everything you see fill your mind. I want to see what you're seeing. I need to know where Octavian and his men are. Slowly, *kara*, slowly."

As he tried to calm her with his thoughts, his head filled with images of the market square that surrounded the Saepta Julia. Once a place for Roman citizens to vote, the building had become a market, and an unruly mob filled the square. Octavian was clearly inciting the crowd as he saw an image of the traitor pointing and shouting. The images shifted and he saw three Praetorians at the entrance to the square, then three more at the foot of the platform where Octavian stood. His thoughts pulled away from her, but her terror returned, and he reached out to soothe her.

"I'm coming, *mea amor*. Just a few more moments. I promise." *Slowly and gently, he retreated from her thoughts. He looked over his shoulder at Tevy and Titus.*

"*There are three of Octavian's men near the Via Flaminia and three more are with him at the pyre where he's holding Cassiopeia.*"

"*If this crowd is anything to judge by, the soldiers at the Flaminia entrance won't be able to reach us easily,*" *Tevy said. Although his friend's abilities weren't as strong as his, Maximus knew he could rely on Tevy's assessment as he focused his abilities on maintaining his connection with Cass.*

"*Octavian has put the crowd in the mood for blood.*" *He jerked his head toward the square.* "*We must move quickly.*"

Without care for anyone in his way, Maximus began pushing his way through the crowd toward the square. He had just reached the square when he heard Cass scream. He was out of time. Ruthlessly he shoved people aside as he fought his way toward the platform he'd seen in Cass's thoughts. He'd already used up most of his ability at the river, and he needed to conserve whatever he had left to save Cassiopeia.

Another shrill scream echoed out over the noise of the crowd. It was one of abject terror, and as his mind connected with hers, he saw what she saw. Horror barreled through him. The image of flames curling among the brush beneath Cassiopeia's beautiful feet turned him into a madman as he plowed his way up the steps of the platform he'd reached. A Roman soldier stood at the top of the stairway, his sword drawn.

The soldier was no match for Maximus's speed and skill. In a blur of movement that reflected the strength of his special ability, Maximus pulled his blade from the scabbard at his side. The blade had barely left the scabbard before it took a diagonal course across the man's stomach and chest in one fluid stroke. As the man fell, Maximus heard Cassiopeia scream again, and he pushed the man off the stairs into the crowd. No sooner had he stepped onto the platform than another soldier charged at him. He neatly side-stepped the man and sent his blade deep into the man's chest. As the soldier fell, Maximus saw Octavian calmly observing the square where Cassiopeia was tied to a burning pyre.

Raw fury strengthened his muscles as he charged forward. A hard, invisible wall stopped him just short of Octavian's back. The impact knocked the wind out of him, and he sank to his knees. Cassiopeia's screams were louder now, pain drowning out the fear in her cries. Maximus jerked his head in her direction and saw flames snapping at the hem of her gown. He looked up to see Octavian smile cruelly as he drew his sword.

"It appears you've arrived too late, Maximus. As you can see, your pretty wife has been tried and found guilty of heresy. But I'll do you the kindness of sending you to your death first so you can meet her in Tartarus."

"Bastard," Maximus cried as he lunged forward. The moment he hit the unseen barrier, he drained what was left of his abilities to break through the invisible wall between him and Octavian. With a vicious thrust, he buried his sword in the man's thigh just below the hipbone then tugged the blade free. Cassiopeia's screams were now shrieks of agony. He instinctively turned in her direction and failed to see Octavian swing his sword. The first thing he felt was a blow

to the head. He staggered backward, the side of his face throbbing.
He tried to wipe the blood off his face to see better, only to realize
he no longer had an eye.

LYSANDER flung himself out of the chair with a loud cry. The
scarred side of his face hurt like hell. He gently touched the area
then looked at his hand, fully expecting to see blood covering his
hand. When he didn't, he breathed a sigh of relief. *Il Christi omni-*
potentia. This dream had been a little *too* realistic for his taste.
He blinked the sleep out of his eye and glanced at the watch on
his wrist. Oh-eight-hundred. He groaned as he saw the three empty
wine bottles on the table. It was just a hangover.

Last night he'd been miserable as hell, and he'd decided to bury
his problems in alcohol. It hadn't eliminated them. It had just made
his head hurt. In fact, his entire body ached like he'd fought half
a dozen Praetorians. That's what he got for sleeping in a chair all
night. He grimaced as he pushed himself up out of the seat and
rubbed the back of his neck in an effort to ease the stiffness.

The briefing the day before yesterday had produced nothing
new in the way of information, and he'd decided to give the team a
breather from the mission. Emma and Atia were still trying to resolve
the puzzling inscription on the metal plate they'd found in the Circus Maxentius, and the computer was still processing all the digital
images the team had taken of various buildings around the city. Until
those two matters were resolved, there was little anyone could do
except wait.

Tension was running high with his secret now common knowledge, and he'd recognized the need for everyone to get used to the
idea that he had Praetorian blood running through his veins. It had
been at least sixty, maybe seventy, years since a Praetorian had left
the Collegium to join the Order of the Sicari and sire children.

The image of the first leader of the Praetorian Collegium filled
his head. Had Phaedra recognized Octavian as Nicostratus? Jaw
clenched, he prowled a path between the chair and the doorway of
his balcony. What the hell did it mean? It meant nothing. The voice in

his head argued fiercely. It was just a dream. The side of his head still throbbed, and he pressed the heel of his palm against his forehead in an attempt to ease the pain.

His head was aching just like he'd had a sword buried in the side of his face. He grimaced. It was the alcohol talking. That's all. He'd simply been so deep in the events of the dream that he was experiencing the physical sensations that came with the images. His hangover had just made the pain seem real. One hand sliding through his hair, he tried to ignore the tiny voice that was growing louder in his head. He didn't want to admit it, but the voice grew stronger.

Maybe Phaedra was right.

The thought made him release a dark growl. That was crazy thinking. The dreams were just . . . memories. *Christus*, he was totally losing it. The only reason he was starting to think like her was because he was looking for a reason to go to her. If only he'd had the courage to tell her the truth from the beginning.

If he had told her everything, maybe things would be different. *They wouldn't be any different, you stupid fuck. All you did was delay the inevitable.* Phaedra's reaction two nights ago had made it clear that it wouldn't have mattered whether he'd told her the truth sooner than later. Even in the study when he'd tried to explain . . . explain?

What had there been to explain? She'd been right. Omitting the truth was the same thing as a lie. But he had good reason for not telling the truth. There was a monster inside of him. It hovered just beneath the surface. If it ever got loose . . . He shuddered as he remembered the look of fear on Phaedra's face when he'd gotten angry.

Shame rolled over him. Only a Praetorian would have lost control like that. Honor was a trait the Sicari prized above all other things. And his behavior had been far from honorable. He closed his eye. He wanted to hit something. The gym. He'd go and expend his energy on a punching bag. A hard knock on the door made him jerk. He'd not had any visitors over the past couple of days, and aside from team briefings, he'd kept to himself.

"Come in," he commanded in a sharp voice, suppressing the

hope that it might be Phaedra trying one last time to reason with him. Cleo's appearance was a stark disappointment.

"So how long are you going to hide out in here?"

"I'm not hiding. I'm giving people time to adjust."

"Adjust to what? The news that you're half-Praetorian or the fact that the man who raped your mother is a monster?" Her blunt words put him on edge.

"Both." He spun away from her and moved to the balcony door to look out at the Colosseum.

"That's a load of crap. You're acting like you're some sort of pariah. If I didn't know better, I'd say you were ashamed to be seen." Her words drove a spike of tension into his shoulders, but he didn't answer her. She drew in a sharp breath. "You *are* ashamed. Of what?"

"Don't try to analyze me, Cleo."

"Fuck. If either one of us needs therapy, it's me. But you . . . you have nothing to be ashamed of. You're not responsible for who your father is, and you sure as hell haven't ever acted like him."

"Just because you haven't seen that side of me doesn't make it untrue." Angry that she was pushing him so hard, he whirled around and took two steps toward her. "It's not just Praetorian blood running through my veins, it's the Patriarch's."

"All right, let's test your theory."

She pulled a dagger from the small scabbard attached to her thigh and closed the space between them. Her hand grabbed his to place the hilt of the blade in his palm and forced his fingers to wrap around the hilt. Still holding his hand, she placed the tip of the dagger against her throat. Appalled, he tugged his hand backward, but Cleo only leaned into the blade.

"What the hell are you trying to do?" he snarled.

"I'm trying to find out if you're like your father." Her violet eyes flashed with indignation. "And I was right. You're nothing like Nicostratus. That Praetorian fuck would have slit my throat the minute I handed him my blade."

He jerked away from her, the dagger falling to the floor with a clatter that made him jump. A sympathetic gleam in her eyes, Cleo shook her head as she picked up the weapon and put it back into the leather sheath on her leg.

"You got dealt a lousy hand when it comes to who your dad is. No doubt about that. But you're not him, and you don't have anything to be ashamed of. Your heart is Sicari. Nothing else matters."

He wanted to believe what his friend believed, but it wasn't that simple. With a shake of his head, he turned and moved back to the balcony door. Hands braced against the wood frame, he stared out at the rooftops of Rome before ducking his head to study the wood floor beneath his feet. Cleo sighed heavily.

"Look, some people will despise you because of your Praetorian blood. Others won't give a *fotte*. Some will understand why you didn't tell anyone the truth right away. Some might say you're a spy. Other are going to say you acted dishonorably by not being up-front with everyone from the get-go." She paused to clear her throat, and he heard her shift restlessly. "None of that matters because your friends are standing by you. We know you. We know how loyal you are to the Order. *And* you have friends in high places."

He lifted his head to stare out the window, his mouth curled in a slight smile at her last statement. Straight and to the point as always. It was one of Cleo's strengths as much as it was a weakness. Sometimes she didn't know when to be diplomatic.

"So are you going to go talk to her or what?" Cleo's abrupt change of subject shouldn't have startled him. It was her way of throwing someone off balance when she was forming an argument.

"I talked to her after Atia's address to the Order. She—it won't work out."

"Do you love her?" The question made him turn around and glare at her. She raised her hands in surrender. "Forget I asked. I already know the answer."

"Why did you come here, Cleo?"

"I came because I'm your friend, and I know you and Phae belong together."

"You're wrong."

"You know, on the field of battle I've never seen you hesitate, and yet when it comes to Phae, you're like a kid afraid of getting burned by fire."

"Leave it be, Cleo," he snapped.

"If a Praetorian was breathing down my neck, would you just let them kill me?"

"You know better."

"Do I? If you can't trust Phae, how can I believe you trust me? Our friendship isn't worth squat if you don't trust me to watch your back and vice versa."

"It's not the same thing and you know it."

"It *is* the same thing," she exclaimed angrily. "And if you can't trust the people who care about you, you can't trust anyone. Not even yourself."

The staccato tempo of her fiery words made him feel like he was the punching bag he'd considered using earlier. Violet eyes dark with anger, she glared at him before she stalked out of his suite. The door slammed behind her with a crash, and he winced. One of the most aggravating things about Cleo was that she was usually right when it came to things like this. She had good instincts, and it wasn't the first time she'd acted as his conscience. And as much as he hated to admit it, she was right. He hadn't trusted anyone for more than a year now.

Nicostratus had done a number on him in more ways than one. The bastard had made him question everything he'd ever believed about himself. Not only that, the Praetorian had destroyed his relationship with Phaedra before it had even begun. No. He'd done that all by himself. If he wanted to be with Phaedra, he only had one option. He had to take a step into the unknown and trust her. But before he could do that, he needed to win *her* trust. That wasn't going to be easy. He'd created a chasm so wide between them, he wasn't sure she'd forgive him easily, let alone trust him. There was only one thing he could think of that might earn her trust; he just wasn't sure he was ready to accept what it meant. He swallowed hard. He didn't have a choice. If he didn't gain her trust, he'd lose her. Maybe he already had.

Chapter 23

LYSANDER paced the hall outside of Phaedra's suite. Exactly what was he going to say to her? He'd come to his senses? He wanted to tell her about his dreams? *Christus*, if it was this hard just to knock on her door, how hard was it going to be telling her about everything he'd dreamt in the past few weeks.

Steeling himself not to run, he stopped in front of her suite for what had to be the twentieth time in the past fifteen minutes and knocked. It took only a minute for her to open the door, but it seemed like an hour. The smile on her face swiftly dissolved, and her expression became guarded the moment she saw him standing in the doorway.

"Yes?" There wasn't any hostility in her voice, but there wasn't any warmth either.

"Can we talk?" He clenched his jaw as he saw the hesitation slide across her face and he prepared himself for a rejection.

"All right."

She stepped back and opened the door wider so he could cross the threshold. Not about to give her a chance to change her mind, he moved deeper into the room. From the bedroom, he heard the unwelcome sound of a male voice.

"*Carissima*, you're all out of . . ." Luciano Pasquale's voice trailed off as he emerged from the bedroom.

Jealousy made Lysander's blood boil at the sight of the man. What in the hell was this Italian Casanova doing in Phaedra's suite? In her bedroom. His fingers itched as he fought the urge to mentally throttle the man. Instead, he pinned the man with an icy glare.

With a grimace, Pasquale moved toward Phaedra. In bitter silence, Lysander watched as the man took Phaedra's hand and raised it to his lips. He murmured something to her, and Phaedra shook her head.

"I'll see you at dinner."

"As you wish, *cara*. You know where to find me if you need me."

"She doesn't need protection from me," he said with a sharp precision that mimicked a blade being honed.

"For your sake, *il mio signore,* I hope not." Pasquale's response added more fuel to the fire streaming through his blood, increasing his need to hurt the man. Badly. Instead, he remained silent.

A moment later, the suite door closed behind the Sicari warrior, leaving him alone with Phaedra. His jaw ached from the pressure of keeping his teeth clenched so he wouldn't say something he'd regret, but the minute Pasquale was gone, he exploded.

"What the fuck was he doing in your bedroom?"

She bristled with anger. "You don't have any right asking that question."

"Maybe not. But I want an answer." He moved quickly to put himself in her path as she appeared ready to walk past him. Her beautiful brown eyes flickered with something he immediately wanted to shy away from.

"All right, he needed to use the bathroom."

Defiant. That's what she was. She actually expected him to believe that *bastardo* had been in her bedroom for no other reason than to take a leak. He flinched. Trust. He'd made up his mind to trust her, and that meant believing her when she said something. *Christus*, he wasn't sure he could do this without screwing things up worse than they were. Not to mention how bad his jaw was hurting again. He blew out a harsh breath and turned away from her.

"Okay," he growled.

"Okay?" The incredulous note in her voice forced the muscles in his shoulders to go tight.

"I believe you, okay?" he snapped. "It's just that Pasquale's been looking to find a way into your bed since the first time he laid eyes on you. And I—well, I don't want you making some sort of mistake where he's concerned."

When she didn't answer, he looked over his shoulder at her. The expression of amazement on her face made him grimace. Was she that blind? Pasquale hadn't been able to keep away from her since day one. She narrowed her eyes at him as he faced her again.

"And this concerns you, how?"

"Because you belong to me," he growled as he wheeled about and closed the gap between them until he could feel the heat of her body penetrating his clothing. "You're mine, and I don't want him anywhere near you."

"You arrogant *bastardo*. I don't belong to anyone, least of all you."

He knew he sounded arrogant and possessive, but it was how he felt. He was jealous as hell of Pasquale, and he wasn't going to let go of her without a fight. He leaned into her, his nostrils breathing in the sweet honeyed scent of her. *Deus*, she smelled incredible. And he knew she'd taste just as good as she smelled. Desire clouded his brain as his gaze studied her mouth for a long moment before he noticed her breathing had suddenly become ragged. Breathless even. His gaze scanned her face, noting the way her eyes had widened, and a familiar emotion fluttered across her features.

"I might be arrogant," he rasped. "But you *do* belong to me, and you know it."

She shook her head, but he could see her wavering as he reached out with his mind to lightly drag an invisible finger down her throat to the base of her neck. His erection thickened in his pants as his body responded to hers. *Christus*, he wanted her so bad right now.

"Why are you doing this, Lysander?"

"Doing what?" he muttered, well aware that he wasn't playing fair with her. Not a good way to earn her trust.

"Toying with me," she whispered.

"Believe me, *carissima*. I'm not toying with you. I'm trying to make you see how much I need you. When I say you belong to me, I'm really saying that we belong to each other."

He swallowed hard as he ventured out into a place he'd never gone before. It was one thing to say she was his, but to take the chance that she wouldn't reject him was unfamiliar territory for him. Surprise widened her eyes, and he flinched, waiting for her to drop the hammer on him. An instant later, her hands tugged his head downward, and she kissed him hard.

The unexpected response opened a floodgate of emotion as he wrapped his arms around her and pulled her tight. Her lips parted against his, and his tongue swept into her mouth savoring the sweet, cinnamon flavor of her. She tasted like hot, spicy apples. Damn, how was it possible the woman could twist his insides with just one taste of her?

Warm and soft in his arms, she pressed her hips into his until his erection was pressing into the apex of her thighs. She immediately swiveled her hips against him. It pulled a deep groan from his throat and filled him with the need to strip her clothes off and make love to her right here in her living room. Her fingers worked frantically at his sides as she tugged his shirt free of his pants and pushed it upward.

The minute she touched his bare skin, he was on fire. A shudder rocked his body a second later as her mouth blazed a fiery trail across his stomach. Desperate to remove every article of clothing separating them, he pulled the shirt up over his head and tossed it aside. At the same time, he used his mental ability to remove her clothes just as quickly.

As they undressed each other in a state of frenzy, he deepened their kiss until need, hunger, and desire consumed him. In that moment, he knew she was a part of him. He was incomplete without her. The tiny mewls of pleasure escaping her sent him tumbling toward a place only she could take him. Hands clutching her round, lush buttocks, he picked her up and carried her toward the bedroom.

With her long legs wrapped around his waist, the heat of her core seared him through the scrap of silk she wore. His cock rock hard, he ached to bury himself inside her and feel her hot folds squeezing him until he exploded from the sheer pleasure of it. Her mouth broke away from his and slid along his jaw and down the side of his neck. A moment later, her teeth lightly nipped his shoulder. It tugged a growl from him as she came back to his mouth, her tongue insistent on teasing his again.

The moment his shin hit the edge of the bed, they tumbled downward onto the mattress. Before he could pin her beneath him, she escaped his arms and straddled him. The sultry look on her face made his mouth go dry. Scooting backward until she was sitting on his thighs, she made short work of his pants then moved forward until the only thing between his cock and her heat was a wispy piece of silk.

Not willing to wait for her to remove them, he visualized her panties ripping at the seams and flying out from between them. She gasped, her face darkening with desire as he quickly lifted her up and seated her on his cock. The hot, creamy center of her clenched hard around him, and he released a cry of pleasure. Unable to hold himself back, his fingers dug into the soft flesh of her hips as he rocked back and forth against her.

Sleek and velvety smooth, her body gripped him like a hot vise, the pleasure of it pulling him over the edge and down into the abyss. The entire way down, his body cried out for her, until he went rigid and throbbed violently inside her. Slowly the haze of passion drifted away, and he rolled her onto her back.

Color heightened the beauty of her cheekbones, and he lightly ran his fingertips across her face. He was never going to get enough of her. She was the light to his darkness, and if he ever lost her, he'd descend into a madness from which there was no return. She smiled up at him with a mischievous sparkle in her eye.

"That was wonderful. Can we do it again?"

"*Il Christi omnipotentia*, woman. Give me a few minutes to recover."

She laughed, her hands lightly rubbing over his shoulders only to stop on the pinkish scar on his arms. Her fingertips traced the line of the scar as a haunted look flashed across her features.

"He could have killed you."

"But he didn't, *carissima*. And there are worse things in the world than a cut." He dropped his head until his forehead pressed against hers.

"I don't want to lose you to that *bastardo*." Her fingertips edged the line of his mutilated jaw as she forced him to look at her.

"You won't, *inamorato*."

He kissed her gently as the whisper of a sigh echoed out of her. The need to reassure her swept through him. How could he make her understand that he was willing to enter the darkness of Tartarus itself if it meant keeping her safe? His mouth trailed its way along her beautiful jaw to glide down her neck. She was beautiful, and she was his. He wasn't going to let any other man take her from him. Another sigh slipped past her lips as his mouth tenderly feathered her shoulder with kisses.

"Do you have any idea how beautiful you are, *carissima*?" He nuzzled the soft spot between her neck and shoulder. "You've got the softest skin imaginable."

"I think you're delusional," she said with a laugh, but there was a breathless quality to her voice that he liked. "But I love it."

"Everything about you is soft and sweet. I don't think I'll ever get enough of you, *inamorato*." At his words, her hands grasped his hips, and she reached between them to stroke his cock.

"Will you please stop talking and make love to me again?"

The moment she touched him, he was hard. *Deus*, the woman simply had to touch him and he was lost. His heart skipped a beat as he raised his head to look down into her eyes. The warm emotion shining there tugged at his heart and took his breath away. Unable to speak, he kissed her again, his heart in every caress, every kiss, and every touch of his mind.

More than an hour later, she stirred beside him, her fingers lazily trailing a path across his shoulder to the pink scar on his chest. He caught her hand and carried it to his mouth to press his lips in her palm. She sighed.

"So where do we go from here?" she asked softly.

His jaw clenched for a moment before he released the tension holding it tight. Now was the moment to show he was willing to trust her completely. To regain her faith in him. He swallowed the knot of fear swelling in his throat.

"We could talk about . . . about these dreams we've both been having."

She stiffened beside him then shot upright to stare down at him in astonishment. In the back of his mind, he noticed how beautiful her breasts were, but at the moment, he was too fucking nervous to do anything about it. In the next instant, his heart sank as she scooted off the bed to pace the floor. Pushing himself up on one elbow, he watched her stalk the small area beside the bed. He loved her best this way. Beautiful. Naked. Her hair tumbling past her shoulders to sway against her skin like black silk.

"Why now?" she demanded as she came to a halt and faced him with a fierce expression on her face.

He closed his eyes and fell backward onto the pillows. Here it came. The truth. The mattress bounced slightly as she returned to the bed and moved toward him. A moment later, she'd straddled him. Surprised, he opened his eyes to meet her wary gaze.

"Well?"

"Because you want me to trust you," he said hoarsely. "And I don't know any other way to make you see that I do."

Unable to bear the possibility that she wouldn't believe him, or worse, dismiss his display of trust, he looked away from her. A moment later, something wet hit his stomach, and he jerked his head back toward her to see tears rolling down her cheeks. Horrified that he'd made her cry, he rolled her off him onto her back and hovered over her to wipe the tears from her eyes.

"It's all right, *cara*. I know it's not much, but it's the only card I have in my hand at the moment. I'll try to do better, *carissima*. I promise."

"*Deus*, you really can be dense sometimes, you *bacciagalupe*." She sniffed and gave him a watery smile. "I'm crying because it shows you *do* trust me."

Relief raced through him as the impact of her words hit him. She did understand. He lowered his head and kissed her gently. Lifting his head, he grimaced.

"So where do we start?"

"Why not the beginning?" she said quietly. "Tell me the first dream you ever had about Maximus and Cassiopeia."

With a nod, he rolled onto his back and shared what he could remember of his first dreams about Maximus. As they talked about their dreams, he began to see a pattern emerge. Based on everything Phaedra had told him, their dreams had followed a timeline that in many ways paralleled their own relationship and the people they knew. But when she shared her dream about Octavian, he knew he couldn't tell her about his last dream. It had been difficult enough for him to experience, he didn't want to alarm her or make her think they were going to endure a similar fate. He wasn't going to lose her like Maximus had lost Cassiopeia.

"Do you think Octavian had anything to do with the death of Cassiopeia's father, like he . . . like he did with my parents?"

Her question caught him off guard. "What?"

"Octavian. Nicostratus. They're one in the same."

He turned his head to study her pensive expression. It was the first time she'd mentioned the two men were connected. It hadn't been until his latest dream that he'd realized it himself. Without agreeing or disagreeing with her, he simply watched her. The palm of her hand cradled her head as she propped herself up on her elbow, and she was staring off into space. He knew she was remembering the death of her parents. It cut deep to know the man who'd sired him was the monster who'd caused her so much pain. Suddenly, her gaze focused on him with a look that indicated she expected a reply.

"I don't remember anything in my dreams about Cassiopeia's father, but if the *bastardo*'s true to form, I wouldn't be surprised."

"Have you noticed that everything we've dreamed is almost like someone showing us a chronological record of events?"

"Events you think we've already experienced in another life." He winced at the words. He still wasn't ready to believe their dreams were a depiction of their lives together in ancient Rome. The thought was unsettling, and he didn't like the sensation.

"Yes," she said quietly, a somber look on her face. "What if we're doomed to repeat the past?"

The words were a sword running him through, and he didn't know how to answer her. He knew he'd give his life for her, but if he believed the past would repeat itself in the now, it meant he had to believe he was Maximus reincarnated. Worse, it meant he would fail her just as Maximus had failed Cassiopeia.

"No," he rasped. "I can't believe that. The future isn't written yet, and I'm not going to let anything happen to you. I'm not going to fail you."

"Why would you think that?" She narrowed her gaze on him. Although he kept his expression neutral, he didn't fool her. "There's something you're not telling me."

He knew better than to lie. Instead, he looked up at the ceiling again to avoid her penetrating gaze. In a flash, she was hovering over him, simply glaring at him in a way that made him realize she wasn't going to let him off the hook. Frustration tugged at him.

"I haven't told you about the last dream I had."

"Why not?" The question was gentle and without judgment. "Did you see Cassiopeia's death?"

"No, I didn't see that." He dragged in a harsh breath. "I couldn't see her because Octavian buried a sword in Maximus's head, blinding him in one eye."

"Just like you," she breathed softly as her fingers reached out to touch the scarred mass of tissue that had once been his cheek. "We have to tell Atia."

"I was afraid you were going to say that," he groaned.

"She needs to know. As *Prima Consul* she's entitled to know. Besides, with the exception of my brother, she knows more about Sicari history than anyone else in the Order. If there's anything to these dreams of ours, she'll have answers."

He knew she was right. If anyone knew what their dreams meant, it would be Atia. The woman had asked him weeks ago whether he was dreaming; the *Prima Consul* knew a hell of lot more than she let on. He just wasn't crazy about the idea of spilling his guts to anyone but Phaedra. His gaze met hers, and he agreed with a sharp nod.

"All right. We tell Atia." His resigned response made her smile mischievously at him as she gave him a quick kiss. Her gaze drifted toward the clock, and she gasped loudly.

"*Christus*, it's almost noon. Atia called for a team meeting at one, and I'm betting she and Emma have come to some conclusion about the artifact. Maybe Emma got a vision when she touched the plate. She was wearing gloves when she dug up the plate at the circus, so I doubt she saw anything then."

Moving quickly, she got out of bed and hurried into the bathroom to turn on the shower. She poked her head back into the bedroom, her expression one of sultry invitation. "Aren't you going to join me?"

He didn't need a second invitation, and with a grin, he climbed out of bed to join her in the shower. When he reentered the bedroom a short time later, he waved his hand to straighten the tousled sheets and put the bedspread back into place. As Phaedra emerged from the bathroom, she laughed.

"I always said you were a neat freak."

"I am *not* a neat freak," he growled. "I simply like order. Something you clearly need when it comes to your clothing."

With an arched look in her direction, he pointedly turned his gaze to shoes scattered in various places in the room, shirts tossed over a chair in one corner of the room, and a nightstand cluttered with a collection of everything under the sun. The dresser had a drawer half closed with something silky draped over the top edge. He didn't know how she could find anything in all the chaos.

"When we get home to Chicago, you're going to have to get used to seeing female clothing lying around, and *not* just where you peeled them off me." Her playful tone didn't create the amused reaction he was certain she meant to incite in him. Instead, his muscles knotted up and his gut twisted in a sharp, painful reaction.

"Right," he muttered in an effort to avoid her noticing his sudden tension. He was dressed before her and headed toward the door.

"I love you, Lysander." Her soft words stopped him dead in his tracks. Il Christi omnipotentia, *what was he supposed to say to that?* He glanced over his shoulder at her.

"I know, *carissima*." His response made her pale, and he wanted to kick himself. She'd put herself out on a limb, and he'd practically cut it off to let her fall to the earth.

"Do you love me?"

The question brought the stark emotion he'd felt for a very long time to the surface. Until now, he'd never had the courage to name the feeling, let alone openly express it. And with good reason. The minute he confessed his feelings, his gut told him she'd eventually expect the blood bond. He was willing to do whatever else she wanted commitment-wise, but he had no intention of mixing his Praetorian blood with hers.

It wasn't just the thought of polluting her with his tainted blood that troubled him. Sealing the blood bond meant the odds of her getting pregnant were extremely high. The thought made him queasy.

No kids. He wasn't going to inflict his blood on an innocent child. No. A blood bond between them was out of the question. Slowly, he turned to face her, and one look at her face sent his heart plummeting downward. It was like he'd taken two steps forward, only to realize he was about to go back three.

Chapter 24

PHAEDRA'S heart was pounding as Lysander slowly turned to face her. She couldn't believe she'd actually said she loved him, let alone asked him if he felt the same way. The expression on his angelic profile was almost as twisted and tormented as his demonic half. *Deus*, what was he thinking? Had she made a mistake? She'd been so certain he cared for her, but what if she was wrong? She bit her lip nervously, as with each passing second she grew more certain he was going to break her heart.

"Yes," he rasped. "I love you."

She swayed slightly as relief weakened her knees. *Gratias Deus*. She was beginning to think she'd made a terrible mistake. Warm with the knowledge that he loved her, she took a step toward him. His mouth became a hard, grim line, the scarred tissue of his face twitching slightly, and her heart sank as she hesitated.

"Why do I see a 'but' coming?" she asked with more than a hint of trepidation.

"There's something I want to make clear before we go any further. If you're expecting a blood bond—don't."

The words scraped down her spine like a Praetorian sword splitting her in half. Why would he say he loved her in one breath and in the next say he wasn't about to commit to the blood bond? Confused, all she could do was stare at him while half a dozen questions danced around in her head. The man was going to drive her mad.

"Why?" She wanted to shout her question, but instead she kept her voice low and calm.

"I don't want kids." Sharp and to the point. No kids. She could deal with that.

"Okay, so we don't have kids." She shrugged, ignoring the slight twinge she felt at the idea that she wouldn't ever feel his baby growing inside her. She'd live with it if it meant being with him. "There is something called protection, you know."

"It doesn't matter. It's just not going to happen." His emphatic tone made her flinch.

"*Va bene*, it's not going to happen," she said sarcastically. "Happy?"

"Yes," he growled. "You?"

"No, because I'm trying to understand how you can say you love me, and yet you don't want to blood bond with me." She raked her hair back off her forehead and glared at him in frustration. "I think I know why you don't want children. You're afraid you'll pass on some terrible gene of Nicostratus's to any child you father, but me? If we take precautions, why would sealing the blood bond be a problem, unless . . . having children isn't what you're really afraid of, is it?"

"Take care, *carissima*. This isn't a path you want to tread." His gaze narrowed at her, and his beautiful green eye was a hard gem.

"And why *is* that? Could it be you're worried you're somehow going to infect me with that Praetorian blood you have in you?"

She saw how her words exacerbated the strength of the tic in his cheek. She'd hit the target. He hadn't come to terms with his Praetorian half, and he didn't want to drag her into his personal hell. She loved him all the more for wanting to protect her, but she wasn't going to let him get away with it. When he didn't answer her, she shook her head slowly.

"Bonding with me will *not* send me over to the dark side."

"It's not up for discussion." A deep, rumbling growl echoed out of his chest as he turned away from her and stepped toward the door. Damn it, she hated it when he walked away from her or a problem between them.

"Then there's no point in us staying together, is there?" The question made him come to a dead stop. His features unreadable, he turned his head to look over his shoulder at her.

"Not if you're going to insist on something I can't give."

The cold, inflexible note in his voice sent her reeling. Her bluff had failed. He'd give her up rather than give way on the blood bond. She swallowed hard. Could she live with him without that commitment? Could she accept it without resenting him for not loving her enough to take that extra step and overcome his fear? The fact that she didn't have an immediate answer scared her. She closed her eyes, and when she opened them, he was gone.

Deus, she wanted to deck the hardhead. She quickly braided her hair into a single plait then sat on the bed to pull on her boots. Finished, she buried her face in her hands, trying not to cry. She understood his fear, but she didn't know how to help him overcome it. The torture he'd endured at Nicostratus's hands had changed him in ways she'd not comprehended until now.

She'd always known the emotional torment of that night had stayed with him. But how was she supposed to make him accept he wasn't responsible for the Praetorian blood in his veins? How did she make him understand that he was the sum of *all* his parts not just one piece? It wasn't his Praetorian side that defined him.

He was convinced that his relationship to Nicostratus made him part monster. And she was convinced it terrified him. Well, the one thing he wasn't factoring into the equation was her. If he thought she was going to give up on the two of them without a fight, he was wrong. She'd given up the last time. She'd walked out of the hospital that night more than a year ago without fighting for the two of them. This time she wasn't giving up so easily.

Somehow, she'd make him see reason. She'd find a way to help him see past the fear and to conquer the demon he thought resided in him. The resolve in her gaining strength, she got to her feet and left the bedroom. The empty living area of the suite said he'd already gone to see Atia. She tightened her jaw with determination. Quite soon now, Lysander Condellaire was going to find out that his Sicari heart was stronger than his Praetorian blood.

She left the suite and hurried down to the study Atia had made her temporary office. When she arrived, she saw Lysander seated in one of the chairs opposite the *Prima Consul*. Without saying a word, she simply crossed the room and sat down next to him. Atia's gaze narrowed on her.

"Lysander tells me the two of you have been dreaming about Maximus and Cassiopeia."

"Yes. We compared notes, and it appears we lived"—she shot a glance at Lysander, whose face remained emotionless—"might have lived as the first Sicari Lord and his wife."

It was the first time she'd referred to Maximus in the manner most Sicari would refer to the ancient Roman general. Beside her, Lysander stiffened. The emotions running beneath his cool façade made her swallow hard. Saying he wasn't happy with her comment would be an understatement. Atia nodded, a pensive look on her face.

"Lysander has some misgivings at saying you're the reincarnated couple." Atia arched her eyebrows at the two of them. "What do you think, Phaedra?"

"If we're not, then how do we explain the dreams? Mine are life-like in their imagery, and I believe Lysander's are just as vivid."

"There are other possibilities." Lysander cleared his throat. His response made Atia frown. She immediately reached for an aging, leather-bound book on the table to her right. Carefully, she turned the pages of the thick volume until she found the spot she was looking for and turned it around to lay on the table in front of Lysander.

"Sometimes the most improbable becomes the obvious. Read it," she commanded. He leaned forward as she pointed to a passage in the book. When he began to read to himself, Atia stopped him. "Out loud, please."

" 'When the Sicari Lord is Mars to the Nazarene's *templum*, the search for the *Tyet of Isis* will be won only if he accepts the truth Somnus shows him, and to regain what he's lost, he must be prepared to use his lady's dagger.' "

Phaedra leaned forward to look at the book, and her arm accidentally brushed against Lysander's. An electric shock raced up her arm at the touch, but when she glanced at him, there was nothing on his face to reveal that he'd even noticed the slight bump. Was he already starting to shut her out? Lysander looked up at Atia with a puzzled frown and shook his head.

"Is this the prophecy that Atellus has been citing for the past couple of weeks?"

"No," Atia said quietly. "This is something only a *Prima Consul* has access to, although I'm certain this is what *Prima Consul* Julius Marchio used to create his version of the Sicari Lord's prophecy. This was written by Tevy. He gave it to the first *Prima Consul*, Antonius. I only show it to you because of who you are."

At the mention of Tevy's name, Phaedra froze. Tevy was the tribune who'd served under Maximus. If Lysander hadn't been convinced he was Maximus reincarnate before, she was certain *this* would change his mind. She turned her head toward him. His features were devoid of color, and he looked as though someone had dealt him a numbing blow.

"Tevy?" he choked out in a harsh whisper.

Without thinking twice, Phaedra reached out to him with her senses. It was like hitting a wall of darkness. He knew she was reaching out to him and was intentionally keeping her out. But it didn't hinder her ability to feel the bleak horror he was struggling with. Atia eyed him carefully as she nodded.

"He survived the Battle of Milvian Bridge, along with another officer. Both of them served under Maximus after Octavian denounced all of Maximus's followers as Sicari. The second officer, Crispian, was instrumental in saving a large number of Sicari from Octavian's persecution in the days after the battle," Atia replied, her expression filled with gentle compassion.

In a violent move, Lysander was on his feet, the chair flying through the air to crash against the bookcase on the wall behind him. Fear crested over his angelic profile as he backed away from the table. It was easy to see just how pale he'd become, because the scarred portion of his face still retained a small amount of color due to the pink muscles beneath the thin layer of scarred skin. Concerned, Phaedra started to stand, but Atia forestalled her with a wave of her hand.

"Pick up the chair and sit back down, Lysander." The calm, soothing sound of Atia's command echoed quietly through the room.

The silence in the room vibrated with tension, and the *Prima Consul*'s gaze didn't waver from Lysander's face as she waited for him to obey her. Dismay had replaced his fear as he slowly did as he'd been ordered. Seated once more in front of the table, he leaned forward, arms on his knees as he cupped the back of his head in his hands to stare at the floor.

"Knowing you as I do, Lysander, I am sure this is not an easy thing for you to accept. For the past year, you've believed yourself unworthy to be called Sicari. But I know differently. Your heart is Sicari, and you *are* the Sicari Lord Tevy wrote about in this prophecy." Atia tapped the page of the book.

Instinctively, Phaedra stretched out her hand to lightly touch the back of his head. His body flinched at her caress, but he didn't try to avoid her touch. After a long moment of silence, he sat upright to meet Atia's sympathetic gaze. His features composed with a stoic expression, he looked at the *Prima Consul*.

"Even if I accept this idea that I'm . . . I'm Maximus. This"—he swept his hand in the air over the book—"doesn't make any sense at all."

"If you break it down, it makes perfect sense," Atia said. "Mars was the son of Jupiter. You are the son of Nicostratus."

"Nicostratus isn't a god." Lysander's icy words were a harsh rejection of her explanation.

"No, but he represents the Collegium within the Church, the Nazarene's *templum*, which in many circles is representative of a god."

"Don't you think that's a bit of a reach?"

"Is it a reach that Somnus is the Roman god of sleep and that dreams are his domain? Tevy says that Somnus will show the Sicari Lord the truth. The dreams you and Phaedra have had are a clear indication of the connection the two of you have with Maximus and Cassiopeia."

"And the dagger? Exactly what does that part of the prophecy mean?" A thin veil between acceptance and denial layered his voice.

"Emma never told you this, but while she was at the estate in White Cloud, she had a vision when she held Cassiopeia's dagger."

Atia hesitated then continued. "She saw a man who could have been your twin holding the dagger."

If she'd not been convinced before, she would have been now. Phaedra looked at Lysander's still stoic expression. A quiet resignation vibrated off him that revealed more than his expression did. He drew in a harsh breath.

"And what do you suggest we do with this . . . information?"

"I've sent for Cassiopeia's dagger. I want you to carry it with you at all times."

Lysander paled again and shook his head. "If you're expecting me to use it on her again, I won't."

Phaedra started at his emphatic statement. He'd spoken as if he'd already used the dagger in the past. He believed. He finally believed. Her hand reached for his, and in an instant, his fingers were crushing her own. She didn't protest. How could she? He was dealing with so much. Even she was having a bit of an adjustment with the reality that she was Cassiopeia reincarnated.

But she hadn't fought the idea like he had. Hearing it confirmed had been a slight shock, but it had not stunned her in the way it had Lysander. The moment he'd heard Tevy's name had been the moment he'd accepted the truth. Her fingers began to ache, and Lysander's grasp immediately eased as if he'd read her mind, but he didn't let go of her hand.

"I think you're meant to use the dagger to save Phaedra. Then again, the prophecy might be telling us that you're to use it against Nicostratus. Who, if I'm correct, is Octavian reborn." This time, they both stared at the *Prima Consul* in amazement, and she smiled slightly. "You seem surprised."

"How could you possibly have known?" Phaedra shook her head.

"It's quite logical, actually. The man is second only to the Monsignor, and Gregori is growing old. Nicostratus is the real force behind the Collegium now. It makes sense that those who were with you in the past are with you now." A mantel clock on one of the bookshelves chimed the quarter hour. Atia picked up the book and headed toward the door.

"I believe you have a briefing to lead in a few minutes, Lysander. I think we're quite close, perhaps only hours away, to finding the

Tyet of Isis. When Emma shares her research about the plate you found at the Circus Maxentius, I think you'll agree."

The *Prima Consul* disappeared through the door, leaving them alone. They sat together in silence for a long moment before Lysander released her hand and stood up. He crossed the floor of the study to stare at the Sicari icon carved into the wood between two bookcases. As she watched, his fingers traced the sword intertwined with the chakram.

"Are you all right?" she whispered.

When he didn't answer her, she went to him. Without speaking, he pulled her into his arms, the scarred side of his face buried in her neck. The confusion pulsating out of him made her heart ache. He'd been through so much in the past year, and now he was coming to grips with another shocking revelation. But this time she was with him. He straightened to look down at her, and she lightly caressed his scarred cheek. A shudder ran through him.

"I love you," he rasped. "No matter what happens, I want you to remember that."

"If you're worried the past is going to repeat itself, it won't."

Despite the confidence in her voice, a shiver raced down her spine, and she swallowed the lump of fear rising in her throat. He didn't agree or disagree, he simply kissed her. The heat of him warmed her, eased the dread that chilled her.

His mouth was firm and hard against hers. It wasn't a kiss of desire or passion. Her senses opened up to him and recognized the kiss was an expression of all the emotion in his heart that he couldn't speak to her. As he lifted his head, she clung to him, suddenly terrified at the last bit of unknown she'd tasted in his kiss. She didn't know what he was planning, but she was certain she wouldn't like it.

"Come on, or we'll be late, *carissima*." Without giving her a chance to speak, he grabbed her hand and pulled her toward the door of the study. When she hesitated, he stopped and turned his head to look at her over his shoulder. "You asked me to trust you, *il mio amore*. Now, I want you to trust me."

She swallowed hard. This trusting thing wasn't quite so easy when it came to trusting him not to put himself in harm's way. And something deep inside her said it was exactly what he was planning. Reluctantly, she nodded.

"I trust you, *caro*." She forced a smile to her face in spite of her misgivings and followed him out of the room.

Chapter 25

THE briefing room was quiet as Lysander gently pushed Phaedra through the doorway. The team sat quietly at the table, their uneasy manner telling him that despite Atia's backing, they still didn't trust him. He understood that. Ares and Emma sat to the left of his place at the head of the table, while Phaedra sat down on his right next to Cleo.

The fact that his staunchest supporters were seated near him wasn't lost on him. It was a show of support the rest of the team would find hard to ignore. He was too restless to sit down, so he folded his arms across his chest and looked to his left.

"Emma, why don't you share what you and the *Prima Consul* learned about the plate we found the other night."

"Angelo, would you mind pulling up your map of the city and layering it with the ancient city map, please?"

Emma looked across the table at the historian who nodded and quickly went to work on the laptop in front of him. As he worked, Emma unwrapped the artifact in front of her then carefully held it up for everyone in the room to see. The bronze plate had been carefully cleaned and a large part of the brown, crusty matter that had covered it was now gone.

"This is the artifact we found the other night at the Circus Maxentius. We found the plate under one of the *spina*'s foundation stones. Whoever placed it there dug out a hole beneath the original marble that encased the *spina*. The plate was shoved under the stone foundation itself then a base of mud mortar was added over top of it before dirt was layered on top."

Gently returning the plate to the center of the cloth it had been wrapped in, Emma glanced up at the wall screen as the maps popped up. She stood up to walk around the table as she continued her explanation.

"Based on where we found it, and the condition it's in, I'd say it dates back to the time of Constantine's rule in Rome. We've been able to clean the artifact enough to make out the complete inscription. It's in Latin, but the *Prima Consul* translated it for me. It says 'The *Tyet of Isis* is safe from Octavian, and if one follows the signs, it can be found at the center of all that is Sicari.'"

"So we're right back where we started with one more clue added to the list," Marco said with a grimace. The *Primus Pilus* leaned back in his chair and sighed in disgust.

"Not at all." Emma shook her head. "I actually think this clue is the strongest we have. In fact, I think it's the one that will lead us straight to the *Tyet of Isis*."

"That's what we thought about the last two clues, but none of those have panned out either," Cleo said quietly. Emma sent Lysander's friend a sympathetic smile before turning to Angelo Atellus.

"Angelo, would you mind triangulating the two maps here with the icons that have been found, please." As the historian clicked away at his keyboard, Emma looked around the room. "I understand your frustration and your skepticism, but I'm convinced this plate tells us exactly where the *Tyet of Isis* really is."

"There you go, *Domina*." Angelo's tone was one of respect as Emma smiled at him.

"Look at all these places where we've found a Sicari icon." With two fingers, she pointed to the various pinpoints on the map that indicated where a symbol had been found. "Does anyone notice anything interesting about their placements?"

"They're all over the city," Pasquale said as he waved at the map. "We find one clue, only to have it send us off in a chase to find a new tip. It's like chasing butterflies."

"*Fotte.*" Cleo sprang to her feet and joined Emma at the wall screen. Her fingers touching one location after another, she looked at Emma. "If you connect the dots, they surround the Field of Mars area."

"They're place markers," Emma said with a smile before she

turned to Angelo. "Can you draw a line between the icons found at the Mausoleum at Augustus and Pompey's Theater?"

"Sure." Angelo shrugged slightly as he drew the line with the mouse.

"Right," Cleo exclaimed with excitement as she turned back to the map. "Here's an icon we found at the Trajan Forum and the Bridge of Hadrian. Draw a line between those two. It's like X marks the spot."

"Exactly, the *Tyet of Isis* has to be in the Pantheon. It was the central worship center for all Romans who hadn't converted from their gods to the Church's teachings. In other words, *all Sicari*. Now we just need to know *where* the artifact is inside the building."

As Lysander stared at the screen, the images from his last dream rose up to haunt him. Maximus—he'd gone to the Saepta Julia to rescue Phaedra from Octavian. The small alleyway he knew about had been the only way he'd been able to reach her. An alley he'd found when he'd moved the *Tyet of Isis* and placed it with Vesta. Emma's voice penetrated his consciousness.

"It's in the niche that once held a statue of Vesta. It's between two icons etched in the base of the columns bordering the niche."

By the time he realized he'd spoken out loud, it was too late. The sudden tension in the room only exacerbated his own. The muscles in his face tightened painfully at the looks of amazement and sus-picion on the faces of the people in front of him. *Fotte*. This wasn't going to be any easier than the other night.

"How in the hell do you know that?" Pasquale was staring at him like he'd grown two heads.

"Maximus," Angelo said with a note of awe in his voice.

Emma hurried around the table to a satchel beside her chair. She rooted around in the depths of the brown bag for a moment. When she pulled out the item she was looking for, Lysander recognized her father's diary. With a sense of urgency, she flipped through the book, until she stopped about three-quarters of the way through.

"Lysander's right. There are two icons directly opposite each other on the niche's columns," Emma said with quiet excitement as she sent him a smile of reassurance. "The center of all that is Sicari would be the *Tyet of Isis*, which is at the center point of those two icons."

"So exactly how did *he* know that?" Pasquale's tone was belligerent. The minute Phaedra leaned forward to speak, Lysander gestured for her to remain silent.

"Because he's Maximus reincarnate."

Atia's quiet words made the room grow silent as she walked toward him. It was one thing for Angelo to say he was Maximus, but for the *Prima Consul* to say it was a different matter altogether. He swallowed the sudden rush of fear rising in his throat as he saw the slender, velvet-wrapped item she carried. The Dagger of Cassiopeia. When she reached him, she laid the artifact on the table.

"Angelo was right recently, when he suggested a *Primus Pilus* of mixed blood would find the *Tyet of Isis*. Lysander was *Primus Pilus* for Ares in the Chicago guild, before he assumed command of this guild for the purpose of finding the artifact. As everyone now knows, his mother was Sicari, but his father Praetorian." Atia paused for a moment as she looked around the room. "The actual prophecy, handed down from one *Prima Consul* to the next, makes it quite clear that Lysander is Maximus."

Gently, she removed the weapon from its metal scabbard and laid it on the velvet beside the sheath. Embedded in the middle of the grip was a ruby. At the top of the hilt, the squared-off pommel was roughly scarred and misshapen. It looked like someone had dropped it in a forge for a few minutes. Surprisingly, the blade itself looked as pristine as the day he'd first held it. The thought startled him, and he almost recoiled from the table. Instead, he drew in a deep breath and turned his head to look at Atia.

"*Bis vivit qui bene moritur,*" she said in a strong voice.

There was reassurance in her gray eyes as she met his gaze. *He lives twice who dies well.* The Sicari motto. It was often spoken before a warrior entered into a battle with the Praetorians. He knew it was Atia's way of saying she believed he was Maximus, but he wasn't sure he was capable of living up to the reputation the Order had built for the first Sicari Lord over the past two thousand years. Even his abilities were a far cry from what Maximus could do.

The sound of a chair rolling away from the table made him jerk his head in the direction of the noise. Luciano Pasquale eyed him with respect as he offered him the traditional Roman salute.

"*Bis vivit qui bene moritur.*"

One by one, each of the team members stood up and offered him the salute. The last member of the team to stand was Ares. The salute he gave was all the more powerful because of the brotherly affection Lysander saw in his friend's eyes. Taken aback by the gesture of acceptance, he locked his jaw against the emotion the sign of respect created in him. Finding it hard to speak, he gave everyone a sharp nod and cleared his throat. Fists pressed into the tabletop, he looked around the table.

"All right, everyone. We've got some planning to do."

For the next two hours, the team laid out a plan for accessing the Pantheon in the middle of the night. When it came time to decide who would actually go on the mission, he leaned back in his chair and closed his eyes. He knew everyone wanted to go, but he was certain Nicostratus was watching the house.

Any sign of the entire team heading out on an assignment would alert the *bastardo* that something was up. They'd be followed, and things could get uglier than usual. What he needed was a bare-bones squad of the best members in the installation, and he knew he wasn't going to be popular when he announced his selections. His gaze met Atia's, who had sat quietly and patiently in the corner of the briefing room, offering the occasional input. She suddenly rose and gestured for him to follow her out into the hall. When they were out of earshot of the team, she eyed him steadily.

"You know I have the right to select team members for this assignment, but I wish to create a united front." There was an inflexible note in her voice, and he knew better than to argue with her. It just wasn't worth it at this stage of the game.

"I take it you have someone in mind?" he asked in a low voice.

"I intend to go with you." He jerked back from her in angry dismay, but she reached out to touch his arm. "I intend to take Ignacio with me. The *Prima Consul* has the right to be a part of any mission a Sicari team undertakes. You know that. It's just not done very often."

"I don't give a fuck about your right of office. I'm responsible for your safety as well as my team, and I say you're not going."

"You don't want to argue with me on this, Lysander. I'll simply follow you, and that could easily jeopardize the mission. I intend to exercise my right in the matter, and there's nothing you can do about it."

"It's insane."

"It's necessary." A flash of pain flitted across her features before she met his gaze again. "You also know that Phaedra must come."

"*No.*" He released a sharp hiss of air as he objected.

"She's your best healer. This mission is too critical for you to leave her behind. Violetta's incapable of healing life-threatening wounds, and if we send our best people on this assignment, I want someone capable of saving a life."

His heart sank at the thought of putting Phaedra in the kind of danger they might face tonight. If something happened to her . . . he swallowed the fear inside him and nodded sharply.

"Emma stays here. Her skills aren't strong enough. It's a miracle she escaped harm at the Circus Maxentius the other night."

"Agreed," Atia murmured. "I assume you want Ares to come."

"Yes. And Cleo." The minute he mentioned her daughter's name, Atia stiffened and shook her head.

"No. I won't risk—"

"Cleo, short of Ares, is my best fighter. I need her. Your safety is paramount, and the Order will have my head if something happens to you," he growled. "She goes or you stay."

"*Va bene.*" With a sharp nod, Atia agreed.

"Then I think we have everyone we need." The minute they returned to the briefing room everyone went silent. His gaze surveyed the expressions of everyone at the table, and he steeled himself for the protests.

"After consulting with the *Prima Consul*, the following people will be going to the Pantheon tonight to retrieve the *Tyet of Isis*. Ares, Cleo, Phaedra, myself, and the *Prima Consul* with her *Celeris*. We'll meet here in the briefing room at oh-one-hundred for last-minute instructions. That will be all."

The moment he finished speaking he heard the loud crack of someone slapping their hands against the tabletop. Everyone jerked their head toward the sound, and he saw Cleo jump to her feet with a look of angry fear on her face.

"Are you out of your *mind*, Mother? You haven't gone on an actual mission in years. It's too dangerous."

"You forget your place, Cleo." The icy tone in Atia's voice made Cleo flinch, but she didn't back down.

"And you forget yours, *Mother*. This isn't a little jaunt out to one of your archeological sites. If you fall into the Collegium's hands, what happened to Lysander will be a picnic compared to what they'll do to the Order's *Prima Consul*." Cleo didn't wait for a response, but stormed out of the briefing room.

After just a few seconds of tense silence, everyone quickly gathered their things and left the room. The disruptive moment had made everyone uncomfortable, but Lysander understood his friend's anger. Lysander turned his head toward Atia, whose features were a bit pale, but serene. He had to admire her for her ability to remain composed under her daughter's blistering attack.

Atia had to know Cleo was right, which made him wonder what was really driving her decision to join them. As *Prima Consul*, Atia occasionally took risks, but never any this grave. His thoughts slammed to a halt. The Sicari Lord. She was going to contact Marcus. He couldn't help the rush of relief that surged through him.

He wasn't a fool. The odds of them running into Gabriel and Nicostratus tonight were high. And they could use all the help they could get at this point if that happened. There was too much riding on this. The artifact had to remain out of Octavian's hands or everything the Sicari held dear would be lost. He wasn't sure how he knew that, he just did.

He turned toward Phaedra and winced at the sight of her talking with her brother. Impulsively, he reached out with his mind to caress her cheek. She turned her head toward him the moment his invisible touch brushed across her skin and smiled. He'd never seen a more beautiful creature in his entire life. His gaze drifted away from her face to the dagger on the table. His body tensed and grew cold as he looked at it.

This had killed her once before. What if he was forced to do the same again? Fingertips pressing into the tabletop, he closed his eye for a brief moment at the unbearable thought. A warm hand captured his, and he could feel the beat of her heart through her fingers, while the sweet, buttery scent of her brushed against his nostrils. Without a word, he pulled her into his arms, uncaring of what anyone might think. She was his, and he'd do whatever necessary to keep her safe. No matter the cost to himself.

Chapter 26

THE stone wall against Phaedra's back was chilly as they waited for Ares to signal he'd opened the rear door of the Pantheon. Her nerves on edge, the three clicks in her earpiece made her jump with surprise when they came. Beside her, Lysander quickly ordered Cleo across the narrow street that wasn't much more than an alley. She watched her friend disappear down into the fosse that surrounded the sides and back of the building.

When Cleo vanished, Lysander ordered Atia and Ignacio to cross the street and follow her. The older couple didn't waste time and disappeared in seconds. A warm hand clasped Phaedra's in a silent message of love and reassurance. In the dark, she couldn't read his expression, but his whisper was warm and comforting.

"I'll be right behind you, *carissima*." He released her hand. "Go."

She didn't hesitate. With a quick push of her hands, she shoved herself away from the cold wall and raced across the cobblestone street. She slipped past the crumbling wall to drop down almost six feet into the trench that surrounded the monument. Several feet away she saw someone slip through the door into the Pantheon. She took a step forward and froze. Someone was nearby.

"Lysander." It was a struggle to keep the panic out of her voice.

A dark shadow dropped down into the trench, and her heart slammed into her chest with fear. Pressed into the outer wall of the monument, she tried to control her racing pulse.

"It's all right, *cara*." Lysander grabbed her hand and pulled her toward the door as he bent his head toward his shoulder mike. "Atia, your company is waiting for us."

In seconds, they were in the building, and Lysander closed the heavy metal door behind them as quietly as possible. The darkness complete, she shivered as the powerful individual she sensed seemed closer with every forward step she took. The muscles in her body grew taut as her senses registered the strength and power of the man.

She'd never sensed anyone this powerful before. Not even Gabriel had made her senses react this way. The hairs on her arm were standing on end, while her skin was warm from the blood rushing frantically through her veins. Lysander tapped his flashlight on then quietly ordered her to follow him. Somehow, she managed to jerk herself out of her stupor to do as he commanded.

He didn't seem the least bit concerned, even though she was certain he sensed the person who currently had her senses wired for overload. They quickly passed through the narrow corridor and emerged from behind an altar into the temple. Overhead, the dome's paneled ceiling rose up to the oculus, which was open to sky and elements. Moonlight spilled onto the temple's marble floor, and the beauty of the building was breathtaking.

It was an incredible work of art, and despite the fact that it was almost two thousand years old, it hadn't changed much in all that time. The only thing missing were the statues of the gods. It created a sense of loss in her, even though she followed no particular set of religious teachings.

What had once been home to the worship of the gods had become something altogether different. Now it was a tomb and place of worship for another faith. It seemed almost sacrilegious, and she recognized the longing inside of her for what it was. Cassiopeia had worshiped here. The soft whisper of a sound from the far corner of the temple jerked her out of her lapse of concentration.

The moonlight illuminated the majority of the temple's interior, although most of the niches were out of reach and dark as midnight. She saw Atia move toward one of the darkened recesses in the building's wall, and Phaedra suppressed a gasp as a tall figure stepped into the light. Instinct made her draw her sword as she leaped forward to protect the *Prima Consul*. No sooner had she done so, than Lysander stayed her.

"It's all right. He's with us," he said quietly as Ares and Cleo moved to join them.

"Who the *fuck* is that?" Cleo jerked her head in the direction of the man who towered over her mother.

"He's a Sicari Lord." From the sound of his voice, Ares was clearly in awe of the man.

"Well, it's clear Ignacio doesn't like him."

Cleo pointed at the *Celeris*, whose body was rigid with tension as he watched his charge engage in an animated, almost heated, conversation with the Sicari Lord. At that instant, the Sicari Lord's head came up, and he stared at Cleo. Immediately, her friend fidgeted beneath the penetrating look.

"*Christus*, why the *hell* is the *bastardo* looking at me like that?"

As the Sicari Lord stepped away from Atia and headed toward the four of them, she heard Lysander draw in a sharp hiss of air and mutter a harsh curse. Atia bolted after the Sicari Lord, a worried frown furrowing her brow. Phaedra's gaze left the *Prima Consul*'s concerned expression to return to the man coming toward them in clothes typical of what Sicari Lords were reported to wear.

The man was dressed like a warrior monk from the past, his flowing cape cloaking his dark apparel, and she was certain his boots came up almost to his knees. It was an old-fashioned form of dress, but on him, it was intimidating. He stopped short of their small group to study their faces and removed the hood from his head to reveal his handsome features.

There was something so familiar about him. Somewhere in the back of her head a dim memory of a young tribune playing with Demetri filtered its way into her head. She gasped. He was older, but it was still the same face of the man she'd known in ancient Rome. The Sicari Lord nodded at Lysander, who bowed slightly in deference.

"Well, Maximus. Isn't it time you stop bowing and recognize me for who I really am?"

The Sicari Lord's question made Lysander start in surprise as the man pulled up his sleeve and extended his arm. In the moonlight, it was easy to see the lightly colored birthmark in the shape of an eagle. The legion's mark. The same faint-colored stain Lysander had on his arm. He stiffened as his gaze took in the Sicari Lord's amused expression. Astonishment made Lysander's green eye open wide as he quickly stepped forward and grasped the man's forearm in a timeless Roman greeting. The smile on his face didn't surprise her, but the dazed expressions on her brother's and Cleo's faces almost made her laugh.

"Tevy. Is it really you?" Lysander said with an air of disbelief.

"I always said I would come back stronger than you, if simply to save you from yourself. It seems I was right." The Sicari Lord released a soft laugh. "Although it took you longer to realize the truth than I did. You always were stubborn."

"I should have recognized you the night I fought the Praetorian Dominus," Lysander exclaimed as he gave the Sicari Lord a boisterous brotherly hug. "By the Gods, Tevy, it's good to see you, old friend.

"And you, my friend, but it might be less confusing for everyone if you call me Marcus."

"Confusing is an understatement," Lysander said in a wry voice.

"It's good to see you as well, *Domina*." The Sicari Lord she recognized as Tevy turned to her and bowed slightly. At a loss for a proper response, she nodded her head at him, and he laughed again. "It is a bit unsettling, isn't it? I almost envy those who don't remember their past existences. There are distinct advantages to not remembering the failures of the past."

His voice had taken on a serious note, and she stepped forward to touch his arm. "Regrets are for the past. The present is what's important now."

"Agreed." He nodded his head.

"Will someone please tell me what the fuck is going on here?" As always, Cleo's colorful language was a shock to those who didn't know her, and the Sicari Lord eyed her carefully.

"That will take far more time than we have to spare, *carissima*." The term of endearment made Cleo narrow her eyes at the Sicari

Lord, while behind him, Atia and Ignacio both jumped with what she could have sworn was fear. The man didn't seem to notice and turned his head to Lysander. "I believe you know where the artifact is."

The man didn't even question Lysander's knowledge, he simply believed. With a nod, Lysander headed toward one of the darkened niches. Instinctively, Phaedra knew it had once housed a statue of Vesta, the goddess Maximus had always prayed to. The sensation of Cassiopeia's memories fluttering to life inside her was unnerving, just like Tevy . . . Marcus . . . had said. Not to mention confusing.

As Lysander and his friend from the ancient past quickly crossed the temple's marble floor, she followed them. When they reached the niche, Lysander squatted over a central spot in front of what was now a tomb. The beam of his flashlight moved slowly across the marble flooring in an obvious search pattern. A second later, the light stopped moving, and with a gesture toward Marcus, Lysander silently directed the Sicari Lord to hold the light.

She immediately sensed the escalation of tension in the temple as Cassiopeia's dagger flashed in the moonlight. Her own heart skipped a beat as Lysander looked up at her. The hesitation in his gaze made her nod at him with a smile of encouragement. She saw his throat bob with emotion before he turned his attention back to the marble tile in front of him.

As the group's varying degrees of excitement and nervous energy assaulted her senses, she blocked the vibrating emotions in a natural effort to protect herself. With careful precision, Lysander tapped the tip of the blade along one of the spidery brown lines spilling across the white marble. He tested first one line and then another. The soft tapping noise continued until the dagger's tip dipped below the surface.

Atia drew in a sharp breath, and Marcus sent her a look that made Phaedra think there was more between the two than anyone else realized. Phaedra's gaze shifted back to Lysander. As she watched, he wiggled the tip of the weapon under the marble, and she could see a piece of cracked tile slowly pushing upward under the pressure. A moment later, the tile popped out of the marble floor like a single puzzle piece.

Hidden among the copious number of brown spidery lines winding their way across the white marble floor, the cracked tile had remained virtually undetectable for centuries. Carefully, he set the tile aside and leaned forward. One hand braced on the floor, Lysander slowly reached into the small hole until his entire arm disappeared from view. He grunted as he strained for something that seemed to be just out of his grasp.

With another sound of exertion, his entire shoulder dropped toward the hole in the floor as he reached for whatever was hidden beneath the tile. A whisper of excitement drifted through her head, and she recognized his thoughts caressing her.

"*It's here*, carissima. *We found it. We found the* Tyet of Isis."

"*No*, caro. *You found it. You did it.*"

With a triumphant grin, Lysander pulled the artifact free of the floor and held it up in the air with a low cry of excitement. In his hand was a small box, about the size of a jeweler's necklace box. The tangible sensation of someone forcing her to reach out for the artifact made her gasp, while the avaricious need sweeping through her chilled the back of her neck. The jubilation she'd felt in Lysander evaporated as he was on his feet and at her side in a split second.

"They're here," he said in a terse tone.

The invisible touch on her hand slowly trailed its way up her arm to slide across her shoulder to the side of her neck. The terror slogging its way through her veins churned her stomach, and a vicious tremor rocked her body. Beside her, Lysander growled as his gaze met hers. He couldn't see Gabriel touching her, but he could read her fear, and she sensed the darkness in him fighting to take control of him.

"Don't, *carino*. They want you to lose control. It will make you vulnerable."

She wasn't sure how she knew this, but she sensed the level of frustration rise in Gabriel the moment she spoke. The Praetorian Dominus immediately squeezed her neck in a brutal grip, and her fingers grabbed at her throat in an attempt to stop the unseen hand from choking her. As she gasped for air, the Sicari Lord turned to study the wide expanse of the darkened nave.

"Are you so afraid of me that you find it necessary to attack a woman?" The quiet taunt brought her immediate relief as a low snarl echoed through the air from the other side of the temple.

"Tonight we end this once and for all, you whoreson." Gabriel's response sent a wave of sorrow blasting through her, and she wasn't sure whether it came from across the nave or from the Sicari Lord himself. The moment the Sicari Lord stepped forward, Lysander stretched out his hand to stop the man.

"Tevy—Marcus . . ."

"It will be like old times, my friend," the Sicari Lord said with a slight curve of his lips.

It was still hard to think of the man as Marcus when her memories of ancient Rome told her different. The man she'd known as Tevy so long ago bowed slightly in her direction before he turned his head in Atia's direction. The intense look of sorrow and resignation darkening his expression equaled the pain on the *Prima Consul's* face as he nodded in her direction.

"*Mea gladius non voluntas concidi, mea kara.*"

Phaedra jerked slightly in surprise. *My sword will not fail, my beloved.* The words surprised her as much as they did Ares and Cleo, but there wasn't time to make any observations as the Sicari Lord moved toward the center of the temple. Out of the darkness she saw Gabriel striding forward, his cloak streaming out from behind him due to his fast pace. Marcus raced toward the Praetorian Dominus, drawing his sword out from under his cloak. With blinding speed, the two men leaped into the air, their swords crashing together like a steel thunderclap inside the nave.

As the two men battled in the center of the temple, shadows on the opposite wall shifted and moved forward to stand at the edge of the circle of moonlight that spilled out from the oculus above. She pulled in a sharp breath of horror at the sight, and the reactions of everyone around her filled her ears as their emotions slammed into her like a runaway train.

"*Merda.*"

"*Figlio di puttana.*"

"*Stronzo.*"

"Oh, we are so fucked." Cleo's voice, along with Lysander's, Ares's, and Ignacio's, rang out in a simultaneous sound of pessimism.

"*Il Christi omnipotentia*," Ignacio muttered. "Am I counting right? There's at least twelve of them."

"Thirteen if you count that *testa di cazzo*, Nicostratus. *Christus*, this is *not* good. How in the hell do we keep the *Tyet of Isis* out of their hands?" Cleo looked at Lysander, who immediately handed off the artifact to Atia.

"Ares, you and Ignacio get the *Prima Consul* out of here as quickly as you can."

"I'm—" Atia broke off her response and nodded beneath Lysander's glare. "You're right. The *Tyet of Isis* mustn't fall into Praetorian hands. But Ares stays. Ignacio will return once he sees me safely out of the temple."

Lysander didn't argue with her. Instead, he eyed the Praetorians walking steadily toward them, and she was certain he'd singled Nicostratus out of the group. Cleo grimaced and turned her head to look at the *Prima Consul*.

"I love you, Mother. Ignacio, I . . .take care of her." She jerked her head back to watch the enemy heading toward them and drew her sword. "Watch the floor. The blood I'm going to spill will make this marble pretty slick."

The observation made Ares smile slightly. "I second that optimistic point of view."

"*Ti amo con tutta l'anima.*"

Lysander gently touched Phaedra's thoughts with the vow of adoration. He didn't just love her with all his heart. He loved her with every fiber of his being, and he intended to do whatever it took to keep her safe tonight. He watched her draw her sword out of the scabbard on her back and reached out to her with his mind. The telepathic connection between them was surprising in its strength as she opened her mind to him. Her love for him filled his mind, and he sucked in a quick breath at the strength of her love and her belief in him. He wouldn't fail her.

"*Bis vivit qui bene moritur*," Lysander growled as he drew his sword. *He lives twice who dies well.* The Sicari motto had never seemed more appropriate.

Seconds later, the Praetorians were on them. Steel crashed against steel, and when two Praetorians targeted Lysander, it forced him to go on the defensive. In a quick move, he ducked beneath a sword slicing through the air in the direction of his chest. Spinning lightly around on his feet, he dragged his own blade across the first Praetorian's chest and continued to swing his body around in a tight circle until his sword sliced open the second Praetorian's stomach.

It was a mortal wound and he knew it. With a thrust of his hand, his ability sent the first Praetorian flying backward to land hard on the marble floor. A loud crack told him the man had hit his head and wouldn't be rising any time soon. Before he could turn to the man near his feet, two more Praetorians leaped in his direction.

Saving his mental reserves for his inevitable encounter with Nicostratus, he cleared his mind to focus and deliberately threw himself between the two approaching fighters. His sword raised above his head, he feinted to the left and then the right. The Praetorians responded with counter swings and just before his sword connected with theirs, he sent his weapon sliding across the floor then quickly tucked himself into a tight ball and rolled past the enemy fighters. As he sprang to his feet, his fingers wrapped around the leather grip of his sword as the weapon flew back into his hand.

Unprepared for his move, the Praetorians found it impossible to stop the momentum of their blades, and they sliced into each other almost simultaneously. Their resulting grunts of pain tugged a grim smile to his face. His satisfaction vanished as his gaze darted to where Phaedra was battling two Praetorians of her own. It was obvious they were holding back with her, which meant they were under orders to simply subdue her. He tried to maneuver closer to her but found his way blocked by one of the Praetorians he'd outmaneuvered.

"Sorry, Unmentionable. We've got plans for the bitch."

The Praetorian's words struck a sharp blow to his gut at the thought of Phaedra in the hands of these *bastardi*. The smile on the man's face said the other fighter had seen his slight slip in control. He tightened his focus and strengthened the shield covering his thoughts. The Praetorian's expression suddenly turned gleeful, and Lysander immediately sensed the second *bastardo* charging him from behind. He opened his senses a little more, and just when his attacker's sword was about to fall, he jumped to one side and swung his blade up and across the Praetorian's throat in one smooth stroke. Not bothering to watch the *bastardo* fall, he offered a taunting smile at the other fighter.

The dead Praetorian's partner roared with anger then leaped forward. In a surprise move, Lysander's opponent jumped high into the air, and his foot slammed into the scarred side of Lysander's face. Pain erupted inside his head as his head snapped backward, and he reeled to one side in an effort to remain standing. He failed. On his knees, he barely managed to block the sword aiming for his neck, and before he could recover, the Praetorian deftly switched his weapon to the opposite hand.

The moment the other fighter's blade dug deep into the muscles of his arm, a searing pain eclipsed the throbbing in his head. Fuck. *How in the hell was he supposed to fight a sword-carrying southpaw?* Rolling away from the Praetorian, he stumbled to his feet, fighting to isolate and ignore the pain in his body. His arm limp at his side, he glanced in Phaedra's direction to see one of her attackers slam an elbow into her head before his sword splayed her leg open just above the knee.

She didn't cry out, but he heard the scream of pain in her mind. A cold rage pounded its way into his veins and muscles. It energized him, and as his opponent strutted forward with confidence, Lysander filled his thoughts with images of defeat to disguise his real intentions. The man's arm flew upward with a slight laugh of triumph. The gleeful chuckle died in the Praetorian's throat the instant Lysander thrust his sword up into the man's chest. He almost didn't perform the Order's rite of *Rogare Donavi*. As if she could read his intentions, he felt the soft whisper of Phaedra's thoughts drifting through his in protest. He gave in to her plea.

"I ask your forgiveness. Do you give it?" The mechanical note in Lysander's voice indicated how little he cared whether the man answered yes or no. But he waited for the man's answer. The Praetorian denied him.

"I hope you . . . rot in . . . hell, Unmentionable."

"Then I'll see you there," he said grimly.

He threw his foot up to brace himself on the Praetorian's thigh as he jerked his blade out of the man's body. Not waiting to see the man fall, he whirled around to cover the short distance between him and the Praetorian about to strike Phaedra from behind. Adrenaline filled his uninjured arm with brute strength as he impaled the man with his sword. The fighter looked down at his chest, and Lysander didn't have to see the man's face to know how surprised the Praetorian was. In slow motion, the man slid off Lysander's blade and fell to the marble floor. A low laugh echoed out of the darkness as the Praetorian crumpled to the blood-slicked floor. The sound made him wheel about to face the new danger.

"Well done, boy. You continue to impress me." Nicostratus strolled casually out of the shadows to where Lysander could see him. The moment the Patriarch smiled, Lysander knew his mental shield had slipped and the man could see the hate seething inside him.

"I'm not here to impress you," he snarled as he glanced in Phaedra's direction to ensure she didn't need help with the last Praetorian threatening her.

"Nonetheless, you do. I can't help but believe there's more of me flowing through your blood than you'd care to admit."

A red haze clouded his mind for a moment before he heard a soft whisper of warning in his head. Whatever connected him to Phaedra had allowed her to remind him that Nicostratus wanted him to lose control. If he wanted to defeat the *bastardo*, he needed to remain calm and collected.

Immediately shielding his thoughts, he thrust his hand outward and directed an unseen pulse of energy that sent the Patriarch flying backward. Nicostratus hit the floor with a loud thud. It was a satisfying sound. As he strode forward, his father scrambled to his feet in an agile move. The man leaped forward, and a moment later, their swords crashed into each other. Sparks flew as the steel blades scraped upward and away from each other. Nicostratus was stronger than he looked, and with one arm out of action, it would be harder to defeat the man, even with his telekinetic ability. Any other time he would have had the advantage, but now the playing field was fairly well balanced between the two of them. As his weapon slid off Nicostratus's blade, he spun around on his heel to whip his body behind the man. In his mind, he visualized the man's legs buckling beneath a vicious kick to the knees. The Patriarch released a loud oath as he fell forward.

"You surprise me, Nicostratus. That kind of language is hardly becoming of a man in your exalted position within the Collegium."

With a quick twist of his wrist, Lysander flipped his sword in a downward direction, intent on plunging it into Nicostratus. Mocking laughter echoed in his thoughts as the Patriarch swiftly rolled out of harm's way and got to his feet.

"There are many things about me that would surprise, my son."

"I told you before—I'm *not* your son."

Lunging forward, he parried Nicostratus's thrust, and the tip of his blade scraped across the Patriarch's shoulder blade. Another oath flew out of the Praetorian's mouth, before he countered and swung his sword toward Lysander's blind side so quickly there wasn't time to react. Fire bit into his wrist as Nicostratus's sword sliced the tendons controlling his grip. His hand incapable of holding a weapon, the sword clattered to the floor. He heard the man's thoughts echoing through his head.

"*But don't you see, Lysander? You are everything I would expect from my son. My greatest regret is that I didn't know of your existence until it was too late.*"

Lysander didn't waste his energy on answering the man, instead he extended his hand to slam an unseen fist into Nicostratus's jaw. The Praetorian grunted with pain, his head popping backward from the hard blow. As the man recovered, a gleam of something akin to respect glittered in the Patriarch's eyes, and he shook his head.

"*We're very much alike, Lysander. We know what's expected of us, and we do what we must to achieve our goal. The question is . . . what are we willing to give up when it comes to attaining our goal?*"

The odd question confused Lysander as he stared into a pair of green eyes similar to his own. The *bastardo* was planning something, but when he tried to read the man's thoughts, Nicostratus's disciplined mind prevented him from seeing anything. If the *bastardo* thought he was defeated simply because he didn't have the ability to hold a sword, the son of a bitch was deluded.

In a sudden, unexpected move, Nicostratus leaped forward, and instinct saved Lysander as he ducked beneath the wide arc of the man's sword. The instant he dodged the deadly blade, the Patriarch opened his thoughts to him. The move had been a diversion to hide his real intent. As the man's mocking laughter filled his head, Lysander released a shout of agonized fear.

Chapter 27

PHAEDRA somersaulted away from the Praetorian attempting to take her head off. The boot the man had viciously planted on her chest had made it difficult to breath. Merda, *had the* bastardo *managed to collapse one of her lungs with that kick?* Her entire body ached. She'd never healed as quickly as those she served, but now would be a good time for that particular quirk to take a hike.

Between her leg hurting like hell and her difficulty breathing, she was ready for a little respite. Not to mention that when it came time to heal others, her own injuries were going to make it even more difficult to help the others. And considering the amount of blood on the floor, she had a feeling her friends weren't without their share of injuries.

She came up in a crouch with her back to her attacker, her senses blocking everything out around her except the hum of furious determination in her veins and the movements of the man she was fighting. When he was within a foot of her, she spun around on her haunches and dragged her sword deep into the man's lower leg. The Praetorian crashed to the marble floor with a low cry, and in a flash of movement, she was standing over top of him, the tip of her sword pressing hard against his heart.

"I ask your forgiveness. Do you give it?" The *Rogare Donavi* echoed softly between her and the Praetorian. Despite the anger in his eyes, there was a resigned expression on the man's face.

"Granted."

The moment he spoke, her blade pierced the man's chest and drove its way into his heart. Immediately, her stomach lurched and bile rose in her throat. *Deus*, even in self-defense it never got easier. Only harder. The sudden sound of Atia's cry jerked her attention toward the center of the Pantheon. What the hell was the woman still doing here? She glanced around, searching for some sign of Ignacio. Her heart sank as she spotted the *Celeris* collapsed on the floor near the altar. *Christus*, they hadn't even gotten out of the temple. She followed Atia's stricken gaze to where the Sicari Lord and the Praetorian Dominus were fighting.

It was easy to see the younger man was winning, his blade a silver flash in the moonlight that streamed down from the building's oculus. With a wave of his hand, the Dominus hit the Sicari Lord with an invisible blow. The older man doubled over as if someone had jabbed him in the stomach. His sword scraping across the floor, the man struggled to regain his balance. As he came upright, the Praetorian Dominus didn't give the Sicari Lord the chance to raise his sword.

"This is for casting me aside, heretic." The Dominus's words reverberated loudly in the temple as the hate, anger, and pain touched her mind.

Horror replaced her bewilderment as she watched the younger man viciously swing his sword upward in a diagonal slash across the Sicari Lord's thigh and abdomen. Stunned, Phaedra saw the Sicari Lord sink to his knees, his hand braced against his leg to stem the flow of blood from his wound. A cruel smile on his face, the Praetorian Dominus lifted his sword up in preparation to finish off his opponent.

"Gabriel, *no*. He didn't give you up. They took you from us. *For the love of God*, he's your father." Atia's cry of fear and pain made the man pause, his sword hovering in the air over his father's head.

About to launch herself forward, the *Prima Consul*'s words made Phaedra freeze with shock. The Sicari Lord murmured something to the man towering over him before his sword flashed in the moonlight. As his blade plunged upward into Gabriel's chest, a stark look of surprise swept over the Praetorian Dominus's face. His gaze locked with the Sicari Lord's for a brief moment before he fell backward to the floor of the Pantheon.

Anguish twisted Marcus's face as his weapon left his hand to protrude from his dead son's body. The Sicari Lord tried to throw himself toward Gabriel in an evident display of bleak sorrow, but it was obvious his strength was gone as his body gave way to fatigue and pain. Tears streaming down her face, Atia raced forward to catch him in her arms as he collapsed.

The older couple's turbulent emotions held Phaedra hostage as she stared at the small drama playing out before her eyes. Behind her, Lysander's cry of anguish cut through her as a warning fluttered through her head. She whirled around just in time to see Nicostratus's sword swinging her direction. Instinctively, she raised her weapon to block the man's blade. As her sword clanged with the Patriarch's sword, experience told her to tuck and roll to avoid the man's next stroke, which would be lethal.

Suddenly, the air rushed out of her lungs in a whoosh as Lysander's body slammed into hers, knocking her aside as he took the sword meant for her. The force of his action sent her sprawling across the floor, and she looked up just in time to see Nicostratus pull his blade out of Lysander with a low cry.

Her heart took a sickening lurch as she saw Lysander tumble forward to roll onto his back. *Care Deus*, what had he done? Blood flowed heavily from the wound in his side, and she started to scramble her way to him.

"Stay where you are, Phaedra." The harsh command made her pause as he forced himself up into a sitting position with one elbow.

"What were you thinking, son?" the Patriarch exclaimed as he quickly backed away from Lysander in what seemed to be actual horror.

"I am *Sicari*. I have *never* been your son."

Lysander's words were harsh with pain and disgust as he violently jerked his head in Nicostratus's direction. The Praetorian immediately stumbled backward and doubled over with a grunt of pain. While his father was struggling to recover from the invisible blow, Lysander tried to push himself up to his feet. *Deus*, the man was insane to think he could fight. She started forward, and in that instant, she saw Cleo racing forward, her sword flying toward the Patriarch's neck.

As if prepared for the blow, the man easily blocked the attack with his sword then turned to plant his foot squarely in Cleo's stomach. Her friend went flying backward across the Pantheon's marble floor. Backing away from them, Nicostratus's harsh command to retreat echoed through the Pantheon. The two Praetorians still alive broke and ran as Nicostratus stared down at Lysander for another brief moment then fled the building. Cleo and Ares started to follow them.

"Let them go. Secure the *Tyet of Isis*," Lysander rasped before collapsing back to the cold marble beneath him. She reached him just before his head hit the hard surface. Fear jumbled her thoughts as she frantically slit his shirt open with her sword to examine his wound. Tears filled her eyes as she worked.

"You dumb *bacciagalupe*. That was a stupid stunt to pull. I could have easily ducked his sword."

"How many times do I have to tell you . . . you're not as good . . . a fighter as I am?" His eyes were closed, but there was a faint smile on his lips.

"Shut up and give me your hands."

"No *Curavi*. See to the Sicari Lord first. Then come back for me." There was something in the whisper that terrified her.

"Goddamn it, I won't let you get away with this a second time, Lysander Condellaire. Now give me your hands."

"Phaedra." Ares's sharp cry made her turn her head. "Marcus needs you, *now*. I don't know how much longer he can hold out."

No. The other man could wait. Lysander came first.

"Give me your hands now," she said harshly.

"He is the Sicari Lord, Phaedra. It's your duty to heal him first."

"*No*, I won't lose you. *I won't.*"

She knew the highest-ranking officer was to be healed first, but she wasn't about to let Lysander die. She didn't care what the rules were. She didn't care what anyone ordered her to do. Determined to keep him safe, she grabbed his hands and tried to calm her thoughts. He broke free of her grasp to caress her cheek.

"I'll be fine, it's little more than a scratch."

"Don't lie to me."

"All right, it's a cut, but it can easily be sewn up." He sent her a stern look. "Go to Tev—Marcus. I'll be right here. I'm not going anywhere."

"Please, Lysander. Don't make me do this. I can't."

"You don't have a choice, *mea amor*. Honor and duty first." The endearment pulled a sharp breath from her as his fingers curled around her neck and he pulled her head down to kiss her. "As *Legatus*, I order you to go."

Shaking her head in protest, she felt Cleo's hand on her shoulder. "The sooner you heal the Sicari Lord, the sooner you can get back over here. Go."

Torn with guilt at leaving his side, Phaedra scrambled her way across the bloody floor to reach Marcus's side. Anguish had drained the color from Atia's face, and the Sicari Lord's head rested in her lap as her fingers lightly stroked his forehead. Quickly Phaedra examined the wound in the man's leg. She met her brother's gaze and grimaced.

The only explanation for the dark blood spurting out of the Sicari Lord's wound was that the arterial vein had been nicked. With every beat of his heart, he lost blood. He had maybe two minutes to live if she didn't heal him. The *Prima Consul* brushed her fingertips across his cheek, and the man's eyes fluttered open to meet Phaedra's gaze. It was Tevy she saw looking up at her.

"Maximus?" The question was a soft rasp.

"He's alive." *Barely.* Riddled with fear, she knew the sooner she healed the man, the sooner she could help Lysander. She offered her hands to him. "With your permission, I must touch you to heal you."

"He's dying." The Sicari Lord's words made her grow cold. "Heal him. I am no longer important."

"He won't let me touch him until you're out of danger," she said through clenched teeth. "Now stop wasting my time and *his*, and accept the *Curavi*."

"He always was a stubborn man," Tevy murmured. "You have my . . . permission."

The moment he spoke, she grabbed his hands and fought to focus on her patient. The warmth flowing through her hands made her skin tingle. Despite her concentration, her heart ached to return to Lysander. Pain sliced through her leg as the Sicari Lord's wound appeared on hers. The danger of healing an arterial wound wasn't lost on her. Her healing was tied to Tevy's wound healing. If she didn't concentrate on visualizing Tevy's wound closing, she could wind up dying along with the Sicari Lord.

Black blood spurted from her leg, and a wave of nausea spread its way through her. Desperately, she pushed the pain away. Focus. She needed to focus on getting Tevy out of danger then she could go to Maximus. Nausea streaked through her again, and this time she had to release the Sicari Lord's hands. Weak from her own blood loss, she glanced down and saw Tevy's wound beginning to disappear from her leg, although the cut above her knee remained dark and ugly.

"He needs you, *now*," Tevy rasped.

She nodded as nausea crashed through her again. The intensity of it signaled she'd reached the end of her healing abilities. *Care Deus*, Lysander. She tried to stand but was too weak. A strong hand lifted her up onto her feet, and Ares half carried her to Lysander's side. Tears streaming down her face, she collapsed on the floor next to him. The warmth of his love flooded her mind, and it made her sob harder as she reached for him.

"Give me your hands," she choked out.

"It's too late, *carissima*." He weakly avoided her grasp and offered her a small smile as she stared down at him. "I have no regrets."

"Don't do this, Lysander. Give me your hands. Let me heal you."

"We both know you don't have anything left to give, *mea amor*."

His eyes closed, and she grabbed his hand. So cold. *Care Deus*, not again. She couldn't lose him again. Across from her, Cleo looked at her with a grim expression on her face as her eyes watered. Behind her, Ares touched her shoulder. She shook off the touch with a vicious twist of her body.

Desperate for a way to save him, she frantically glanced around for some type of inspiration. Something that would keep him with her. His hand was growing icy now, and her stomach churned as grief assailed her. Eyes watery, she caught a sparkle of color near Lysander's leg. Her head jerked up and she looked around the temple. In the dim light, she saw the altar they had passed when entering the temple. She looked at Cleo.

"Is your shirt clean?"

"What?"

"Is your shirt *clean*?"

"No," Cleo shook her head. "But my camisole is."

"Wet it in the baptismal fount *now*!" When Cleo hesitated, she leaned over Lysander. "*Do it. Hurry.*"

"What the hell are you doing?" Ares's voice echoed over her shoulder.

"I'm saving his life."

"*Il Christi omnipotentia*, you don't know that you can. You're already as weak as a newborn."

"Not now, Ares."

She shrugged off her brother's hand and waited for Cleo to return. It took Cleo almost thirty seconds to return with the material dripping with water, but it seemed an eternity. She grabbed the wispy thin material to scrub her hand and then Lysander's. His eye fluttered open to look at her. The horror in his gaze said he'd read her mind. His breathing labored, he tried to speak.

"No."

"You don't have a choice. Now say the words. My life for your life."

He flinched. "No."

"Damn it, say the words. My life for your life."

She waited for his response to drift through her head. When he refused, she reached for the dagger in his boot. With a swift stroke, she made a deep cut in her palm.

"My heart for your heart," she murmured as she ignored Ares's and Cleo's gasps. When she grabbed his hand, he tried to resist, but he had no strength. The dagger sliced through Lysander's palm. As his palm ran red with blood, she stared down into his green-eyed gaze.

"Say the words," she said hoarsely.

"*No. I can't let you do this*, mea amor." His voice was stronger in her head, but she could tell how weak he was by the obvious effort it took to concentrate.

"Goddamn it, say the words," she rasped. "My blood for your blood. Say it, damn you."

"Don't do this, Phaedra. You need to let me go, dolce cuore." His words whispered in her head as invisible fingers touched her cheek.

"Do you trust me, Lysander?" His gaze focused on hers, glazing over slightly, and in the back of her head she heard him whisper yes. It was enough for her, and she pressed her bleeding palm into his, their blood mixing together. "Then if you won't say it, I *will*. My blood for your blood. Our blood and hearts are one."

Her heart beat frantically as she could feel him slipping away from her. In response, she squeezed her hand tighter around his. Eyes closed, she prayed with all her heart that performing the blood bond would give him what he needed. The only thing she had left in her was her ability to heal herself. But if he received enough of her blood, perhaps it would be enough. With every beat of her heart, she willed him to fight—to stay with her.

Weak and exhausted, the first pain when it came startled her into opening her eyes. She sucked in a sharp breath, which only exacerbated the pain in her side. Glancing downward, she saw blood spreading across her stomach. Behind her, Ares uttered a soft curse.

"*Il Christi omnipotentia*, it's his kidneys. Phae, you need to let go. Now."

"No." She barely recognized the sound of her voice. It was weak and hoarse. She focused her gaze toward Lysander. Was it possible his color was returning? Lightheaded, she swayed against the dizzy spell that swept over her.

The nausea returned, and she blinked as Lysander's features blurred. Confused, she fought to keep her hand curled around his as first one wave of dizziness after another rolled over her. As if from a distance, she heard people calling out her name, but she couldn't answer. Then she heard Lysander whispering in her thoughts. When she tried to touch his thoughts with her own, a sudden whoosh echoed in her ears and it made her feel like she was flying backward.

Moments later, the sensation ended as suddenly as it began. It was as if someone had jerked her to an abrupt halt, and the first thing she noticed was her body felt as though it were on fire. A dull roar echoed in her ears, and when she opened her eyes, she recognized the Piazza Saepta Julia. But not the Piazza Saepta Julia of today. *Il Christi omnipotentia*, she was in ancient Rome. *Care Deus*, she was in Cassiopeia's body at her execution. Flames licked against her feet until she could see blisters forming on her skin. The pain was agonizing, and terror streaked through her as she realized she was going to die a horrible death.

"*Cass, mea amor, I'm here. Focus on my thoughts, carissima.*" Relief swelled inside her. He was here. He'd find a way to save her. The heat from the flames abated, and while the pain was terrible, she could tolerate it. The only explanation she could think of for the relief was that he was somehow shielding her with his ability.

"*Maximus.*"

"*That's it, carissima. Look at me, mea kara.*"

His thoughts showed her where to look, and she turned her gaze toward the podium, where she saw him stagger to his feet. The sight of the horrible wound on his face made her strain at the rope binding her to the stake.

"Mea Deus, *what have they done to you?*"

"*I'll survive.*"

There was a tormented bitterness in the thought that made her realize he couldn't reach her. Fear rose in her again as she saw the distance between them, and the angry crowd that kept him from her. He would survive, but she wouldn't. She coughed from the wisps of smoke filling the air around her. He was strong, but not strong enough to keep the flames off her for long.

"Dulcis *Vesta.*"

"*Do you trust me, Cass?*" His calm presence in her head soothed her.

"*Yes,*" she said as she met his gaze over top of the mob. And she did. She trusted him to do whatever it took to keep her safe. "*I love you, Maximus.*"

"*And I you, mea amor. Close your eyes, Cass. The pain will be gone in a moment.*"

She did as he ordered, tears streaming down her cheeks. There was a sharp prick of pain in her chest and then it was over. The pain was gone. Somewhere in the deep recesses of her mind, she heard Maximus—or was it Lysander?—shouting out her name. He called to her, but she couldn't answer.

Chapter 28

MAXIMUS sank to his knees as he saw Cass sag against the stake, his dagger protruding from her heart. Flames rose skyward, and over the cries of the mob, he heard the sound of a wild animal screaming in agony. The cries were his. A rough hand caught him by the arm, but he shrugged it off with a violent twist of his body.

"She's gone, Maximus. She's no longer in pain."

Tevy's voice was a distant roar in his ear as he sobbed uncontrollably. Not even his heart being ripped out of his chest could be this painful. He'd killed her. Her and their unborn child. The agony of it made him rip at his cloak like a madman. Her blood was on his hands, and he would never forgive himself for deserting her.

"For the love of Vesta, Maximus. Look at what you saved her from." His friend viciously forced his head up and made him look at the flames shooting upward. The sight of Cass's body engulfed in the bonfire pulled the air out of his lungs until he didn't think he would ever breathe again.

"You did what you had to do. You saved her from enduring that terrible death." Tevy's hand bit into his shoulder, his friend's voice harsh with emotion. "She wouldn't want you to stay here. One of Octavian's men got the bastard to safety. He'll have this mob after you the minute he realizes what you did. They'll want your head, too."

"It doesn't matter what they do to me now," he rasped. "She's gone. Everything I held dear is gone."

"No," his friend exclaimed with urgency. "Demetri may be

alive. Posca is a resourceful man, and he'd give his life for your
son."

"Leave me be, Tevy." He jerked away from his friend's grip and
sagged forward. Tevy was right. The moment the crowd realized
he'd saved his wife from pain, they'd have his head. He welcomed it,
because there was nothing anyone could do to him now that would
match the agony he was in at this precise moment in time. His beau-
tiful, loving, sweet wife was gone. Murdered by his own hand.

"Forgive me, Maximus." Tevy's voice was gruff, and in his
grief, Maximus didn't consider what his friend's words meant until
a heavy blow hit the back of his head. The last things he saw were
yellow flames consuming his beloved's body and the dagger that
killed her.

LYSANDER jerked upright with a startled cry. He blinked as he
looked around the room. It was morning. Still disoriented, he realized he was holding on to the cold metal rail of a hospital bed. Phaedra. His gaze jerked toward the bed. Desperate to reassure himself
that she was real and not a figment of his imagination, he captured
her hand.

The warmth of her fingers against his eased the pain and horror
inside. Slowly, the dream ebbed away. It was the past. Maximus and
Cassiopeia were long dead. He grimaced. That wasn't exactly true.
Even though he was a believer now, he still had trouble grasping the
fact that he had once lived as Maximus in ancient Rome with Phaedra as his wife Cassiopeia.

He stared down at her. She looked like she was sleeping. When
they'd brought her to the Order's private medical facility here in
Genova, he'd been certain she'd wake up in a matter of hours. But it
had been a month since that night in the Pantheon with no change
in her condition. The doctors still couldn't explain why she was in
a coma, and as each day passed, they seemed less optimistic about
her recovery.

He spent his nights sleeping in a foldout chair beside her bed,
showered in her private bath, and sat holding her hand, reading to
her, talking to her in hopes she'd come to. Unlike the doctors, he

refused to give in to the pessimism the rest of the medical staff had begun to exhibit. Phaedra was strong. She'd fought too hard for the two of them to be together. He couldn't believe she'd give up now.

The steady beep of the heart monitor filled the room, while he could hear the early-morning sounds of the hospital stirring to life beyond the room's closed door. For just a brief moment, he released her hand to lower the railing. Elbows resting on the mattress, he raised her hand to press his mouth to the scar in her palm.

The blood bond between them had worked as she'd obviously hoped. Her ability of self-healing had transferred to him, helping him come back from death's door. In the process, she'd gone where he'd been—the edge of death's door—only she hadn't come back. His body convulsed with grief before he dragged in a deep breath.

"Please, *inamorato*, I can't bear to live without you as I did in ancient Rome."

The warm fingers enclosed in his hand flexed suddenly, and his heart skipped a beat. He jerked up his head, hoping he'd see her looking at him, but her eyes remained closed. *Christus*, what artifact was worth losing the woman he loved twice in two lifetimes? The door whispered open behind him, and he turned his head to see Ares, followed by Emma, come into the room. He turned back to Phaedra.

"Ares and Emma are here, *mea amor*."

He prayed for her fingers to stir against his again, but they didn't. A strong hand came to rest on his shoulder, and he looked up to see Ares's resigned expression.

"Anything?"

The question made him shake his head as he turned back to Phaedra. There hadn't been anything new to report since she'd arrived here in Genova. Occasionally, her fingers would move like they had a minute ago. Then there were the times when someone spoke to her and a slight grimace would twist her features. He hadn't even been able to read her mind and help guide her back to the land of the living versus the twilight she occupied. Every time his thoughts reached out to her, he encountered a barrier between them. Something that kept him out.

"The doctor told me they want to put a feeding tube in." Ares's words sucked the air out of Lysander's chest, and the hopelessness roaring through him made him want to rip something apart.

"What did you tell him?"

"I told him to ask you. The blood bond gives you the right to make that decision."

"No," he said fiercely as anguish slugged its way through him like a hammer pounding every inch of his body. "We didn't blood bond. I refused to say the words. I failed her."

The heart monitor in the room beeped erratically as he spoke, and Phaedra's fingers jerked in his hand. He was on his feet in an instant, leaning over her, his mouth pressing against her forehead and then her cheek.

"I know you can hear me, *carissima*. Come back to me. I need you, *dolce cuore*."

She went still again, and the beep of the monitor slowed to its usual steady pace. His heart sank, just like it did every time she stirred. He dropped back down into the chair. It was agonizing to see her this way. He needed to hear her voice . . . see the warmth in her smile when she looked at him . . . feel her touch on the scars that covered his body and his heart. Needed to hold her . . . love her. Desperate to ignore the pain inside him, he turned his head toward Ares.

"Are Atia and Tevy . . . Marcus . . . deciphering the contents of the *Tyet of Isis*?"

"Not yet. It's going to take some time. The parchment is fragile, and it's falling apart. It could be months before they're able to piece it together. They left yesterday with the artifact. They're taking it to the White Cloud estate for safekeeping and examination." Ares crossed the floor to sit in one of the chairs the hospital provided visitors. "Neither one of them think the Genova stronghold can withstand a full-out Praetorian assault because it's so isolated and close to Rome. Nicostratus isn't going to let the *Tyet of Isis* go so easily, now that he knows we have it."

Lysander flinched at the sound of his Praetorian father's name. Maybe he'd been wrong to keep Ares and Cleo from going after the *bastardo*. No. Nicostratus was his responsibility and no one else's. The Patriarch was unfinished business that would have to wait for the time being. Soon the man's life would be forfeited for all the pain he'd caused. Not only for Phaedra's loss of her parents or for what his mother had suffered, but for Atia and Marcus for the loss of their son, and Ares as well. Even Gabriel had paid a price for being kidnapped as a child.

"I'll deal with Nicostratus soon enough," he bit out. "What about Marcus? Has he recovered fully?"

"Yes." Ares had a grim look on his face as he tilted his head in a slight nod. "If Atia hadn't disobeyed your order and returned to the temple with Ignacio in tow, I've no doubt Gabriel would have killed him."

"Women, they never listen," he whispered.

Phaedra had saved his life because she hadn't listened to him. In return, she'd offered up her life for his. He automatically reached out with his mind to try and breach the mental barrier between them. It was like hitting a steel wall that didn't give an inch. *Christus*, why couldn't he reach her? The possibility that she might never respond filled him with a bleak despair. It was the same sensation he'd experienced the night Nicostratus had told him that he was half-Praetorian.

"Maybe when we don't *listen* it's because our instincts tell us to do otherwise." Emma's gentle chide made him look at her, and she offered him a sympathetic smile. "She saved your life because she loves you, and because she believes the two of you are Maximus and Cassiopeia."

For a second time the heart monitor accelerated rapidly, and Phaedra's fingers flexed in his hand as her features contorted into a grimace he could have sworn was frustration. He squeezed her fingers and scooted his seat so he was closer to where her dark hair spilled across her pillow. Hair he brushed for her every morning after her sponge bath.

"Does she do that often?" There was an odd note in Emma's voice, and he sent her a puzzled look.

"Just once in a while. But it's the second time in the last hour, which is a little unusual. Although the doctors say it can happen fairly frequently."

"When she does move, do you remember what you were saying or doing when it happened?"

"No." He frowned for a moment as he met his friend's gaze across the bed. "Why?"

"Well, it looked to me she heard every word you said and was trying to respond." Emma leaned forward to stroke her sister-in-law's forehead and brush back several stray hairs.

"Maybe, but I'm not so sure anymore," he said with a sense of defeat.

The room went silent again, and he didn't bother to look at either Emma or Ares to see their reaction. The only thing keeping him from accepting the diagnosis of the doctors was the notion of living without her. That thought was even more agonizing than the prospect of sitting here thinking she might never wake up.

"Have you had any more dreams lately?" Emma's quiet question made him jump.

"Nothing significant." He clenched his jaw. What he'd dreamt a short while ago had been a nightmare. Fuck, his whole existence right now was a nightmare. "Why?"

"No reason." Emma shrugged. "Atia asked if you'd mentioned any. She said something about a prophecy she'd shared with you and Phae."

"I did what was expected of me. I found the *Tyet of Isis*, and look what it cost me." He jerked his head in Phaedra's direction, refusing to hide his anger or bitterness. Atia's damn prophecy had taken from him the only thing short of his honor that he cared about.

"Atia doesn't seem to think you've completed the task."

"What more does she want me to do?" He glared at Emma, who didn't flinch as she reached into her purse and pulled out a familiar-looking object.

"She said you would know what to do with this." His friend laid the velvet-covered weapon on the bed.

"Cassiopeia's dagger?" he snapped.

What the fuck was he supposed to do with the damn thing? The thought barely filtered through his head when Phaedra's heart monitor when crazy. Immediately, he leaned forward, his gaze searching her face in the hope he'd see some sign that she was trying to return to him. A nurse burst into the room and quickly made her way around Emma to check the equipment and examine the IV drip.

The minute the nurse pressed the call button above the bed, his heart dropped like a stone into the pit of his stomach. Inside his hand, Phaedra's fingers flexed, and he leaned into her.

"I'm here, *inamorato*. If you can hear me, squeeze my hand."

The only response was the sound of the monitor beeping faster as her heart rate accelerated. *Christus*, what the hell was happening to her? Another nurse charged into the room and ordered everyone out. Ares and Emma tried to pull him out of the room, but he refused to budge. Two more people raced into the room, one of them obviously a physician as she snapped an order and one of the nurses raced out of the room.

A moment later, Phaedra's heart rate made the monitor explode with sound. With a sharp order for him to move, a nurse pushed him away from the bed, and he stumbled backward. Stunned by what was happening, he watched the scene in front of him as if it were a nightmare in slow motion. Someone rolled a crash cart into the room and up to the side of the bed. The sight of it sent bile rushing to his mouth, and his heart clenched as the doctor reached for the paddles.

Disbelief pounded its way through his body as he watched them shock her heart. Her body violently arched upward from the electrical jolt, and he choked back a cry of fear. What the fuck was happening? How in the hell could she go from being in a coma to cardiac arrest? The gentle stroke of a whisper touched the back of his mind. He immediately reached out for it, searching for its source.

"Lysander, I need you. Don't leave me here."

The plea was so soft he wasn't certain he'd heard it. *Deus*, this couldn't be happening. One minute Emma had placed Cassiopeia's dagger on the bed, and the next Phaedra was in distress. The whisper came again, and this time her voice was faint, but distinct. Desperately, he stretched out his thoughts in an attempt to reach her.

"Tell me how to reach you, mea amor. *Tell me what I have to do."*

"Lysander, please. He . . . You . . . saved me . . . Don't let me . . . die again."

Her thoughts were so distant that he wasn't certain she could even hear him, let alone respond. *Christus*, she sounded so alone—so terrified. Angry despair slammed into his chest as he watched the medical staff working on the woman he loved. Suddenly, she convulsed in the bed, and in the very next breath, she was gasping for air, her heart rate dropping drastically.

The sight of her fighting to live sucked every bit of air from his lungs. He could tell by the frantic note in the doctor's voice that they were losing her and they didn't know how or why. Another shock of the defibrillator made her convulse again, and Cassiopeia's dagger, escaping its velvet sheath, fell to the floor with a clatter.

He stared at it for a second. What was it she'd said? *Don't let me die again.* He didn't think, he simply reacted and leaped forward to grab the blade off the floor. He didn't have a clue whether this was what she needed him to do, but if there was any chance in Tartarus that it might save her, he'd do it now rather than later. Roughly shoving one of the nurses to the side, he sliced open his palm, the dagger reopening the cut Phaedra had made on his palm that night in the Pantheon.

"My life for your life," he said fiercely. "My heart for your heart."

With a swift stroke of the blade, he cut her palm open, ignoring the cries of protest from the medical staff. "My blood for your blood."

"*Say it,* inamorato. *My blood for your blood,*" he commanded.

"*My blood . . . for . . . your blood.*" It was a clear, yet ragged whisper in his head as he clasped her hand in his until their blood flowed together.

"Our blood and hearts are one." He squeezed her hand, ignoring the wildly erratic noise of the heart monitor.

"*Our blood and hearts are one.*" Her words rang stronger in his head, and he gripped her hand as if his life depended on it.

"Non posso vivere senza voi, carissima. *Don't make me live without you again.*"

"*Lysander.*" It was a soft sigh in his head, and he closed his eyes, reaching out with his mind to touch hers.

This time there was nothing stopping his thoughts from touching hers. As he reached out for her, the sounds of the hospital room slowly faded. When he felt her, the strength of her love and faith in him was overwhelming. It humbled him. Suddenly, images of ancient Rome and their final moments together as Cassiopeia and Maximus appeared in his head. The memories were painful for him, but in her they generated a sense of panic and hysteria that alarmed him. Gently, he touched her mind, reassuring her.

"*It's the past, Phaedra. Vesta has given us a second chance,* mea amor. *Come to me, I'm here.*"

"*I don't know how.*" It was a soft cry of desperation, and he could feel her slipping away.

"*Yes, you do. You can do this. Trust me, like I'm trusting you. I promise I won't let go.*"

He embraced her thoughts, pulling her toward him as he visualized the hospital room. Suddenly he could feel her again, her thoughts and emotions clinging to him as he fought to focus on the present. It was a gradual sensation, but the present slowly filtered its way into his consciousness. The heart monitor was the first sound he heard, and it beeped a strong, steady rhythm.

"*Ti amo con tutta l'anima, Lysander.*" It was the most beautiful thought ever to flow through his head.

"I love you with all my heart, too, *carissima,*" he said out loud as the hospital room came fully into focus. Her fingers flexed tightly around his.

"What took you ... so long to come ... for me, you *baccia-galupe?*"

Her voice was a hoarse whisper, but it was the most beautiful sound he'd ever heard. His gaze jerked toward her face and her eyes fluttered open. It seemed to take her a moment to focus before her gaze met his, and her smile was little more than a twist of the lips. The physician gently touched his arm, but he shook his head.

"I'm not leaving."

"It's ... all right ... *mea amor.*" Phaedra squeezed his hand. "Just ... tired."

"It's quite normal for her to be sleepy, *il mio signore.*" Lysander shook his head, but the doctor smiled at him patiently. "We'll keep a close eye on her."

He looked down at Phaedra to see her close her eyes, but the slight smile on her face eased his fears. As her thoughts merged with his, he realized for the first time he'd been right about her intuitive ability. His telepathic abilities had enhanced her own power.

"Which means you'll no longer be able to keep secrets from me, caro." Her thought was filled with mischief, and he smiled as he raised her hand to his mouth.

"Never, carissima. Never again."

"I love you, Lysander." It was the last thought she sent whispering through his head before she was asleep.

Slowly he released her hand as the nurse gently pulled him away from the bed. As he stepped back, a strong hand gripped his arm, and he turned to see Ares staring at him with a look of heartfelt emotion. His friend didn't say a word. He simply pulled Lysander into a bear hug. His gaze met Emma's over Ares's shoulder. She was beaming at him while brushing tears out of her eyes. When Ares released him, Emma stepped forward to hug him as well. He was feeling a bit choked up as Emma pulled away from him, and he was grateful that the doctor took that moment to approach him.

"She's asleep now, *il mio signore*. But we'll monitor her response to stimuli over the next twenty-four hours." The physician eyed him sternly. "As for you, you're to sleep in a real bed tonight. You've done everything for her that you can. We'll take it from here."

"Don't worry, doc. We'll see to it," Ares said with a note of steel in his voice. "As my *Primus Pilus*, he knows not to go against my orders."

As his friends guided him toward the hospital room door, he looked back at Phaedra. She loved him, and she'd come back to him. He couldn't ask for anything more than that.

THE sun had dropped below the trees, and in the sky above, the first pinpricks of starlight tried to pierce the bluish purple sky. The small campfire Lysander had made to ward off the evening's chill was crackling softly in the Michigan spring air. Aside from the wind rustling in the trees and an owl hooting nearby, the only sound was the fire.

Phaedra stared into the flames, mesmerized. The physical pain of Cassiopeia's last moments had been excruciating. She shivered.

Lysander immediately wrapped the sweater she'd brought with her around her shoulders. She smiled up at him, and he kissed the tip of her nose.

"Better?"

"Yes," she said as she watched him squat in front of the fire to hold a metal rod with two fat marshmallows on it over the flames. "This sunset picnic idea of yours was a good one."

"I aim to please," he said as he tossed her a grin over his shoulder.

She glanced at the extra-large sleeping bag sitting next to the huge picnic basket he'd carried out to this quiet spot on the White Cloud estate. Even though it was relatively safe, she noticed he hadn't forgotten to pack his sword.

"Are you planning on keeping me out here all night?"

"Maybe. Depends on what my wife thinks of the idea."

"Oh, I don't think she'll mind at all."

The flames caught her attention once more, and as she stared into the fire, an image of Nicostratus flared in her head. In ancient Rome, the Patriarch had been responsible for her death, and if the *bastardo* had his way, he'd do it again. She knew Lysander was determined to destroy the man, but she was terrified Nicostratus would triumph in this life, just as he had in ancient Rome.

"You're thinking about it again, aren't you?" He kept his eyes on the white spongy confection he held just above the flames.

"Listening in on my thoughts again?" she teased, knowing he wouldn't do such a thing without her permission. He shot her a quick glance before he returned his attention to the browning marshmallows.

"No, I'm just beginning to recognize that look you get when you think about those last moments . . ." His voice trailed off, and she frowned.

"I try not to, but there's something about those last few moments that make me realize how terribly lucky we are to have found one another again."

He pulled the marshmallows away from the flames and scooted backward to sit beside her again. He offered her the first treat. She pulled it off and bit into the sugary morsel. Licking her fingers, she watched him pop the last marshmallow into his mouth.

"I talked to Atia today. Apparently, the only thing the *Tyet of Isis* contained was a treasure map."

"*What?*" she gasped. "After all we went through, it's nothing more than a treasure map?"

"She and Tevy . . . damn, I don't think I'll ever be able to call him Marcus . . . they think it leads to the potion that gave the Praetorian Guard their special abilities."

"If it involves going back to Rome, you're to tell her no," she said fiercely.

"You know I can't do that, *inamorato*." He reached out to trail his forefinger down her cheek.

"Yes, you can. Even if you kill that *bastardo*, there will be someone else just as bad to take his place."

"That's not the point. Nicostratus has a personal interest in us. That makes him all the more dangerous. And I won't let him jeopardize either you or our children."

"We don't—what did you say?" She came up on her knees and turned to face him. There was a hesitant look on his face that sent her heart pounding.

"I said Nicostratus was dangerous."

"No. The part about children."

"Children? Did I say something about children?" Lysander lay back on the plaid blanket, his arms folded behind his head. A small smile tilted the corners of his beautiful mouth.

"Are you saying . . . you mean . . . you want children?"

"Yes," he said softly. "I want to see you grow round with child, just like you did in Rome. You're beautiful now, but when you're pregnant, you'll be exquisite."

He reached out to run his fingertips down her throat to where the first button of her shirt was. The button popped off against the strain of his touch. A slow hum spread its way across her skin, heating her blood. When had he changed his mind? He'd been so emphatic about not having children she'd not broached the subject with him at all since then. Now, out of the blue, he'd changed his mind?

"I don't understand. You said . . . But . . ." She didn't know which question to ask first. Confused, she nuzzled her face in the palm of his hand as he cupped her cheek.

"I said I didn't want kids." He grimaced. "I've been thinking about it a lot since we came back from Italy. When I said I didn't want kids, I hadn't fully accepted that I was Maximus. It still makes me a little uncomfortable, but I keep thinking back to those last moments where Max . . . you and I were saying good-bye."

"You knew." She breathed in a sharp breath. "You knew about the baby."

"Not until afterward. Not until . . . you were dead." The memory of that moment sent a sickening lurch through his stomach. Terror is a powerful emotion that can block out pretty much everything except the danger you're facing.

"There was nothing you could do, *mea amor*. It's over now, and we've found each other again. And nothing Nicostratus or anyone else does will change that."

She lowered her head and brushed her mouth over his in a light touch before deepening the kiss. The moment her lips touched his, a firestorm went off in his body. Eager to taste her, he parted her lips, and his tongue mated with hers in a kiss filled with love, but hot with passion.

His hands reached up to undo the braid she wore and freed her hair so it could tumble downward over him. As her mouth left his to wander down the side of his throat, he inhaled a quick breath when she slowly unbuttoned the denim shirt he was wearing.

The leisurely pace with which she explored his chest with her lips sent him up a wall. *Deus*, he wanted her. Her mouth captured his nipple and she gently nipped at it with her teeth. It made him suck in a sharp hiss of air. *Christus*, he loved when she did that. The moment her hand reached for the waistband of his jeans, he rolled her onto her back to hover over her.

"I think we should get the sleeping bag," he rasped.

"Why? Aren't you warm enough?" she said with a mischievous twinkle in her eyes.

Beautiful brown eyes that would always make him forget to breathe. As she wrapped her arms around his neck, he sent her a wicked smile.

"Oh, I'm quite warm, *carissima*."

"Then why don't we get down to the business of making a baby," she murmured as she pulled his head downward.

"With pleasure, *inamorato*."

He let her pull him into her warmth, his mouth seeking hers in a kiss designed to show her that she would have his heart now and always. A whisper of a thought drifted through his head. She was touching him in a way no one had ever done before. As her hands heated his skin, he merged his thoughts with hers, pulling her deep into the heart and soul of him. With each kiss, caress, and every intertwining thought, time stood still. And just as she pulled him over the edge, he realized that two thousand more years still wouldn't be enough time for him to love her.